MW01106180

In A Flicker

A Novel

George R. Lopez & Andrea Perron

authorHOUSE®

AuthorHouse™
1663 Liberty Drive
Bloomington, IN 47403
www.authorhouse.com
Phone: 1 (800) 839-8640

Published by AuthorHouse 04/12/2016

ISBN: 978-1-5049-5396-2 (sc)
ISBN: 978-1-5049-5397-9 (hc)
ISBN: 978-1-5049-5395-5 (e)

Library of Congress Control Number: 2015916309

Print information available on the last page.

This book is printed on acid-free paper.

Dedication

To the women of history who make history.

IN A FLICKER

Prologue
HEADS WILL ROLL

"Is she dead?"

The hum of black rubber on a tarmac has a life like a musical score. There is a tune in it, a melody its grooves create as cool air siphons through the perforations, by divine design. When tires squeal on a sharp turn or in a burst of acceleration, it adds to a symphonic collaboration as any orchestra is incomplete without a piccolo. The year and model of this Mercedes always had the sound of some grumbling wild animal, as stealthy and predatory, in hungry pursuit of asphalt prey. By popularity and dependability, the W140 model of the Benz was so admired they were the stock choice of taxi companies in France and around Europe. In contrast the commonality of this particular model of luxury sedan, its black paint buffed to a high gloss, was often seen driven by many of the populace of means and style. It was only logical to have several of the cars functioning as decoys in front of the hotel, allowing these revelers a chance to slip out the back then escape unnoticed.

The three occupants and their driver probably were not even remotely aware of the orchestral harmony of the inner and outer workings of this masterfully crafted transport, as they likely had custom speakers drowning out the tires, the engine or any other audible distractions beyond the reflective glass. They were insulated and isolated, most likely engaged in some conversation as reflections on the evening's events. Two occupants in the back seat may have been locked in a lover's embrace, sharing a gaze, a passionate kiss, ignoring the concert, the dance of lights and sound surrounding them. Perhaps they remained sitting quietly side-by-side, eyes closed, holding hands, breathing in those moments with the scent of leather seats, taking in the solitude and security of their mobile domain. A blissful state of being, opposed to the origin of their journey at the crowded Ritz, was surely calm by comparison.

Their final turn was onto Pont de L'Alma Road, an unassuming and commonly used route for many tourists and Parisians alike. As August nights went that Sunday evening the sidewalks were aflutter with activities. The lights of streetlamps popped like strobes as they passed by. Apartment houses lined the landscape. People peered out glowing windows, casting silhouettes, catching a nightly glimpse of Paris from a safe distance. Oncoming cars hustled and bustled past black windows on the Benz. Motorcycles buzzing around the car like mosquitoes ready to strike at a food source, flash bulbs snapped that dark night to attention as their increasingly anxious driver began navigating around the pests, flying faster and faster, attaining unsafe speeds in mere moments. The single stationary object visible in the distance was the Eiffel Tower in all its illustrious, illuminated majesty, splitting the landscape in two.

Unknown to them, they had been spotted and followed. As he then accelerated toward a six-degree bank of the road, a rapid dip into the tunnel, their driver seemed unstable, fishtailing into the right lane, nearly sideswiping several other vehicles all rapidly disappearing in his rear view mirror. Everybody in the car suddenly shifted in their seats with the sharp pitch of the road, all at the mercy of centrifugal force. It produced the dangerous equation, one reduced down to its common denominator: speed. He was descending into the depths of hell, taking them along for the ride.

The tunnel alive with lights, well-traveled, echoed the elements making up the mobile musical composition reverberating between solid concrete columns. Faster on the curve then down the hole into that treacherous tunnel, faster into the abyss, suddenly went any unawareness of their surroundings. Jolted by an urgent sense of alarm, an equally watchful couple in the back seat remained as vigilant as were the occupants in the front as men on motorcycles encroached on the sedan's perimeter. Men hidden behind camera flashes attempting to capture *the* snapshot (even though glass barriers protected those inside from such intrusion), they provoked the couple, no doubt hoping they'd roll down a window in anger. Trying to make a quick buck by selling those images to tabloids, they'd made their presence known. Risking life and limb to steal a "still" of the rich and famous, they did so for the money, for the chance a rag mag would cut them a big fat check. All of this madness, so somebody less *fortunate* standing in a checkout line could, for a moment, escape the doldrums of a middle class existence and slip into a fantasy world. "*What must it be like to be a princess in France, whisked away in a luxury Mercedes sedan after dinner?*"

Rolling. Spinning. Screeching.

Who would have thought on that particular assignment, paparazzi on this night would have witnessed what they did, perhaps what they might have even caused? Could this have been a comedy of errors, the tragic scene? Had it been all of these photographers encroaching on their car that ultimately caused the mishap…a little bump that became the big bang? That was one theory. Any chance their driver was impaired? Had he enjoyed a few too many cocktails with dinner or was the accident caused by oncoming lights or the distraction no one saw happening? Or was it that close call with an older model Fiat? Time would tell. Should anybody wonder what the noise of the vehicle hitting a concrete barrier at such high velocity sounded like, caving in the front end, forcing itself up inside the engine, crushed into a dashboard, fracturing the windshield? This dreadful night, the splintering of human bones was not the kind of accordion bringing music to their ears. Who could've imagined such painful, disturbing sounds piercing the ears and hearts of witnesses? The Mercedes Benz impacted the concrete support in that tunnel, one of the solid beams separating them from the flow of oncoming traffic. The head-on crash came quickly, so violent it caused the back end of the vehicle to twist and bend, swinging around to the right. Full stop, settling in place, it came to rest facing the opposite direction of the lane's stream of cars. Photographers raced to the rescue, not to aid the injured and dying occupants of the wreck but to rescue their efforts at getting the *big scoop*.

Traffic came to an abrupt halt. Six minutes later, (right on cue), a multitude of ambulances arrived at the scene accompanied by the French police. They'd witness the deadly outcome of a foregone conclusion. Mangled by the implosion created by a collision between the steel frame of the Benz and a cement barricade, it was hell on wheels.

Sirens wailing, horns honking, many people gathered together talking in hushed tones, some quietly crying, others screaming at the sight. Ancillary figures hovered like ghosts in the ether as noises overwhelmed the lingering paparazzi, scrambling for one last shot in the dark. Hopping onto their motorcycles, vultures scattered in a flicker of light, disappearing through a black hole at the far end of the tunnel under the cover of night, their squealing tires layering more musical instrumentation upon an operatic cacophony of sounds, a passion play unfolding before their eyes. It was a vision seen through the lens of a camera, each viewfinder fixated on that singular, stationary object. Scavengers had captured an accident they'd likely caused on film, death resulting, then took flight as they fled the sickening scene.

It came, a strange, unnatural sound…an out-of-tune tuba…a loud buzzer.

"CLEAR AND RESET" A booming British voice came over the large speakers as the order was given.

"Oh no, not again." The thought uttered as a collective sigh swept through the air then sank into the soul of every witness to the carnage.

All the participants began filing out of the tunnel on cue as other vehicles were then strategically backed up out of sight. They'd done it before in practiced fashion, in fact, a multitude of times. Someone flipped a switch. Instantly flooded with light, the full extent of the crash site stunned even those who had seen it previously. Six men, all in yellow jumpsuits (the initials FTC worn prominently as an identifying emblem) approached warped wreckage in an unemotional, detached manner. Men on a mission, they circled the Mercedes Benz, assessing the damage, inside and out. Peering through its fractured glass, the crew photographed positions of the victims from every conceivable angle until an enormous machine lumbered onto the scene. Team members stepped aside as a huge wheel-driven construction vehicle assumed its proper position. Slowly extending a claw-like arm it savagely ripping the vehicle apart. As opposed to its counterpart, the Jaws of Life, this mechanism resembled jaws of death. Off came the passenger side front door then the rear door, bending solid steel joints in ways they weren't intended to bend. The jumpsuit brigade could then freely access the inside of the compartment of the crushed fuselage.

"Is she dead?" A young technician made an honest inquiry.

It began systematically. Tugging and pulling, yanking four occupants out of the twisted tomb with no regard for the injuries, computers had done the work, reading the head-to-toe sensors which established a cause of death, the full extent of wounds sustained. From the front passenger seat came a right arm, dismembered from the body. No blood, bones or cartilage revealed in the retrieval process, it wasn't that kind of arm. A whispered private thought escaped the lips of the startled FTC team member left holding it. *"Oh, no. That's not supposed to happen."* He cast it aside. Human error.

No need for delicacy. As computations were made, facts and figures gathered, by the time the team approached the car, their experiment was over and all the hard work they'd do was merely an afterthought. For all intents and purposes, they were glorified janitors but what a cleanup crew! Their role was integral to the process. A young engineer reaching into the back seat had more luck. He was able to extricate the victim, removing their test subject intact. Technically still alive, she would die later on in the local hospital. It was beginning to look a lot like death by paparazzi. Ironically, flashes of light continued unabated even after the bikers were long gone. Surrounding the team as they worked striking the set, photographers documenting the results of the reenactment as well as the program itself, recreating an unnatural disaster, they captured it from every angle. It was merely probability and statistics, compiled and cross-referenced to identify then determine the causal connection, all done for the sake of clarifying history, a noble cause.

"This one's still alive. We got it right!" The lead assistant praised the effort.

"He's still warm. They're really lifelike even when they're dead!" An awkward quip slipped from the junior member of the team who fell silent with a glance from his boss. This was serious business. An enthusiast among them was reminded.

"Keep your heads, gents." Perturbed, the stern team leader said nothing more. He didn't need to, as his expression said it all. There wouldn't be a single oversight, no room for error, no distractions allowed. No comments. No joking. This was not a laughing matter. Heads would roll if he heard another word.

I.
DOWN IN THE VALLEY

"The FTC Oversight Committee authorities are at it again, running more bloody paperwork across my desk. Colin, I am sick of it, to the pit of my stomach." Ethan plunged his hands deep into the pockets of his trousers, just as deep in thought.

As glaring floodlights came down, saturating the scene of the crash reenactment of Princess Diana's accident, Ethan LaPierre and Colin Bishop exited the area just beyond the range of the tragic play. For the seventh time, a painstaking process was played out, covering various realms of possibilities and relevant conspiracy theories regarding what actually happened one fateful August night so many years before when a beloved princess perished. Observers and participants alike hoped against hope for a decisive resolution, wishing this would be the last Time Trial regarding a lady long gone but not forgotten. It was traumatic to watch but it was not met with resolve. "Clear and reset" were not welcome words to their weary crew that night. At 1:00 a.m. they intended to run it again.

Ethan was preoccupied with matters of his own, busy looking back in mind over the past few weeks, recalling redundant requests he had received, messages coming from different departments, all pertaining to the same subject.

"Why can't I answer their questions *once* then leave it to them to sort it amongst themselves?" Chuckling aloud, rhetorical in tone, the question posed as a statement didn't require any response. "Doesn't anyone around here ever compare notes?" It seemed a legitimate inquiry. His friend answered the call with a reason offered, one plausible explanation for the delay.

"Perhaps that is just what they're doing, cross-referencing your answers to the same questions from different departments, establishing a consistency they require. They're most likely as cautious as you are, P. They cannot fathom your submission! I think '20/20 Hindsight' boggled their minds! Your project is unlike any other ever proposed. Fuckin' aye, mate, there's a reason your submission has been on the table for so long. Bugger! You wrote the bloody thing! You know the complexities, the variables of the proposal. P! Listen to me! They're still trying to wrap their minds around the concept's construct. Give them time."

It was indeed an equally painstaking process for all petitioners like Ethan. From requesting a "Flicker" research project, granting participants rights to the facility all the way from conception to fruition, every nuance was overseen and dissected. These expansive grounds currently had several projects ongoing at once, each more secretive than the last one. "Top Secret / Eyes Only" was the required protocol. All cleared projects possessed the same primary purpose: clarify history.

"There's a silver lining. I know it! Ethan, listen to me. This is a sign that you're closer than ever to an approval. Final touches to a masterpiece. It will happen."

Colin's encouraging words fell upon a set of recently deafened ears, too much residual sound from the crash still ringing in them, his cluttered mind was too noisy.

"No, mate. They're too cautious. It is never going to happen. They are too afraid of it." Ethan tried to apply logic, watching every step on the moist grass deceptively slick, laden with dew. He paused, turning toward his confidant. "They want to know things I can't tell them until it is all over. Why don't they understand that?"

"Look, you're a historian and a scientist. Some of them are, as well. Facts and patterns will make the final decision here." Colin tried to lighten the mood. "They may reject it just because you're too bloody ugly to be a hero."

"I don't know, Colin, I just don't know." Ethan was looking down, literally and figuratively, removing and glancing at the face of his reliable pocket watch as he'd done a thousand times before, ignoring the luminous face of the full moon above, casting its heavenly glow as it danced atop dewdrops beneath his feet. It was too lovely a night to feel so disheartened. Ethan was not paying any mind to the present moment as his mind's eye remained entirely focused on his project and its future. He had a viable mission, an intriguing scenario being bogged down in bureaucracy, literally wasting time itself.

Secluded, sheltered from the storm of societal knowledge and judgment, these two gentlemen knew they were very privileged to be here. Taking a moment to look back toward the path out into the moonlit night, a spectacular view was breathtaking for both. Although they'd heard it before, for anyone close enough, within earshot, the replay they'd just taken part in left a mark, indelible impressions impossible to erase. Every single time was more shocking than the last, adding insult to injuries, grave mortal wounds. Stopping on the hilltop to take it all in, they silently observed the opulent, sprawling six-hundred-and-forty-eight acre research field before them, providing ample space, privacy necessary for their Flicker test trials. Encompassing the facility, this vast tract of land located northeast of the Oxford University campus was buried within an expanse of lush greenery known as Oxfordshire. Known to all involved, familiar with the project, it was called "The Valley". Within its confines were docks and hangers, roadways and even a mock-up of an airport. Some areas revealed pristine lawns in suburban settings while others had wild vegetation, tall willowy grassland gone to seed. Left deliberately unkempt, the grassy knoll worn as a clever disguise, The Valley was designated to and definitive of different times and locations from all around the globe, created specifically for acts of re-creation.

There were many entrances to and from this bucolic setting but only one for the staff parking. It was quite a hike up the lengthy staircase, framed by metal handrails on either side, painted multiple times over the years, attempting to cover wear and tear. It was a busy place. Situated beside the steep staircase was a tall, wide tunnel with an ascending concrete ramp providing access for numerous work vehicles that transported stockpiles of odd materials for buildings, technical support and the like. It resembled stadium tunnels football teams come running through onto American playing fields, only much larger.

Just seventeen steps into their trek up and out of The Valley, Ethan's breathing became labored. Although six feet tall and slender, he was not athletic in any way, shape or form. Ethan had the metabolism of a scared rabbit and the diet of one, too. His earlier years spent with his nose buried in some book or any journal he could get his hands on and wrap his mind around, for all his knowledge the man was not a bit street savvy. Huffing and puffing, he was also clearly out of shape. Colin felt the necessity to state the obvious regarding this condition.

"Fuck me, mate! What was the course level for *your* fitness requirements?"

"Tier One Level Three." Ethan forced the answer through in one exhale.

"Good Lord! My Gramms could run that with 'er knickers down to 'er knees!" Colin's thick British accent suddenly assumed a more authentic lilt, almost Scottish brogue, with his use of the well-worn phrase. Ethan just shook his head, visualizing a favorite old Monty Python skit of an old lady in a full sprint. His hybrid ethnicity showed only in his humor. Though Ethan's English was perfect, as textbook proper as one might expect, during more improper moments, these two gents would resort to their true nature with ease. Colin frequently told his best mate that he could charm like a Frenchman, possessing that certain *je ne sais quoi* his kind are so famous for, yet he could banter with the best of the Irishmen. Ethan possessed an ideal blend of his parent's distinctly different cultures.

"So? What's your point then, smart arse? It is meant to be...a predetermined, objective observation...like a fly on the wall, my good man, a quiet little fly on the wall." Ethan rationalized.

Between his inhales and exhales, he choked out a response but could not muster enough air to continue on. Winded, Ethan kept account of his steps as Colin teased, deciding to lend support to his companion with a hand under his arm.

"Of course, unless it goes *off course*, then the proverbial fly has no wings left after *that* flight!" Colin was suddenly serious. Tugging at Ethan's arm, both stopped on the stairs. "P. What if you get stuck there?"

They stood, staring at each other in silence. "Nah!" was spoken in unison. Both realized that would *never* happen, a ludicrous notion, at best. Inconceivable! Their training was meticulous. No room for error. No doubt about it.

Funny, sometimes, how the mind works, especially on the staircase. How many times had Ethan counted the stairs he ascended, but only while ascending? A force of habit, always stunned by the number of steps, he counted silently as he spoke. It seemed to quiet his mind…57, 58, 59, 60, 61, 62, 63 and 64…finally!

Graciously waiting a moment for Ethan to catch his breath, the men stood atop the staircase they'd just climbed, peering out across the magnificent "valley". Colin couldn't help but be amused by the sweaty brow of his friend. Ethan couldn't help but notice the moon illuminating the sprawling facility.

The FTC or "Flicker Trials Consortium" was at full force that night, removing vehicles, resetting the field for yet another reenactment. Their second run had been scheduled prior to the initial one, a *just in case* block of time reserved for any such scenario, all ready to commence after initial review and assessments were returned. The computer banks spitting out calculations, giving vital course corrections before the next reenactment could commence, from such a distance it appeared more like organized chaos that would, no doubt, continue until morning's first light. For these two men on the crest of the hill, it was late. Two replacement "Scopes" were already present for the next reenactment, so the time had come for them to go home.

The FTC was comprised of numerous committee-approved videographers and photographers, emergency workers, professional drivers, construction contractors, maintenance, and so forth. Any and all trial participants were subjected to the same intense security scrutiny endured by those in the upper echelon, perhaps more so. As background checks go, this was not a run of the mill, point and click affair, not the standard fare. Drug testing was as thorough as their physical examination was invasive. Intrusions were simply a part of the process. Various clandestine agencies emulated their protocol. It was all quite secretive down in the trenches and tunnels of The Valley. Members of the team knew they were being perpetually scrutinized for any sign of weakness or psychological trauma, watched like a hawk stalking its prey, watched at all times by those who were, in turn, being observed by someone else. That was how it worked and everyone knew it. Here in this form privilege had its lack of privilege. Under severe penalty disclosure agreements, they all collected their hefty "private contractor" salaries and kept their mouths shut. It was just the job.

Ethan and Colin were two of many university professors, scholars, experts and others of proper qualifications who were part of the oversight protocol of every trial conducted at the facility. Their purpose in process allowed them (as electorates and select team members) an opportunity to experience the reenactments firsthand, not from a final report on a desk. One mantra: *"The more eyes on the prize, the better"*. Each and every trial had its Scopes, those there but not there, taking it all in, giving project directors opinions, different perspectives, angles and approaches, ideas they could also implement for their own pending research projects. They'd seen enough that night to make a few crucial recommendations to the FTC team leader, including the suggestion of a re-training order for one young man who could not seem to curb his carelessness, nonchalantly tossing a loose limb onto the sidewalk.

Every Scope invested much time into these trials as one compulsory element of observation and preparation proficiency, one piece of an overall acclimation to the facility. All future progress of their own proposal was contingent upon completion of the task, rotating observer duties between various reenactments underway. Colin and Ethan attended the only Time Trial operating on site that night, participating as conscientious observers. Job done, they were free to go on their way then file the corresponding incident reports in the morning. In the rising mist, hilltops bathed in the mystical white light from above, two men appeared as ghostly figures floating away, heading home across the moors.

Dozens of advanced stadium lights aligned with distant hedgerows at a natural boundary of The Valley. Utilized during nighttime resets, at other times, to simulate daylight, the halogen halo cast from above illuminated the landscape. These stately, stoic fixtures were particularly useful for the occasional time trials that ran over the allotted time on their schedule, though this happened infrequently. The whole team had it down to a science. Having just walked away from the scene of this deliberate accident, the gentlemen paused to reflect on their mutual good fortune, two among only a few dozen people on the planet who knew what was occurring in The Valley. From their shared vantage point, the landscape suddenly appeared surreal, ethereal in nature, glowing from afar like the moon above.

"Beautiful, isn't it?" Ethan murmured.

Colin did not respond in words while they gazed down upon The Valley. There was no need. It was self-evident. Both were overcome by the place in that moment, not only by the lush inviting valley but by all the technology contained inside it, the genius at work within its borders. It was quiet, residual sounds from the crash site unable to carry the distance on the barely perceptible breeze. As they stood on its periphery all video, audio and photographic data was being wirelessly downloaded. Evidence collected from the observation tower at the trial site went straightaway to the secure Flicker database located underground, beneath Fellow's Garden, hidden in plain sight on the main campus at Oxford University. This was where all of their extensive review occurred. All that remained missing was the Scope reports.

"Dr. LaPierre! Dr. Bishop!" Young Maggie was approaching the men, waving her arms wildly in the air, stirring up the night's molecules with a manila folder in hand, so to flag them down. "Oh! Bloody! Hell!" She'd blasted out the words. The two found an instant smile, as there was no curbing the amusement seeing the lass in the predicament she'd found herself on a soft sod path, her high heels penetrating, perforating the supple ground. Each step more awkward than the last, her struggling pace slowing due to the unexpected obstacle course she was improperly dressed to navigate. Sporting the standard suit, a professional outfit suitable only for the site's tall observation platform known as The Tower, it was where she'd come from, her assigned station that night. This young woman was obviously out of her element in the elements. Twisting her ankle, slipping down to the ground on slick grass, knees buried in cold mud, an equally sunken expression on her face was precious for two Scopes observing her stuck in quite a quandary.

"Down she goes!" Colin's voice projected all the way to the damsel in distress. The green-eyed, platinum blond youngling had been swallowed up, as if eaten alive by the muck and mire of marshland, managing to preserve the integrity of the sealed folder by tucking it in her jacket. She then sunk one hand into the ground, hoisting herself into a more dignified upright position. The next steps brought awareness to the absence of both heels now missing from her regretfully expensive pair of shoes. Each of the nubs protruding up from soggy sod, having snapped off where she fell forward, she was a mortified Maggie. Decorum tossed away in the wind along with the satin heels she tried to pry from her saturated feet, clinging like glue to thickly encrusted hosiery, *this* was a comedy of errors not lost on an audience of two highly amused men.

"Fuck! Fuckety fuck! Fuck! Fuck!" In the shrillest tones of pure frustration and an impromptu stomp of one foot, humiliated, angered by the ordeal, Maggie could not help herself. Nor could she extricate herself with grace.

"Ah, a woman of unique linguistic talents. English major? Or perhaps zoology, as that just reminded me of a newborn giraffe trying to walk." Colin quipped in his worst Shakespearean falsetto, "Me thinks the lady doth protest too much!" Sarcasm a strong suit, he had a way about him which disguised this tendency in typical style, a dry wit the British are so famous for, perfected with practice over time.

Poised on the precipice of disaster, bogged down in pasty mud, there would be no escaping the dilemma with her dignity intact, so she sacrificed it along with her fancy footwear. Poor fragile creature, delicate as a daisy, the intern had never been so embarrassed, but for this to occur directly in front of the man she admired, even idolized, added to her awkwardness.

Ethan, always the gentleman, made a sympathetic query. "Are you all right, Ms. Daley?" He called to The Valley review staff member, one of his former students.

"Fine. I'm fine." Shouting back from still a bit of a distance, she was attempting to master the stretch of less than manicured land yet to conquer.

"Mind yourself, mate. Here she comes! It seems there's lady in our midst!" Content in the knowledge that Maggie would never respond in kind, out of respect and a rapport with these men of stature, Colin enjoyed the restrained back and forth repartee between them all, much like a family at the dinner table. Ethan knowingly glanced his way, feigning a parental look of disapproval. He wanted to save the girl from more torture but knew Colin wasn't done with her yet.

"You know, Magpie, someone will have to go fetch those things!" Colin, a bit of an antagonist, simply could not resist the urge to torment the flustered soul while pointing in the vicinity of the final resting place for her discarded shoes. "Protocol requirement: proper footwear must be worn at all times on the property."

Ethan promptly came to her verbal aid, taking the argument to Colin with their usual exchange. "Field maintenance will retrieve them. She's providing job security for the grounds staff." Ethan was especially fond of Maggie. Bellowing his counter response assured she would hear him defending her honor. She had heard him loud and clear. Chastising Colin in the most jovial way, Ethan continued on her behalf.

"Did it even occur to you to go and help her?"

"What? And get myself stuck in the mud *with* her? It's a deathtrap out there!"

Colin grinned as Ethan walked toward Maggie to lessen her embarrassing solo journey through the marsh, taking her hand in his own as added balance for both.

"Ms. Daley, why did you come this route?" Ethan seemed legitimately curious. She had cut across the marshland from the looming control tower constructed near The Valley's edge, to head them off at the pass. Forced to detour from the delivery road due to incoming vehicles, late night deliveries common in The Valley, she had no choice but to tread upon unpaved terrain.

Still stomping along, each soggy step created that suction cup sound effect with the release of her feet from a saturated sod. Maggie wiped her one free hand on the skirt of her fine linen suit. Disgusted, the look on her face was a priceless keepsake, a still life snapshot of her for the ages.

"Because I didn't know it was more of a *deathtrap* out there then stepping into traffic. Beggin' your pardon, sirs. My language." Sincere desperation in her meek little voice was evident as she spoke the truth, hoping for mercy, but none would be forthcoming from the devilish Doctor Bishop.

"Guessing you don't get out much. Nice suit! Perhaps you've reconsidered the standard issue fatigues and army boots?" Colin, relentless in his pursuit of banter, the man lived for it.

As the two approached Colin, Maggie wanted to thank her gallant rescuer. She strained her neck to meet eyes with a man she looked up to in myriad ways, literally. As perky as she was petite, Maggie's stature was, at best, diminutive. Standing only five feet tall barefoot in mud, she was severely eclipsed by Ethan's height. Delicate, flawless features made all the more attractive by drifting moonlight, a speckled and freckled face splattered in mud, her smile beamed with a genuine innocence. That sparkling gaze so full of wonder, reverence and respect, Ethan could not help but notice her huge, green eyes looking up at him in awe. Maggie Daley was a devoted assistant, a fifth-year student as well as a first-year participant in the program.

"You left without taking your documents, sir. The director requests your report be on his desk by midday tomorrow." Slipping the manila envelope from her jacket, she politely handed it to him, only then realizing they were still holding hands.

"Thank you, dear." Ethan smiled sweetly. "As usual, above and beyond the call of duty. We can always count on you." Releasing his grip from Maggie's hand, he opened the seal of the folder.

Both men being much taller could not see the momentary expression of loss in her eyes as he broke the connection. She tried her best to hide her crush.

"Where's my envelope?" Colin whined.

Stunned, petrified in place by the question, Maggie automatically began to tell her tale and cover her tracks, realizing she'd inadvertently grabbed only one of the pre-packaged report forms from the desk as she quickly left the observation tower.

There was an instant, with a devilish look of her own, a glimpse of a grin on her face, Maggie peered at Colin with that *"Ya got me, now don't rat me out!"* look.

"Blast! I was certain I'd retrieved both packets from The Tower." She rebutted.

"Do forgive her oversight, Colin. Besides, technically speaking, she prioritized correctly." Ethan pumped up his chest in a competitive manner.

"Apparently so!" Colin acquiesced, a disapproving consent. "I suppose I'll have to suffer the misfortune of going into my office and printing them off the template. It will take such an awfully long time, one, perhaps two full minutes." The bad actor in Colin, the clown assumed an expression of epiphany. "But wait! Ethan, couldn't you have done the same thing? And Ms. Daley has made this long, arduous trip for you, special delivery, all for naught. What a pity." Dr. Bishop had a point. Empathy was not a usual character strength in him.

"Your efforts do not go unappreciated, Ms. Daley." Ethan was always forthright with her. "As for apologizing for your colorful language, my own vocabulary leaves much to be desired at times."

"You're fucking right about that, Ethan!" Colin continued, attempting to engage her in a debate, to no avail. "You've quite the gutter mouth for such an intellectual. Wouldn't you agree, Ms. Daley? You've worked for him, after all. I'm sure you've heard a slip o' the tongue a time or two, now haven't you?"

"I couldn't say." Maggie hung her head, shifting her gaze at Colin as if to order him with her eyes to stow it before she got painted into an uncomfortable corner of this metaphorical room with a view of The Valley.

"Sure you can! You're among friends." Colin was searching for pressure points to bait the younger mind into banter.

"Well, perhaps a time or two." Maggie regretted the statement the moment she made it. Her face flushing with fire, expecting steam to rise from her porcelain skin at any second as the heat of embarrassment hit the cool night air, Maggie was too overcome with dread to do anything more than smile a shy, sheepish grin.

"Aha! I knew it!" Colin's wicked wit suddenly kicked into high gear. Pointing an accusing finger Ethan's way, he reproachfully exclaimed, "Vulgar bastard."

"Pay no mind to this cretin, Ms. Daley." Ethan's concern for her wellbeing was one of the reasons the young apprentice was so enamored with him.

"Well then, I'll take my leave." Maggie's intense desire to flee the scene could not be interrupted. Pivoting in place, she turned away from the professors, preparing to make a more graceful exit than she had an entrance. Slipping again, her stockings slick with the dew, Ethan grabbed her elbow as she stumbled. Having kept her from falling, he held her upright, gently cupping his hand around her arm, hanging on a bit longer than necessary.

"Thank you, kind sir." Made breathless by his touch, she allowed him to linger. As Ethan released his grasp, sensing his absence once again, she mourned the loss of the moment between them.

"Thank you, Ms. Daley." Patting the envelope, "You'll be in my thoughts now as this added work will keep me up half the night." He followed the statement with a wink of assurance that he was truly appreciative of her efforts. Ethan's sincerity was touching to the blushing young woman. Unbeknownst to him, the man touched her heart long before that fateful night, thrilled by the all too brief encounter shared with Professor LaPierre.

Maggie knew the intrepid trip continued. Retracing her steps back through the magnetic-like muck, she'd needed to return to The Tower. About twenty paces into her trek a moonstruck lass realized it wasn't over yet, not by a long shot, as it was Colin's bad boy habit to throw out the last word, always a final say so in the offing.

"I believe your shoes are in *that* direction, Ms. Daley! Have a safe *trip*!"

Her back turned to them, she raised a hand in acknowledgement, receipt of his comment, once again navigating the soft sod attempting to eat her feet. Colin half expected and definitely hoped for one extended finger on that hand directed at him. To his dismay, he was disappointed, but Ethan was not…not ever.

Waiting for his former apprentice to attain a sufficient distance so he would not be overheard, an ever vigilant, always patient Ethan reflected on Maggie's kindness extended, and at what cost to her wallet as well as her dignity.

"It was good of her to track me down."

"I still think we should have had her arrested."

"Arrested? On what grounds?" Ethan took the bait.

"On *these* grounds, my good man." Gripping Ethan by the shoulders, pointing him toward the field of evidence. "Her shoes! Those heels are still stuck out there somewhere! 'Littering'! Hello?"

Ethan, rolling his eyes, broke free of the clutch. Colin stood there, hands on his hips, gazing across the open terrain as his colleague attempted to make his escape, widening his stride with each step.

Turning to see Ethan long gone, Colin had to run to catch up. A rather symbolic act played out as it had many times before in different ways, the proverbial younger sibling in hot pursuit of big brother. Rushing to his side, Colin continued unabated.

"Well, that was quite the chemistry lesson the two of you just had." Colin added, "And quite the education for me."

"Whatever are you talking about?"

The two men returned to their walk, heading in the direction of the car park.

"We work quite well together." Knowing where this was going, Ethan wanted to nip it in the bud before it bloomed fully on his cheeks.

"Oh! To be sure! But she could have grabbed two envelopes, mate. She knew we had left together. Guess I wasn't on her mind." With a fiendish grin and taunting tone, Colin had made another astute observation. "She is blossoming into quite the attractive young lady, don't you agree, P?"

If you think of her as so blossomed then ask her out yourself." Noticing Colin's expression, Ethan knew he was equal to the ensuing rhetoric.

"Oh, no, I'd never do that! I like her far too much to ruin her. After all, I'd only break her heart. You know me, P." Colin flung his arm around Ethan's shoulders.

"Indeed, I do."

"Why settle for merely one when there are so many young lovelies awaiting my company? Besides, I wouldn't go down that road. I would not stand a chance. She'd never pay me any mind, anyway. She's yours in heart, my good man. I would never presume to cross that bridge."

"You're quite off your bloody rocker tonight." Ethan observed.

"Ms. Daley has been your little understudy for years yet it appears you've never made any moves in that direction?"

"Moves? Get a grip! She's practically a child! She's half my age and twice my class, at least five times yours!" Ethan sized him up with his eyes, causing Colin to have a moment of pause, scanning himself once over, but only for a moment.

"Thank you, kind sir! It's so good of you to notice me!" Mocking Maggie, Colin should've expected the playful shove he received. Colin knew he'd struck a nerve, nudging him back in an almost Masonic-like ritual of acknowledging one another's intentions and feelings.

Inwardly, Ethan's discontent was really for himself, within himself, pertaining to his decided lack of carnal knowledge. Decades spent as a student then a master, from boyhood to manhood, he never pried his nose from those books long enough to behold all the beautiful scenery surrounding him on campus. Abundant examples of the female form on constant display, at his disposal, he'd never looked up. It just wasn't a focal point for him.

Oh, to be sure, there'd been a few brief encounters, interludes in his past as an undergraduate. He remembered one slightly drunken girl at a frat party. Spurred on by his college brethren, her inebriation had made her the aggressor as she thrust her tongue down his throat. What he most recalled was how humiliated he was for her and how agitated he'd been with his friends. It was not funny or sexy. It was sloppy. Nasty. The smell of hard liquor on her breath and the residual taste of it on her lips repulsed him. Ethan was not enticed by her kind, not in the least.

His desires for romance always seemed fulfilled in mind and heart by those women whose lives and accomplishments were recorded in literature. Fascinated, seduced by their words and deeds in earlier times, women who had captured his imagination through their contributions to history had the most profound effect on him. He had always felt an attachment to those long gone; those who'd once made the world a far more interesting place, even though they were no longer a part of it in flesh and blood. They had remained alive in his mind, immortal, companions he would never have to part with for as long as he lived. Their former existence in time functioned as his mental aphrodisiac, a truly emotional touchstone for an otherwise introverted soul immersed in his own world. He yearned only for the same cerebral intimacy attained while spending time among them, keeping company within the pages of a book.

Looking back on it, Ethan wondered why his path had been a solitary venture, a lonely road traveled through time. The females he had been exposed to during the course of his primary education were generally over-exposed, present in the flesh, present day women too *in the moment* for a man desperate to find a common past. How many times had fraternity brothers ridiculed him for his social disinterest with the opposite sex? Over time, some of the same guys flunked out, due to those many distractions, no doubt. Others graduated then moved on into high salary corporate executive positions and most of them later became firmly entrenched in politics.

Professor LaPierre was unique. A studious, serious sort, a fellow dedicated, devoted to the cause of pure research for the sake of advancing human knowledge, his rather high-minded predisposition had left the gentleman outstanding in the field…alone. Several others like Colin Bishop, as friend and colleague, never left the nest either. Academia provided them a sense of home, a safe haven where the heart was spared the ravages of a cruel world and a new discovery was always around the corner.

"You'll be getting on to your flat then?" Colin asked, apparently disappointed to see their adventure come to an end.

"Yes, but I don't think I'll be getting much sleep. This, atop all the other reports I have to do, all due by midday. I expect to be up all night." Ethan replied.

"I could do them with my eyes closed." Colin was a cocky sort.

"Well, that rather defeats the purpose, doesn't it?" Ethan applied logic. "A bad attitude for any Scope to have, I'd say."

Colin ignored the logic but knew he'd have to delay the pomposity for a future time. "Right then. Meet for tea?" Cajoling, he prompted Ethan to respond.

"Uh, yeah. Should be fine, right, ring me up." Ethan was obviously distracted, lost in thought. On autopilot once he opened the envelope to begin sifting through its familiar contents, what he held in hand was not a request. Report forms were to be filed promptly, a requirement at the conclusion of every time trial, whether or not the time trial came to a conclusion. No matter how tedious it had become, Ethan could not afford to be anything less than diligent in his approach, as it might reflect poorly on him otherwise, harming his chances for submission approval. This boring routine necessary to cover all the elements of any reenactment, he began composing his answers to the standard fare questionnaire in his head.

"Don't fall asleep before you finish!" Colin quipped. His risqué double entendre had not escaped Ethan's notice.

"Yeah, I know…you can do it in your sleep."

As always, needing to have the last word, Colin took one more stab at Ethan's cardio-conundrum on the stairs. "Just hoping ol' Jackie was out of shape…and you don't have to chase him!" Sharing yet another knowing grin between them, with a wink and a nod, they parted ways for the evening.

II.
SPARKS WILL FLY

About thirty yards ahead was The Valley car park where a motorcar was idling, awaiting Ethan's arrival. His chauffeur would take him to his flat just off campus. Anyone actively participating in the Flicker project was assigned a private security detail, personnel in place due primarily to the highly sensitive nature of this cutting-edge research. All communications were closely monitored, including in sedans used for transport, knowingly fitted with a recording device, occupants were scrutinized for any breach in protocol. No leaks allowed, no such thing as personal privacy, it was the price paid by those invested in their project.

"Home, Dr. LaPierre?" The driver asked his routine question, anticipating the usual response.

"Yes, then straightaway Sparks, shall we?"

"Right, sir."

Clifton Sparks was once a professional boxer in the United Kingdom with an impressive win / loss record to his credit. Interestingly, he was also one gentle giant of a man, a soft-spoken intellectual who had used his brain as much as his brawn to get where he wanted to go in life. His athletic career came to a chosen end once he received a full scholarship to Oxford University. After graduating with honors he'd stayed on, having overheard his department head whispering about the new Flicker program, an ambitious project being developed on campus. Fascinated, he wanted in on it in any conceivable way. Since this research was still pure and in its infancy, untouched by any military influences, he had hoped to explore the possibilities of participating in its development.

There wasn't to date any candidate proposals available for a former prizefighter with a degree in philosophy. More than willing to accept any entry-level, ancillary assignment to begin with, he did not consider it insignificant, as a subordinate role. Instead, he'd considered it his contribution to the cause. When Clifton Sparks was assigned to Dr. LaPierre as his personal security detail, it was that rare and welcome opportunity to wedge his formidable foot in the door. An imposing six-foot-four-inches tall, Sparks towered over Ethan. Hovering above him, he opened the back door on the driver's side of the black sedan. Coincidentally, the vehicle was another Mercedes Benz, the later model of that forty-year-old version once fit for a princess. Assuming a position behind his driver, Ethan was a creature of habit. Maneuvering his not-so-slight six foot frame into the back seat, he began focusing on the pile of files a green-eyed lady had handed over to him. Forms he was all too familiar with appeared to consume his attention, though his mind was on more pressing matters.

As Sparks reassumed his position in the front seat, the car's balance shifting in an easy heave, a heavyweight settled his hefty torso securely into place. The interior light dimmed with the closing of the door but not before Ethan glanced up to see the sheen off his driver's closely cropped haircut. His dark black skin decorated the pudgy cheeks of his round, glistening face as Mr. Sparks appeared to glow beneath the beam of white light shed from above the dashboard. He did not really fit, space provided in the sedan inadequate to receive someone of his size. The musclebound mass of flesh in his upper arms appeared stuffed into the sleeves of his suit jacket, causing it to bulge at the seams. Ethan's keen powers of observation, undoubtedly honed by being an experienced Scope, an inordinate awareness of his surroundings suddenly swept over him. He noticed everything, including details of an easygoing traveling companion who had patiently awaited his late arrival.

"No rest for the wicked, sir?" Sparks made his query in jest, spying the pile of papers on his passenger's lap while readjusting the rear view mirror.

"No rest, indeed. I do take exception to the *wicked* reference." Ethan peered up over his reading glasses into the gaze of smiling eyes he found in the mirror.

"Indeed, sir. Yes." Sparks acknowledged the comment with a bashful nod in an amused tone. Though Ethan could not see his entire face, Sparks was grinning. He'd grown quite fond of his charge, a man with whom he often exchanged such quips as idle chatter, something for The Consortium to record on the drive home.

Revving the engine a bit before shifting it into gear, Sparks embarked on their journey in silence, the distance between The Valley and Ethan's flat almost twenty minutes, less at that time of night. No traffic. The stereo system was turned on and tuned in to the BBC. The news, broadcasting as low-level noise in the background during the short transport, the newscaster spoke on an array of topics from politics and agriculture to weather and entertainment, providing the narrative for inattentive Ethan to tune out. His mind was preoccupied with a previous encounter.

"Would you like the dome light on, Doctor LaPierre?"

"Not necessary. Thank you, Sparks." These forms were all the same after every trial. A series of multiple-choice questions followed by a section provided for any commentary or recommendations, it was all a rather mundane, repetitious exercise if a Scope was expected to review the same scenario again and again. Redundant at best, Ethan dreaded the process. As the method of submitting ideas and suggestions, the plethora of paperwork served a valid purpose, a way of exhausting any and all possibilities, positing ideas until every last angle was approached in the trials. All candidates for the Flicker program were compelled to participate in each trial, as it was presumed to assist them in reexamining their own submissions. Staff and field workers initially created the affectionate nickname for observers chosen, tagged as *Scopes*. It stuck, a reference made to telescopes, microscopes, those peering deeply through a lens, eyes scrutinizing every aspect of what they witnessed. Dr. Ethan J. LaPierre was one of only eight Scopes with his Flicker petition submitted, currently under review. Exhausted by the prospect of yet another all-nighter ahead of him, he closed his eyes for a moment, listening to the sounds around him.

"The Prime Minister is scheduled to meet with dignitaries from several African nations...." The broadcaster's voice had a regal sound about it, his education likely procured from the very same institution they were driving through at that moment. Pondering the considerable requirements of candidacy, Ethan had been relieved to learn his participation as a Scope in The Valley was actually an exercise in mental acuity, a pure reflection; opinions, nothing more. His assessment was not subject to interpretation by the Review Board, a panel of experts who'd ultimately decide to either approve or

reject his submission proposal. If any of his observations proved beneficial to the program overall, all the better, but his project's acceptance was not contingent upon said assessment. With such a comforting notion firmly supplanted in mind, a road-weary traveler opened his tired eyes and began checking off boxes beside the questions he had memorized months before.

As they passed beneath the luminous streetlamps on campus, the strobe effect danced across the paper like a copier scanning through the car windows. As Ethan glanced from the corner of his eye, barely attentive to the task at hand, from time to time, he'd see a few of the students out for the evening strolling along the campus sidewalks. Surprised by how many of them were still mulling around, it brought to light how late that hour really was for Ethan, recalling those days of his youth as a student when all-night study sessions were merely a matter of course. The Valley was northeast of Oxford University; his flat, southwest of it. Deciding to save the "comments" section of the report for his destination, if he completed it at home, at least the handwriting would be more legible.

Eyes feeling the strain, his focus blurred, Ethan inadvertently raised the same hand that held a mechanical pencil to rub his itchy eyelids, almost poking himself in the face with the implement. Never one to multitask once he had become engaged with the written word, this aging scholar suddenly recalled his schoolboy teachers, often accusing him of daydreaming in class. When they would call his name Ethan would fail to respond. Such concentrated effort was reflected in exemplary grades. Forgiven all transgressions in the classroom, his apparent inattention suggested he was engrossed, deeply submersed with the curriculum of those books his nose was buried in. He absorbed by osmosis the lessons being discussed. His favorite history professor once joked that the Russians could invade England right under that nose while he remained oblivious to the tanks rolling in around him. The young master LaPierre was, indeed, a creature of habits established long ago.

"Up next, the agricultural report and then local weather. You're listening to the BBC...." Breaking into Mozart's Clarinet Concerto in A Minor, Ethan paused to reflect on events of the night, laying the files and pencil aside him on the seat. It was such a luxurious piece of music. He leaned back against the head

rest to take it in, closing his eyes again. A lover of classical music, the period piece allowed him to drift off. Accessing his "history" education, Ethan imagined himself going back in time to when these brilliant compositions were created. Pondering its true origin, he entertained a progressive concept of theorists (and a belief of some theologians) that composers such as Mozart, Brahms, Beethoven, Vivaldi and the like were not the *true* composers but were merely vessels through which angels from above were channeled to create such ethereal works, celestial gifts given to the world.

There's that moment between wakefulness and sleep when, through no process of thought or effort, the body will flinch, jumping as if catching oneself just before taking a leap off a tall building. Ethan braced his hands on each side of his legs just to stabilize himself, thinking he might have dozed off for hours when, in fact, it was only a few minutes. Startled, his eyes opened wide to determine his reality.

"…as it was on the subject of economic pressure anticipated for the succeeding Minister of Agriculture based on autumn projections…"

Talk about a transition of tunes! In his absence, the stereo booming out news of the pending reports, his thoughts quickly shifted from Mozart to one of his favorites from younger days. Thinking of drifting off or trying not to again, the classic song "Drift Away" by Dobie Gray popped into Ethan's mind. It would be stuck there for the rest of the night.

"Are you all right back there, sir?" Sparks knew what happened, as it happened a lot on their brief ride home, often at the end of an inordinately long day.

"Yes, yes, right as rain." Ethan replied, readjusting himself, sitting up straight in the back then clearing his throat, slightly embarrassed by the incident.

"Almost there, sir." Sparks was always reassuring, a comfort in the night.

There is much to acknowledge and to respect when it comes to the condition of mental fatigue, as basic skills almost always remain intact in spite of the exhaustion. Present and accounted for in mind even when the brain begins to compartmentalize and reprioritize, still attempting to function at optimum level within the parameters of necessity, it's an amazing machine that knows no bounds, even when disoriented. Ethan was on overload. He routinely reached a point of cerebral fatigue as a matter of course, more times than he'd care to admit. So common a threshold to cross, the bridge too far, he knew the route and could actually estimate how much more time he had to be productive before he would have to either shake the cobwebs loose or lay his body down. Physical exertion was one thing, mental fatigue, quite another.

His mind began wandering back into the past, his own, recalling his childhood, one structured primarily around academic endeavors. A curious lad, his youth was wrought with few perils, nothing more dangerous than a paper cut. Whether it was time spent reading the classics or, decades later, composing his first doctoral thesis, Ethan's predisposition was established early in life. He was not a star athlete during his formative years but that did not mean he wasn't in good shape. In fact, if not for his intellectual nature, he could have taken many directions in terms of his physical development but those years had quietly slipped away. Once Ethan began teaching, his only consistent form of exercise came in walking the college grounds, as several of his classes occurred on opposite sides of the campus, keeping him on his toes. It counted, in the same way he'd counted the steps up the stairway with Colin, though he wondered if that is what knocked him out, their hike across The Valley. He then caught himself projecting into the future, coming full circle, dreading all the work ahead of him. *"Paperwork...more bloody paperwork."*

Ethan anticipated exiting the car, emerging from the dreamy warmth into a fresh slap of cool night air, sure to revive him. Scaling the two sets of stairs up to his flat should get the blood pumping again. Ethan did the math. He figured ninety minutes – tops – before he'd have to intervene with caffeine or give up the ghost. Knowing he would need to get to work straightaway or risk slipping into a coma from sleep deprivation, with that vision, he laughed.

As the story of his life flashed before his eyes, the car began to slow, turning into the parking area for his building. Ah, home at last. Sparks opened his own door, preparing to do the same for a passenger when Ethan called out from the back seat.

"No bother, Sparks. I can manage it." Ethan gathered all of his belongings then stepped out of the vehicle, closing the door gently behind him.

"Yes sir, have a pleasant night, Dr. LaPierre." Closing his door, Sparks settled himself in the seat, opening his window. Ethan paused beside the car, as always, to utter the same words as he took his leave, a creature of habit.

"Thank you, Sparks. No loose women tonight, now."

"No promises, Doc. I don't have to get up for class anymore."

"There it is, then."

Their anticipated words came in a timely manner, precisely placed, an expected punctuation mark, words that indicated the end of their journey on any given night. With a tip of his imaginary chauffeur's hat, his standard response was a sweet, silent gesture of respect. Having made the familiar, understated exclamation point, Ethan winked, turning toward the pathway leading to his door. Sparks beamed his bright smile so broadly, it lit the path and warmed the chilly air.

It was his pleasure and privilege to transport the great Dr. LaPierre. Contracted by The Consortium, security details were assigned to post-classroom hours, usually from five in the evening on for transportation to and from the research facility and various locations off-campus. However, the contract also stipulated the shadowing of primary researchers who preferred to drive themselves while going off-grounds to shop, have dinner, etc. Essentially, Sparks was a bit of a spy and bodyguard. He remained in the idling vehicle ever vigilant, following Ethan with his eyes.

The residence was lovely, a three-story luxury apartment complex of Victorian descent. The entire stone façade adorned in lush English ivy, floral window planters full of blossoms, a variety of purple, yellow and red splashes of nature's creativity, it was always a wonder to behold. As Ethan approached the familiar five stone steps up to the solid oak door, Sparks remained diligently at attention, sure his passenger was safely inside behind it before calling it a night. Counting steps as he ascended, Ethan arrived on the landing where he stood beneath two bright electric porch lamps fashioned in the style of old gaslights. Reaching into his pocket, he retrieved a key ring cluttered with a collection of school, staff and safe keys. He always meant to mark them but time did not allow. Flipping to find the one for access to his building, he finally did. Unlocking the door, he waved his chauffeur on. Safe and sound.

Watching as Sparks departed, Ethan knew full well the probability of his driver spending the night alone was certain, identical to his own statistical routine. It was an unspoken connection between them, tacit understanding that each was a creature prone to introversion, both very comfortable with solitude. Sparks would more than likely head straight home then submerge himself in another classic film *noir*. Ethan wasn't as lucky. He had no time to escape into any such misdirection of energy and diversion of attention. He still had work to address in earnest. Indeed, that evening the air was reinvigorating, infusing Ethan with enough oxygen to awaken his brain and tickle his fancy as he recalled the events of the night. There he stood, taking it all in, surveying the landscape as he had on the knoll of The Valley. This apartment complex, the place he called home was comprised of twelve contemporary designed private domiciles with all the most modern conveniences, yet brilliantly in keeping with an Olde English motif, appointed with hardwood floors, ornate crown molding with a fireplace in every unit. Amenities aside, it was quite cozy.

All of Ethan's neighbors were connected in one form or another to the college, lending to the majority having the same sleep schedules. Definitely not a good thing to have a cranky professor due to sleep deprivation, yet, they all seemed to suffer it as it was not uncommon to look up from the street at this time of night and see most lights still on as they graded assignments or planned the next day's proceedings. It comforted him to know he wasn't alone in the dark. His place was on the second of two levels, twelve steps ordained with a rough running rug stapled all the way down the staircase, a handrail carved of rock maple, stained to perfection. Three entrances in front of the complex meant only two apartments per floor, per section. Ethan's was on the right side of the second floor. The door to his abode, appearing antique by design, was actually a heavily constructed imposter with far more durability and safety features provided than those it was modeled after. Be it ever so humble....

Once inside, his shoes came off, a conscientious routine, as the hardwood floors would echo the strikes of hard heels. As a show of respect for two colleagues who dwelled in the apartment below, it was also a welcome relief to let his feet breathe for the first time at the end of a long day. Suit jacket draped over the coat rack near the entrance, Ethan began gliding along on his socks like an Olympic speed skater, traveling across the combination living and dining space.

The contemporary furniture created an interesting juxtaposition with the elegant grandeur of the apartment. Clean, sleek lines against a backdrop of Victorian design with all the latest state-of-the-art electronic gadgets at his disposal, the man was in his comfort zone. With the entire campus wired to the hilt with Wi-Fi, almost every device programmable through a smart phone, Ethan barely needed to budge from his office. Lights, coffee timer, thermostat, security system. All set.

"Music. Tchaikovsky. Play."

The voice-activated wall mounted stereo accessed desired pieces from over one hundred thousand saved in a digital format. At the speed of thought, Ethan selected this evening's choice, retrieving it from his vast array of classical compositions, a 19th Century Russian composer. Volume preset at its lowest level, (so not to disturb the neighbors), a full orchestral ambience filled the room. Ethan continued past the kitchen then through a doorway to the right leading into a bedroom combined with an adjacent study. Most of the ample space was reserved for his project, only a twin bed crammed into the right corner of the oversized room. Appearing inadequate for his tall frame, to him, it was a creature comfort, a return to humbler days and nights spent sharing the campus dormitory during his undergraduate tenure. The plain gray wall-to-wall carpet accentuated the lack of personal décor. His closet was a study in academic discipline, presented in the manner of a serious student. All of his suits or casual attire were hanging evenly, neatly organized, suit jackets donning Oxford insignia. Professor LaPierre's personal space spoke of propriety. A study in modern minimalism, the right side of the room was sparse, the picture of simplicity.

The opposite view to the right side of the room provided a very stark, startling contrast, almost reflective of another personality, someone scattered or cluttered in the extreme. To an unaccustomed eye it would appear chaotic, not the least bit tidy. Upon closer inspection, one might recognize a process, the method to the madness. It looked like a forensics research project. Hundreds of unframed pictures all strewn across a two-tier desk, scores more taped to the back wall from desktop to ceiling. The office seemed to belong to an investigator, one sleuth on the prowl for a culprit. Old case files from Scotland Yard and the London Police stood at attention between wire dividers but the photographs and drawings referenced another era not his own. There were stylish images of old English menswear, pictures and maps of the streets of London from an earlier century, books stacked randomly titled by various topics, including medical reference books. From criminal forensics to autopsy procedures, his library littered the floor and covered the gamut on the subject at hand. Ethan's office chair was worn leather, aged and used regularly, daily, for hours upon hours. Once an opportunity to take the lead on a Flicker research proposal / submission of his own surfaced, since he saw the chance to become history himself, it had become his one and only passion, his life's work.

"Hello boys!" Saluting as he addressed the instruments of his work, Ethan had taken to acknowledging the tools of his trade as colleagues; his partners, his team. As Symphony No. 4 played subtly in the background, he pulled out the loyal leather chair from beneath his desk, once again settling in for at least ninety more minutes, an estimation of the necessary effort according to his calculations during transport. He'd now complete the comment section of those field assessment forms he would not escape but couldn't complete in a moving vehicle without them looking like the illegible scribbling of a nine-year-old boy on a candy high.

By this time, the Princess Diana crash reenactment had been done enough times to leave barely any room for criticism, yet he had remarks to make. Still, the forms had to be filled out, discrepancies noted then submitted in a timely manner. Almost immediately Ethan's concentration began to wane, not simply from fatigue but also because he always considered the reports made on his own time trials. His was one of the first research requests, his proposal submitted when the program went online. Was there anything he'd missed? Were the other project reviewers careless in their review of his project, focused on their own? Did budget constraints factor into the delay? The details he was not privy to distracted him most. Ethan needed to know.

"Christ, I must be awfully tired." Forty minutes or so had passed since he'd last glanced at his pocket watch, rubbing his eyes to make sure he saw the correct time. Could it really be 2:36 a.m.? Filling in the final void box reserved for his comments, his input of words, a critique in support of what had transpired earlier in the evening at The Valley was invaluable to the research and any subsequent conclusions drawn by the FTC team. No matter how tedious, it *did* serve a purpose.

Once finished, he reloaded the forms into the corresponding envelope and set it aside. Suddenly inspired to continue, in spite of the late hour, Ethan began delving into his backlog of papers to grade. History students tend to go on (and on) and he quickly tired of the task. Considering these young, facile minds, he wondered what adventures, what breakthroughs awaited them over decades to come. Opportunities are boundless when an imagination and curiosity collides with knowledge at an age when the mind is fertile ground and the appetite to know more is insatiable. In the reading of a few pages he determined the sad fact that some of his newest History students obviously required tutorials in English! Hunched over in his leather chair, Ethan shook his head, appalled by their linguistic foibles and ample spelling errors. *"Didn't they even look at the computer screen before printing out their text? The program does the bulk of the editing work for them! Did they not notice the colorful squiggly lines?"* Laboring to rise from his seat, Ethan wandered the room, worried for the future of the planet when all these hormone driven kids take over the world. He murmured to himself, "God help us. God help us all."

Having worked far longer than intended, Ethan called it a night. Retiring to his bed, the struggle persisted, the strain on his brain finally taking its toll on the eyes. His mind in flux, still reeling with recollections of an eventful eve, Ethan attempted to quiet his thoughts. Relaxing into a prone position, descending into ascension, he suddenly realized the adverse effects such a long day had on his physical form, as every single atom in his *not so young anymore* body screamed then surrendered to the call of a soft mattress. His feather pillow serving as an amazingly regenerative device, it was almost magical the way it enveloped his head, ushering him into the blissfully unconscious splendor of sleep. After one more habitual check of the time, Ethan replaced his pocket watch on the night table. It was never beyond his grasp, practically a part of the man. Rolling over on one side, he made a few primal sounds that are perhaps the only verbalizations still able to bridge all languages at any time in history. Moaning and groaning with the efforts required to move his aching body comfortably into position, he counted the hours remaining for him to rest before he had to begin his daily grind all over again. Closing his burning eyes, Ethan pictured the weary Sisyphus, a tragic figure condemned to rolling his rock up a mountain.

The timepiece that had controlled his life for the past six years, ever since he'd found it in an old London antique shop during one of his late night research walks, it was both a friend and a foe. Structuring each day according to its delicate features, slender arms pointing to Roman numerals he'd adhere to in his travels, it functioned as a reminder of a chronically tight schedule, sometimes doing so with disapproving overtones, the face of it glaring back at him whenever he was running late. Cordial when he was right on time, a metaphorical pat on the back seemed even jovial when he was running ahead of schedule, a rarity. It seemed Ethan was always on the run. And so was his pocket companion, right there beside him. It was as if the timepiece owned him instead of the other way around. He was a slave to its rhythm, the ticking tock of a clock in perpetual motion, as much in need of it as his own beating heart. Quickly addicted to the feel of the silver watch in his pocket, it added to his weight and measure as a man.

Ethan didn't know much about the watch because the shop owner knew little to nothing about it himself. The design was, by the cogs and clock face, French. It was pure silver, cover embossed in the likeness of a three-legged horse, breed unknown. With no inscription or family crest to divulge its origin, just the three-legged horse standing alone in the field, it was a unique, anomalous piece of craftsmanship and was undoubtedly a one-of-a-kind design, perhaps a commemorative piece in honor of a special pet. Regardless of the reason why, Ethan was instantly drawn to it. The moment he saw it in the window, it spoke to him. Tick tock. The following morning he was waiting for the owner to unlock the door. Ethan knew it was meant for him.

He associated the image on the watch cover with his time spent around horses. At the age of eight, Ethan's parents whisked him away to a boarding school where he'd spent a good deal of his time working in the equestrian stables to earn money and keep fit. (Obviously it didn't stick, the "keeping fit" part.) Even at Oxford, he seemed to link with people involved in activities such as the Polo Club or the Horse Riding Club. Observing the majestic, towering creatures trotting along a manicured track, some strapped in harnesses with someone in tow, others set free to roam in a pasture of clover, they were blissful to watch, even more splendid to touch. Some clopping along through *the cobblestone alleys, only the shadow of its titan form bouncing off dimly lit warehouse walls. He came into sight, the stud, steam rushing from his flaring nostrils on a cold, moonless night, silently, but for hooves striking stone. In full view, fiery eyes glowing red with pure fury, black wings extending from his sleek body, the Pegasus of doom emerged from darkness, fulfilling his role as the harbinger of death.* Ethan shuddered beneath the sheets, urgent realizations coming with an evil image, a bizarre, manipulating memory invasion from within his subconscious mind. He was falling asleep, drifting off into dream state, floating on the feathers of a pillow. He thought it best not to fight the feeling. Well past time to let go. Gone.

Wet cobblestone streets glistened under clear, moonlit skies through the early morning fog, rolling around corners, following the breeze. From this vantage point Ethan can see everything, allowing him to blend into the narrow alley, a shadowed walkway off the main street. The hollow sound, the shoes of a bobby approaching, dancing off the edifices of wood and stone surrounding him. Raising one hand to his uniform hat as a couple pass him in the other direction, Ethan's heart begins to race. Hearing the pulsing of blood in his eardrums, pumping faster and faster, matching the rapid increase in his breathing, he waits in anticipation of discovery. The officer turns left, disappearing down a side street as the couple moves further down the main road, strolling out of sight. Simon and Garfunkel begin singing "The Sound of Silence". Playing in his head, an eeriness in the atmosphere begins to toy with his imagination. Senses tingling with the passion of the piece, the pleasure of it calms his rattled nerves. Aware that his familiarity with music is a safe haven, an escape from his fears or phobias, it directs him to focus on the notes and lyrics, to listen. "...because a vision softly creeping left its seeds while I was sleeping..." The shadows, someone around a corner reflects off buildings illuminated by the gaslight streetlamps perched overhead. "And the vision that was planted in my brain still remains..." Following shadows, the echo of footsteps, faint at first then increasing in volume, coming ever closer then increasing in speed, from a standard cadence to a fast walk then a run in some haste and urgency. No, wait. The footsteps stopped. Had he made some sound he'd been unaware of? Did he give himself away? Had someone else scared them off? Pause, holding his breath, there are footsteps again, immediately running from a dead stop. One, two, three, four, five, six, seven, eight, stop. One, two, three, four, five, six, seven, eight, stop. One, two, three….

III.
STICKING THE LANDING

"Ethan?" The distant voice jarred him awake.

"Oh shit! He knows my name! How the hell does he know I'm still here?" As the words swirled in his mind, he could not speak them aloud.

"Ethan, open the door! P, it's me! Open the door, mate!"

The sounds of rapid footsteps continuing, Ethan suddenly began to feel himself being sucked backwards out of the shadows of the dark alley into a vortex, his brain readjusting to the sound he'd mistaken. Jolted into consciousness by the real origin of the noises he'd heard, someone banging at the apartment door, he woke from his disturbing dream. Pounding resumed, matched only by the throbbing in his temples. A clearing of cobwebs, he laid quite still in his bed listening intently, trying to make sense of it. Ethan recognized a distinctive voice as that of Colin Bishop.

"Oh, shit! Shit! Fuck me!" Slamming both feet to the floor, not thinking of the tenant beneath him at the moment, Ethan immediately reached for his pocket watch on the nightstand, frantically concerned that he'd overslept, missing his first class, picturing students gazing at a desk void of a professor. With a sigh of relief he saw the time. It was only 6:39 a.m. As quite another category of panic arose within him, wondering what on earth happened that Colin would be banging on his door at such an ungodly hour, in a rocking motion Ethan projected his body upward, launching himself from the side of the bed. Tilting his head backward in a stretch, coming to his senses while coming to his feet, Ethan yelled "Hang on, Col!" hoping his voice would resonate throughout the apartment to reach the front door. Gliding along the wooden floor in his thick woolen socks Ethan realized the music he'd enjoyed hours before was still playing. "Music. Off." The system obeyed his verbal command and the classical composition went mute. Morning light subtly seeking entrance through his kitchen windows, it illuminated the room enough for Ethan to navigate the path safely to his door.

"Colin Bishop! Sweet Jesus, mate! This had damn well better be an emergency of epic proportion...you'd better have a coffee with you!" Yelling through it while he unlocked the door, Ethan yanked it open to find his friend propped in the alcove, casually standing there, a coy grin betraying a secret on his lips.

"No, I don't have 'a' coffee. I've got two!" Holding up one of the two cardboard cups in his possession, Colin handed the hazelnut blend over to Ethan. "For you." Strolling across the threshold right past a sleepyhead, Colin put his cup in Ethan's other hand. "Here. Hold this for me, will you?" Doing as requested, Ethan perched himself on the arm of a chair, watching as his impetuous, uninhibited friend began dancing like a performer at a Greek festival, one who'd sipped a bit too much ouzo. Arms outstretched, snapping his fingers, this was too much Zorba, too early. If only separated in age by two years, Ethan being the eldest, Colin obviously retained most of his boyish charms, qualities he'd exemplified when they were still students.

Dancing wildly around the apartment to some nonexistent tune in his head, he abruptly stopped. Sticking the landing, he struck the pose similar to a gymnast after a difficult dismount. The class clown was out of breath, clearly a little out of shape. Colin placed both hands by his sides, attempting to calm his nerves and contain his excitement. Only one thing would've dragged him out of bed and across campus at this hour. Only one thing mattered that much. Looking his befuddled brother in the eyes, Colin's contented smile said it all. Ethan raised his eyebrows, seeking further confirmation of a suspicion. Nodding his head, returning the coffee, two men faced one another in amazement, as if they had both been told they'd just become a father. Gestation period over, the baby is born! Touching cups together in an early morning toast, one project stuck up in the air far too long, the waiting game was over. Ethan's Flicker project was a "GO!" His proposal submission finally approved. Colin began by boasting.

"Anson called *me* with the news! He thought I'd like to be the one to tell you, in person. Damn nice of him! He's flying in this morning from the site to meet with you on campus. He suggested we meet him in the conference room at the museum."

"My morning seminar..."

"Covered. Dr. Ellis is taking over all of your classes. You're done for the semester. You've got places to go…things to do…people to see. Start packing, Doc!"

Like the release valve on a pressure cooker, Ethan exhaled.

"He's a good substitute. My students know him and he knows my syllabus. So, when did Anson call you?" Begging the question, "What time?"

"Final approval came just after midnight, Geneva time. We didn't get word until sometime after 2:00 a.m., just before he left for the airport. Naturally, the military consignment was the alleged holdout, problematic component with *security*, as we expected." Colin explained.

As jovial as Colin was in those moments, Ethan was his antithesis, ignoring the little quips and comments that would normally make him laugh. Mood and manner as serious as the mission, he got right down to business. He wanted details.

"What about the Ethics Council?"

"They were the first chips in the game." Colin stepped closer to Ethan, placing the coffee-free hand on his shoulder. "P, they always considered you an honest and responsible, even a respectable candidate for the Flicker project, regardless of your questionable ethnic heritage." This time Ethan had to laugh, relaxing a bit.

"Not ethnic, Col! I said *Ethics* Council." Playing right along.

"Oh, them!" Playing into his hand, Colin countered and raised. "They gave you a pass right away, though how anyone could trust a Frenchman…"

As a term of endearment Colin had been calling Ethan "P" since their days spent together as students, referencing the capital P in LaPierre as punctuation. Being of French and Irish descent, Ethan's mixture was his schoolmate's favorite target for antagonistic banter, describing Ethan's tenacity and passion with a letter, no matter how consistently he played those emotional cards, always close to the vest.

Ethan was in a momentary daze. He slid down into the red fabric chair, modern style design, a chair he barely ever used. It was kept for company, though he rarely entertained. But the room needed furnishings should that day ever come, and it had come at dawn. His lapse of attention from Colin was nothing personal. He was lost in thought, riddled with emotions. It was an astounding feeling, like the first day of school all over again. Over six years of trials, proofs, reports and research. Finally, the time had come. It was what every candidate dreamed of manifesting. Yet, only in that moment did the full impact and magnitude of what was now going to happen give him chills, even though he'd always known the profound responsibility of it. Ethan's heart jumped into his throat with an acute awareness. His Flicker project was no longer a hypothetical proposal. Humbled, honored, knowing precisely how massive this endeavor was going to be, the difference his research would make to recorded history, it was as if Ethan had just awakened from a dream. He rubbed his head while Colin made mental plans around his friend's accomplishment.

"We've got to hit the pub, have a few pints!" Colin insisted. "Tonight! What ya say, mate? Maybe even invite Magpie along? Oh, c'mon P! It's time to celebrate!" Colin began dancing to his own tune again.

"What are you talking about?" Still bewildered, this was a legitimate question. Ethan hadn't processed the previous statement. It didn't make any sense in his mind because he was thinking logically. There was only one imperative for consideration.

I've got to review my work. Right now! I've got to go over everything again."

Colin abruptly stopped dancing mid hip thrust, frozen in the most awkward but comical position possible, a posture that had to hurt. Enhancing the overall effect of his staid reaction to a comrade's judgment call, Colin paused, stuck in his shtick. Dropping his arms, untwisting his warped torso, the man hung his head in defeat. "Buzzkill." It was the only word that sufficed and it seemed apropos at the moment. As the air in Colin's lungs drained out with one long sigh, Ethan could literally hear his disappointment, lingering like dense English fog on the moors.

A wave of compassion swept over Dr. Bishop as an uncharacteristic expression of caring took hold of him. Looking down upon his friend, it occurred to Colin that he should say something encouraging, sincere. Squatting down in front of the chair, placing both of his hands upon Ethan's knees, with reverence and respect he rarely displayed, effusive heartfelt empathy, Colin found precisely the right words for the poignant moment.

"P, you know this project better than anyone in the field. You've covered every square inch of it, been over every detail for years. It's been your baby from the very beginning, *your* project right from the start. You needn't worry about a thing, chap! You're a bloody fucking SCOPE! The real deal! You've got this!"

Colin's epiphany wasn't lost in delivery. Ethan bolted upright from his chair as his friend sat back on the drab gray carpet, giving him room to roam. Then came a knowing smirk, that familiar quirky grin Colin claimed as his lifelong expression. Before Ethan could divulge the plan of action, his classmate broke into an English drinking song they knew well and sang together at a few of the local pubs over the years, back in the good old days of youth.

"As I went down to Derby town,
All on a summer's day,
It's there I saw the finest ram,
That's ever fed on hay...."

With only the slightest prompt, a shake of the hand, Ethan joined in the revelry.

"And if you don't believe me,
And think I tell a lie,
Just you go down to Derby,
And you'll see the same as I...."

Taking a minute to catch his breath, Ethan paused after their duet. It was a new beginning, a new chapter, personally and professionally. Standing beside Colin, as he silently reflected on his lot in life, Ethan pondered marvelous, magical moments which had seemingly all conspired to transport him to this singular moment in time. A brilliant flash of total recall, memories made over the course of a lifetime passed through his mind, a series of snapshots or slides feathering through the light which curiously illuminated each from behind the image captured. He not only saw these images, he could see the light.

IV.
UNDER THE RADAR

It begs the question and poses an argument regarding the human mind in all its inherent complexity. Those of good character, an honest nature will make decisions based on positive outcomes, contributions made of the results, or will at least claim the premise as true. How does one really know, though? Most folks go on the basis of hope that when someone trusts another, that trust has been earned and is returned in kind, repaid in good will, always the best of intentions.

To the dismay of history, one common theme has been the selfish intent of man. In a group setting, men will talk, debate and argue for the betterment of all society. However, the singular individual, one man or woman, will seek the personal interest at heart first. It is human nature, for good or evil. Mother Theresa, Gandhi, Mandela and those few others in history who've stepped beyond a pattern of selfishness and made the world a better place for it, leading by example, have been too few and far between, leaving the world otherwise "off balance" and clearly leaning toward the diabolical. Throughout the course of human history many world leaders, pharaohs, kings, queens, soldiers who have appointed themselves as "president" have had the proclivity for meeting their needs through the exercise of power, governing for one instead of the masses in the most self-serving way. These were the concerns of the Ethics Council.

Having been subjected to numerous psychiatric evaluations over six years, per the Flicker Project Oversight Committee, his acceptance was a stamp of approval, having determined that Ethan, being of sound mind and body, was ready to take the deep plunge into the past. The Ethics Council was an integral, compulsory element of The Consortium, mainly comprised of psychiatrists, psychologists, physicians, theologians and even military intelligence. Their primary concern was to establish what kind of individual every candidate was at the core. All tolled it was a grueling process, nearly dehumanizing. Methods used to derive information were, at times, downright brutal. According to the powers that be, it was necessary to preserve the integrity of the program as a whole and if someone wanted to gain entrance to the Flicker, they'd have to be willing to endure some humiliations with the intention of protecting this sensitive project. Interrogations often involved a loss of control, so to observe and verify how a candidate reacted under pressure, in adverse conditions. When subjected to prolonged periods of sleep deprivation, malnutrition, coercion, enticement, seduction and myriad other stress scenarios, the circumstances imposed upon them enabled the gauging of candidate durability. It was imperative they knew every risk to define any potential hazards posed by the project selectees. Possessing profound implications, including its potential military applications, it was much too significant a discovery to place in jeopardy with one faulty decision. Flicker was much more important than the sum of its souls on either side of assessment tables. It could only prove to be a gift to humanity if the discovery was handled with care.

Colin was correct. The Ethics Council had been the first of these high-powered committees to sign off on Ethan's project submission, a real peacock feather in his cap. It was recognized as quite an accomplishment by all involved in the project. A normally headstrong section of the committee, it was considered the largest hurdle by all petitioners and had denied many proposals in the past. With his usual stoic resolve, Ethan had committed to remain true to his principles during the grueling process, come what may. It paid off in the end, which was only the beginning. His was one of only three project submissions to survive such intense scrutiny, that is, since the Van Ruden incident which occurred when it all began.

Back in the year 2008, September 10th to be precise, a consortium of scientists, physicists, mathematicians, theorists and a support staff gathered from universities and laboratories. Through the miracle known as the internet more than ten thousand people from over one hundred countries witnessed history in the making: the first tests of the Large Hadron Collider (or LHC). Built by the European Organization of Nuclear Research (or CERN), this massive new machine built along the border of Switzerland and France was the world's largest, most powerful particle collider. It took a decade to construct and it was built primarily to test the endless theories and predictions regarding particle physics and high-energy physics while connected on the worldwide web to thirty-five countries. All the initial trials went very well, moving particles within milliseconds of the speed of light, smashing them together.

Everything changed on September 19, 2008 when the quench incident occurred. There was a bending of one hundred giant magnets. Six tons of liquid helium leaked out with the impact of a massive explosion. Were they tinkering with elements too unstable and unpredictable? Were they playing God? The LHC took its first hit, its first hiccup, or was it their first warning? For the next fourteen months the program was halted.

The LHC went back online and testing resumed in November of 2009 but prior to that, back in December of '08, CERN released a *complete* analysis report of the quench incident. It was incomplete. What was released to the public was press-safe, an explanation regarding the mechanical issues leading up to that event. What they neglected to include in the public report was the "anomaly" that occurred during it, lasting only .0009 seconds. This was ascertained during damage assessment review. Only then did they discover the anomaly when its monitoring cameras were slowed down and scrutinized frame-by-frame. Something strange occurred, something that was momentarily visible. Like the flash bulb from an old-fashioned camera, it was there and then it was gone. Thermal imaging cameras in position, there to read heat variations, fluctuations during particle testing, detected a doorway, not a manmade construction but more of an opening, a vortex.

CERN immediately found itself compartmentalized, their new Top Secret label stamped above this occurrence. Until they could discern what this was, or was not, the nature of it had to be studied. Until they could determine if this was a perpetual threat or some uncontrollable benevolent occurrence, by necessity it would remain cloaked in secrecy, available only to key members at the facility. Of ten thousand people involved in the original project, only about two hundred and twenty-five had knowledge of or any access to it as it morphed into something else entirely. Those privileged to be involved were instructed to comply with a newly drafted, enforced protocol. Though there was no designation for it at the time, it eventually came to be known as The Flicker Project…or Flicker.

Almost immediately after the anomalous event occurred, new project directions and a subsequent cover story emerged on December 15, 2009. It was an experiment in ion collision to determine the nature and qualities of phenomena known as quark-gluon plasma. Theorized to have been in existence since the "early" Universe, still in existence in some compact form in current times, it was presumed to be more of a rediscovery of "The God Particle". The method utilized for particle collision was designated ALICE and the "looking glass" it created appeared to be an example of the theoretical Einstein-Rosen Bridge. What was once merely a hypothesis would transform into reality before the eyes of a select few who could barely believe what they were witnessing.

Many attempts were made to recreate the doorway, yet, it was not until May of 2011 when they'd actually succeeded. The general research access was open to all but the results of that primary research were, in fact, secondary to this discovery. Flicker remained clandestine, flying under the radar. The area where this anomaly consistently reappeared was restricted, guarded, claiming it to be hazardous during testing. Nobody outside the scope of the initial team was allowed to observe, those who had been there since the inception of the covert project. There were only a few "necessary" people to inform from both operations logistics and security protocol. They were aware of what was happening but were not technically involved, not for the first two years, anyway. During that time, there were countless offline *off the grid* experiments to attempt to sustain the vortex, to keep the door open. Successes were slow but consistent. A minimal military presence was required and they wore civilian clothing, always on the scene should something enter through the doorway. Nothing ever did. Instead, once they could control the opening, their research team began breaches with robotic probes, cameras attached. All they saw was the facility but there was a slight time delay. It was calculated that eight seconds had elapsed, or, in other words, what they were observing was eight seconds in the past.

For the next year they tried all variants of testing to effect a change so to control and perfect the length of time the door could remain open. Measuring the collision speeds of particles, by increasing the intensity of additional magnets placed around the anomaly, they were finally able to intensify, specify and regulate the depth back in time and the duration of the opening as well as the geographical destination. That took a little more time to perfect. Time exploration of space would, no doubt require more power than imaginable. The initial trials made the quantum leap from probes to people in a relatively short period of time. Like a child playing with his father's gun, it wasn't long before the first shot was fired. Only then did scientists, all giddy with success, wake up to its stark reality. The Van Ruden incident was that gunshot.

Anson Van Ruden was candidate number four during their early trials. The first brave men were involved in a *"step in step out"* scenario which they did at various points and locations in time. Every opening of Flicker was designated for arrival in late night hours, so to lessen the potential for human contact with the one jumping through. The return trip was surprisingly simple. As long as the doorway remained open and the traveler knew its location then he needed merely to walk back into it. The portal was, on either side, undetectable to the naked eye. Only through thermal imaging could it be seen. So, it could be in Times Square or located in the center of a soccer field and no one would know it. The traveler need only remember where he'd entered to exit.

The third had taken the longest trip, two hours away halfway around the world on an uninhabited Pacific island. The fourth trial involved the candidate Anson Van Ruden, a physicist. He was scheduled to take a six hour trip. The doorway in time took a massive amount of energy to open but sustaining the opening required both proper and precise magnetic positioning and amplitude. Like thrusters on booster rockets of the Space Shuttle, Flicker used an immense amount of energy to escape the gravitational pull exerted from present time before it could freely float in the zero gravity of the past. This was a two-fold stress test of Flicker's capabilities for depth of time and geographical distance. A plethora of run-throughs had to be made to see how long the door would stay open and how far back in time it would reach before the portal would "flame out" requiring days or even weeks to reformat the collider for yet another gauging of its potential limits. Thus far the farthest back the vortex seemed to remain stable, not in flux, was assessed through a series of probes and stellar computations to be the year 1947. Any attempts to probe deeper into the past was akin to a breaker box on steroids tripping off. CLEAR and RESET! These tests and experiments helped the think tank begin calculations on the engineering adjustments necessary to breach the current limit.

Dr. Van Ruden had a stocky, six-foot-three build. If not for his brilliant mind, he could've easily passed for a fifty-six year old lumberjack with his ruddy cheeks, flaming red hair, a beard and handlebar moustache. He was a trusted and respected member of The Consortium. His destination was also scaled and recorded for the farthest geographical point the quantum leap would reach. As a previously visited location during the last venture, a remote deserted island in the Pacific was a likely choice. It was widely theorized that when the amount of energy expended for *depth* of time was minimized the geographical opportunities would increase substantially, but repeated trials proved when the *timeline* was stretched to its maximum capacity their window of physical or global distance and duration actually narrowed. Anson Van Ruden's trial was expected to go just as uneventfully as the others had, were it not for the fact that three hours into his excursion, he came upon a scared Japanese soldier who thought World War II was still an ongoing conflict. What ensued was a wild chase through the jungle, a *foreign* soldier repeatedly shooting at him despite Anson's attempts to explain his presence as harmless in the six languages he knew, none of them Japanese, trying to convince the man the war was over.

As Anson reached the doorway he had pre-marked for his exit, he was attacked by the younger, though much weaker combatant. His rifle ammunition depleted, he went after the larger Anson with his bayonet, thrashing and screaming incoherently. As they wrestled Anson finally got the upper hand as the warrior was malnourished. Grabbing the handle of the blade, Anson twisted it inward, penetrating the soldier's abdomen. As the pitiful soldier looked up at Anson in shock, his woeful life fading away, he tumbled backward, taking Dr. Van Ruden with him. The direction of that fateful fall carried both of them right through the doorway of the Flicker.

Both men came through the portal, crashing to the floor in a pool of blood. For a moment everyone froze, dazed and confused by the sight. Several members of the team ran over to them to find the combatant dead.

Anson was physically unharmed, though obviously in shock. Four of the senior staff immediately decided to assist in helping him carry the body back through the doorway, making sure before and after that they did what was necessary. No physical evidence remained in the past of the altercation with someone from the future. The major issue: what *other* harm might have occurred? For several minutes everybody stood around staring at one another as if they had just broken their mother's favorite vase in the cosmic parlor.

The timeline being disturbed, fears surfaced, beyond knowing whether (or not), one by one, each of them would begin to vanish like those in the photo Marty McFly carried with him of his siblings and himself in the classic film "Back to the Future". They were in uncharted territory. Who was this young Japanese man who just died sixty-five years ago? Was he supposed to be rescued, perhaps become a war hero? Go into politics? Was his destiny to become president of Mitsubishi Corporation or was he just an average "nobody" whose offspring was now a part of their coalition? Like Scopes, everyone watched everyone else.

Fortunately, not. Their next few days were spent feverishly researching his dog tag identification, a scouring of war records for him or his lineage to determine if his body was ever recovered and if any potential descendants were in existence. It was an exhaustive effort made through every conceivable resource at their disposal. Relieved that the lost, deceased soldier named Michio Tamakusuku had been listed as "missing in action" at the end of the war, it appeared Dr. Van Ruden had only hastened his inevitable demise, his quick death, a mercy.

A false sense of security was instilled in some while other members among The Consortium still theorized, wondering if their actions might have disrupted history. Could it be the reason why that soldier was never found? The conundrum was itself a vicious cycle. Nervously waiting to see if what occurred had altered them, if there was a "change" back in 1947 (due to their interference), there would be no possible way for them to recognize this change had occurred if it did. Most suffered a brain freeze over the incident, something akin to sucking down a Slurpee too fast. Many of them were burdened by it, over-processing a paradox, the intrinsic consequences of time travel as they reckoned and reconciled it against the advancement of science for the betterment of humanity. Some of them quit while others requested (and were granted) reassignment off-site, away from Flicker.

There would be no turning back, no stopping these opportunities for discoveries concerning the mortal mistakes made in the past. To determine what was accurately documented in history and what was not: it was too crucial and far too precious an opportunity to abandon because of one glitch. As the saying goes, history is written by the victors. It was the first time this technology was available for scientists and other scholars to peek through the looking glass of ALICE, to witness actual history as it occurred. Flicker was an altruistic endeavor. To dismiss a great gift, this virtual "microscope" capable of peering into the living history of humankind would be an abomination regardless of the inherent risks imposed by the discovery. For them to forsake their effort would be plain irresponsible, an act of wanton disregard for the human race. Events in history which may not have played out precisely as recorded in the annals of time could be exacted, clarified; rectified for future generations. An ability to leap through time was not a reckless endeavor. On the contrary, from the moment the ability to do so existed it became an imperative act of conscience. Poets know the truth. "Those who cannot remember the past are condemned to repeat it." (George Santayana)

Anson Van Ruden resigned from the candidate program and immediately began forming the Flicker Trial Consortium Oversight Committee (FTCOC) to ensure the establishment of strict protocols, standards, inquiry, as stringent training regimens, so every candidate was prepared, made fully aware of the responsibilities and risks involved with time travel. It was imperative that each candidate be trusted implicitly with such a sensitive and truly provocative discovery. For over a century scientists, theorists, university scholars, writers and, of course, film producers have posed the concept of the potential consequences of traveling back in time. The notion that the linear event of time could simply be redirected or changed by the slightest act of a time traveler became a concern of frightening proportions. The FTCOC made this the top priority on a long list of alterations built into this institutionalized think tank and subsequent program, rapidly expanding into the collective of councils and sub-councils, each committee created to serve a specific purpose.

The Ethics Council was the penultimate panel, the spearhead committee of The Consortium. Anson took the lead role, ensuring those chosen as candidates were of good stock, strong stable mind. Those selected completed a plethora of compulsory questionnaires and review forms from test trials to remove any doubts. Anyone void of moral fiber could conceivably, for purely selfish reasons, contaminate a process, jeopardizing the program. Whether due to a political persuasion, a religious agenda or otherwise, whatever the impetus, deliberately tampering with the timeline of the past to change the known present or the unknown future would be a disastrous, epic failure. If The Consortium let even one bad seed slip through the crack in its barrel the results of such an oversight could be catastrophic for humanity. Knowing these inherent risks, candidates selected would have to be approved by the entire group. The vote was anonymous and had to be unanimous for acceptance into the program, no exceptions made. It was the prerequisite of paramount importance. Essentially, the Ethics Council called all the shots. Their responsibilities were the most difficult, tasked with peering into the heart, mind and soul of another human being.

Until their discovery of the portal, the scientific community almost uniformly theorized that any devised method of time travel would require some machine that would likely have an adverse effect on any and all electronic devices utilized in its function. Just as the electromagnetic pulse in a nuclear detonation overloads every device impacted by it, a time machine would shut down the electrical impulses of the brain and body. A perfect indication of what mankind does not yet know about the Universe, the Flicker had no such drawbacks. It was simply a doorway. Anyone carrying anything could merely walk through it, experiencing no ill effects but there was concern for the return.

The Medical Review Board, staffed by several top minds in modern medicine, included specialists in world medical history. They, along with their support team, would be responsible for examining and approving all the candidates. History itself was one critical component, another valuable resource for the committee, providing documentation of plague and pestilence, epidemics, pandemics afflicting the world, pinpointing a specific virus down to the week of the outbreak then exactly where it occurred yet, viruses mutate. Diseases presenting during various stages across ages of human existence have evolved along with mankind. Of course not every calamity was chronicled, so it was a bit of a crap shoot, after all, the deathly serious guessing game of Russian roulette. To insure these landmines were avoided precautions were taken, yet there was no immunity anybody could build (like muscle mass) to guard against past plagues which ravaged Europe hundreds of years before these travelers were born. Ironically, having been born into a world currently riddled with disease had its benefits. If one survived the exposures of childhood into adulthood, chances were their immune system has sufficiently developed enough to provide a modicum of protection for candidates who proved worthy of taking the leap.

It was imperative that time travelers not deliver or receive any infectious illness. It was likewise essential these candidates comply with its rigorous medical training, expecting each to become proficient in triage techniques for "in the field" treatment. Should they succumb to any physical injuries they needed to have specialized skills, patching themselves up enough to allow for mobility to return to the portal location. "Medical" had to approve everything returning to the present, to make quite certain there were no pathogens or parasites hitchhiking a ride. Maintaining sterility within the project environment, going and coming, was the major focus of this department. The only cross-committee professional was one psychologist who was copied in on reports to the Ethics division. The mental stability of all project selectees was tested then retested for stressors, memory issues, phobias and a multitude of other criteria as the training occurred and progressed. Unlike the jump, it wasn't a one-shot deal.

Then there was the Military and Security Committee. Their multitasking unit, this council comprised of civilian and uniformed representatives from twenty-two countries was a force to be reckoned with and a necessary evil. Dr. Van Ruden was extremely cautious around them, quite clever in his design for the use and limits of this division of their coalition. The LHC project designated its home near Geneva, Switzerland. Although the bulk of underground operations of the particle collider was actually located beneath

French soil, in fact it was always a neutrally controlled operation. This being inarguable, the committee could and did control the military's involvement at every step without having to concern itself with the historical record of them muscling in on projects of science, soon thereafter weaponized. Anson and his constituents understood the necessity for occupancy and the scope of their reach. From background checks to surveillance capability, the on-site security specialists were there to protect key members and candidates. Anson believed there wasn't a single member in the military department of the organization that could ever pass the ethics requirements they so stringently enforced.

The Debriefing Council was the most difficult committee to staff. This was the post-event group, those charged with sifting through a candidate's documentation, given full access to the individual for all subsequent interviews and examinations. Anson wore a secondary hat, holding a high position in this office, his own Flicker experience leading him to request all debriefing materials be copied to him. Yes, even the military got their crack at the returning travelers. This was the only sector of the process which integrated representatives from various religious institutions. Considering history's sordid recording of religious involvement in political affairs, senior members of the committee felt pressure to glean all information, impressions from the time travelers; a faith-based assessment of events from their own unique perspectives. Discussions were encouraged but only after travelers had been fully debriefed, cleared for discharge. It was presumed that atheists would make the best candidates, logic at the core of a belief that there is no God. Instead, having *faith* in the "scientific method", they relied on it to tell the truth. Those travelers with a foundation in a belief system involving a specific religious affiliation could expect some fascinating, spiritually significant conversations with the theologians after the fact, sharing their moments of epiphany about the project as personal revelations.

The remaining committee members were support staff, more involved with the ongoing time trials in The Valley. So many project requests being submitted from all over the world, The Consortium could afford to be selective, downright picky. It took years to get to the *go ahead* point in the process and the importance of trial runs at The Valley factored heavily into the equation, essential to it once a research submission was approved. The fact that it was in England on the grounds of Oxford University mattered little to influences of the opposition against the project overall, as it was only preliminary "plays" and not the real thing, located in neutral Switzerland. However, to The Consortium and its candidates, the play *was* the thing. The critical element of recreating specific moments in time allowed them to witness the event but also acclimate to the conditions surrounding it. Likewise, it allowed for further contemplation and questions to arise that may not have been considered prior to the trials, asking all the "what ifs" remaining before the actual event became a reality.

On July 4, 2012 the LHC posted the detection of a new elemental particle called Higgs boson so it became their *new* cover story. This critically important discovery provided the justification for expansion of the Flicker project, buying enough time to obtain considerably more magnets intended to enhance a depth, length and reach through time. If The Consortium's acquisition of additional materials for the still clandestine Flicker project was the *easy part*, attaining the doorway's cooperation required two full years of calculations, coaxing and coercing to open the portal at a specific point in time. Then, to convince it to remain open as long as necessary was the objective, no small feat. The electromagnets actively pressuring a doorway to obey a human command, the huge magnets increased the functioning of the particle accelerator, reinforcing both the structural integrity and stability of the portal. As was theorized and anticipated, developing the ability to manipulate the doorway, to control the collider to such an extent was a significant breakthrough, a catalyst for all future Flicker endeavors. From that moment on, a new element of "control" was established. Submissions were being accepted from various fields of expertise and The Valley test trials at Oxford began.

On February 14, 2014 the LHC announced an extended "shut down" to prepare the collider for a higher energy and luminosity. It was the second public cover story released as The Consortium's covert program became fully integrated with the LHC published project directive. Then, on March 20, 2014, the time trials went public. A release of information was simply a matter of going through the motions for The Consortium that had all of its security measures and primary protocols routinely in place. Well-prepared, public relations representatives were there to handle any and all concerns regarding various implications of disrupting the time continuum. Any biased reporting was contested, scrutinized long before reaching the court of public opinion. They had an answer for everything when questions arose.

Then it became about money and power. What a surprise. People of wealth and influence wanted access to the publicly-funded project, some, all but demanding to be granted permission to submit their proposals. Permission granted! (All that was granted.) These forthcoming submissions soon revealed secret agendas, banking on Flicker to be used for personal gain. Once their hefty contributions were transferred, secure in The Consortium accounts, "The Donors" (affectionately known in-house) were bombarded with reams of paperwork, overwhelmed by stipulations, rules and regulations as requirements of the program. From the Legal and Ethics departments to the prerequisite military clearance necessary to go forward, it was made clear to the fortune seekers, those pursuing access to Flicker, this was a commitment unlike any other. Those accustomed to maintaining their privacy at all cost were suddenly thrust into a new reality, their personal lives scrutinized with good reason, read like an open book. In spite of their investment, any attempts made in earnest to buy their way into the program, it was shocking how fast they would abandon ship once they realized the depths of its intrusion and duration of the process, a seemingly endless ordeal. No refunds were allowed. There was nothing altruistic about their proposals. Self-gratifying submissions were never destined to see the light of Flicker. Since humble taxpayers had been footing the bill for the research all along, it seemed only fair for the rich and famous to start kicking something into the coffers, an excellent way to subsidize the project without jeopardizing it and at the expense of those who could most afford it.

As they held back going public, The Consortium had daily conferences off-site to discuss every nuance of intent, scrutinizing those who would utilize this portal, revisiting the reasons why they'd be going and for what duration. The team created nomenclatures for every department of review then broke down various duties and responsibilities of each oversight committee during the specific trip taken. Overall, the primary ideology was to function as an "Objective Observer", a.k.a. *Scope* when referencing the candidate who'd met all the criteria for approval to go back in time. Above all else, the understanding was consistent: no matter who was chosen, they were not to do anything that might affect the timeline as recorded in history. In fact, it was so driven into the psyche of every selectee, it became almost religious fervor. It became their belief system, their creed and code of honor.

Ethan LaPierre had as much faith in his trial submission as he did in the Flicker. He was one of the few original selectees handpicked by Anson Van Ruden who had met and exceeded the criteria. They'd been introduced at Oxford back in 2008 after Ethan's graduation, with honors. His curiosity piqued by the chronic over-achiever, Anson was interested in knowing more about this man, specifically why his course of study appeared so eclectic, having earned several degrees in Theoretical Physics, History and Philosophy. Anson attempted to recruit him into their research program at that time, to no avail. Ethan had other plans which included teaching, continuing to walk the hallowed halls as a professor at the same institution where he had spent his entire adulthood attending class. Turning down his initial offer, he instead chose to accept the adjunct professor position available in the History Department. Ethan LaPierre was satisfied, prepared to wait his turn to rise in the ranks of academia, no higher aspirations haunting him. Nothing was lurking in the back of his agile mind. Anson would not take "no" for an answer, approaching him persistently, reminding his acquaintance and new colleague of the real opportunity awaiting him.

It was not until The Consortium went public with the program that Ethan took notice, reconnecting with Anson Van Ruden at that time, still firmly entrenched in the project. Anson was delighted to hear from him, his graveled voice exclaiming: "Well! Doctor, I knew you'd come around!" Truthfully, Ethan never discarded the invitation extended nor did he shrug off the concept. He simply never expected this rocket to launch. Now, with their project in orbit, how could Ethan pass up such an incredible opportunity to witness history firsthand then be able to report on it? To rewrite history from a first person perspective seemed sinfully self-indulgent, were it not for the pertinence of his unique proposal, the intrinsic meaning regarding the time and the events addressed in his submission.

They'd had a number of promising trial scenarios submitted to The Consortium but most would never be realized because the selectee ultimately proved to have a rather questionable, perhaps unscrupulous past. Choosing somebody to be a Scope was serious business, indeed. To assign such a position to someone without them enduring the long, painstaking process of intense scrutiny, without knowing every nuance of their psychology and morality would be the height of irresponsibility. It would be as dangerous as someone wielding a loaded gun in a drunken rage. Were it not for some of the most brilliant minds on the planet converging on this project, a collection of characters as diverse as their fields of expertise, Flicker would not have progressed past the point of theoretical inquiry. Anson at the helm, there were many other hands at his disposal to help steady the wheel of history when it turned. Without their learned participation there would be no possible way for this program to be fully embraced by the scientific community, let alone beyond its parameters. Powerful voices provided the credibility required, igniting the spark of curiosity to move Flicker forward.

From March 20, 2014 to present, August 2020, one thousand and sixty-four trial submissions from various individuals or organizations around the globe crossed the desks of those designated to receive them. It was a little too popular a project! Many from the ultra-rich were intending to satisfy a debt, including business and property disputes, ancestral lineage, several financial entitlements and even one who wanted to catch his wife in the act of infidelity. There were governmental submissions, too. No preferential treatment was extended.

There had also been a slew of passionate pleas, heartbreaking submissions from people who were looking for their lost or missing loved ones. These applications to the project were limitless and these issues had to be handled delicately. None of the proposals ever made it to a *selectee* status, processed out of contention because of the emotional nature of the trial requests. Should any of these scenarios forge some steely resolve for revenge once facts formerly shrouded in secrecy were revealed, should such knowledge result in an act of blind rage, the ripple effects that followed would be devastating. No one was allowed to travel through time subjectively.

The Legal Department handled all the political jargon when a submission was denied, accompanied by a rather large stack of assessment forms, files and reports, all submitted by the Review Board in response to applications, explaining a "cause and effect" regarding the trial rejection. Keeping it all in perspective wasn't always easy but it was a necessary evil done in the name of doing something *good* for all of humanity. Judging by the number of appeals and resubmissions or the attempted lawsuits, there was nothing frivolous about it. The Consortium paused to reflect on the process, considering the concept of doing more harm than good. Many members of their team had taken the Hippocratic Oath and intended to uphold it. Reviewing the body of evidence, they finally declared themselves entirely justified, absolved of blame for refusing emotionally charged submissions. One thing could rightfully be said of the members of The Consortium. They always maintained their integrity and always had the best of intentions.

After six years and over a thousand submissions, only seventeen made the cut, having met the criteria to move onto candidate interviews. Of these, only eight went on to time trials in The Valley and from those, only three received final approval to proceed on to Flicker. The first two selectees had thus far passed through the portal, objectively recording their chosen time frame in real time. The first successful run of the project coincided with the public announcement of the second startup of the particle collider in April of the year 2015.

"All the experiments conducted at the LHC so far are part of 'run one'. This week, after several years of upgrading the LHC's magnets (which speed up and control the flow of particles) and data sensors, it'll begin 'run two': a new series of experiments that will involve crashing particles together with nearly twice as much energy as before."
Vox.com news article: 16 April 2015

Though the public statement was regarding the source energy being doubled for particle discovery, the impact for Flicker was far greater and remained Top Secret. The additional magnets used to coerce the doorway were actually installed late in 2012 and the potential for length of time and location seemed boundless. As if they had invented an endless battery, an exhaustive array of experiments and probes had confirmed that the window into the past was wide open with a virtual reach of two millennia or more. Over the next eighteen months, test trials continued with a focus on perfecting the collaboration of all three aspects of the time jump. Formula after formula written on chalkboards was then fed into their supercomputers to exact the equations so a date, location and duration of Flicker's projected target was executed flawlessly. Once its precise calibrations and subsequent calculations were presented to The Consortium they could proceed with the true nature of the research, sending an explorer back in time. The first was a brilliant gent from Cambridge by the name of Dr. William Fontaine, a linguistics professor and archeologist. A man of superior moral fiber and impeccable reputation, known personally by a number of top brass in The Consortium, his soaring intellect and adventurous spirit caused the decision makers to label him as "good stock" then passed the word around. He sailed through the approval process.

Dr. Fontaine's event for Flicker was so intriguing, benevolent in nature, its only obstacle, mastering the language through phonemic awareness of ancient Egypt, so to grasp the intrinsic meaning and true substance of what he might hear and witness during his excursion. Flicker took an intrepid traveler back in time testing the limits of the doorway's reach to an era during which the Great Pyramid of Giza was being created, circa 2570 BC, a project "currently" under construction. There were a great many test "jumps" made prior to the actual project approval, all of which transpired without incident. Dr. Fontaine's first words upon his return through the portal:

"Sorry, chaps. No aliens in sight!"

The success of man's first walk on the metaphorical moon of time left FTCOC members popping the corks of champagne bottles in celebration! The world? It was still intact. Planet Earth did not stop spinning on its axis and explode (or some other fearful manifestation of Hollywood filmmaking at its worst) but continued on. With a collective sigh, they cried and sang songs, a festive occasion. None of them were so naïve as to believe every Flicker episode would go as smoothly but it was a check in the win column for the process that was still very much a mystery. Their ALICE project and subsequent phenomena it created was all accidental, its origin unknown. How could a particle collision not only be coerced but controlled? Deemed "a force of nature" by the team of scientists who could barely comprehend it, they were all well aware that, historically, forces of nature are not something mankind has had much success controlling. Everything hypothesized from cloud-seeding to HAARP turned out to be another fruitless endeavor, wasted attempts to control the elements. Delving into the smallest particles known to science, man should rightfully expect a few surprises along the way but nobody anticipated opening up a vortex as a portal to the past. With one tiny flicker of light, a new world was revealed.

The second mission launched on July 19th in 2017 was, well, yet another hiccup. A situation arose that, in spite of all the time trials and criteria requirements for the candidates, was never considered. A famous billionaire philanthropist had become selectee number two. He had performed exemplary charity work lifelong, donating much of his time to global causes. Canadian born, David James Cox had passed all pre-trial formalities with superlatives. As their time trials in The Valley produced hard facts, formatting all the necessary guidelines for his Flicker project, this man's pragmatic rationality and level-headed approach made it easy for every committee to approve his submission. Allowed to proceed, on the day he had been scheduled to go back in time, to step through the gateway, he froze in place at the threshold. Like somebody facing the anxiety of their first rollercoaster ride, David Cox could not have been dragged, pushed or pulled through it. Sometime during an exhaustive selection approval process the burden of personal responsibility got to him, fear he associated with any potential altering of the timeline continuum. He told no one of this feeling during his early screenings, even in The Valley trials. Cox truly believed his innate intelligence would gradually override this anxiety so he could rationalize the newly developed phobia and press on. His subconscious mind had other plans.

David managed to disguise his trepidation with their prep team earlier that day. However, from the moment he stepped toward Flicker, Cox was overwhelmed with fear. Although he could not visibly perceive the gateway entrance, it was designated by a series of lines on the floor leading to it. From his unique vantage point he could see all of their monitors, thermal imagery of himself displayed on multiple screens simultaneously as these dramatic events unfolded, being recorded from every angle. *Never let them see you sweat*? One could hardly miss it! Alarms ringing in his head signaled a sense of urgency. Cox panicked. Suddenly overcome with raw emotion, drenched, nauseated, a veritable tidal wave of terror swept over him.

He stopped. Suspense rising in the lab, David Cox broke his momentum, staring at a computer monitor, an alternate perspective. Everyone could see the heat rising, radiating off his body. Petrified, he began again, focused instead on the line leading up to an open portal unseen by the naked eye. Walking toward this invisible vortex, following the trail, his gaze never deviated from it as he approached the final mark. Nearing the threshold he paused to reflect on his precarious predicament. No. There were too many variables in this equation. No. Operations were immediately halted.

Unprepared after all, fear triumphed. A stoic pragmatist succumbed to a human emotion. Though they wanted to try it again, before he could, Mr. Cox had to revisit the psychiatrist, a physician required to address this underlying issue. If there was any hope of him achieving his desired objectives, they'd first have to successfully rewire his thought process so he could identify then confront his insidious nemesis. It took nearly two months of mental restructuring to reveal the culprit. Defeating it took some effort. When his "fight or flight" mechanism kicked into high gear, Cox flew the coop. It was time to fight the feeling. Fear stopped him dead in his tracks.

During this reprogramming, the Flicker door remained open into the past as a team of scientists took the *glass half full* approach, using this down time to test the stability of the vortex. It never flamed out. This window of opportunity to test the extended duration the doorway could remain open was a serendipitous contribution to Ethan's project which required more than two months to complete.

It was true. There were many variables. Stepping through the portal might prove to be a step in the wrong direction, past the point of no return. An exclusive form of human experimentation came with conditions that may not always be duplicative in a controlled setting. This research project still in its infancy, others had gone and come back unscathed but there was no guarantee, no implicit promise of safe return. It was virtually impossible to predict. No scientist at the LHC facility could assure a selectee that the portal would preserve its structural integrity in their absence. As a natural phenomenon, the vortex could close as inexplicably as it had opened with no prior notice. The team had to trust the conditions they so consistently recreated to keep a doorway revolving as travelers had to place their trust in the team to get it right. They had to be willing to go in spite of this awareness, disregarding inherent risks. They had to be willing to take the plunge into the past, into the deep end of the pool. A natural fear swirled around the knowledge they might not come back up for air, not in the 21st Century. Diving in meant overcoming it, perhaps in spite of it.

Like astronauts soaring into space with no guarantee of a safe, soft landing, an uncommon courage is called for in committing an act of insane bravery so extreme, it appears as reckless abandon. All explorers want to know they can go home again but that is not the nature of true exploration. Great discoveries often result in great losses. Archaeologists in pursuit of artifacts, digging up history to find the answers they seek, have been lost to harsh elements or unseen perils at the excavation sites. Anthropologists have been lost to the hazards of the Amazon. Astronauts have been lost in space, sacrificed to the Universe for the sake of knowledge, human progress. Yes, the potential existed for travelers to be lost in time, abandoned to another age. They were risking their lives. No denying it. Yet, the deepest, darkest fears revealed in therapeutic sessions with the candidates involved a concept more frightening; a fate worse than death. Their fear of being left behind, alive and well, lost to history itself on the other side of a disappearing doorway is what scared them the most. It is what kept some of them up at night. Not all fear is irrational. In search of eternal answers, few are capable of answering the call of destiny, requiring an unwavering faith, an uncommon valor in the face of potential adversity.

In order to fulfill his research proposal, David Cox had to conquer his own fears, defeat a doubt or whatever trepidation had abruptly halted his forward momentum. As it turned out, there was nothing "personal" about it. He was not afraid to die or, by some quirk of fate, live on in another time. His concerns were the same with the project as they had been for all mankind, a testament to his character. Devoting his lifetime to the betterment of society, this soft spot for humanity proved detrimental to his effort on their behalf. He was scared to death he'd inadvertently do something imprudent, perhaps out of ignorance, something that would permanently disrupt the timeline. Altering the established course of history was not the way he wanted to change the world. The Van Ruden incident had left an indelible impression on him. If it could happen once...what if...how to subjugate such an insurmountable sense of impending doom. Dread in his heart is what stopped him at the door, overcome in the moment by overpowering worry, an inability to trust his own judgment. If he made a mistake...one mistake... it could result in an incalculable loss.

David was an altruistic human being, a rare individual who harbored only good intentions for his fellow man. There was an innocence about him, an aura of purity, an otherworldly essence easy to detect and hard to dismiss. In his heart, he knew he would not deliberately do anything to disturb the timeline and would do everything in his power to preserve it. Once he had accepted the truth of his circumstances, he reconciled himself to the fact. No guarantees? No problem. By embracing his fear, it dissipated into the ether through which he would travel on his way to elsewhere. Reluctance waned, replaced with his personal conviction, a newfound determination. Finally ready to pass confidently through the portal, he knew he would do the right thing while *there* so to prevent a tragic, irreversible mistake *here*. As for the rest of it? He rested it in God's hands.

From that point, what came to be known as the "Cox Paradox" was systematically integrated into the Flicker program, so to prepare other candidates for any particular internal conflict of this magnitude. Cox ultimately completed his event flawlessly, as predicted. Coming back to the future right on time, as a triumph of the scientific method, probability and statistics saved the day and the man. His research project? Stonehenge, circa 3100 BC. Once again, no aliens reported.

Dr. Ethan LaPierre was the third approval and the next individual from present day to step into the past under the FTCOC guidelines. Who knew exactly how long mankind's luck was going to last tempting fate?

Was it human arrogance to actually believe they could harness this power and control it, in a way, package it and market the concept? After all, that theory worked so well with regards to the atomic bomb. Still, a determined necessity to know the truth of the past persisted. What errors in judgment had been made? Likewise, if mistakes were made recording those events, it seemed the perfect opportunity to clarify these errors then set the record straight, virtually rewriting the history book, removing the dark clouds hanging over a shady human past. Some argued since humans were still here, no one had yet to blow up the world, it was a good reason to leave well enough alone. *Flicker was too risky, tampering with what had already transpired.* The Consortium rejected this narrow mindset. It was time to explore "time" itself. If the excited scientists were aware of the implications of this discovery, they were so enamored with its assets they never fully considered the liabilities, overlooking the obvious concept attached to it. Just because they *could* did not necessarily mean that they *should*. It was not splitting hairs to split atoms nor was it a small matter to deliberately cause matter to collide. This is the true nature of exploration.

V.
HEADIN' DOWN TO DERBY TOWN

At the conclusion of the duet with Colin, the two of them decided they'd head on down to *Derby Town* a bit earlier than usual for the customary meeting after an announcement of this magnitude. Dr. Bishop waited patiently, quite comfortably in the red chair, humming the lyrical limerick while Dr. LaPierre took a quick shower. He emerged donning his most dapper duds, prepared for what would inevitably be an eventful day ahead. Grabbing the manila envelope of forms from his desk, in all the excitement, he was surprised he'd had the presence of mind to remember it.

Leaving the apartment building, carrying half empty cups of lukewarm coffee, two jovial gentlemen were taken by the sight of the courtyard on such a delightful morning. Stepping over the threshold through the oak door, there they stood, taking in the view, drenching the senses with brilliant August air. Competing essences of floral bouquet in early morning mist, Ethan found the intoxicating aroma as enticing to him as the scent of a woman was to Colin. Ah, perfect timing! Breaking into their infamous pub song, both drunk with joy, as the first rays of sunlight filtered through trunks of trees across the road, the merry men embarked upon a six street jaunt to the campus of Oxford University.

Admiring the splendid view along the way, natural beauty spawned by ancient, fertile, English soil, both felt blessed to witness this event. Shards of light split the sky, illuminating a multitude of colors splashed along the sides of buildings, Mother Nature's murals. Ethan could still feel the stroll even though his feet were barely touching ground and his head was in the clouds. Warm rays beamed like a spotlight directly onto his face. Drinking it all in through every open pore, he paused, closing his eyes. As if God was smiling down upon him, the moment was something sacred. Colin waited for his friend, watching a sublime awareness sweep over him. Ethan's expression said it all, revealing his sense of supreme satisfaction. When he opened his eyes again Colin was standing beside him. Hoisting up his cardboard cup, Ethan returned the gesture in kind, a toast to welcome the new day.

"Well done, mate! I'm proud of you. Now, let's go get a refill and a bite to eat. You'll need a good breakfast in you to face this day."

"Thanks, Col…yes, let's!"

For Ethan, it was a *new* day in every respect. It seemed different, almost surreal. The antiquities of the campus were, as always, inviting to the eyes. Both men shared the sense of being *at home* there, welcomed, embraced by the academic community. But there was something different in the air, the sweet smell of success, cajoling an eager professor to notice everything. The first stop was breakfast at the Grand Café on High Street. Accustomed as the British are to the chronically cloud covered sky, bright sunlight accompanied this new day dawning. It was an unexpected pleasure, a warm and welcoming presence so early in the day. Others mulling around campus were taken by its radiant glow, the force of nature compelling them to don an array of stylish sunglasses kept at the ready but rarely necessary. The campus looked like a Hollywood movie premiere, all glitz and glamour.

Students and faculty alike gathered daily at the Grand Café. Leaning up against its gray marble pillars, each topped with gold leaf inlay, they'd await an open table at the oldest coffee house in England. Its famous history wasn't the only draw to its doors. The cuisine was contemporary, delicious and nominally priced. Said to be a favorite place of Chelsea Clinton while attending Oxford, she'd brought her famous father there on occasion. Fine custom ground coffee and loose-leaf teas kept a café and its clientele buzzing morning, noon and night. As the hostess for their breakfast crowd continually rotated tables as guests came and went, customers stood patiently awaiting their turn. They'd politely file in then pile in together, gravitating to a four top table or the bar stools, there to begin yet another day of learning and teaching.

"Top o' the mornin'!" Dr. Ellis tipped his hat but not his hand. He too had gotten an early start, having received news of his inheritance overnight. Coming out of the café as Ethan entered, in passing through the alcove they'd paused, blocking traffic in a moment of recognition. "Professor LaPierre. Congratulations." Understated, as usual, his typical tone, he knew about

Flicker and Ethan's rare opportunity, having covered for him in the past. Likewise, he knew it was nothing to speak of in public.

"My students are, indeed, fortunate to have you, sir." Ethan's sincerity beamed like the morning sun as he leaned down to share his sentiment with this short, stout Irishman. Detecting the sweet scent of pipe tobacco, it rushed his senses, reminding him of how pleasant his campus office would smell upon his return.

"My pleasure, Ethan. It's the least I can do." On the verge of retirement, he was anxious to participate, gladly accepting the interim assignment, his contribution to a noble cause. He whispered, keeping a secret secure. "They'll adjust to this sudden sabbatical. Besides, they like me. I'm old but feisty."

"With age comes wisdom, sir. I'll drop by your office later this afternoon."

"Looking forward to it. We'll celebrate!" Dr. Ellis kept a stockpile of vintage Irish whiskey on hand for just such occasions. There was always *something* to toast!

Feeling Colin tugging at his coat sleeve, the men parted ways for the moment. It appeared normal, just another routine day on campus but looks can be deceiving. For one professor and his colleague it was a very special day filled to the brim with anticipation, dripping with adrenaline. Both feeling like school boys again charmed by their surroundings, Ethan was a pensive man most of the time but this morning he could barely contain his youthful enthusiasm.

Maneuvering through the crowd to a window seat, by happenstance, claiming a favorite spot, they settled in for a meal. This café, an ornate eclectic mix of period design had the blissfully sinful atmosphere of a church, a classroom and a nightclub all rolled into one. Old English style chairs and bar top stools decorated the place. Aesthetically pleasing beyond the creative vision, it displayed an authenticity hard to resist. A grand café, indeed! Vaulted ceilings of stained marble were evangelical, a befitting image for ascending minds pursuing higher education. They needed only to look up for inspiration.

While unfolding his napkin, Ethan glanced out the window, noticing a familiar object in the road gliding slowly past the glass. They had been followed by the same unobtrusive black sedan that drove him home the night before. It crept off, parking across the street. Ethan knew the driver. It was Sparks keeping an eye on his charge. Motioning toward the vehicle, he brought its presence to Colin's attention.

"I should go tell him the good news."

"He already knows. That's why he is here, P." Colin was right. "Get used to it. You're the hottest commodity on campus. A shame. I used to think it was me."

As a young man approached, neatly dressed in his freshly pressed black Oxford shirt, trousers and an apron, Colin grimaced with disappointment. He was the waiter assigned to service their table that beautiful summer morning. The lad was pleasant enough, welcoming the two men by filling their glasses with ice water. His offer of a warm smile and a hot cup of coffee simply wasn't good enough to satisfy Colin's voracious appetite...wrong item on the menu.

"Oh, bloody hell! Tell me, P. Why do we always get a male, not the pretty girls? It has been four years since they introduced female servers here, yet we still get the blokes!"

Ethan tugged at the corner of his reading glasses, shooting a lowbrow look at Colin, a scolding expression resembling that of a parent whose child is acting up in public. Their server ignored the dry comment as if he'd already heard it from every sophomoric male student since the first day of employment.

"Proof of its existence! The Immutable Law of Attraction or Repulsion. Perhaps your reputation precedes you." Ethan teased.

"Ouch!" Colin winced. "Touché!"

"Serves you right! With your appetite, be happy the café opens at 7:00 now!"

While Ethan ordered his usual, an almond croissant with fresh fruit, Colin went for broke with the Grand English breakfast, consisting of sausage, bacon, scrambled eggs, balsamic tomatoes and toast. It was not any sort of surprise to Ethan that Colin could put away so much food in one sitting, almost comical the way the man could eat. Ethan sat quietly for a moment studying the person he considered to be his long lost brother. There were many fascinating aspects to Colin, including his ability for absorbing life, its many gifts embraced with reckless abandon. Overindulgence was his natural overindulgence. He knew what he liked and he liked to enjoy it in fruitful portions. Colin's conspicuous consumption of a veritable cornucopia of delights his life had to offer, all things tolled, took proper measure of the man.

Ethan admired Colin's irrepressible, unabashed freedom. Never a dull moment, never a sense of remorse expressed for any actions taken, never the pangs of regret, including the aftermath of a hangover, just as cherished as the festivities the night prior that brought on the cloudy, hazy morning in its wake. It was another memory to reminisce about. His inordinately high metabolism produced a constant, raucous display, an abundance of energy unleashed on the world. Based on the vast amount of food Colin could consume, it was the only thing keeping him thin as a rail. As tall as Ethan, similar in stature the true differential as one distinction drawn between the two was Colin's blonde, short cropped hair as opposed to Ethan's jet black hair, cut in a far more moderate style. By contrast, they were as dissimilar in personality and social relativity as possible, in some ways, opposite ends of the spectrum. Ethan grinned. Together, he thought, they made one well-rounded man.

"What are *you* looking at?" Colin felt Ethan's stealthy gaze fall upon him.

"Just admiring the view." Mustering his most effeminate voice, Ethan ribbed.

"Who could blame a bloke? I am so bloody attractive. Give us a kiss, love."

"Not now. You know I abhor public displays of affection." With a wink, Ethan redirected Colin. "As for admiring the view, there's plenty to see this morning."

"I know! Now, you see, P? Right there!" Gesturing with his fork, pointed in the direction of a young and lovely lady, Colin's complaints were obviously justified. "Why couldn't *she* wait our table?" Ethan cast a discreet glance up as the ravishing redhead passed, ignoring the comment she'd heard just as her male counterpart had earlier. They were all used to it. In his morning glory yet frustrated, not nearly close enough to his heart's desired server,

Colin observed those around him while Ethan observed Colin. They were both Scopes, after all.

Having placed their order, Ethan then requested another cup of coffee from their waiter, asking that it be delivered, "to go" across the road, indicating the black Benz parked within eyesight. As he did so, he'd lifted a paper napkin from the lad's tray. Scribbling a note on it, he handed it back to him.

"Please make sure he gets this, too."

"Will do, sir."

"Thank you…what's your name?"

"Terry."

"Thanks, Terry."

The café was vibrant, filled to capacity. Students, faculty and visitors alike, the crowd was fueling up for the day with selected cuisines and favorite beverages. The air laden with the aroma of fresh ground coffee as well as an assortment of culinary delights, he could have his appetite sated merely by breathing in the fragrance of it. Ethan loved the old café. Moving through that colorful crowd was always an event, a sensual experience. Anybody passing through its doors was immediately privy to a pleasure, instantly detecting a wide variety of aromas. Some subtle and innocuous, barely there, others more pronounced, wafting through the air of the unique eatery. Each step taken was a flight of fancy, a new encounter with the next scent.

The social gathering, as primal an instinct as any of mankind's idiosyncrasies, is an ancient ritual engrained in the DNA. Wandering a crowd feeds that craving to belong within it, to share and compare. Some guests dined alone, seeking solitude amidst the hordes, faces buried in laptops or smart phones. Others paired off, teams of two, not unlike Ethan and Colin, while others made breakfast a gathering of the clan, seated around four top tables, some pulled together to accommodate the crew. Sitting shoulder to shoulder, presenting a unified front, stalwart companions were determined to face the day together. These folks were resolute, perfectly willing to pack it in, there to feed off of one another's energy. They were tight, literally and figuratively, loyal to each other's causes, reinforcing the notion that they could all overcome the forthcoming day, come what may.

Quietly studying his surroundings, Ethan noticed everything, committing it to memory as a series of snapshots. There he sat at the table, making picture postcards. They hadn't spoken in several minutes while waiting for their food to arrive. Colin finally piped up, noticing the brooding expression as it crept onto Ethan's face. He'd have none of it. This was to be a day for celebration. Colin would not allow any slipping backward into a reflective pool.

"Look at that one. *She's* new." Colin fancied himself an aficionado of fine wine and women. He spotted the recent hire immediately.

"You have a one track mind, Dr. Bishop."

Watching the waiter crossing the street, Ethan waited for some response. Sparks opened the door to receive his complimentary cup of coffee then read the napkin it arrived with, plunging his huge thumb high into the air above the hood of the car.

Arrival of their luscious breakfast a welcome sight, Colin plunged into it before Ethan could adjust the napkin laid across his lap. Typical! Resisting an aggressively persistent urge to comment, Ethan chose to hold his tongue, reserving it for another, more useful purpose. Meanwhile, Colin lunged at his plate in attack mode, as if he had not dined in a decade. Gesturing with his fork again, this time a piece of sausage attached to a protruding prong, he was emphatic, disagreeable about his lot in life.

"That one's been here for years and she never waits on me!"

"I wonder why." Nothing like his dry sense of humor, Ethan perfected practice of it with Colin, an easy mark to target. "Yes Colin, I see your point. She obviously *must* be a better server than the bloke who politely brought us a delicious meal in a timely manner. I'm sure she does a better job of it, no doubt, in spite of the constant barrage of courtship invitations she receives from men and, I imagine, some of the women, too. I'm certain it is her primary source of satisfaction every morning."

Colin stopped chewing his sausage mid-link, staring at Ethan in utter disbelief. "Do you really think she gets hit on by women?"

"Oh yeah Col, of course. You're so naïve for a worldly sort. Your competition just doubled." Ethan went back to his water glass, leering over the rim, hiding his smile. Colin stared off into the distance, considering the moment of epiphany as a revelation he could have lived without.

"Bloody hell, P." He continued gnawing on the thought along with his sausage.

Having finished his much more conservative menu prior to Colin, who was still negotiating with the sausage, Ethan thought it an opportunity to write in his journal, a simple, three-by-five inch black leather bound book. It was his written record of significant moments, appointments and questions to ponder and reflect upon later. As an ardent student, then a professor, he was already fascinated by and dependent upon the written word. "Everything everyone does is history." It had been the creed instilled in every student of the science of history for eons. As the dawn of Ethan's journey approached, coming ever closer, so came this thought, how significant the most trivial event can become over time. How one discerns what single occurrence or individual act could do to affect the future when every action has an effect.

Today he would meet with his friend, Anson Van Ruden, facing him along with select members of the FTCOC panel, going over their schedule leading up to the Flicker proposal day of launch. Reaching into his breast pocket, he retrieved the mechanical pencil he so regularly relied upon for most things relating to his classes and those unrelenting report submissions for test trials from The Valley. Seeking the next undisturbed page of white with black lines, he sifted through previous notes and illustrations that once again brought him back to those exact memories, the cause or reason for these entries. Ethan always had a romanticized, old-fashioned fantasy that every soul on the planet had a journal just like his to record every one of life's experiences as their own personal history book. Alas, Colin didn't have one. If a form was placed in front of him, he would complete it fully. If Colin had a questionnaire that required attention, he was on it, but asking him to *freely* record experiences that should be denoted, logged for posterity? Ethan meant to ask him why he'd never kept a journal but Colin was preoccupied at the moment, distracted by two young ladies from Italy at the adjacent table. (They had been hiking Europe.) It was a ridiculous notion to think he would consider doing some writing, unless it was in a specific journal predominantly filled with phone numbers, his little black book of conquests.

Ethan wouldn't be surprised if Colin submitted a second Flicker proposal to have carnal knowledge of Cleopatra and Joan of Arc.

***

Journal Entry ~ 17 August 2020

This morning my wake-up call was an alarm sounded by Colin pounding on my door with news! Late last evening The Consortium gathered to finalize the approval for my proposal! This was my moment of realization that this was going to happen. All my research, my studies, my perseverance was encapsulated in a single moment of decision making and I didn't even know it as I filled out forms as it happened.

This morning, I'll stand before the panel and accept full responsibility with the utmost seriousness, a respect for the power and danger of Flicker. My research is, without a doubt, of paramount consideration. I've labored long, sacrificed much to have this privilege of recording, potentially rewriting history from my own unique perspective then, once I return, have it published in every scientific journal known to the civilized world. Yet, overshadowing that notion of recognition and respect is the supreme responsibility to the non-interference directive. I was a fan of Star Trek in my youth. I always wanted to call it the Prime Directive which was a mandatory order of the Federation: no interference allowed to indigenous planetary life while studying them. So it is with the past. This directive is driven into the psyche of every selectee from the inception. I have the utmost confidence that I can commit to this endeavor with no incident of timeline displacement due to any actions on my part. Just finishing breakfast with Colin the Café Conqueror. The time has come to face the respective music.

***

Returning the journal to his coat pocket, Ethan noticed he had Colin's attention again, as the two ladies were moving on, undoubtedly to conclude their hike across the continent and Colin seemingly always had to talk to *someone.* Ethan was up.

"Anson will probably be there waiting for you." Colin suggested, taking another nonchalant sip from his freshly refilled coffee cup. "I'm sure he'll be there waiting. He represents The Consortium but you're his favorite, most special project."

"Well, at least I'll have one bloke on my side...besides you."

"Bloody hell, P! What are you worried about? Enjoy the moment! Your project is fucking approved! The event is a GO!" Resorting to his falsetto tone reserved for special occasions, Colin leaned in close to Ethan's face. "They say it's a GO, mate!" Leaping to his feet, clearly over stimulated by caffeine, Colin began dancing wildly around him, circling their table. "Good to go! He's good to go!" Heads turned.

"Have you no shame, my good man?" Peering over the rim of his spectacles, scanning the local vicinity, a few female students walked by giggling as Professor Bishop continued dancing like a lunatic or an extra from the Broadway production of "Fiddler on the Roof". Ethan smiled awkwardly, humiliated by the shenanigans he could not control. Clearing his throat to make the jester aware of his audience, Colin responded with a post-performance bow toward the gathering crowd. There wasn't a pair of eyes that did not recognize Dr. Bishop's animated personality. This was his teaching style, as well.

"Will you please sit down, you clown!" Ethan was embarrassed but never cross.

Obliging the request, Colin reluctantly took his seat, speaking in hushed tones. "It's only the FTCOC wanting to congratulate you! Sure, they'll need to look over the project once more but that's to be expected. They want to cover their own *arse*! I can see those gears turning in your head. Stop it! You're worried about nothing."

"Don't be such a twit, Colin. There is no need for them to cover anything at all. The test trials and committee procedures did that. They want to pick my brain. They will want to know *why*, aside from the obvious reasons, of course. Colin, you know the inner workings of Flicker just as well as I do. I can get *tossed off* right at the moment of the event, at the doorway, the plug pulled for the smallest infraction, the least conflicting issues. I won't be happy until I pass through the portal. In fact, my comrade, I will be much happier long before you will ever be born to cheer me on!" Taking a sip from the lip of his cup, Ethan smirked, pouring the rest of the hot brew into the paper cup he'd arrived with, apparently a "to go" cup. Rising from his seat, leaning in to speak privately with his cohort as if preparing to share a secret, Ethan winked, whispering "Pay the tab, mate. Breakfast is on you, including your shirt."

Taken by his discordant comment, Colin scrambled for his wallet while wolfing down the last of his scrambled eggs, hurriedly swiping the crumbs from his chest. Meanwhile, his companion glanced at his pocket watch then abandoned him at the table, making his way toward the exit. While navigating a narrow passage through the tables, Ethan looked down upon several of the fresh, young faces he knew, some of whom he had tutored over time. Suddenly the tableau transformed in his mind's eye, something akin to Pink Floyd's "The Wall" – a bunker scene. As if he were their commanding officer, he found himself surveying the troops in what appeared to be a World War I fortification. Bombs impacting above the cave shook earthen walls, showering dust on everyone huddled together. Walking past his foot soldiers, gazing into the scared faces of young boys, each tipped a salute as he passed. Dirt on their brows, fear in their eyes, he'd been the one chosen to lead them into battle.

Departing the establishment, Ethan bolted across the main street to spend a few minutes with Mr. Sparks. When Colin caught up they decided to pass on a free ride, resuming their trek across campus. It was quite a hike to the Museum of the History of Science. His spirits lifted, Ethan picked up the pace. Colin sprinted from behind to keep up. That man was on a mission. Dr. LaPierre wanted to get on with it. Broad Street was set in his sites. Ethan always took the initiative to arrive for appointments on time, punctual by nature. This morning he intended to be earlier than expected, a sign of respect.

"Ethan, are you having a good laugh at my expense? Ethan! Wait up!"

"I don't know, Colin." Ethan stopped in front of the monument erected to honor a man who would still be alive when he passed through the portal. How interesting! As he stood there reading the inscribed dates carved in granite, the thought occurred to him. "I may have to have a chat with your ancestors, try to persuade them not to procreate, make my life easier. Certainly quieter."

"That's not funny, P." Colin remarked, feigning the tone of someone seriously wounded, cut to the core.

"Don't be offended, mate. It's on me. My burden to bear. Who knows?" Ethan continued taunting. "I might even fancy a night with your great, great grandmother and become your great, great granddad!"

"Now you're just being mean, you fucker." A *grin and bear it* smile on his face, Colin suggested, "You could marry the Queen then *fucker* too! Put me in the will!"

"You know something Dr. Bishop, you're a man of clear conscience and moral fiber, but then, I jest."

"Not to mention my exceptional intelligence and model good looks."

"Mmmm, yes, there's that." Taking another sip of lukewarm coffee, completing the thought, Ethan remarked, "Not to mention your modesty, such a humble sort!"

Colin paused, poking out his chest like a peacock, strutting his stuff, posturing, proudly displaying his imaginary feathers. Ethan was so very fond of Colin. In fact, he loved the man far more than a friend, more like a brother, the comic relief in the room. Everything Ethan lacked in social skills, Colin possessed in abundance. Yang to his Yin, his oldest and dearest was also his nearest friend, someone to confide in, share with and count on. Trust is everything. Ethan could trust Colin with anything. His companion had been a continual source of encouragement when Ethan became impatient awaiting the fate of his project in the hands of The Consortium. If Colin knew the intricacies of Flicker like Ethan did, he knew, as well, the inner workings of Ethan. It wasn't like the Cox Paradox but rather, an internal reflection regarding this rare opportunity. Still humbled by the prospect of it, even after all these years invested into the program, it had not sunken into his thick skull. His Flicker project was one of the committee's favorites and he knew every facet of it, every detail of the history, every nuance of the mystery, the tale left to time itself to solve. He had earned the respect and confidence of his colleagues. It was his baby, right from the point of conception. They could almost hear it wailing from across campus when it took its first breaths, demanding to be acknowledged, begging for attention. Ethan was about to receive copious amounts of attention for his efforts. Approaching the museum, he chastised the naughty circus performer prancing beside him.

"Straighten up and fly right!" Ethan warned Colin to behave in the company of The Consortium panel, thereby having one less thing to worry about.

Truth be told, there was no way he could have mustered the patience to see this through, especially during those early stages, had it not been for Colin, there to help him keep a level head and some semblance of brevity in light of such pressure and responsibility. On certain long nights at his flat, having spent countless hours in the big leather chair at his desk, Colin would appear at the door like a cavalier of sanity to rescue him just prior to his leap off the edge of reason. Off they'd go for a walk or a stiff drink at some unsavory pub where Ethan could unscramble his brain and decompress. Colin was an anchor for Ethan, his first and best mate long before the Flicker proposal originated and he would be evermore. Cognizant of his faults and frailties regarding his social skills or lack thereof, Ethan felt comfortable, far more uninhibited in the presence of his friend. Although he was a well-spoken, brilliant individual, in a social scheme he often portrayed the wallflower. He could speak to anyone about anything, but basic human interaction of frivolous banter was never part of his répertoire. It did not come naturally to him and Colin never allowed him to be placed in an awkward position, always watchful, ever mindful of Ethan's shy demeanor. He was a pensive, insightful man, the strong, silent type depicted in old films as the leading man. Colin admired these attributes, protecting him at all cost.

The two turned west on High Street towards the University Church of the Virgin St. Mary. Oxford is so much more than just an educational institution. Dating back to the 12th Century, it has had the distinguished history of having some of the most influential people around the world walk its halls, receiving a variety of degrees in many fields of study. In some respects, Oxford University was a popular destination for tourists, especially those who were fans. From Lewis Carroll to Harry Potter, it was a way to feel a connection to their heroes. High Street was a main thoroughfare, a passageway to class for the students, staff and visitors. Although in modern times its sidewalks were paved, the asphalt and design of High Street was modernized so to accommodate the constant barrage of buses, cars and endless bicycles parading between majestic, truly historic structures, some dating back to the middle 1500's. Overwhelming stone architecture lined the streets, as if telling the story of ages and wisdom encompassing the roads and walls. No one traveling its streets could remain unaware of Oxford's significance. Ethan was still in awe of its ancestral echo.

Turning right onto Catte Street heading north along a side road, Colin began to feel the effects of the large morning meal he had just ingested back at the café. Out came his trusty smoking pipe, a perfect addition to any overindulgence, punctuating the proclivity. Stopping for a moment to light up, Ethan hadn't noticed his absence, moving onward toward his well-defined goal with single-minded purpose. It was a veritable quick step. Colin's turn to pick up the pace, smoke trailing behind him, as he huffed and puffed his way back, catching up with Ethan as they passed Radcliffe Square, he reached out, placing his free hand on Ethan's shoulder. He'd had an idea he felt compelled to share.

"P, tell me, when you're horribly rich and famous, doing the lecture circuit, you WILL remember the little people you left behind, won't you?"

"How could I forget, Col? I'll need to collect at least two thousand pounds for all the breakfasts I've bought for you at the café."

"I picked up the tab this morning!"

"Wow! One whole day in a row! And *only* because I told you to get the check!" Well of course Ethan was only teasing but Colin took it to heart.

"You keeping track, mate?" Colin inquired nervously, suddenly concerned by the comment, hoping he hadn't been perceived as taking advantage of a friend.

"I'm making tracks! YOU might try to keep *track* of me, if you can!" Ethan's long legs stretched out like the neck of a giraffe, his stride widening with each step, he left Colin behind in a matter of milliseconds. Checking his pocket watch again, a slave to time, it was not a matter of being late as much as a force of habit. Getting ahead of it was his objective, dispelling concerns that something or someone would impede his progress. Ethan sprinted away from every delay.

Racing to catch up with his friend, Colin became winded keeping pace with his impatient companion. He managed to duplicate Ethan's cadence while they passed through one of the many open plazas located just south of the Sheldonian Theatre. Reaching the side door entrance into the Museum of the History of Science just off Broad Street, Ethan paused then placed his hand on the door knob. Closing his eyes, he took a deep breath. This was no longer a paper acknowledgement, phone call or e-mail. He was about to hear it from The Consortium director himself. He was about to receive news of his submission acceptance from Dr. Anson Van Ruden.

"Uh, P?" Leaning in toward Ethan's ear, Colin whispered, "You've got to turn the knob for the door to open."

Ethan snapped out of his momentary paralysis. "Right. Yes." Turning the brass knob, he pushed the door open and they entered the museum.

This enormous cathedral-like structure housed an amazing and unrivaled array of historical artifacts honoring the instruments used in the development of science. Many of the items had been donated by the museum's benefactor Lewis Evans back in 1924. On the ground level, Ethan and Colin continued along the polished marble floor past a plethora of science-based technology, displays including the collections from the Royal Astronomical Society and the Royal Microscopical Society. At the center of the ground floor they turned left, facing a set of ascending and descending stairs. Their journey continued downward as each footstep echoed through a narrow stairwell heading toward the basement level galleries. Ethan envisioned the future, counting footsteps in his mind as more a metaphorical excursion into the past. What would he experience once he stepped through the portal? Would he actually go into the past as the present or would it be the echo of an era long gone?

His mind was reeling, though he did not share a single word with Colin. Ethan's thoughts were loud enough to create an echo! Considering the definition of the word pertaining to the resonance of sound, it was a sound repeated, duplicated after cause of the initial sound, mimicking it as effect. This journey would also have to include the visual echo of past events. Of course, science would eventually contest a theory, inevitably so, as sound and light travel at very different speeds. Be that as it may, accepting current science, no one to that day could formulate the equation otherwise known as Flicker. The doorway, in all its aspects, was exactly that. It was not some sort of Divine intervention nor extraterrestrial in nature. Due to human imagination, a natural curiosity for advancement of science, he'd be an accidental tourist in time, passing through a portal revealed as a by-product of research, a fortuitous moment of serendipity. They were not searching for it because they did not know it existed. The LHC was not designed for this purpose and those who never planned for a fluke of natural law or a rip in the fabric of the Universe did not have to understand it to utilize it. Regardless of its origin, if their discovery was predestined or preordained, whether this was caused by the power of atoms colliding or something else entirely, the door now existed and Ethan was destined to step through it.

Reaching the end of the stairway, Ethan opened a door to the basement gallery. It was one of his favorite areas, where Einstein's blackboard was on display, as well as a wide selection of items and instruments contributing to the research of physics, chemistry, medicine, microscopy and photography. They would bypass this section as their destination was through the "C" gallery, a revolving exhibit display. At the moment there were no displays of anything, as the area was cleared for this meeting. Straight through the "C" wing to the end of the hall, a sudden left turn brought them to the conference room. On the other side of the door was Ethan's future in the form of five Consortium representatives. Anson Van Ruden was expected to be there but it was anybody's guess who accompanied him on the flight from Geneva to Oxford. This was the last hoop to jump through before his giant leap into the past. Although it was just a formality, the reps were there to ensure that Ethan, or any selectee, for that matter, was mentally and physically prepared to go forward with the research. The incident that happened when Anson went through the portal as well as the Cox Paradox had never been concealed or sugarcoated at any time during the project's existence. In fact, it had become an integral part of the selectee screening process.

The conference room smelled of fresh coffee and old books. Ethan stepped into it first as Colin trailed closely behind, trying to be invisible, to shrink into oblivion. It was Ethan's moment of truth. Colin *had* to be there. He wouldn't have missed it for the world, though he wanted to be as unobtrusive as possible. To both, it seemed like an anxiety-ridden trip to the principal's office, or worse, into the coach's office to see if they'd been cut from the team. Strange how pessimism can sneak into even the most confident mind, in spite of all the cards on the table indicating the ultimate winning hand. It was never an aspect of self-doubt for Ethan. He knew who he was and what he brought to the table. His thoughts were more of a preparatory mentality to expect the worst, especially when one's future lay in the hands of another. Within those four walls, confirmation of Ethan LaPierre's destiny would come, at last. Five men stood chatting around a table at the far corner of the conference room, enjoying coffee and extras served for their pleasure, nibbling on crusty scones and fresh fruit. One of them took a particular interest in the new arrivals, looking over his shoulder, a familiar face with a reassuring smile.

"Aye! Ethan! Right on time! How are ya, buddy?"

There was an ease in Anson's demeanor as he finished stirring cream and sugar into the hot brew. His jubilant expression provided Ethan a deserved sense of relief. The "barrel-chested Swede" (as Flicker personnel affectionately called him) made his way over to Ethan, extending his hand in a warm and welcoming gesture. It was an immediate signal to Ethan that all his predisposed trepidation was unwarranted. The air was suddenly lighter, more vibrant; easier to breathe. Glancing past Anson, Ethan recognized the other Consortium members still jockeying for their coffee. In attendance, Dr. Anthony Galli of Switzerland, a brilliant physicist, Dr. Lars Linsin of Sweden, an incredible particle scientist, Dr. Franco Carmalini, a psychiatrist who had been with the project from its inception and Dr. Devon Murth of Australia, who was not only an amazing physician but also a selectee in the program.

"Dr. Van Ruden, I'm so delighted you were one of the members coming today." Ethan spoke with a tone of humility, sincerity while reciprocating, shaking the hand of this great scholar. Anson's vice grip was legendary, having puddled blood in the fingers of most recipients. The man did not know his own strength.

"Anson, please Ethan. Call me Anson. I wouldn't have missed this! Actually, I am the reason for recent delays. I wanted to be here for this, so had to fit it into my schedule. I beg your pardon."

"Told you." Colin made his presence known, poking Ethan gently in the ribs.

"Dr. Colin Bishop, good to see you!" Anson grabbed his hand with such force, it was like getting caught in the *Jaws of Death* in The Valley during time trials.

"Was your flight in a smooth one, gentlemen?" Ethan asked out of concern.

"Like a baby's bottom." Anson replied with an enormous smile.

"Fantastic to hear."

Ethan began moving towards the four other members of The Consortium with whom he was very familiar, holding them in the highest regard. His respect for their accomplishments was unparalleled, actions before and during the Flicker program. Each of them greeted Ethan with unbridled enthusiasm. He sensed their excitement for him, filling his heart. He hadn't expected to feel so emotional, trying to disguise the lump in his throat. With each handshake he knew this project was not only going forward but those involved were so encouraging, supportive of this Englishman of Irish and French descent. Likewise, Colin greeted them as he made his way over to the table to have another caffeinated beverage, as if he needed it! Ethan needed his moral support, Colin by his side. His attendance at this briefing was, if for no other reason, to work his magic misdirection of Ethan's mind should something shocking or disappointing be announced. Colin was the cockeyed optimist he counted on for some balance in his life.

"Did you get enough rest? I know both of you were out at The Valley last night." Anson asked with some concern, aware of the ridiculous hours they kept as Scopes.

"Oh, yes. I'm just fine." Ethan responded by handing over the manila envelope to the project director. He then reached for a fresh cup of coffee, mixing in an extra sugar cube into the brew, taking one sip to test it before committing to the cup, the consummate scientist.

As a scientist himself it was in Anson's nature to be observant yet he was a kind man, as well. His generous comments, thoughtful gestures of support were heartfelt, nothing cold or clinical about him. Over time he had developed a specific empathy, compassion for those assigned to this formidable task, the link established between gentlemen who would walk in his shoes. It was the bond of kinship, having been in that identical position before, one in which Ethan stood, examining the examiners for any signs of strife or doubt. Leaning in to comfort a kindred spirit, Anson knew few mortal souls would ever pass through their portal. Selectees became a tightly woven family over time, individuals who were the intermingling threads, there to enhance the big picture, to be the strands that expand the tapestry of the Universe.

"Not to worry, this is just a formality." Anson whispered the words as if sharing a secret kept. "You're good to go on your way." As a father would comfort his son, a few lyrical words functioned as a lullaby, ushering Ethan into a daydream.

Closing his eyes, Ethan dropped his head in relief, chin to chest as his shoulders relaxed for the first time in forever. A chronic tension headache as his nemesis, one sign of the stress he'd carried all morning, it suddenly evaporated into languid air. A burden lifted, Ethan smiled. Perhaps it wasn't eye strain after all! Anticipation is almost as powerful as fear, and is, in fact, borne of it. An insidious fear, it creeps in through the back door, a worry, not that something will happen but that it won't.

The center table in the room was an exquisite replica of a 17th Century trestle style, made of a lighter material for easier mobility and relocation. Surrounding it, eight *built for comfort* modern desk chairs, luxury made for such meetings as their own; the one about to occur. Anson motioned to everyone present to take their seats. The time for not so idle chatter having passed, the moment to begin was upon them and everyone sensed the gravity of it, especially Ethan, sucking him down into his seat as dead weight.

Removing a small digital recorder from his breast pocket, Anson used it strictly for dictation purposes, as was done for every Flicker interview by every committee leader during the application process since the beginning. Redundant, perhaps, as the museum had security video with audio in virtually every room of the building. The Consortium was filming these proceedings and would secure all the recorded data of their meeting. This was Anson's personal accounting for his report. Pressing a button on the recorder, noting the date, time and every member in attendance for the event, Anson announced commencement of the closed door conference.

"We have gathered in this formal capacity, as required, to finalize all remaining details prior to initializing the third Flicker Research Project, '20/20 Hindsight' as spearheaded by candidate Professor Ethan LaPierre of Oxford University, England. During his endeavor as Scope, in pursuit of objective real-time observations, events in history which have transpired are to be scrutinized by Dr. LaPierre, requiring his transport via Flicker to the established time frame between the dates of 28 August 1888 and 9 November 1888. Regarding these five similar unsolved criminal cases, known as the Whitechapel murders, Dr. LaPierre's intention is to clarify history, to determine a culprit, thus identifying the infamous Jack the Ripper."

The atmosphere in the chamber suddenly shifted. Anson abruptly fell silent, as if pausing to reflect on the process, allowing those present to reabsorb the nature of one intense research project as the dense air thickened further. It seemed to possess an intelligence. A memory was awoken by the spoken words. It became oppressive, unbreathable as Dr. Van Ruden continued, consuming what oxygen was available.

"Candidate LaPierre will be provided vintage attire, currency and identification indigenous to the era. He will be entrusted to faithfully and accurately execute, duty sworn, accounting these events from a non-invasive vantage point to such a degree that a proper conclusion may be drawn as to the identity of the notorious assailant. Professor Ethan LaPierre, are you of sound mind and body and do you completely comprehend the responsibilities inherent to this endeavor in the name of puritanical research and historical documentation?"

"I am sir, and indeed I do." Ethan responded with confidence. No doubt.

"Note that on this day, 17 August 2020, Professor Ethan LaPierre's affirmation of the project directives and procedures as provided in the Flicker Legal Doctrine that all candidates have been previously required to read and sign, acknowledging a full understanding of the responsibilities and requirements prior to their project launch. Dr. LaPierre, do you have any questions, comments, concerns regarding acceptance of your candidacy and forthcoming duty?"

"No sir, I do not." Ethan responded in a somber tone of deep commitment. He'd taken his pledge of allegiance to the program long ago, years before.

"Does any member of The Consortium Final Review Panel have an objection to this project or to the candidate we are addressing on this date at this time?" Anson inquired of his colleagues, knowing their answers in advance, a collective response of "No." For the recipient of a ringing endorsement, it instantly reiterated the most powerful word in the English language.

"This concludes the final project review with candidate Dr. Ethan LaPierre. We thank you for your time and patience, professor. Launch preparations are currently underway. Its countdown has commenced. Ethan, you are scheduled to go forward. Congratulations, sir. Your destiny awaits. Meeting adjourned." Anson grasped the candidate's hand then held on, smiling warmly at his protégé, sharing his own sense of satisfaction with the professor as the culmination of this final confirmation.

Turning off the recorder, they sat in silence, taking in this momentous occasion. The spark of inquiry ignited, Anson wanted to know the long elusive answer to the question as much as anybody else at that table, solving the ultimate *whodunit* once and for all time. He wanted his acolyte to be the one to reveal a secret kept by time itself and he knew Ethan was destined to become a witness to history in the making, albeit a series of gruesome observations. He would wander the streets of London in disguise, focused on the one who prowled the dark alleyways in search of his prey. With the eyes of a detective, just like any bobby walking his beat, Ethan would be privy to events as they unfolded, present at the scene of the crimes as they occurred. Intriguing beyond measure, it was a fascinating proposal right from the inception, captivating those who knew the details and ultimately approved the petition request. As the anticipation continued to rise, it erupted out of Anson with one rogue gesture as he threw his arms up like a football referee signaling a touchdown.

"Tonight we drink to your success!" It was a proclamation. Dr. Van Ruden had made plans for the evening, a customary celebration the burly Swede insisted upon, as a good luck toast to the selectee as well as a tribute to Flicker.

Much to Ethan's delight the other panel members followed Anson's lead, all of them cheering him on. Their outburst caught Colin mid sip, dazed and confused, as if he had been warped into an alternate Universe. Again, he was the comic relief in the room, a priceless expression on his face for all to enjoy. Placing his coffee cup and saucer at the edge of the table as elegantly as possible, he finally sent his arms sailing into the stratosphere, better late than never. His colleagues howled, a rather standard response to Colin's antics. It broke the tension.

Beyond the door of a basement conference room, up to street level and all along the campus, then out to all of England, the United Kingdom, Europe and the planet, the vast unawareness of what had transpired within the confines of those walls was staggering when considered. For only the third time in the history of any species, the ability existed to travel into the past as a witness to firsthand accounts of events long echoed in time. The "Laws" of physics had been rewritten and redefined, never more vitally so when applied to the discipline and dangers related to what humanity had discovered and what had discovered humanity. If those chosen to comprise The Consortium allowed a research project to continue without taking every precaution they would be irresponsible, knowing what could happen to those assigned the task. The result would be nothing short of catastrophic, fracturing linear time. Their final decision had ramifications beyond borders.

"So, Colin will lead your project team then?" Anson queried.

"Yes, yes sir, he will." Ethan responded. "He's been with me from the start and knows my research better than anyone. I trust him implicitly."

"Very well, then." Anson continued. "Ethan, as you prepare for the event I will correspond with Colin regarding protocol and any program fluctuations which may occur in the offing, freeing you to mentally plan without further distraction."

"Thank you." Ethan responded with blissful contentment.

Anson knew Ethan need not be told how to prepare for this "timely" adventure. He had not seen a more focused and logic driven individual selected as a candidate since the program went public. His research was faultless and broad, covering every angle and approach a Scope would need to consider for this journey, and then some. There was no allowance of apathy for any candidate tasked to breach this doorway. When it comes to due diligence required to conduct research of the past by a living strand of its content, someone from a time not yet in existence during the time it is conducted, suffice to say Anson Van Ruden always placed his bets on Ethan, quite confident he was the perfect candidate for the task at hand.

"Colin, I'll have Rita Drocman from my office in Geneva get with you via email to organize flight arrangements and shipping priorities for the project."

"Right, sir. Any idea when *we* will be in Geneva?" Colin asked sheepishly, not wanting to push but anxious for an answer on behalf of Ethan as well as himself.

"You'll have a charter from Heathrow the morning of the twenty-fifth. Rita will bring you up to speed this week."

"Thank you." Colin glanced at Ethan who'd momentarily closed his eyes while lost in thought, perhaps lost in the concept of time itself.

As the gentlemen stood and shook hands with one another, it was clear to Ethan that this incredible opportunity was upon him. The entire meeting had been surreal. His research was no longer a pen and paper affair, no longer relegated to the realm of the cerebral, no longer a figment of imagination. It was manifesting, taking form, shape-shifting, morphing into a new reality. It was made tangible with one meeting. It was happening, after all. Anson collected the files and recording device from the table, leaning in towards Ethan and Colin once more.

"I have a few things to attend to over at The Valley. I'm hoping we can all meet later on at The House sometime around four o'clock?"

"Yes, right. Four o'clock then at The House." Ethan shook the hand of a friend and colleague, yet felt humbled in the presence of the great Dr. Anson Van Ruden.

The two men once more shook the hands of their counterparts as Anson ushered the other four members out the door, following behind them. "The House" he had spoken of was the popular Oxford pub off of Blue Boar Street, a faculty favorite. Anson's thick Swedish accent could not conceal his intentions, to share a few pints with them in celebration and, in some way, a preparation for the weeks and months ahead. As the door closed, a moment of serenity settled into the silence of the air. The two remaining men altered their blank gazes from the door toward each other. Colin and Ethan stood there like statues made of stone, allowing time to lapse of its own accord as the consequence of the meeting was absorbed. Mount Vesuvius had nothing on Colin. He spontaneously erupted, spewing forth a yell that undoubtedly could be heard across campus! Reminiscent of two soccer fans seeing England win the World Cup, Colin jumped into Ethan's arms, wrapping his legs around his torso like a toddler clinging to his mother. Ethan embraced Colin as they reveled in pure, unbridled joy. Rapidly losing his grip to the force of gravity, Ethan yelled, as well:

"Col? I'm falling. Col? I'm losing my balance.....Colin!"

And down they went.

VI.
DOWN TO THE LAST DETAIL

Journal entry ~ 25 August 2020

Colin and I landed in Geneva earlier today. Their private jet was all about the publicity, pomp and circumstance. I would have flown commercial or taken a boat to get here, as long as I eventually arrived. The onboard meal was quite a delicacy, though. We were then chauffeured to our private quarters on the LHC property. As living conditions go, this is meager, no doubt typically reserved for full-time staffers who are living abroad, away from their families.

For the past week, contrary to Colin's persistent attempts to distract me and to continue the celebration started at the pub with Anson, I've now revisited all of my research and historical timelines relating to my Scope mission project. Anson was spot on when he said I knew all of my materials and would perceive my research to be flawless, but that is reason enough for the redundancy, reexamining the minutia in all things relating to this time jump. I'm reluctant to take for granted that nothing was missed in my work. There's always something.

A surgeon sees the operation in his head prior to the first incision. An Olympic skier navigates the imaginary slopes in preparation for the physical actions. I, too, over and over in my mind have walked the streets of Whitechapel. I have also visited these narrow passages personally in my physical form a multitude of times to gather a first person perspective of the crime scene locations and potential vantage points from which I may covertly observe, a witness to the savage slayings that eventually came to be known as the "Autumn of Terror".

There is a sense of anticipation, of exhilaration in my body for what is to come. There is also a need for justice to be done, the mystery solved for the victims whose assailant was never truly named. Speculation about him being a physician, my best disguise in order to gain any necessary access to research and medical records, it suits me well. The Consortium has acquired all the credentials, attire, instruments and currency of the era so that I may more easily blend with the time and its people. Into the breach I go with a sense of social invisibility, merging with the background, with walls and streets in shadows cast by oil lamps, wearing my cloak of obscurity. I'll be able to witness, document and report the true identity of Jack the Ripper.

***

During the week leading up to his Flicker jump, there came a point (at the tip of a needle) when Ethan had lost his identity as a well-educated, level-headed Scope and was transformed into a veritable pin cushion, covered in puncture wounds. It was necessary to immunize candidates prior to their time travel events. In this case, it was specifically for the prevention of disease, pathogens associated with late 19th Century London. He needed to have an innocuous journey so the research could go on uninterrupted by sickness which could restrict him to a bed or worse, hospitalize him, exposing Ethan to the barbaric conditions of medicine in that archaic era. Even upon return he'd face an onslaught of sharp syringes during a customary quarantine period, test procedures mandatory, including numerous prophylactic inoculations. Scouring his blood to ensure he had not become infected, thus protecting everyone involved, Ethan expected to open a vein when he stepped back through the portal. Without stringent oversight, time travelers could return contaminated, conceivably unleashing an epidemic comparable to the Black Plague.

Flicker project participants and Consortium staff administration were all housed in the facility about twenty minutes off the LHC property, located at CERN. Setigny, Switzerland was where all the other pre-project examinations, conferences, testing, scoring and staging were conducted. Once their Candidate Program was introduced (after the Van Ruden incident), the FTCOC explored all conceivable contingencies. They'd left nothing to chance. Everyone felt quite confident there was *nothing* The Consortium failed to cover prior to the final approval stage, including that meeting Ethan had at Oxford in the basement of a museum.

There would be one more "final" meeting, this one with their staff psychiatrists. A formality for Ethan yet, an imperative inquiry regarding any issues related to the jump, ranging from phobias to his moral stance on the project, it was an interview that had to be conducted. No stone left unturned, they had to know beyond a doubt that Ethan could emotionally handle watching five women being butchered on the streets of Victorian London. He'd have to be prepared to hear them scream, crying for help, yet remain stoic, making no attempt to intervene on their behalf. It would be tough to stomach were it not for the years of mental conditioning, programming a Scope to understand his role in conjunction with the natural timeline. There'd be no interaction with a killer or his victims, no temptation to rescue them or forewarn local authorities. To do so would be a blatant breach of the continuum, presumably resulting in severe ramifications for an unknown future. Logic had proved to be the ultimate dictator, demanding proper scrutiny of the project, start to finish.

For years, Ethan had been exposed to surgical autopsy photographs and videos, having access to cadaver research from the medical college at Oxford University. Anything and everything they'd brought to bear was introduced to desensitize him to such an extent, he'd learned to process events like a trauma surgeon would assess a patient. No panic, no reaction to the victim, just initial observations. The analogy ends at the point when the examination begins and the surgeon plunges in to assist in saving a life. Ethan had only one option, to stand back and watch someone die.

The concept was uncomplicated. Ethan was trained to look at these events as if peering at images projected onto a movie screen. It worked. He readily dissociated himself from the characters involved, what he witnessed, so to preserve the integrity of its recorded history. In his mind, these were images captured on film, unalterable, not real. He'd found he could remain detached, unemotional when confronted with such macabre pictures. Every effort was made to eliminate the element of surprise, every angle approached with purpose, to compel Ethan (or any other candidate) to comprehend the laws of physics as they pertained to the timeline. Non-interference was the law of the land. Breaking it came with a permanent penalty.

For Ethan, his certainty of duty, strict obedience to "the law" was unquestioned. He understood the rule and his role right from the start, before submitting a petition. His entire project proposal was predicated upon the non-interference directive. All his field trials at The Valley were based on this rule of law, yet he remained steadfast in a multitude of run-throughs, never once a waiver, adhering to his responsibilities not to respond. Everyone involved in the project had the utmost confidence in this candidate. There wouldn't be an event such as what Anson Van Ruden encountered, no episode akin to the Cox Paradox. Ethan would not freeze at the portal, unable to initiate the mission. The only thing icy was the blood in his veins, a rigid resolve to complete the mission assigned: raw research, observation and documentation. From a psychological standpoint, he was ready to go.

The Medical Department took him to task long before he arrived in Switzerland. After the incident with Anson, The Consortium deliberately implemented a protocol to expose any weaknesses in their candidates. As a Scope, Ethan was subjected to the SERE Program: Survival – Evasion – Resistance – Escape. Designed by the U.S. Navy Seals, it was grueling, nothing short of a test of will, pure human endurance. Though he'd always been an active man, Ethan was no athlete. This element of the training proved to be the most trying for him. He barely made it through. There was no pass or fail. Instead, it was an evaluation technique, its results turned over to The Consortium to be factored into their final decision, approval or rejection of a Scope. In the event of detection, they needed to know he could make his great escape back to the portal and back to the future without collapsing from exhaustion. Had Ethan's Flicker proposal involved documentation of Moses crossing the desert, he may not have made it out-of-committee. Taking into consideration that this project required little more than hiding, biding his time in the shadows of a few Whitechapel alleys, he was perceived to be safe enough, at relatively low risk of overexertion.

For the past three days, Ethan proceeded through every interview and examination The Consortium threw his way. He was now just twenty-two hours from the jump. Isolated within his austere surroundings, the room was drab, dreary. Military gray floors and steel blue walls. Ethan reclined on his bed, eyes closed, walking through the foggy alleys of London as he had physically done a hundred times before. He'd visualized the murders, bearing witness through countless photographs and reports burned into memory describing the crime scenes in all their lurid detail. It brought to light how important the redundancy factor and these mental exercises were, after all. He would not react counter to his training once the event went *live*. Still, it was surreal, pondering the events about to unfold, the historical unveiling. Being one of the first human beings in history capable of traveling back through time, from this first person perspective, he'd actually witness the grotesque murders committed in 1888 by someone who remained nameless, who'd come to be known worldwide as Jack the Ripper. His reflection was abruptly disturbed by a knock on his door.

"Open." Ethan declared.

The knob turned, the door cracking slightly open before a familiar face appeared like a bodiless apparition sliding through the opening. Colin had come to call.

"You decent?"

"Well, if I'm not, you'll be the first to know!" Ethan was in high spirits.

Colin stepped into the room, closing the door behind him. Not one to be lost for words, there was an awkward silence, nervousness in the air not unlike a first date scenario where two people begin sizing each other up, not yet knowing if they had a connection on any level. Sliding his hands into his pockets, Colin wasn't Colin.

"Hey."

"Hey?" Ethan returned the word with an equally curious tone.

"How…how are you feeling, P?"

"Alright Col, you know, all things considered. Perhaps even excited. You?"

Colin moved further into the small quarters, rubbing on the top and back of his short cropped blonde hair. He appeared to Ethan as if he was about to attend some sort of support group meeting where he'd reluctantly disclose an addiction, a secret he had kept hidden for years. Pulling the desk chair from its place beneath the metal table, positioning himself aside the bed Ethan was laying on, he sat with his hands together in prayer form, wedged between his knees. Taking one deeply heavy sigh, it appeared Colin was avoiding any eye contact between them.

Ethan immediately sensed uneasiness in Colin's demeanor. Having been close for so long does tend to lend privilege to unspoken communication on many levels in many different situations but this was new to both of them. It didn't fit any of the previous models they'd encountered over the years.

Ethan felt it pertinent to entice Colin to verbally define the reason for his awkward posture.

"Come Colin, don't dillydally. What's on your mind, mate?"

Colin continued to silently stare at the floor for a few seconds more, then, turned his sight toward Ethan. "Why?" Colin paused for a moment. "Why do we feel this compulsion to fray the edges of reality? Why do we challenge the borders of sanity with the risks we take? What is this madness we pursue, thinking that we can be so arrogant as to control forces of nature in the enormity of time?" Colin turned in his seat, facing Ethan directly. "Why – when there are so many wonderful mysteries to explore on *this* side of the doorway you are about to walk through, P, the Universe, the ocean's depths, women, the mountains, the valleys…the women?"

"Col?" Ethan interrupted. "You said women twice."

"Oh, yeah. Right." Colin flashed a quirky grin, raising an eyebrow with his tone of voice. "I rather like women."

Ethan turned his horizontal frame on its left side, propping his head atop his left hand. "Seriously, what are you trying to tell me?"

"I'm scared!" Colin exclaimed. "I'm scared that we both submitted our petitions around the same time and that my number will be called next." Colin slumped back in the chair. "I'm scared I'm going to fuck it up."

"Oh, c'mon Col, you're just…"

Colin put his hand up, interrupting the thought. "Ethan. I wish…no, I want you to take over with my trial when you come back."

Ethan immediately sat up, facing Colin head on but before he could speak, Colin jumped in deeper with his heartfelt plea.

"Please. Hear me out. I may present myself as, I don't know, a man of the world, confident with the ladies, well-educated in many aspects…"

Ethan smiled. "I was just going to say that."

Leaning in towards Ethan once more, he continued. "I don't want to be the next bloody Van Ruden incident or Cox Paradox. I can see it now. Bishop's Blunder!"

"Nonsense Col, now you're just being paranoid."

"Yes, exactly! You're not even on the board of evaluations and can see through my façade. I do not have your stoic nature. You are the poster child for this project, personally groomed by the 'great and powerful' Anson Van Ruden to guarantee the future of this research program. There is not a single aspect of this jump you haven't considered and conquered. You're about to go through Flicker and spend fucking months in the past tracking Jack the Ripper! And you're about to witness multiple bloody murders and document them as it happens and you act as calm and collected as if you were going on fucking holiday! I do not have that fortitude, P. I'm fooling everyone, including myself."

"Not me." Ethan smiled empathically, his sincerity felt as he placed a hand onto Colin's stooped shoulder, a compassionate gesture of encouragement among men.

"Only because I told you." There was despair in his voice. That would not do.

"Col, I have those same fears." Dropping his voice along with his eyes, Ethan's plan went off without a hitch.

"Really?"

"No!" Incredulous in tone, any tension shared was released with their laughter. Ethan leaned back again relaxing on the bed. "Look mate, you're here as my second in command, my support system. It begs logic that you'd be having delivery pains with me and for me. Sympathy pains. It'll pass when I pass through the Flicker."

Colin stared, listening intently, as if trying to comprehend a new language.

"You're not me," Ethan continued, "but you're projecting, trying to labor your emotions through my project. Problem is, you do not know *my* jump-research the way I do, so your uncertainty is translating into emotions about *your* project."

"Sorry I didn't have *smart food* for breakfast. I nuked a bowl of sauerkraut."

"Well, that explains a lot!" Ethan raised his eyebrows insightfully.

"What are you getting at, mate?"

Explaining further, momentarily holding his nose barring any pathogens, Ethan continued. "If your trial was approved first, I would feel the same way. It is healthy and expected by the panels. They prefer a little self-doubt to cocky overconfidence. From the inception to completion of our projects, our brains are working overtime. I am always working it over in my mind, thinking on my feet. You, too? How well do you know your Flicker project?"

"I go through it in my fucking sleep."

"Do you know every angle and false step, every precaution?"

"Intimately." With renewed vigor, Colin slowly sat up higher in the chair, as if being lifted by some unseen force. His expression went from lost in the dark to the proverbial light bulb going off.

"Yet, I'd be terrified." Ethan confessed, sitting upright, placing his hands on the shoulders of his confidant. "Colin, this is *my* woman. I know her every nuance, each and every aspect of her personality. I know her body and her soul. I know her heart. I'm comfortable with her. She's unique just as *your* woman is unique and…"

"…and hot!" Colin added for emphasis.

"Yes Col! Very hot! I'd be nervous to even be in the same room with her, much less make love to her."

Colin suddenly thrust Ethan's hands off of his shoulders then stood up with his hands planted on his hips. "You bugger! I can't believe you'd fancy *my* woman!"

Ethan stood in counterpoint. "Well, she *is* hot. C'mon, Col, give us a kiss."

They began wrestling in their lighthearted way, eventually leading to the kind of machismo hug men give each other, avoiding the slightest hint of emasculation.

It was an unspoken conceit from Colin, to admit to his foolish fears, to concede that Ethan was absolutely right in his assessment of the situation.

"Fucker." Colin used the vulgarity as a common term of endearment.

"Fucker back." Ethan used it as punctuation.

VII.
A DECIDED LEAP OF FAITH

Journal Entry ~ 28 August 2020

This is my final entry before my jump which is scheduled in less than two hours. The moment of truth. How interesting to note on the eve of a jump back in time that the time since meeting with Anson at Oxford, until now, has seemingly sped up in total opposition to the timeframe prior as I waited for it to happen.

I am ready. I have been ready for weeks, for months. For years. Where my mind goes is to the intangibles. Does it mean Colin was right about uncertainty? Not in the least. For me there is nothing about the jump I am not ready for and then some. I think more so about the science of this endeavor. There have been myriad tests, so many jumps confirming the Flicker's stability and continuity. The Consortium and LHC teams have perfected the exactness of the duration and direction of the doorway. I cannot stop, however, dwelling upon the forces we are trying to harness. Can this be the day that, as I walk through the portal, some sort of cataclysmic, unforeseen alignment shift in physics occurs and all of my molecules explode? My thoughts also go on to the return point. In two months I will be finished with my research and return to the area where the gateway will be waiting for me. What if, during those months, there is a global war or a natural disaster that debilitates the Flicker permanently? It is not about my survival in the slightly more primitive time of London or, in fact, the world. I have the distinct advantage of knowing the times intimately well, a crystal ball of sorts, having both the privilege and the curse of being a being from a future time. It would mean having to watch every step, every action for the rest of my life, constantly having to be on guard, knowing the slightest historical involvement from me would create ripple effects on the future timeline in an undeniable, unknowable way. I would have to disappear or die to assure events didn't change due to my presence in the past, my existence. Existence is a bigger concept, a word of consequence, of greater weight when you are about to hold that word in your hands. As a schoolboy I read about earlier, simpler times in London. As a child, your imagination is enough wonderment to fill the Universe and never have to violate anybody or anything for answers because all was there to savor in the simplicity of thought. Nothing and no one to be responsible for, I'm just trying to peer into my future trip to examine the past.

***

Ethan was never one for church, in spite of the fact that he'd found monuments erected to God amazing, a testament to mankind's imagination. He worshipped the genius of creativity, admired achievements in majestic architectural design, edifices built as places to gather in devotion to the Almighty, including structures at Oxford. Certainly there was faith, perhaps on a more practical scale. God, for Ethan, was an ideal. As a university man, so much of the literature on the subject of the Supreme Being was available to him. He understood the ideology of religion and its power, constructive and destructive to cultures which have risen and fallen by the faith they supported. His inspiration came in walking those hallowed halls.

There was a foundation to his belief system that was a variation of forced-logic. Having accessed so much on the subject throughout his academically driven life, it seemed self-evident from his educated perspective, leading to a conclusion that the evidence that God exists is inarguable. For those who'd dispute God's existence, it was Ethan's scholarly way to meekly inquire, "Why?" In having faith, a belief that there is an all-seeing, all-knowing being, guidance from the heavens above, perhaps humanity could comprehend existence, overcome fear then achieve understanding. There was a certain solace in the feeling that there was *someone* who would always be playing a supportive role behind the scenes of life. As a pragmatist, having faith seemed to him, logical, far more astute, more beneficial to body and soul than not.

In the time remaining before his jump, as part of the time allotted by the project powers that be, Ethan used this personal time for reflection. Speaking with himself internally, addressing the depth of his own faith, it became incumbent upon him to reconcile the science with spirituality, what it meant during this insightful hour and beyond, in the magnitude of the moment to come. He had found peace long ago, so his humble prayers covered any intangible issues before departure. At the doorway there would a clergyman present, someone to bless and release him to the journey; the striking similarity to The Last Rites before execution was a little bit unsettling. Leave it to superstitious banter, a necessity for "public relations". To have someone of the cloth on hand would avoid any atheistic accusations by the press.

Now to address the press, something Ethan knew was forthcoming, dreading an inevitable encounter at the facility. Since the launch of the LHC there had been film documentation during particle acceleration tests. Much of their funding for Flicker was motivated by footage captured during sequential modifications, tests leading up to an introduction of the Scope candidates. Those given press access were hand selected by Anson and other top brass as well as LHC directors for their credibility and prior security clearance / access background. If the military cleared these men and women they were on the recording team, allowed to disseminate the report only after a Scope had returned from the jump and the event was concluded, to keep any disastrous incidents in-house. God forbid something went amiss, the slightest detail misconstrued, any and all opponents of "Flicker" would bring to bear everything in their arsenal to force the program to permanently shut down.

Thus, the ineludible requirement for the Flicker trials on the outskirts of Oxford. Every aspect of event preparation thought then rethought with a surgical precision and exacting calculations, it was a process, a prime example of the phrase "no stone left unturned" in search of scenarios. The poorest of analogies is Lamas classes for the most important "labor" in the history of science. The world would be watching the film of this birth. Ethan would be the newest to breach and all of his family felt confident he would come out the other side head first, ready for the world in 1888. Ethan preferred to think of it in terms of a familiar sports metaphor, as the pressure brought to bear was no different than telling a coach if he did not have an undefeated season he'd be terminated. The stress rested squarely on Ethan's shoulders. He was the quarterback of this game, left to his own devices to make calls on the field.

Time to close the journal and lock it away, In fact, anything from "present day" had to be left behind. Draped on the desk chair was the 19th Century suit he'd wear for the jump. The Consortium provided Ethan considerable currency from that time period, generously donated from collectors around the world for this specific event. It was intended to be used for additional period clothing as well as perishables and living accommodations, enough funding to sustain him for months.

Resting on the floor beside the desk was his medical bag. An authentic antique, it contained all the expected instruments and his corresponding credentials. These items, pristine and protected from time by the keepers of antiquities, most of which were likely purchased from a high-end auction house. Each was part of someone's collection, all to present the visage that Ethan was a visiting physician to old world London. In duality, a new false identity was value added, providing accessibility to prohibited areas of medical facilities which may or may not be necessary depending upon the theories that Jack the Ripper was a skilled surgeon. Other diagrams from this case of Scotland Yard of old profiled a butcher and multiple assailants, to which end his false identity would be for naught. In this case it was "better safe than sorry" in terms of deciding on an identity: Doctor Arthur Bridgeman. The prudent decision was to use the occupation that had the title of "Doctor" as the prefix to his fictitious name. Additionally, it would also help to substantiate the amount of currency he'd be carrying with him during the jump, should he be detected straightaway.

Finally, Ethan would find his travel journal on the desk, also indicative of that era with the proper paper stock, authentically aged leather hardbound cover, another charitable contribution to the cause that could not and would not be returned to the donor. Intending to transfer its contents to his current journal upon return before he turned it over to The Consortium, once again, everything was being considered and reconsidered to avoid any connection to the present.

Thirty minutes had mysteriously passed since Ethan donned his period attire. In that time he'd stood facing the closet mirror. Less than an hour remained before his decided leap of faith. Peering into his own eyes, this was not a psyche out session before the jump, nor was it a doubt about his research knowledge regarding the era or the target. It was not even about the concerns of mechanical failure of the Flicker during his departure or return.

No. It was the conjuring of this character he needed to become that captured Ethan's attention. He'd been given all the credentials and identification for the name "Doctor Arthur Bridgeman". As a graduate of the Royal College of Physicians (in documentation only), Ethan had to take the surname and persona to such a degree of belief so as not to raise any suspicion. His identity and the knowledge base to qualify this title of "physician" was one of the initial design blueprints adopted when this project was submitted. So, too, was the considerable research he had needed to master, as if he were obtaining the scholastic degree as a specialist in his field of study. Staring into the mirror, Ethan fixated on suppressing his own identity and embracing this new persona. The surname was a familiar one, from the annals of English medicine, one of hundreds of small details scrutinized during his pre-submittal planning.

In his mind he imagined being in a variety of scenarios, perhaps an encounter with a stranger who had a background in medicine of that time or London's "finest" were to begin questioning him. Looking in the mirror, as he'd done countless times, he once again rehearsed his responses in those probable situations he would likely encounter. Selling it to himself meant selling it to anyone else who might approach him. Character acting 101! He thought, *"I should've done more theatre in school."*

Then came a knock on the door. Ethan took one long last look at a mirror image, and in reflection, took one last long breath. It was time. He looked around the room. As dull and drab as his quarters had been, they'd become a sort of sanctuary, a place of solitude where everything was certain, in its place. As another friend he'd have to say goodbye to, he did so silently while opening up the door. There in the hallway staring at him were nearly two dozen pairs of eyes, some scrutinizing, patronizing and even criticizing. Then there was Colin. His eyes, smile and body language were supportive, protective. He was the first to step forward into the room toward Ethan, leaning in to whisper an important message.

"The green-eyed brunette from the tech team wants me bad."

"For fuck's sake mate, please don't have me returning to a wedding invitation."

Two ardent men reached out, grasping one another firmly by the shoulders. Any unspoken conversation between them served to reinforce mutual confidence in this day, one of such historical significance. A shared smile, acknowledgement that both of them were ready for this jump, a simple nod concluded their nonverbal dialogue. It was time to go *site* seeing at the most sophisticated scientific facility in the world.

Ethan quickly grabbed his 19th Century belongings and they were out the door, escorted by security personnel, medical staff checking the traveler's vital signs one more time in transit. Flicker techs surrounding him, Ethan would've normally been squeamish around this many people in such close proximity but the experience was surreal, almost magical; he noticed everything and everyone, including Colin's new love interest. The distance between their quarters to the jump site was about twenty minutes, less during their late night excursion, like crossing the campus at Oxford.

Outside the staff housing complex, lining its circular drive, three vans sporting LHC insignia awaited their charge. Standard transport, it was nothing special but it felt so to Ethan, glancing at his own reflection in a van window as they approached.

"I did ask them for a limo." Colin boasted. "They said it was too conspicuous." His mouth drooped into a petulant pout.

Looking over his shoulder at the cast of characters accompanying them, Ethan replied, "A circus clown car may have been more appropriate for our troupe."

The entourage piled into the three vehicles which already hosted the driver and two additional armed security guards (per van) for their fourteen kilometer journey to the LHC facility. Every person presently involved with the Flicker program was playing a supporting role to Ethan.

Support. That word had numerous faces, some Ethan may have never even met, not even so much as basic conversation with people who held his fate in their hands throughout this entire project. Most of them were strangers to him yet they felt like close friends in his moment of need. It was imperative they do their jobs efficiently to get Ethan where he was going. Launch time for Flicker was slated at four o'clock in the morning, the best shot for him to reach the other side without being spotted.

Even at such an odd hour of the morning and still a couple of kilometers away, the LHC compound illuminated the night sky like a small city. Ethan never tired of the dramatic visual effects of the approach to this facility. Poetically reminiscent of returning again and again to the "New World", seeing the Statue of Liberty in New York City as some fictitious literary immigrant boy from the classic story, this place *was* the new world. To these explorers, the ones who came before and would come afterward, the discovery of new lands, new frontiers and new opportunities was no less frightening and exciting to them as those who sailed across the Atlantic Ocean to a place both foreign and familiar at the same time.

The surrounding property was vast. Ten minutes earlier merging roads funneled the vehicular traffic of workers, press and security cleared dignitaries into the main artery leading to all the different entrances from Route De Meyrin 385. At any time on any *normal* day this property was cluttered with thousands of cars belonging to its employees covering shifts at all hours in every department the place required for operation. This incredible location was composed of dozens of separate buildings. If The Consortium hadn't limited access, the number of attendees to the event could have gotten out of control. Everyone with a security pass to the facility would have arrived prior to their shift (or remained after their shift was completed) to hopefully witness the early morning leap through time. For security and safety protocol, there would only be a communion of thirty people actually present during Ethan's jump. He had wanted a rather understated affair, an exclusive group of invited guests but the turnout was more than he'd bargained for, in spite of his humble request. It was Anson's call to make, as these events were so significant and rare. The Consortium had to use these jumps as demonstrations for promotional purposes, fundraising for further proposal research grants and to finance amongst other things, the time trials of future Scopes back at The Valley.

Arriving at the facility just past 3:30 a.m., soft breezes blowing in from the west cooled the summer night otherwise adorned with phosphorous streetlamps lining the pavement. As three LHC vans made their way through the security gate, a guard read the drivers' manifests then signaled someone in their gatehouse to make a call. Once inside the gate their vans took an alternate route from other traffic to access one garage large enough to allow passage of five semi-tractor trailer trucks entering side-by-side. The concrete floor inside the building was polished to a sheen. Tires on the vans (moving at a slow pace) made a high-pitched screeching sound with the slightest turn of their steering wheel. Sixty or so yards into the large warehouse the vehicles came to a dead stop. As all the passengers disembarked Ethan immediately recognized the nearly deafening sounds of the turbines and generators. Standing in the LHC Engine Room, they were there, inside the driving force behind the particle accelerator. Cooling systems, air conditioning units, gigantic water pumps: dozens of massive machines serving either a primary or a redundant purpose lined the walls of what appeared to be a futuristic miniature city.

A small, bald man in a lab coat and wire framed glasses approached Ethan with one hand extended, the other holding a walkie-talkie.

"Dr. LaPierre. Dr. Bishop." The man greeted them in a heavy Austrian accent, attempting to be heard over the cacophony of electrical noise.

"Dr. Eschmann, hello." Ethan replied as he reciprocated the handshake.

"Everything is ready."

They all began walking, following the lab coat and six additional assistant lab coats that accompanied Dr. Eric Eschmann. He was initially a project director with the LHC until the first "event" that began the Flicker trials. From there he willingly took a demotion in position to join The Consortium with a fire rekindled, a passion ignited for the project and keen curiosity regarding what possibilities may await on the other side of a doorway.

"Flicker's up and running perfectly!" Gesturing toward an access door, the good doctor led the way in advance of Ethan's support team. Ethan knew his way around the building but he deferred, following dutifully behind. It was one of the few jobs Dr. Eschmann had, to escort him like a dignitary as if it was his first visit to the site.

Once through the entrance, the last of the group (which looked like an entourage following a prize fighter to the ring) hit the security pad, closing the oversized slab of metal behind them, effectively muffling the heavy whirring of machinery.

"Dr. Van Ruden has been here all night greeting visitors, heading up the Public Relations team." Eric continued in better audible conditions.

As they walked along Ethan looked over his shoulder at Colin.

"You think Anson brought beer?" Colin asked rhetorically of Ethan who shook his head and smiled, recalling their night of celebration together at The House.

Turning his attention back to the corridor ahead, little by little, employees began to emerge from office and lab doors aligning the walls of the hallway.

"Good luck, Dr. LaPierre." One head popped out.

"Viel Gluck, Arzt LaPierre." Several of the workers spoke in unison.

"Bon chance, Medecin LaPierre." It was an international Bon Voyage party.

Ethan never felt more uncomfortable. He was the player at center stage, yet the spotlight felt too hot. He had no appetite for it, no craving of attention from others. Even in his familiar classroom setting his methodology of teaching was minimizing eye contact, keeping the focus of young minds on the work at hand. He was acutely aware of the significance of the events unfolding and the electricity it was creating. Anson would tell him to hold his head high and play the role of Ambassador for the project, star of The Consortium. Once again, regret fell upon him for never pursuing thespian training. He was a very shy man and a very bad actor.

In an understated corridor, an incredibly vast maze of halls, tubes and humming, whirring, buzzing walls, all vents and equipment, Ethan could hear the faint sounds of muffled music like a distant echo chamber. He did not recall seeing any speakers being installed in his presence but the sounds had permeated his mind for a moment. As the entourage continued forward, the soft repetitive snare drum and bass became instantly familiar. Ethan and Colin looked at each other and began to snicker, saying the same familiar name at the same time. "Anson."

"One pill makes you larger and one pill makes you small
And the ones that mother gives you don't do anything at all
Go ask Alice, when she's ten feet tall."

Anson was a prideful product of the 1960's and always made an effort to remind everyone (twenty years younger or more than he) that the greatest era of music and of revolution was in *his* time. Booming one final reminder of his plight, Anson had Jefferson Airplane's "White Rabbit" piping through the communication system that broadcasted in this section of the LHC, the magical place where the ALICE project became a true and legitimate looking glass into the past. They were going down the rabbit hole to "Go ask Alice". Perhaps, just perhaps, Anson was spot on.

Music continuing to play, Ethan was also greeted by the sounds of spontaneous applause from a group awaiting his arrival. Past the sounds and showcase, past the people in attendance there was a doorway, an invisible doorway into the past. Ethan reflected back to the first time he saw the Flicker, or did not see it, until he looked at one of the thermal imaging screens. The control room was a simple moving pod transformed into a makeshift operation center. Standing in front of a monitor, Ethan stared at the portal, amazed he was about to create a path for his future by stepping back into the past. Though not visible to the naked eye, on the screen he could see in multiple spectrums the barrier he would soon breach.

The doorway was fluctuating, oval to circle to oval, a free-flowing form pulsing in the light spectrum, from yellow to blue to red, indicating temperature variations. An energy access gate to another time and place, it was so beautiful. For practically every moment since its accidental discovery in the ALICE system, so many of the world's greatest physicists and mathematicians labored in cooperation with LHC directors to harness it, calibrate the collider's energy, speed, heat; any and all other factors regarding manipulation, perfecting Flicker's timeline, duration and location. Achieving accuracy to a percentage point, flawless in the mechanics of operation, it was the crowning achievement of mankind working in harmony with a force of nature never before witnessed. Ethan gazed at it with wonder, humbled by Flicker, his ride into the history books.

Ethan was not one to look the proverbial gift horse in the mouth. The facts were set, data compiled and analyzed. Flicker was so precise in specificity of calculation, he could have gone through at any present time to the planned arrival date and time in the past. There would be questions regarding the timing of this jump, scheduled three days before the anniversary of the first murder. He'd been told only three days prior, informed upon his arrival at the LHC, exactly why this project had been held up for so long, biding its time. Only then was it disclosed as a deliberate delay, their intention to synchronize the dates. Basically, The Consortium had been stalling for time and "20/20 Hindsight" was waiting out a calendar. It would be the first attempt to correlate the past with the present, pertinent for the sake of testing new theory.

Of course, there was no such thing as Daylight Savings Time in 1888, although these slight variations were considered inconsequential by the scientific team when compared to the impact made by being able to accurately measure deviations to the second from Ethan's departure to return. Having concocted this very scenario while dissecting the delay in his mind over months, Ethan had his suspicions but nobody confirmed them. Anson explained his decision to withhold such vital information with one line composed of nine simple words:

"Less time for you to be mad at me." Then he winked.

Knowing Anson's warped mind enough when it came to his Scopes, Ethan also assessed that by keeping the time short between project approval and Flicker jump limited the Scope's tendency to overthink and stress about their project submission. Never known to hold a grudge, Ethan accepted Anson's rationale with good humor, no hard feelings. Being present at the site certainly softened the blow. Actually, Dr. LaPierre applauded the concept. There was a perfection about it he could not ignore. In spite of the realization that this approval could have come sooner, it all appeared meant to be in an exciting moment of exploration. Anxious to get on with it, Ethan longed to arrive at his ultimate destination to make his appointed rounds. Dates and stars had aligned and his date with destiny had arrived.

Framing the invisible Flicker anomaly was something new and different, quite necessary from the perspective of the Medical Department effectively arguing their point. Considering the premise of this project, the expected proximity between the Scope and people of the target era, a vital precaution was taken with the installation of the sterilization chamber positioned directly in front of the vortex. On loan from the World Health Organization

(WHO), the chamber was a preventative measure, another step taken to assure there would be no pathogen hitchhikers into the past or brought back from it. Nothing was left to chance. Just to the left side of the invisible portal was a large digital clock box displaying red illuminated numbers.

00:12:41

"Ethan!" Anson's forceful, familiar barrel-chested voice echoed throughout the facility, followed by his roaring laugh. An offering of camaraderie for all to witness, watchful eyes enjoyed an embrace between the two men.

"Good morning, Anson." Ethan barely uttered his greeting, trying to catch his breath while locked in another Swedish bear hug.

"A great morning! A wonderful morning!" Anson exclaimed.

PR was Anson's forte. Leading Ethan up to a glass barrier separating them from the uninoculated audience all present, the crowd he was expected to "hobnob" with included various dignitaries, program contributors, heads of state, religious leaders and other media and marketing targets. No need for a formal introduction. They all knew precisely who he was and what he was about to do: make history. Ethan felt dizzy, overwhelmed by the social circle of admirers. The transparent partition was more for a dramatic effect. Ethan had been sufficiently immunized against virtually any *bug*. Anything external would be wiped out in the sterilization chamber before his jump. Anson thought keeping their guests behind a glass wall added impact and would diminish Ethan's stress level. Though well-intended, it failed. His awkward stance and sweaty palms could be diagnosed as agoraphobia were he not a professor at a prestigious university. This was all just too weird. He had always been eager to get on with this project, to go back in time, never more so than in those few fleeting moments, feeling quite like a gorilla caged in the zoo as humans stared at him. The only visual distraction for countless eyes in the room was the minister standing off to the side, softly praying for and bestowing a blessing upon this event as pomp and circumstance with the Almighty present, another Van Ruden maneuver.

Ethan always considered Colin Bishop his friend, a colleague, even his brother. Never before had he been his hero until the instant he approached, wrapping an arm around Ethan's shoulders, easing his discomfort, protecting the man from himself.

"Sorry, ladies and germs, but our man of the hour has already had his shots and, I for one am not sure all of you are free from infectious disease so I think it best we press forward before his overexposure to all of you *filthy* rich people!"

The crowd laughed, exploding into applause as Colin whisked Ethan away to a secure location far from the enthusiastic crowd, a small room off the project floor.

"Any more of that nonsense and you are going to demand your own trailer with fresh flowers in your dressing room." Colin often joked even when he should not.

"Bollocks. Well, I DO want a personal assistant. You, perhaps?"

"Yeah, you know what you can do with that fucking idea, mate."

Both men laughed then, for a moment, stood silently, each avoiding eye contact with the other, looking around as if the words to speak next were floating by on the air, awaiting someone's grasp.

"Look, Col." Ethan began.

No one understood Ethan better. "I know, P. I have got everything covered for you. There'll be a pint waiting here when you get back. I'll be the one in the hazmat suit with a cane and top hat doing the Bishop Bounce, my moves you most enjoy."

"Well, that'd be a dead giveaway, wouldn't it, and quite a sight for the rest."

The affection between them was so obvious, almost painful. Having bonded as brothers in their youth, this separation would literally be the longest since they met. Though neither said it, they both knew it. Should something go dreadfully wrong, they may never see each other again.

"Well." Colin abruptly extended his hand. "Best be off with you, then."

Ethan stared at Colin's gesture with confusion then embraced his best mate, his friend, his brother, his hero. A comrade in arms.

Leaving the anteroom behind, they walked toward the chamber entrance. Colin turned, an astonished expression on his face.

"I just got it, P! Your project title is '20/20 Hindsight' but you could not have known it then, could you? I mean, you filed your submission years ago. Now you're leaving in the year 2020! It's a good omen, mate! It's as if you'd known it all along. Ethan LaPierre! Come now, give us a kiss."

"You're a twit."

"You're a twat."

00:08:19

Sharing one final laugh before separating, Colin led Ethan back into the project room, which was now cleared of all unnecessary personnel. Anson remained in the room. As the Consortium's PR man, he knew the project's future was only as stable as its last project success. Each jump was a chance to promote and sell the concept to the next group of financiers and charitable donors. Oh, but his heart was in it this time. Anson walked towards Ethan with his arms open wide and gave him another giant-sized bear hug. His coffee and cigar stained smile was gleaming through his rust colored handlebar moustache and beard, peeking through like the early rays of sunshine. As he embraced Ethan he made sure his back was to the isolated audience.

"Alright, Ethan. Let them see a confidant smile from you! When I let go of you laugh like I'm capable of saying something fucking funny, lad."

Ethan looked up to see all these unfamiliar faces through the glass partition. He mustered a smile to hide the awkwardness of the role he represented and the burden he bore at the moment. Anson, still with his back to the viewing room slowly altered his facial expression, gazing at Ethan like a proud father. No microphones nearby, no one behind the glass could hear their exchange.

"I hate my fucking job." Anson continued. "You know I have four daughters."

"Yes sir."

"I couldn't be any prouder if you were my own son."

Ethan felt uneasy, never hearing or seeing this side of his mentor before.

Anson grabbed both of Ethan's shoulders. "Be invisible, be safe and come back home or you're going to have to answer to me. Understood?"

"Understood."

Anson, still holding Ethan's shoulders, did not speak but kept staring at him.

Ethan, looking to his left then to his right, cautiously queried, "You're not going to head butt me now, are you?"

Anson burst into his hefty laugh once more then turned to the curious onlookers, keeping his arm around Ethan's shoulders, one final sale made to the buyers.

00:05:33

The dull, scuffed gray flooring of the area around Flicker's invisible doorway and sterilization chamber was painted with yellow caution lines, a framed doorstep leading to the breach's entrance. A Flicker support team member passed Ethan his period medical bag. Another handed him his aged bill fold with a generous amount of currency. Finally, he was presented credentials establishing his false identity, the documentation validating his medical education and citizenship. Ethan tucked away the billfold and paperwork into his 19th Century jacket pocket. Opening the medical bag, hoping there was some sort of gift left by Colin or his students or even Anson, Ethan knew all too well The Consortium would never have allowed anything to slip past them, as risk of contamination of the past was priority one. It was just wishful thinking, only the journal and surgical tools inside it.

00:02:59

The time had come. Within a few seconds of standing in front of this doorway, Ethan reconsidered the Cox Paradox. He could not see that which would transport him to a time he'd never been, walking the streets he knew so well in the year 2020. How horrifying it must have been to reach *this* point then, in the last moments, lose his nerve. It must've be demoralizing, that sudden loss of confidence. Had he failed to overcome the disability, David Cox would have suffered a lifetime of regret.

Ethan had no such issues, no lapse in personal or professional confidence. Only for sentimental reasons had he, once again, glanced over his shoulder, one last time, first spotting a good friend. Anson was still in the room. As they made eye contact, he wondered if this far journey would prove to be somehow redemptive for him. A flawless mission executed, a seamless return may further bury Anson's frightening experience with a Japanese soldier years ago. Then he looked toward Colin. Again, no words. Just a smile exchanged. Colin, true to form, grabbed his crotch and made a "peace" sign with his free hand, mouthing the same line he'd used on Maggie as he yelled across The Valley: *"Have a safe trip!"*

00:01:51

Returning his focus to the task at hand, Ethan watched the digital clock ticking down to a series of zeroes. It was time. Stepping up to the yellow line designating the edge of the breach, this was something he'd had the opportunity to do before on seven prior occasions. During trials he'd been whisked away to preselected, remote locations. This would be no different. Flicker really was an Einstein-Rosen Bridge between two times and locations, yet no movie or theory ever described or depicted it correctly. There was no tunnel or worm hole, no molecular alteration or derivative pains such as exiting the birth canal. Clothes did not burn off the body and the brain did not get scrambled or fried. Nothing with an electronic pulse ever short-circuited, not a thing lost in translation or transportation. As Ethan recalled, it was more like being a celebrity walking through a door to find a paparazzi using a high-resonance flashbulb to take his photograph. That was it! A bright, blinding light then he'd be through it. All the Scopes who ever made the jump described it as "anti-climactic" for an event of such historical significance. Yet, there it was, so the focus on impact became the event on the other side, no longer the many events around getting there. So be it. Ethan stepped into the chamber. Pausing for a decontamination process to work its magic, once concluded, a light flashed then Ethan stepped through time.

00:00:00

VIII.
TIMEPIECE

It hit him like a boxer, a straight jab to the nose then into the gut. Noxious odors immediately brought the time traveler to his knees. Retching in the shadowed alley, gasping that putrid air in between the vomiting only made the stench worse. He and The Consortium medical staff and historians had anticipated this physical reaction but could not duplicate its fullest capability for debilitating the Scope who'd have to breathe this air. As his nostrils stung, his lungs slowly began adjusting to the new pathogens. The faintest echo, the sound stilled the man. Approaching footsteps. But who the hell was walking through this unsavory part of town at four o'clock in the morning? *"It is four, isn't it?"* Ethan reached for his trusted companion, his antique pocket watch.

"Fuck me!" Shocked beyond belief, he inadvertently shouted. Ethan suddenly realizing that he had left his confidant, his *friend* behind in the closet! The precious timepiece remained where he'd left it, tucked away in the pocket of his 21st Century suit. Hanging there, awaiting his return, it languished unused in a dark, drab corner of the living quarters Ethan called home while preparing for the jump. Not that the timepiece miraculously GPS synchronized with the correct time in this presumed century. It served no real purpose in that respect. That aside, he couldn't believe it! How could he have possibly forgotten his closest inanimate object? And especially considering Anson had given him permission to take it along, only because it was authentic to the era.

"I sure didn't expect to find you alone using that type of language." The voice came from a distance, a dark figure standing at the entrance to the alleyway, carried through the dense fog laden corridor by moist, unbreathable oxygen.

Walking closer, the man continued. "I could hear ya getting sick from down the way. Had a bit too much, have we?" Approaching closer, Ethan could make out the uniform, custodial helmet, insignia and baton indicative of one of London's finest, a bobby on the beat.

Ethan said silently, *"Well, at least the uniform fits the target period."*

Attempting to focus, Ethan rose from his knees. "To the contrary, I think I might need a pint or two." Mustering a laugh, "I'm fine, officer."

"Begging your pardon chum, but the contents of your stomach on the ground in front of ya tells me otherwise."

"Right, well, that being done I feel much better now, thank you."

"What's your name, sir?" The constable noticing this man wasn't dressed in the typical attire for that part of town was busy sizing him up. In fact, Ethan's wardrobe was something someone of means would be wearing.

"Doctor. Arthur Bridgeman."

"*Doctor* Bridgeman, is it? Well then, it seems we've begun inviting a far better class of boozer to our end of town." The constable leaned back on his heels, letting out a rather sardonic, judgmental snicker he didn't try to hide.

Remembering who he was by title in the future and his present time, it was vital Ethan not stand out and any "doctor" allowing himself to be belittled would come off as strange to an officer patrolling the slums on the graveyard shift. Ethan stood tall, poised and confident. Adjusting his clothing, he picked up his medical bag.

"Perhaps you didn't hear me, sir. I've not been drinking. In fact, I'm quite sober in mind and body and would readily recall details of your features and this dialogue should I happen into a discussion with some of my friends over at Scotland Yard."

Feeling his position of authority challenged, quickly losing the upper hand, the bobby's body language and sarcastic tone shifted to one of a subordinate.

"Well sir, best be on your way then, doctor."

"Yes, constable. Thank you."

As the bobby continued along down his East End beat, Ethan retrieved his clean handkerchief, wiping off his face of sweat and any residual remnants of the ordeal. If the first few minutes were any indication, his attempt to "keep a low profile" was failing miserably. Ethan took heed of the constable's advice and began to make his way out of the alley. He was absolutely certain of his location in old London. It was a moment of recognition, having walked the same streets countless times more than one hundred years in the future, during his research and planning phase. *"Well, they got the location right. Two down."* Having personally selected the "jump" site, he assessed its obscure, *off the beaten path* location as safe. During the FTC trials in Oxfordshire the construction crews duplicated these streets from the late 1800's as depicted in photographs from the era. It was the time in which he found himself but there was no facsimile for what had sickened him, no replica of the pungent smell they couldn't imagine, let alone mimic.

Under the shroud of night and fog, gaslight streetlamps barely offered a warm glow or a guidepost to each street corner introduced into the scene as he passed but at least Ethan knew he was in Whitechapel. Still flustered by forgetting his watch, he could only surmise that the Flicker calibration was accurate to the second on this jump and it was, indeed, just past four in the morning, 28 August 1888. Looking through several trash heaps along his route, he located a discarded newspaper dated 27 August 1888. Assuming that this morning's papers had yet to hit the streets, it stood to reason but he needed definitive proof. His discovery of the paper proved he was in the vicinity of the correct time, at least on the same block, metaphorically speaking. How old was this discarded post? A day or a week? He had to be certain. Verify before worry. Follow the clues. Each breadcrumb helped lead him to the fact that he was where he needed to be.

The first item on the agenda was to obtain lodging. Ethan had walked this route endlessly in 21st Century London, his initial destination planned to be in the vicinity of Flower and Dean Streets, seeking a "males only" dormitory that housed only the local warehouse employees. The area surrounding Commercial Street, Bucks Row, and Thrawl Street (where, by consensus, Jack the Ripper's first victim Mary Ann Nichols resided last before being evicted for not paying the daily rent of four pence) was especially seedy. The lodgings of that period in a dark, villainous, crime-ridden East End of London were primarily gender specific, an attempt to identify and avoid prostitution activity, though many inns had no choice but to offer double occupancy to accommodate married couples, making it nearly impossible for local police and proprietors alike to distinguish who was whom.

With good fortune and keen observation, Ethan saw a man sitting alone reading in a dimly lit recess of one dormitory on Dorset Street. Historical records identified this man as the innkeeper. Someone of a sullied reputation trying to rehabilitate into society, he'd been hired, no doubt, cheaply by the owner of the property who would never be caught dead in this part of town. He appeared to be a rather shady character though he seemed harmless enough.

"Good, eh, morning sir?" The man seemed puzzled in not too different a manner as the bobby Ethan encountered, due to his attire and his early hour of arrival.

"Yes, I was wondering if you might have a room available." Ethan inquired.

"Yes sir. The rate is sixpence per night. Coming in at such an early time, I have to charge you eight to cover the extra."

Ethan reached into his billfold, careful not to expose the total of his funds. He could've easily paid for his lodging until his time for departure but that again would stir suspicion. Additionally, in this unsavory part of the city, word could get around regarding a gentleman of means residing among them and his safety would become of paramount concern. To lay low and play it safe was the passive plan of action.

"There you are." Handing the innkeeper exact currency, Ethan smiled.

With an indecisive look, the man handed Ethan a modest key crafted from lesser metals with the room number "319" carved into it.

"Up the stairs, third floor, down the hall to your right."

"Good on ya. Do you have a working common kitchen on the first floor?"

"A sitting area." Having been paid, he no longer seemed interested in engaging in banter with this stranger so he went back to his paper.

Before he stepped away, Ethan noticed the front page of the newspaper the man was reading was the same he'd found in the trash.

"Is that today's paper, perchance?" Ethan probed.

"Yesterday." Shaking his head in disbelief for a daft question. "Today's don't come out for a couple of hours yet." He was in the right and proper time and place.

Entering through the guest doorway, whatever critical remarks he made silently earlier about the smell of the streets immediately abandoned his mind with what hit his nose as he entered the stairwell. A composition of odors that, in the 21st Century from whence he'd come just minutes earlier could have been used as toxic chemical weaponry, it was nothing less than an attack on the senses. Feces, urine, mildew, sex, animals and some sort of nasty cheese, Ethan held onto the railing as his knees buckled. Turning right then down the hallway of the third floor, the early morning hours presented a surprising cacophony of sounds. Coughing, snoring and a subtle murmuring was all he could discern before reaching his room.

Opening the door, it was a pleasant surprise. The space was relatively well kept, aged, but well kept. Though bare, the walls and ceiling were stained but thankfully, not the sheets. A narrow closet was just in the entryway to the right. A small writing desk was flush to the left wall with the bed and night table positioned at the far end of the room. If time travel had jetlag, Ethan certainly suffered the ill effects of this malady. It was time to rest. He reclined on the bed, instantly falling sound asleep.

Morning was hazy, as though the fog of nighttime air had made its way through the window past the flimsy curtains, creeping into the room as a shrouded vampire. Was it still morning? Ethan wondered, reaching for his timepiece, a force of habit. Missing in action, every reminder of that oversight left a festering thorn in his side. The momentary calm, a relative quiet in the lodge soon transformed into sounds of arguing, crying, laughing, an array of tawdry emotional outbursts. Sliding his legs off the bed, he allowed his feet to strike the wooden floor with no concern for the tenant beneath him. Rising to his feet required effort. The only window was just on the other side of the night table, facing Dorset Street. Pacing himself, Ethan slowly walked in its direction, still nauseated from his landing on this strange planet, forced to breathe the atmosphere. Peering down, whatever the time, the street below was a parade of activities. A typically bustling city street on any 21st Century Tuesday, why wouldn't it be the same for this 19th Century Tuesday, as well? Oh! The smell! For a minute he'd forgotten until it slapped him in the face again.

Ethan was not yet prepared to leave any of his items in the room, even though it would probably be his lodging for the next few months, barring any incident that may necessitate moving to avoid drawing undue attention to himself. He thought it best to always bring his medical bag along or find somewhere safer to keep it. The job at hand, the purpose of his visit was overrun with responsibilities in these few days leading up to the first believed murder victim of Jack the Ripper. But first, he wondered how a cup of coffee in this century would taste. Locking his room even though he left nothing behind to steal, Ethan meandered down a disgusting stairwell again, listening to the sounds of life around him. Reaching ground level of the inn, he was met by a different innkeeper who'd likely relieved the night watchman.

"Good morning, sir." The much older gentleman with white overgrown hair and a beard framing his chubby face seemed pleasant enough. "You're not from around here…need any directions?"

"Yes. Good morning, sir." Ethan said. "You wouldn't by chance have the time? I seem to have forgotten my watch."

"If you're accusing one of the tenants of stealing from your room I will have to get the local magistrate." Suddenly on the defensive, the man scoffed at Ethan.

"No, no. Not at all. I actually forgot my watch in my, eh, travels."

"Don't own a watch myself." The man said calmly. "It's around nine or so."

"Thank you, kindly. I need to find a new watch. Is there a jeweler in the area?"

"Several located on Commercial Street a few streets over."

"Of course, over on Commercial Street. Thank you, sir." Ethan felt dimwitted not thinking of it himself. Instead, feeling like the stranger in a strange land, he had to remind himself that he'd researched the locale and knew these streets intimately well. Yet, he found it oddly disorienting, being there in real time.

Indeed, there were a few jewelry shops on Commercial Street but there was also one quaint, unassuming little shop. It captured his attention. Drawn in by an awning, it called to him from across the road, his best bet to find a dependable timepiece to replace a treasured keepsake. Ethan felt its conspicuous absence. He felt undressed without it, exposed without being wrapped inside a chronological security blanket he needed to function normally.

Greeted by a brass bell attached at the top of the door, the shopkeeper notified as someone entered his establishment, Ethan closed it more gently. Most repair and design shops did the bulk of their craftwork in a back room out of view of the public and the front of the shop displayed items reserved for sale. As Ethan began looking around, both hands holding the medical bag behind his back, the good doctor was startled by the deep, bellowing voice coming through a doorway, originating from behind heavy black drapes. Listening to an inflection in the first few words uttered, the irritated intonation was unmistakable. The man behind the curtain sounded a bit annoyed, distracted by the interruption of his handiwork by a potential customer.

"Yes, yes...I'll be right there."

Ethan continued to scan the superior craftsmanship on display, wall clocks hung beside grandfather clocks standing tall and proud. Other assorted timepieces tucked away inside glass cases, as he walked through the shop his awareness was drawn to the music, a cacophony of sounds blending together like members of a symphony. The *tick tock* was mesmerizing, the sound of time keeping itself. Every timepiece synchronized, he smiled, admiring the obsessive / compulsive precision, attention to detail, imagining what it must sound like at the stroke of noon...and midnight! Loud enough to wake the dead, no doubt! He finally had the correct time: 9:42 a.m.

Emerging from behind the curtained door a little old man with a cane appeared. The elderly gentleman propped himself beside the sales counter. Donning a pair of horn-rimmed glasses, crafting spectacles attached to them, snow white hair cropped short, his receding hairline and liberal moustache were timeless. He could've easily passed for any one of a variety of professors back at Oxford University. Holding an object inside a buffing cloth, his hands were moving, stroking the metal surface in a circular pattern. As Ethan approached he could see the shopkeeper's intense focus was on polishing a pocket watch with great skill and care.

"Are you from the tax office?" Obviously suspicious, he raised an eyebrow.

"No." Answering the question inquisitively, Ethan realized he was being sized up again, head to toe, as finely adorned as the timepiece the man was holding. In a manner much like the way he'd been scrutinized by the constable and the innkeeper, Ethan suddenly understood that he was too polished for Whitechapel.

"You look like a tax official." His apprehension had not subsided.

"I assure you, sir. I am not."

"Scotland Yard, then?" He did not attempt to disguise his skepticism.

"Goodness, no! I'm just a patron hunting for a pocket watch."

Looking somewhat less dubious but guarded, keeping a keen eye on the stranger in front of him, the gentleman came around the counter. Laying the watch aside, he extended his right hand in a less hostile, more cordial greeting. In so doing, Ethan placed his medical bag on the counter to free the hand he needed to reciprocate the gesture. With that, the shopkeeper achieved clarity, his trepidation put to rest.

"Well hello, doctor, is it? Drakes. Joseph Drakes at your service."

"Arthur Bridgeman. How do you do?"

"Fine, fine. You said you're looking for a pocket watch, sir?"

"Indeed. Something sturdy and reliable."

"Are you speaking of a watch or a woman?" Drakes joked, cutting the tension he'd originally infused between them.

Ethan smiled broadly in response to his humorous comment. Even though more than a century separated them, funny was still funny. The old man disappeared once more behind the curtain into the mysterious back room. Ethan heard him shuffling things around on his bench, in search of something. Since his arrival, this was truly the first time Ethan felt at ease, looking at the situation for what it was. Surrounded by ghosts from over a hundred years ago, people who were living spirits, long dead before he was born, this was that rare gem of a privilege to speak with living history, an amazing opportunity. After a few minutes the watchmaker reappeared, grinning, about to make the sale. Holding a wooden case lined in soft, dark velvet, filled with pocket watches, he placed it open on the counter. Gold and silver embossed casings, some with the fobs attached, others not, it was a fine *vintage* collection.

"These are my finest watches, sir. Not much demand for them lately, I'm afraid. The pricing is fair, not for style but rather the precision-timing within each piece."

"I don't care about the style. Accuracy is invaluable to me."

"Oh there's a value, to be sure. It is how I pay my rent."

Laying the watches out on the counter, one after another, Ethan suddenly found himself in a weird time warp, a distorted reality. His body went numb with his mind. Bracing against the edge of the counter with both hands, he stared in disbelief, sheer bewilderment at what laid on the velvet in front of him. His antique pocket watch, what he'd forgotten in a suit left behind at the LHC quarters, was staring right back at him, its silver cover embossed in relief with a three-legged horse. His most prized possession, a one-of-a-kind piece had found its way back to him.

"Are you alright, sir?" With no response, Drakes asked again. "Dr. Bridgeman? Is anything wrong?"

"Where did you find this one?" Ethan queried as he pointed out his familiar old friend, almost afraid to touch it, should it disappear through the veil, the shear fabric of space and time torn asunder, strands unraveling with the paradox.

"I know a chap who owns a shop in Paris. He trades with me to suit my requests for foreign designs. This one's an original. Never seen one like it before. A beauty."

"Indeed." Still in shock, Ethan could barely utter the single word. His mind was cluttered with thoughts. How did *this* happenstance fit into the cosmos? What were the calculated odds that he would randomly choose this shop to enter then be given the timepiece he'd found six years *earlier* in the window of an antique shop during one of his many late night walks? He did not believe in coincidence. No such thing. Time was on his side.

Drakes handed him the timepiece, as his customer was obviously attracted to it. Rolling it over in his hand, relishing their reunion, its weight in his palm, there was no doubt about it. The pocket watch was his own. He knew it the instant he touched the case. It was his three-legged horse, a long lost companion inexplicably returning to him.

"To me, you *are* Father Time, Drakes." Ethan chuckled, opening the cover to admire the delicate features of a miniature clock he'd sorely missed.

"Oddly enough sir, that's what my wife calls me."

"I'll take it, Drakes."

"Oh! Don't you want to know the cost of it, my good man?" Curious, Drakes wondered why his eager customer was so charmed by this particular pocket watch, though he was more than ready to make a monetary transaction, suddenly excited by the prospect of a sale, funds to add to his meager coffers and so early in the day!

"How much for it then?" Ethan reached for his wallet before the answer came.

"Twenty schillings."

Shaking his head in disbelief, Ethan reached for the correct currency without a word, pulling an ample amount from his billfold.

"It's a fair price sir, I assure you." The jeweler misinterpreted Ethan's reaction.

"Without question. I expected it to be more. Here. A tip for your trouble."

"No trouble, sir. Happy to be of service!"

Generous even before he'd been born, Ethan made the day, perhaps that entire week for a humble shopkeeper scraping out a living in the shabby East End.

"Would you like it wrapped, Dr. Bridgeman?" Drakes kindly offered.

A bit startled, Ethan knew he would have to adjust to being directly addressed by his *new* name. He'd have to get used to this 1888 identity, a whole new persona. It is one thing to rehearse a role and quite another to step onto the stage in front of a *live* audience!

"No, thank you, Drakes. I'll keep it on my person."

"If I may, while you are in Whitechapel, perhaps you *should* keep it concealed. Your attire is advertisement enough that you're a man of means. Keep your distance from others…there are more than a few who'd like to pick a pocket or two."

"Duly noted, sir." Attaching the fob to his trousers, Ethan tucked his *new* watch discreetly away into his pocket, where it belonged and where it would stay.

In 2014 he'd paid nearly three hundred and eighty pounds for this timepiece the first time around, giving all new meaning to the word inflation. Approximate to the time, twenty schillings was equivalent to two weeks average pay. Basically he was paying for the watch again with what he was taxed on the purchase as an antique in the future, a very small price to pay for something he considered priceless.

"Thank you, sir." Mr. Drakes tucked the money away beneath the counter.

Glancing down at his attire once he'd attached the watch, Ethan understood why Drakes took the trouble to forewarn him. The Consortium's decision to provide him with such high class clothing for leverage sake, assuming the persona of a physician should he be in the precarious scenario of being questioned by local authorities, he stood out in a crowd. Having precisely the opposite effect intended, Ethan knew he was far too conspicuous, an easy mark. He did not blend into the environment at all and he needed to for his research. Time to readdress the dress and make a change.

"Yes, of course. By any chance…"

"I'll give you the address of a tailor on Hutton Street. The bloke who owns it is named Thomas Clemens. He will put you in more appropriate attire for this area."

Ethan saw the wisdom in Drake's eyes and heard the perception of his words. He'd found a confidant, a ghostly friend from the past with whom he could confer over the coming months. Though Drakes was aware this man wasn't indigenous to the area, to what degree, he had no idea. Writing a location on a scrap of paper, he handed it to his *a little too well-to-do* customer then sent him on his way, ready to return to his former task at hand, the watch he'd just repaired, polishing off his own fingerprints from the timepiece.

"Thank you, Mr. Drakes. How very kind of you. I bid you a fond farewell."

As Ethan began to make his way through the shop toward the door, he paused, listening once again to the soothing sounds surrounding him, each clock precisely set. Turning back toward the jeweler, Ethan smiled then made an amusing comment of his own.

"By the way, my good man, would you happen to have the correct time?"

The shopkeeper laughed heartily as he glanced around his noisy shop.

"I can see your dilemma!" Drakes played along, popping open the timepiece he held in his hand. "Looks like 9:58, Dr. Bridgeman. Right on time. Wait a moment! You will hear what ten o'clock sounds like in my humble business establishment!"

Adjusting his precious timepiece, his new, old pocket watch, Ethan graciously waved goodbye then walked out the door, brass bell tinkling as he closed it behind him. Standing there beneath the unassuming pale green awning that had called him across Commercial Street that morning, he listened as the chimes inside the shop began tolling the ten o'clock hour of his first full day in the 19th Century.

"For whom the bell tolls…it tolls for thee." Recalling the words of Hemingway, Ethan smiled and shook his head in earnest, knowing a favorite author wouldn't be born until 1899, in another eleven years. A fortuitous day, to say the least, Ethan's mind was still reeling with the notion that he'd reacquired his trusted companion as he left what was now a safe haven. Turning back toward the direction of his lodging, should he continue down Commercial, the tailor shop Drakes recommended would be a few streets over on the other side of Whitechapel Road.

If memory served, Ethan also recalled another fine establishment along the way. Feeling slightly lightheaded, hearing the beginnings of the grumbling coming from his stomach, he knew he wasn't too far away from the famous Ten Bells Pub. Being more attentive to his surroundings, he soon came upon one of the few landmarks of old London's East End business district, a place still standing and in full operation in the 21st Century. Over the centuries of existence since its grand opening in 1752, "Ten Bells" had worn many hats, only to return to its roots as a common drinking spot and victual house, popular with locals and tourists alike. Claiming its notoriety as one place Jack the Ripper's victims were known to frequent, the pub was located on the corner of a row of four-story buildings a stone's throw away from his abode. It was calling him, the perfect spot for some much needed nourishment. And coffee!

The word "pub" originated from the word "public" noting that the upstairs also housed tenants as a common domicile, therefore, the eatery was open at all hours for every meal, including breakfast. Including coffee! For a time, from 1976 to 1988 the pub had a change of name to "*The Jack the Ripper*" but was later restored to the original name with no negative connotation and it has remained so ever since.

Stepping into history within history, Ethan was greeted by a woman who rivaled any stein maiden working at a German beer festival.

"Mornin', love. Don't you look fancy? Come in for some dining, sir?" The bar maid bowed in mild mockery, speaking *proper* English in reaction to Ethan's attire.

Ethan thought silently, *"I've got to get to that tailor next!"* then spoke aloud, "Yes please, some coffee to begin."

"Sure thing, love. Be back to ya right away. Find a seat...doc."

A medical bag gave away his *identity* again. Wondering if it was a friend or foe, Ethan located a small table by the window then pulled the journal out of his vest pocket. The Consortium held all of his items, including his personal journal, stored in his tiny LHC quarters, safe and sound. Supplying him instead with an authentic antique, the beautiful leather-bound journal of premium quality, befitting a man of means, he loved the feel of it. The pencil, also indicative of the era, felt a bit slight in his hand compared with his own but he admired its slender elegance. The doctor was satisfied with selections made on his behalf. He knew if he needed to replenish anything he could do so directly from this time period, an age when anything he'd need was available to him. Instructed to bring all items back to the future with him, with that passing thought, Ethan began to make his first entry in the 19th Century.

***

Journal Entry ~ 28 August 1888

The sensation of the surreal has melted away. In my first six hours I have come across a cast of characters Oxford thespians would salivate to observe and embody their existence on stage. From the constable to the innkeeper to my newfound friend the watchmaker who returned a good old friend to me! I've seemingly been able to speak to the dead as one of them.

As this is my first journal entry during my research, I am compelled to note to The Consortium that future trials in The Valley must, and I strongly urge, must add more focus to recreating the pungent odors relating to the Scopes research timeline and destination. Holy hell! The bloody smell!!

Three days until the first JTR victim. I will do multiple walks in daylight to find my best vantage point so not to be seen yet have an escape route afterward with the same advantage. I will only survey the area one time at night. Tonight. It will allow me to determine where the shadows are darkest. Too many returns to the scene of the crime increases the chance of being spotted and becoming another suspect.

For the time being my priorities favor far less conspicuous clothing and fewer public appearances. I intend to restrict my movement to my lodgings and this place to dine and caffeinate. Only by necessity will I initiate dialogue with those I deem a priority for local assistance. I will only alter from my normal routine to get to the scene of each sequential event. In the meantime, the coffee I ordered here at Ten Bells Pub has arrived. GOT MY WATCH BACK! Was I supposed to leave it behind? My brain hurts. Too much deep thought before coffee.

***

IX.
DRESSING THE PART

Order restored! His simplest creature comfort of being able to check the time at his leisure made Ethan feel much more in control of his surroundings and actions, totally understandable for a man who had lived by the motions of the hands of time. Having had the first meal and coffee of this visit to the 19th Century, Ethan's next order of business was a visit to the fabric shop on Hutton Street, a short walk down Commercial Street then left onto Whitechapel Road then a right onto Hutton to his destination. Along the way as midday was fast approaching, these main streets were rapidly becoming more congested with traffic of vendors, vagrants and vagabonds, protestors and prostitutes. Horse drawn wagons and wooden push carts were filled with any and all sorts of trash and treasures, serving poor and needy souls.

Horse-mounted and foot-patrolling constables created a visible deterrent to any lawlessness in the streets of Whitechapel. History recorded the Whitechapel police beefing up their attendance after two murders of local women had already occurred this year. On 3 April 1888 a forty-five year old prostitute named Emma Smith was attacked and bludgeoned by three men considered to be a local gang. Although she made it away from them, she died from her injuries that following morning. Some historians labeled this the beginning of the *Autumn of Terror*. Only a desperate few from local gangs attacked women. In fact, violent offenses against females during this period rarely made it into double digits in a year's time. On 7 August, however, the local law began to pay attention when another prostitute by the name of Martha Tabram was found stabbed to death on the landing of the George Yard buildings at 5:00 a.m. The two women never made the profile of Jack the Ripper's methodology of killing, yet remained on the radar. Both being unsolved and so close in proximity to others yet to come, Ethan's research indicated (and The Consortium agreed) that Mary Ann Nichols was most likely the first true victim of Jack the Ripper, that this would be the focus of the Flicker jump.

He couldn't make it to the tailor shop fast enough. Even struggling to avoid any and all eye contact, he could feel countless eyes on him, prostitutes and pickpockets alike sizing him up for the taking. Were he not a man of tall stature he surely would have been targeted for a robbery by a group of street thugs. Fortunately, he made it to his destination without incident. Entering the shop that, on the outside, had the address Drake's had given him, Ethan was one of several customers patronizing the place. Three counters lined the three walls of the shop, rolls upon rolls of fabrics of low to decent quality materials standing up on end, as if standing at attention. Some customers were buying material for clothing, some for furniture and others seeking matching material for patchwork. Positioned in the back left corner of the shop were two racks of clothing made by the in-house tailor, Thomas Clemens. Sitting behind a sewing machine was the man that could have been the watchmaker's twin. Ethan rubbed his eyes in disbelief wondering if the man was having a joke on him and ran over there while Ethan was eating. As all the other shoppers were looking to bother the fabric clerk, Ethan approached Drakes' clone while he was patching someone's jacket where the elbow section of the sleeve had become tattered with wear.

"Pardon me, sir? Drakes, the watchmaker, sent me to see you regarding some local attire."

"To answer your question, no, he is not my twin brother." Clemens anticipated an inquiry, having been asked countless times before.

"I'm sorry?" Ethan played innocent, not wanting to pry.

Thomas Clemens stopped sewing then stood, walking around a bulky apparatus. There was a thud with every other step. With the assistance of a cane, he approached Ethan who immediately saw the wooden left leg.

"It's funny when men reach a certain age we all begin to look alike. White facial hair, all hunched over, we become a species of bleached imps."

"I'm somewhat stumped. What I mean is, uh, I'm surprised how similar…"

"Perhaps a restart, sir?" Clemens could barely contain an outburst of laughter.

"Please." Ethan said, sounding relieved. "My name is Arthur Bridgeman."

Ethan chose not to use his title since he'd already provided enough information in his style of dress, still carrying the medical bag. No need to state the obvious.

"Well, what can I do for you, Mr. Bridgeman?"

"Well sir, I'm to be in town for an extended period of time as to require some additional attire. Something more, shall I say, 'common' to this region of London. Might you help me with this?"

The tailor looked Ethan up and down. Pulling a pipe out of his coat pocket he placed it in his mouth unlit. It seemed to help him think better.

"What is it you'd like, sir?"

"Well, I suppose the whole works if you can. Shirts, trousers, vests and jackets, even the customary hats. Two of each for now and more if they do the job."

"I suppose I could provide two full matching wardrobes from what I have here today unless you are particular about the fabric or style."

"No, thank you, but I'll take what you have for now." Ethan said, trying not to sound too desperate to get out of his current clothing.

"I'll see what I can put together for you, sir." Clemens seemed amenable.

As the old man hobbled off, relying on his sturdy cane for support, Ethan looked down, realizing he had forgotten one more important detail.

"I'd ask you about a place to buy shoes but I tremble at the thought of triplets."

"Trust me. Two of us is quite enough." Clemens had "sized him up" at a glance, no need for any measurements. He plucked everything Ethan would need from the racks in a matter of minutes. Laying two full outfits across the counter, he grinned.

"Well my good man, Drakes sent you to the right place. These are to your liking, Dr. Bridgeman?" (Yes, it was that obvious.)

"More than suitable for my purposes, thank you."

With that, the two gentlemen completed the transaction. Clemens had his clerk wrap the clothing in brown paper as they chatted jovially for a few minutes. Ethan bid him farewell, leaving the shop with his new attire bundled beneath his arm. So far, so good. Ethan was beginning to settle into the 19th Century.

The medical bag was clearly a problem, drawing unwanted attention wherever he went. Likewise, Ethan was carrying an inordinate amount of cash on his person, an invitation to disaster should he be robbed on the seedy streets of the East End. If he was going to blend in, he needed to do himself the favor of finding a safer place to stash the bag that routinely gave him away as a man of means. As he did not trust leaving it behind in his room, he decided to make one more stop.

On his way to the tailor shop, Ethan had passed a financial institution close by on Whitechapel Road, no doubt established in service to the area slum lords, a place for their local managers to make rental deposits so they'd have no need to come to that part of town. This time he'd use the conspicuous medical bag to his advantage. Entering the bank, his presence was noted instantly, his stylish attire commanding attention and respect from the employees. He was approached immediately.

"Good day, sir. How may I be of service to you today, doctor, is it?" With that, he extended his hand. "Horace Edgewood, bank manager, at your service."

"A pleasure, sir. Doctor Arthur Bridgeman." Ethan gave him a firm handshake and a warm greeting to begin their association. "I've a sizeable deposit to make and my bag needs safekeeping, as well."

As it turned out, Mr. Edgewood could be more than accommodating and would, in fact, give Dr. Bridgeman not just a tour of the bank but a safe deposit box ample enough to receive whatever he should need to store during his stay. Opening a bank account required only the documentation he had in the bag which promptly moved to the vault once he'd signed the papers. Retrieving his personal identification from the banker, there was never any question regarding its authenticity. It was all quite cordial, good fortune for Ethan to make his acquaintance as another ally in his quest to scope out the Ripper. A necessity to place the bulk of his considerable financial assets behind the walls of a bank, it was Mr. Edgewood's good fortune as well. One deposit made his day and week, providing Ethan with one less thing to worry about on a day-to-day basis for the many weeks of his stay.

"Glad to be of service!" Shaking Dr. Bridgeman's hand once again, Edgewood would remember the gentleman who'd come to call that day.

Returning to his residence on Dorset, Ethan rummaged through the clothing he bought. The materials used for the trousers, vests and coats were rough, scratchy to the touch, no doubt the same material his bed sheets were designed from. The shirts and ties were made from flimsy cloth that would surely stain and wear down within weeks. He would definitely need to visit the tailor again over the next two months. At least he'd blend in with the locals, assuming the role in an unassuming way.

On the way to his room he'd paid yet another disinterested innkeeper for another night's stay. A younger lad, it mattered not. A paid innkeeper is a happy innkeeper. Once again avoiding any unwanted attention as he made his way up the stairwell, Ethan decided to sequester himself in his room for a while, taking some time to try on his new clothing and acclimate to the itchy fabric in private. As predicted, from the moment he slipped on the shirt and pulled up the trousers, his tender skin reacted to the offense. So began the scratching. He began to peel the clothes from his body, an instant relief. Ethan made light of it when an unexpected epiphany came to light. He chuckled softly, considering the notion that there might be a fringe benefit with these untenable trousers. Scratching various portions of his anatomy in public might draw some unwanted attention or may work in the reverse, warding off people who might fear he had an infectious rash! Absolutely no reason to torture himself while in the privacy of his own room, his cotton briefs and undershirt would do him well for the time being. A sudden pang of regret, Ethan wished Colin was there with him so they could both have a good laugh over it together.

Time enough for a short nap before dinner, Ethan crawled into bed. He'd meant to log his activities into his journal but decided to do it later, knowing he'd spend a great deal of time writing once the morning of August 31st arrived and he'd witness the first slaying of Jack the Ripper's victims. He would be quite busy logging those observations into his journal, keeping him tucked away in his room and out of sight for the better part of each day. There would be plenty of time to record every event, as his interactions were already impaled in his memory, easy to recall. He was tired.

In the midst of his dreams, Ethan had something similar to that cross between actual experience and subconscious creation occur. At one point he dreamt of being a celebrity, *walking the red carpet, the multitude of photographers taking snapshots like the ones beside Princess Diana's Mercedes. Cameras flashing, going off like a thousand lightning strikes, it was a constant barrage, only brighter, more akin to the flash when crossing through the Flicker. In fact, exactly like that but over and over, repeating like an instant replay of the event. Yet, he kept on walking as if the Flicker doorway never ended. The red carpet beneath his shoes suddenly sounded like liquid, as if he was stepping in puddles and indeed, as he looked down, realizing the carpet was flowing with blood. Although he stopped walking, he could hear the footsteps of someone behind him. As the tempo of these steps increased, his brain told him to pick up the pace. Run! But the blood was getting stickier, making it harder to lift his feet. The heavier his feet felt the faster the running came from behind. He had no strength left in his legs. Just as he was about to collapse, the bloody carpet came to an abrupt end and the source of the crimson path was revealed. Just ahead, crawling away in terror was the one-legged tailor, Mr. Clemens, his wooden leg gone, blood pouring from the stump. He looked back at Ethan, horrified. No. Wait. He was not looking at Ethan, he was looking past him at whatever was running up behind him, catching up rapidly. Ethan felt the same compelling need to look over his shoulder. As he did so, an arctic chill ran down his spine, an absolute loss of logic. Out of the shadows, splashing over the bloody path was Mr. Clemens! No! It was Mr. Drakes! Wielding a blood-drenched knife, laughing maniacally in a high-pitched squeal, he was moving very quickly in spite of his short little legs, coming directly toward Ethan! Turning to run, the blood had dried and he was stuck in it. Coagulated, glued to his feet, Ethan was frozen in place, no escape. He tried yelling but no sound came forth. In front of him, Clemens was gone and in his place was all of his forensic evidence, photographs from the desk in his bedroom at Oxford. Losing his equilibrium, Ethan fell forward onto the pictures, coming face-to-face with Jack the Ripper's victims, his hands landing on the pictures that seemed to be floating atop the pool of blood. So was he, bobbing on the surface and trying to use the photographs as floatation devices. He pawed at them like some frantic animal drowning, attempting to make it to shore but there was no shoreline, just blood and the autopsy images beginning to transform into motion pictures with sound. Their corpses began looking at Ethan and screaming at him over and over again, "He's coming for you! He's coming for you!" Just as Ethan was about to ask them WHO was coming for him, he felt someone grabbing him by the back of his hair. For that moment, just a fraction of a second, he thought it was somebody pulling him from the murky red death, until he felt the blade touch his throat. All Ethan could do was stare at the images as they looked back at him with soulful remorse, his own blood spraying all over them to such an extent, he could no longer see their faces. Drakes pulled at Ethan's hair harder, causing him to stare upward into the dark, starless sky. Severing his head from his neck, the geyser of blood shot straight up and back onto his face like a rainfall. Drakes continued to laugh as all Ethan could see was the man's face, his own blood raining down. Raining on him.* Raining. *"Holy fuck! It's raining in my room!"* Ethan came out of his dream to find himself drenched to the skin from leaks in the ceiling. It had begun to pour during his nap, syphoning down from the fourth floor. In any other scenario this would have been upsetting, but for him, it was a blessing. He'd kept his head through the ordeal. The curse had been the nightmare coming out of nowhere in the middle of the day.

Ethan immediately reached for his timepiece. Luckily, it was still in the pocket of his vest safely draped over the night table and not exposed to the inside waterfall. Checking the time, it was just past four in the afternoon. Most of the leak was near the wooden headboard dripping down the wall, forming a half moon shape on the ceiling around the size of a saucer. The dream, a bona fide nightmare left him sitting on the edge at the foot of the bed, away from the leak, soaked at his feet as the water puddled, failing to drain down through the floorboards to the second floor. Instead, it accumulated, certain to make it quite slippery and tricky to maneuver once he had to move around the room. So, for the present, he stayed put, deciding how to resolve the omnipresent dilemma overhead.

Still shaken, stirred by the imagery his mind could conceive, it could have only been some side effect of the Flicker. He used both hands to wipe away the rainwater dripping from his hair and forehead, smearing it over his eyes and face in an attempt to clear the images from his mind. It did not help. The picture of swimming in blood permeated the pores of his skin. He decided to clean up for dinner. Pulling the bed away from the waterfall wall while minding his footing on the trackless wet floor, he flipped the mattress over and around so any part of the cotton stuffing that still remained drenched went to the foot of the bed. Most of his new clothing was still wrapped in the brown paper sack on the top of the desk against the opposite wall. He unwrapped them and separated the items by shirts, trousers, vests, hat and coats. Looking for the best matching collaboration of each item, he picked out his evening wear then refolded what he did not need. More than anything else, Ethan needed to wash away that dream. A man prone to self-reflection, he had to consider where in bloody hell it came from! Jack the Ripper could be anyone he'd passed on the street!

Usually, every floor of a lodging house had a community bath where the tenants could go clean up or shave using a large water basin that had to be hauled down to a pump in the street, then heated. Within that basin lay the contents of a self-body wash and shave, normally in that sequence. Dental hygiene would not be discovered for another twenty years or so. Ethan would have to use a combination of soap and peroxide and a cloth for his teeth. The privy was a publicly shared outhouse, a shed with a single box, a hole cut into it and was located in the alley behind the building. Ethan was well aware of the barbaric conditions compared to the year he'd stepped out of, but the true reality always seemed to revert back to the indescribable stench.

Having completed the somewhat daunting task of performing personal hygiene in the year 1888, it was time for him to don his authentic, not-tailored-for-him attire. A size larger, more than a century behind his normal threads, he looked as verifiably local as anyone he'd seen without seeing himself in a mirror, but he felt more of an uncomfortable synchronicity with the history he was living in. The only remnant of his doctor's attire were the shoes. Perhaps in his procrastination was an impending sense of dread, anguish associated with wearing any indigenous footwear. Not the best conditions to break in a new pair considering how much stealthy footwork was ahead of him, numerous trips scheduled over the next nine weeks or so. His wasn't an unreasonable expectation of blisters and pain. The notion of wearing itchy socks inside unpadded soles brought a sense of foreboding to his psyche. For the moment he would enjoy the one creature comfort remaining.

Many a time in a man's life when, from such a primal place as the male ego, he finds everything rides on a moment. How quickly it shatters like glass. In an instant, it is put together like a steel frame. The male ego is the biggest, most sensitive organ of his anatomy. Dressed in his new timeline attire, Ethan ate a huge piece of humble pie. A necessary evil for the sake of anonymity in his research, but for a man of few vanities, this was rough, though not nearly as rough as the feel of the fabric against the hair on his body. He walked around attempting to adjust to the prickly sensation. Even though he kept the comfortable underwear on, from the upper thigh down the material declared war on Ethan's leg hair. More like a tug-of-war with every strand. The more he focused on it, the worse it became. Somewhere between pinching and scratching came an absurdly brief period of relief, followed by the next distracting, annoying tingle. If he couldn't find the will to resist reacting, people would, indeed, clear a path for him! It couldn't be a more perfectly unplanned plan.

With his medical bag safely locked away in the vault, identification papers with him, the only things Ethan had no choice but to leave in his room while he went out for dinner were the clothes off his back, the comfortable outfit he wore for the jump and these lesser quality replacements. Neatly folded on the desk, he could only hope his paranoia about an innkeeper with sticky fingers was far from the truth. The rain had begun to subside while he was washing up. Something told him stopping at the manager's window to bring the leak to his attention would be a fruitless endeavor, a waste of his breath. He chose to make as little noise as possible, saying nothing.

Locking the room door behind him, Ethan was eager for dinner back at the Ten Bells Pub. With any luck, he would navigate the one street journey without any of the previous attention he'd received earlier in the day. Stepping past the innkeeper's cubbyhole, nodding to one of the familiar managers, he stepped onto Dorset Street and made an immediate left toward the corner. Using the hat he'd bought to obscure part of his face, looking down at the ground felt covert, adding an extra asset to his subterfuge while out in public. Blending into the surroundings, his main objective, the need to remain faceless and nameless was critical to the mission. Except for the nasty names he was called once he'd reached the corner of Dorset and Commercial Street, an altercation he couldn't avoid. Head down, appearing a little too much like a spy, Ethan almost knocked over a lady as she rounded the corner, toting a sack of potatoes among other things. She couldn't see any better than he could, considering what she had in her arms but he definitely caught the blame for the contact.

"You bloody twit! Are you daft or just a witless bugger?"

"Apologies, m' lady, 'twas my honest mistake." Tipping his hat to her, yielding the path as he tried out his even *older* English accent, she seemed to accept it.

"*Honestly*, toss off if you know what's good for you!" She scolded the man.

Tipping his hat once again, he fit right in! The woman huffed off to his right as Ethan turned left onto Commercial Street, heading toward his dining destination. If for a second he'd smiled at the encounter with the lady it was because this bump in the night was the first time Ethan felt like he could really pull it off without a hitch. What he said to Colin in that little room at the LHC compound needed to be said to his friend, but Ethan knew he would run into variables of an unexpected nature and would have to think quickly on his feet, adapting to situations, as necessary. It was literally his first obstacle while in his new change of clothes and it went quite well.

For the remainder of his short walk to the Ten Bells Pub, Ethan appeared to be no different than anyone else strolling this main road. Commercial Street was abuzz with activity at the time, characters on foot and horseback alike, making their way to some destination of importance or profit. In the 19th Century in East End London the only true and constant form of entertainment for its inhabitants and visitors alike was, well, themselves. In a day one could witness musicians, protestors, lobbyists, lawmen, pickpockets, prostitutes and orphans running amok. It was one tremendous opportunity for opportunists to gain capital and for those breaking the law to receive swift justice. Oh, there were simply those trying to get through the day going from their job to home hopefully without incident, but the best military obstacle courses paled in comparison to the amount of ducking and dodging required in this part of one of the largest, most populated cities in the world, successfully avoiding the law breakers while evading the law keepers. Life in the Whitechapel district was not for the meek or faint of heart. It was dangerous to speak with strangers or worse yet, to ignore one's immediate surroundings. To do so could prove perilous when on every corner, in every dark alleyway, a predator was waiting for the right prey to pass by.

Ethan's research had indeed given him an advantage, knowing the considerable historical record of lawlessness, who exactly to watch out for while in the company of thieves and scoundrels. Reaching his destination he'd navigated the task without incident and arrived fully intact. The pub was far more active for the evening meal and drink than earlier in the day. The staff was four or more times the number there to serve him previously. Barmaids making their way through crowds, heaving mugs of drink above patron's heads, heaving their breasts into the men, a gratuitous tactic to up their gratuity. Ethan looked for a familiar face but did not see his server from breakfast. He assumed she had finished her shift.

"Seat yourself, love. Someone will be with ya." A voice came from the crowd. Momentary eye contact confirmed that the barmaid was speaking to him. Ethan had to acknowledge that message, so he waved, no point in trying to converse. Looking around he saw nothing free. Most of the center of the room was furnished with long warped wooden benches and beverage stained tables, all appearing quite occupied. As he walked along the length of the pub he spotted a small nook in the back with a block table and two chairs. Making a slalom motion through several intoxicated patrons, he was able to claim the small space as his own. Many town folk frequented the Ten Bells for the chance to mingle, grumble, gripe and drink away their troubles of the day. Ethan hoped being blocked from view in his little corner didn't mean he would be ignored, neither seen nor served.

Although his schedule was not highly regimented over the next two days, Ethan certainly needed to eat well before his reconnoiter of the Bucks Row area later on, and more coffee was an absolute necessity. He was slightly relieved his first cup of coffee in this century (that morning) was not as dreadful as expected. It was a strong mix, a blend of chicory coffee, hot tea water and most likely, mud. A bit gritty, but it did the trick as a caffeine fix. A woman artfully dodging in and out of the crowd, she approached, spotting Ethan tucked away in the innocuous nook.

"Evenin', sir. Ya fancy food or drink?"

"Coffee. Please. To start."

Off she went as quickly as she'd arrived. Ethan pulled out his journal and began to review his prior entry when the server returned, cup in hand.

"So, feeling a bit peckish, are we?" She asked with seemingly genuine interest.

"Perhaps an idea of what's good?" Ethan curiously inquired.

"Are we still talkin' 'bout food, sir?"

Ethan's expression turned from confusion to discomfort as he realized she was hitting on him, offering more than a hot meal. The woman sensed his awkwardness. Although enjoying the tease, she got right down to business.

"We gots duck, rabbit or chicken with carrots, onions n' potatoes. Ya could try our 'three penny ordinary' if ya like. It's a meat in broth n' a beer. Don't know if ya can afford more than that, sir." The server spoke with an empathy in her voice. She probably went hungry in her life, couldn't even afford to eat where she worked.

Her indelicate statement was music to her patron's ears. Ethan realized she was referring to his clothing. It worked!

"That sounds just fine, thank you." Ethan said. "I'll try the chicken."

As his server headed to the kitchen Ethan pondered the next meal of his travels. It had been over twelve hours since the jump and he needed nourishment before his work tonight. Based upon his reaction to the first smell of the land, he'd anticipated as unpleasant a surprise with the first taste of it but his breakfast had been delicious, reason enough to return to Ten Bells for dinner. When his server returned with the big bowl of broth filled with meat and fresh vegetables, along with a slice of fresh bread, the aroma was the most appealing he'd experienced thus far. He dug right in and the first bite had him intrigued and delighted in equal measure.

"How did you cook this?" Ethan questioned, hovering his nose over the bowl.

The server looked puzzled by the question, wondering if he noticed or intended to object to the substitution. "Why it's boiled, sir, for hours by now, I s'pose."

"This chicken is so tender!"

"It's rabbit, sir. Hopin' ya don't mind. Chicken wasn't ready yet."

"Fine. Is it the whole rabbit or the rabbit hole?" As an awkward silence ensued between the two, Ethan continued. "Just, please, don't tell me your name is Alice!"

Wondering if her customer was daft, she had hoped he, at least, had tip money to spare for her trouble. Looking at him cockeyed, she noticed something odd about this interesting man in her midst, something different about him.

From first taste to the bottom of the bowl, he devoured the meal. He looked up to see the hopefully non-Alice returning.

"Will there be anythin' else, sir?" She received her answer with one nod of his head as he lifted his bowl with both hands, the eyes of an innocent child staring up at her. She had no idea he was paying homage to Charles Dickens and Oliver Twist.

"Please, ma'am, I want some more." He was suddenly insatiable.

Taking the bowl from his hands, she aimed to serve and please so she aimed for the kitchen. Smiling as she maneuvered through the burgeoning crowd, the woman shook her head. An expression belied a thought: *"How curious...definitely daft!"*

Ethan did not know how it was seasoned and didn't care. He'd had rabbit before but never with such bold flavors. Perhaps all the chemical additives in the food he'd eaten in the past (in the future) deadened the natural taste of things. He'd absolutely inhaled the broth, a bit more cautious in the dissection of the rabbit meat, insuring there was no pink left inside. Food poisoning was a consideration on this trip. Ethan needed to be fit and healthy to remain as light on his feet as possible. Even though he'd found that the Ten Bells Pub did it right, one night when the cook was off and someone else stood in and *didn't* do it right could be disastrous for his research. He decided for the duration of his stay to stick to the basics, definitely the coffee! Using his piece of bread to sop up the broth drippings remaining on his plate, his gracious server had perfect timing, arriving with a refilled bowl, more bread and a fresh glass of water. Diving right in, it was pure comfort food.

"Thank you, kindly." Ethan made a muffled sound through wet bread. Gulping down the water, he was all ready to return to his coffee then get back to his journal, perhaps even make another entry. At this point, Ethan believed there was far more to document than the research or the murders. Drakes. Clemens. Edgewood, already a colorful cast of characters had made his acquaintance, even in blood red dreams! There was much to note, experiencing the era for every nuance it provided. If there were Scopes who have research submissions pertaining to this timeframe awaiting approval from The Consortium, his notes may give them even more insights, more of an advantage than what he was privy to as a historian. If this research ever went public in the future (one hundred and thirty-two years in the future) at least people would hopefully appreciate their creature comforts in the 21st Century. On second thought, they would still take everything for granted, just like he did. Ethan grinned. Never mind.

About to open his journal, once more the woman serving him returned.

"Like more coffee, would ya sir?"

"Yes, thank you. That would be lovely. Please." Ethan was quite impressed with her attentiveness considering the congestion in the pub as more folks filed in by the moment, the talking, laughing and singing growing louder as time passed.

Returning quickly with a fresh cup, she placed it directly in front of him. Ethan smiled in appreciation then dropped his eyes, scanning the pages of his journal. It took him by surprise when his server, without invitation, claimed the opposite chair. Ethan looked perplexed, wondering if this was a common occurrence.

"Not from 'round 'ere, are ya?" She seemed mesmerized by him.

"Why do you ask?" Cautious, Ethan did not want to answer questions by telling lies to cover his tracks across the centuries.

"Ya stick out like a sore thumb. Where ya from?"

"London. Well, Oxford."

A look of pity came over her face. "Aww, lost yer job, 'ave ya? Not t' worry, love. Yer not the first nor will ya be the last. Hard times. It'll get better."

Ethan looked confused then remembered what he was wearing. His outfit was actually misrepresenting him, certainly not as a vagrant but more a man struggling to make ends meet. "Oh, yes, well, I can see how you may come to that conclusion."

"See? There ya go! Who bloody talks like that in Whitechapel, I ask ya?"

Ethan realized he hadn't kept consistency in his accent or verbiage. "Guess I'm not cut out for espionage, after all." Ethan joked.

"Love, as precious as ya are, don't matter. What's ya name?"

"Arthur. The name's Arthur." Ethan responded. "And yours?"

"Maggie." Drying her hands on her apron, she reached across the table to make a more formal acquaintance as he cordially extended his own hand.

Another Maggie. Ethan reflected back to the last time he saw the mud-splattered assistant at the Flicker time trials in The Valley.

"A pleasure to meet you, Maggie."

"So, Arthur." Maggie said with a hint of sarcasm as if she knew he'd lied about his name. "What brings ya to Whitechapel?"

Ethan could not tell a stranger the truth, not even his fictitious title of "doctor", as it wouldn't help and may yet harm his need to lay low. His fake title was intended only to provide access to areas where physicians would be allowed to enter.

"I'm a historian. I'm doing some research for a book on the history of London's vast cultural origins, thus explaining my desire to fit in." He tugged at his lapel.

"Well, ya've come to the right place, love." Maggie waved down one of her co-workers and asked her to bring along a pint of beer.

"Aren't you working?" Ethan asked, a logical assumption.

"Me? Nah. Been off for near an hour now."

The quizzical expression on Ethan's face made her erupt with laughter. She had been waiting for him to finish his meal, hoping she could spend time with him.

"Then to whom should I pay my tab?"

"Tab? Beg ya pardon?" Maggie looked as puzzled as her patron.

"So sorry. I meant, who is it I must pay for the food and drink?" Ethan corrected himself for his out-of-century terminology.

"Why, this lady right here." Maggie said as her friend returned with the beer.

"Oh, then I'd like to pay for her drink, as well."

"Well, who's this generous gentleman, Maggie?" Inquiring as she set down the pint, she was a cheerful sort, appearing tired around the eyes.

"Rose, meet me new friend…Arthur."

"It's an honor m' lord." The second server curtsied as if standing before royalty in a mocking fashion, giggling.

Ethan gazed at the woman hovering over the table, waiting for payment. She'd bloomed long ago and clearly, the blush was off the blossom but there was a beauty about her that could not be denied. Reaching into his wallet below the table, Ethan removed the money for the meal and drinks, including a tip for Rose. When she left he passed a tip to Maggie, as well, in addition to what was covered on the bill.

"Ya not propositionin' me, now are ya, sir?"

"What? Heavens, no. You brought me coffee, water and my meal. It's a simple gratuity, a gesture of thanks, nothing more." Ethan said nervously.

Maggie laughed aloud again as she downed her beer.

"Oh, you're a fun one to mess with, ya are! Have a beer with me but allow me to pay. My pleasure. Yer a delightful sort, if a bit mysterious."

"That's not proper. I should pay." Ethan argued the point.

Holding out the tip from Ethan, Maggie asserted, "But sir, ya already did!" She flagged down Rose in passing, having her fetch another pint for him.

For the next several hours the two of them chatted, Ethan always being on guard not to reveal anything of his identity or purpose for being here, even the persona he assumed for the jump. He was strategically probing Maggie for information about this strange land he was in and getting a perspective from a living person from this time. After all, it didn't *all* have to be about the murders and his research. This was his opportunity to learn the back story of the actors in a grand stage play.

Ethan was always fascinated with women from history. He had his own opinion and perspective, coming from a time, an era when the opposite sex had more power, position and choices in everything. A history of the species was confusing for both sexes. Women no longer fulfilled a typical *role* in society. For most of the civilized world those times were gone forever. From corporate executives, combat soldiers, politicians and professional athletes to mothers who'd deliberately chosen to work even harder at home raising their young, the women from the 21st Century were the first of only a few generations to achieve some semblance of freedom in their lives.

In the 19th Century, women lived in constant survival mode unless they'd been born into aristocracy, provided the wealth of a name, hence entitled. For all the rest there was always the necessity to fear men. From a young age they were taught by other women, mothers and siblings or, for orphaned girls, by experience, that they were the weaker sex and needed to be strong in other ways. They had to develop a *skill* set. Unless they had access to education, the females of society were destined to serve the males through skills in cooking, cleaning and seduction, servicing their dominant male counterparts. They had to learn to manipulate situations to their best advantage, conceived to prolong their survival in the midst of a bleak existence.

Amazed by having this woman *Maggie* sitting across the table from him, Ethan could get a firsthand description of her reality, the tale of her daily struggle. Maggie shared little of her personal history but spoke of women in plural, giving examples of friends, fictitiously named or not, detailing the strife she'd seen them overcome or succumb to over time. He was captivated, his rapt attention fixed on every word she uttered. Ethan was studying Maggie, memorizing her, taking mental snapshots of his companion, spellbound by the subject matter. She had an earthy appearance. Her life here had taken its toll, along with the drinking which, by Ethan's estimate, was definitely a regular part of life, considering the way she'd already thrown back two mugs and ordered another round. She appeared to be in her thirties but he would never ask such an improper question. She was a woman more on the heavy side but shapely. She knew her size and carried it well with jovial charm and wit. Ethan was impressed with her, using what little empathy he could relate to, her strong will and determination, not allowing rough living conditions to shake her foundation. In fact, she knew no other way to live.

Her intense eyes were the most intriguing part of her, filled with a wisdom and pain and joy. Of course, Ethan was only able to use his life as reference in this real time scenario, not having this resource of live interaction with the literary works he studied at Oxford as a student, teacher or Scope. He found her enchanting, her many anecdotal references to the colorful people of town, riveting. She even brought up Drakes and Clemens, although Ethan chose not to acknowledge his familiarity with either man or anyone else he'd encountered in his travels. He just let her garrulous nature flow. There was no romantic attraction, nor could there be, considering their *age* difference, though he was definitely enticed, drawn to a lifelong dream fulfilled as he spoke with somebody who might as well have been a ghost. He was engaging in a living history lesson. For Ethan, theirs was a cerebral connection, although she continued to flirt while sharing story after story. Slowly nursing his pint, caught up with the beguiling character sitting across the table from him, Ethan felt like a small boy sitting in the cinema for the first time, watching the magic of moving pictures, enthralled with every nuance of the moment. Maggie didn't seem to mind.

They spoke, or rather, she did for nearly three hours. In that time the pub patrons had become considerably inebriated, a rowdy crowd, yet all the noise was absorbed before it ever reached Ethan's ears. He was oblivious to his surroundings, listening only to Maggie. Of course, with a few more pints, she too became more boisterous, to a point where the stories were becoming redundant, as cloudy and incoherent as the crowd. Ethan checked his pocket watch, more than a force of habit.

"Ya've someplace to be?" Maggie seemed disappointed, sensing their evening together was coming to an end.

Maintaining his demeanor, Ethan's heart jumped a little knowing he was deeply into the first full evening of his stay and needed to depart the scene, deferring to the pending reconnoiter he'd yet to complete, the alley where Jack's first victim would be found. Ethan apologized to Maggie, excusing himself, explaining that he needed to return to his room to document as much of her story as he could recall. Maggie offered to help him remember anything he forgot the following night, as she would be working the same shift. Pretending to be a socialite, extending her hand for Ethan to kiss, he preferred the cautious approach, reciprocating with a proper handshake.

"See you for dinner tomorrow, then?" Ethan confirmed the appointment.

"Are ya asking me t' dinner, sir?" She flirted in jest, knowing his intention.

"No. I mean…sure if.…" Ethan was placed in an awkward position.

Maggie laughed, quickly vanishing into the crowd like a ghost into a wall. Ethan once again navigated his way to the exit. The time had come to go to work.

X.
TIME WILL TELL

Ethan's plan was to take a nonchalant stroll, wandering the path to Buck's Row where the murder took place, but first he had to scratch his itchy legs. Noticing the streets were still quite congested at 9:19 in the evening on the chilly Tuesday night, under cover of darkness, Ethan felt an advantage of anonymity that the daylight had robbed him of earlier, as he'd felt exposed to the eyes of all he had passed by. Now, shrouded in the shadows of dimly lit streets and alleyways, it didn't trouble him to have his fancy physician shoes on. Sadly, they would still have to go, to be replaced by lesser quality footwear of these times, more prevalent in Whitechapel.

Having taken countless walks in a London of the future, sometimes attempting to deliberately get lost then find his bearings once more, to familiarize himself with every major road and narrow alley, his safety was not an issue in the 21st Century. Most of the areas he now walked would eventually be cleaned up and restructured for businesses to thrive and tourists to enjoy. What he found in this time was a need to be more aware of his surroundings because of the depravity, destitution and sheer desperation running rampant. The local gangs in the vicinity were also a major issue for anyone holding valuables. A dark alley and one club to the head and possessions were gone along with the assailants, perhaps a life lost in the process. Walking these side streets was the quickest route to Bucks Row. Traveling by Old Montague Street onto Bakers Row then onto Whites Row (which turned into Bucks Row) took Ethan roughly ten minutes, his brisk pace maintained, interrupted only by a few brief stops to scratch his tortured legs.

Once Ethan reached the location of the first murder it all became quite clear. It was "real" even in the dark of night. Walking through this narrow passage, workers' housing on the left and large warehouses on the right, it was easy to see the strategic value of committing a violent murder in this area of town. For a predator of women, this environment was superb. A series of sick acts diagnosed as cowardly in nature, the obscurity of the dark not only allowed the assailant to remain unseen but added to the fear of his victims leading to the horrific attacks. In the distance, Ethan saw shadows moving through the rolling fog, a backdrop of lights coming from an open window or one of the few streetlamps. Scratch the legs. Scratch the legs.

According to detailed historical accounts, the corpse of Mary Ann Nichols was discovered on Bucks Row between 3:40 and 3:45 a.m., 31 August 1888. Found near the gate of an immense building being used as a boarding school, Nichols was first spotted by a warehouse worker by the name of Charles Cross who thought her body, because of the lack of light, was a discarded packing tarpaulin he'd hoped to use or flip for profit. Ethan could only imagine his surprise when realizing it was the body of a woman. Cross then waved down another workman on his way to a warehouse. Robert Paul and Charles Cross approached the victim, crouching near the woman's body which lay prone on her back, the layers of her dress pulled up to her waistline. They both felt her face, which was still warm, but the hands and feet were cold. Her lack of a response confirming the woman had expired, neither of them had noticed the brutality of her demise, only that she was dead. Both men went in search of the police, leaving the body which would soon be discovered by Police Constable John Neil. Walking his Whitechapel beat, the constable wasn't half an hour into his shift before coming upon the corpse, a rude awakening in the wee hours of the morning. Using his lamp he could see the blood and cuts to her throat.

Ethan knew this story like it was his own biography. Neil spotted a uniformed colleague passing the end of Bucks Row. Using his lamp to signal Police Constable John Thalin, letting him know of the gruesome discovery, he sent him to fetch Dr. Llewellyn. Meanwhile, the two warehouse workers, Paul and Cross, located Police Constable Mizen, alerting him to the location of the body. PC Mizen arrived shortly after PC Thalin went for the doctor who'd arrived at the crime scene at four o'clock. Examining the woman on site, he declared her deceased.

Having read all the reports, all the books, having seen each autopsy photograph released by the coroner's office, imagery of these five victims branded on his brain, the history was ingrained in the man. Having studied every documentary made on the subject gave him a familiar sense of Whitechapel, not to mention the meticulous recreations conducted during numerous Flicker trials at The Valley. No arrogance to Ethan's persona, in fact, quite the opposite, his natural humility was an attractive characteristic, a trait known to all. However, when it came to his knowledge of this case, there was no one dead or alive who knew it better. Ethan was confident in his belief that he had the upper hand, able to observe, even second guess a coldblooded killer, doing justice to due diligence of his research. It mattered not whether "Jack" had been street vermin (which was doubtful) or somebody politically connected or, by conjecture, someone in the medical profession, it was entirely irrelevant.

There were thirty-one suspects in the Whitechapel murder cases, yet the police never compiled enough evidence on any of them, failing to secure a conviction for even one of the murders committed during the Autumn of Terror. Ethan would be the only person to ever identify this killer but, more importantly, determine whether or not these women all fell under the same knife or if there were different assailants involved. Either way, he felt he'd have an advantage against any adversary, singular or plural. There were only a few more blank pages left to fill in for the history books of the future to be accurate.

Quite curious about the routes the killer used in and out of each murder scene, circling around his present location where Mary Ann Nichols (also known as Polly) was found by workmen then constables, Ethan paid close attention to all the details in the vicinity. Examining the periphery like a forensics specialist, he was trying to determine which direction the culprit had come from and which way he later exited the scene of the crime. Gaining perspective would give Ethan the best vantage point to observe from while *scoping* out the one responsible for the carnage. He'd scoured this locale a multitude of times in the 21st Century leading up to his jump but this was different, as he expected. This area had been torn up and rebuilt so many times since then, there was no way to get an accurate "first-person" perspective until now. Bucks Row was eventually renamed Durward Street, paved over in lieu of historic cobblestone. The boarding school remained intact though in considerable disrepair but it was still the best reference point for late night excursions back in the future. Being there in the "present" Ethan could not help but recall those solitary walks. It did not feel the same in 1888 as it had in 2020. Many a night he'd sensed the eerie sadness of the place as if the ghost of Mary Ann Nichols was right there beside him, helping him identify her killer. On this night he felt very much alone. There was no sense of her "presence" because the woman was still alive, dwelling somewhere in the East End of London, but not alive for long.

Ethan began to feel a few raindrops zapping him on the head. This was, indeed, London in every aspect, including the gloomy weather. Having been there at night, now he was eager to return in daylight to get a different perspective and detect any dangerous obstacles such as loose cobblestone that may later inhibit him during his observations. Ethan smiled, thinking *"No stone left unturned!"* He could not afford to succumb to any accidental loose footing in his arrival or departure from the scene of the crime on that night. The raindrops began falling in faster succession, causing Ethan to cut short his trip, expecting the miserably moist journey back to his room. He had no intention of retracing the same path he'd taken to Bucks Row. In all his training with The Consortium the one thing its military advisors drove home to him and the other Scopes was their first rule of reconnaissance: always believe someone is watching and never travel the same route twice.

Deciding to walk the two streets over from Bucks Row to Whitechapel Road, a route where the foot traffic was heavier, he could disappear into a crowd. The road took him back toward a main intersection at Whitechapel Road, Commercial Road and Commercial Street where he turned right toward his destination. Over the time required to travel to his lodging, the skies fully opened up and he was unavoidably drenched. Mud was splashing all over his shoes and newly purchased trousers were wet all the way up to his knees. At least the itching below the knees had subsided. Literally mud-stomping along Commercial Street returned him to his domicile just past midnight. Due to the late hour and a pouring rain, the streets had quieted down considerably. Passing through the door, the old, cranky innkeeper made some snide remark about his tenant being wet to the bone, accusing Ethan of tracking mud into the place. Ignoring the comment, he kept on tracking.

Up the stinky stairwell he went, leaving a trail behind him. He'd felt guilty until opening the door to his room, met with a worse roof leak than he'd been introduced to earlier in the day. Now the *other* side of the mattress he flipped over and around was soaked and the original drenching had yet to dry. That corner of the room had standing water on the floor…again. Ethan pulled the *water bed* farther away from the wall so he could at least attempt to get some sleep on the saturated mattress, one of many hardships the Londoners of this period had to contend with on a daily basis. For Ethan, he was certainly out of his element, conditions he considered *roughing it*. No electricity. No running water. No indoor plumbing. Candles and oil for light. Peeling off wet clothes, layer upon layer, like moist filo dough, a recipe for disaster if, due to exposure, should he catch a cold! Thankfully, his identification had been spared, tucked securely in a dry inside pocket. Sliding the documents underneath a pile of dry clothing on the desk, his journal had not fared quite so well. Pulling it from his pocket, he tossed it on top of the pile. The towel felt like coarse sandpaper against his soft skin but at least it scratched away the itchiness of his new wardrobe! Like his clothing, he'd have to air dry overnight to be ready for his morning jaunt. Soggy shoes were his greatest concern. No way would they dry! Ethan knew he'd be taking a suction cup-like stroll to the cobbler. He had a flash, a snapshot image of young Maggie heaving her blue satin heels across The Valley.

Curling his six-foot frame into a ball so to avoid the worst of the wet spots, he'd try to preserve some body heat cocooned in a blanket for the night. Even the pillow was unusable as the half-moon shaped drip from the ceiling focused its attention on the feather-filled head rest. With just over two months of this kind of night to look forward to, Ethan wished he just supervised the project and sent Colin in his place. Grinning in spite of his circumstances, truthfully, Ethan would not have missed this for the world. A few months of sacrifice for a lifetime of literature seemed a small price to pay for the privilege of putting pen to paper, scribing the actual account of the true identity of Jack the Ripper, not to mention his real time experiences in this century. As Ethan slowly drifted to sleep he imagined what his writing would entail, what he would have to share with the world. He dreamt about scratching himself in public, how his tailored pair of pants would feel. At the risk of appearing a bit too posh, perhaps he'd return to his original traveling clothes. It was only a dream.

Wednesday morning light poured in through the dusty windowpanes as rain had streamed through the ceiling the long night before; a bright and cheerful ray of hope delivered with the sunshine, greeting him cordially. Something Ethan didn't usually say "hello" to without the accompaniment of coffee, he opened only one eye at first as if afraid it may burn his retinas. Naked as a newborn baby, he was unaccustomed to sleeping in the buff, never knowing when Colin might show up at his flat. There was a dull ache in his neck, no head support due to the waterlogged pillow. Sitting up, wishing he had a mental broom to clear the cobwebs, Ethan stood to take a look around. Assessing the damage done by the free of charge in-house waterfall, other than the ensemble he'd worn the night before, still dripping wet, the clothing Ethan purchased from Clemens was spared this drenching, as was his more formal attire. The "doctor" outfit was draped over the desk, some items folded on the chair tucked beneath it, safe and sound and as dry as a bone. Oh, how he longed to slip his itchy legs back into his luxurious trousers. Then again, he'd stick out like a sore thumb!

The clothes and hat, even the underwear he'd worn the night before during his inspection of Bucks Row were hours away from wearable again but the concerning part was his shoes, the only pair he had. There was no way around it. He'd have to wear them along with his soaked socks to go and get another pair or two of the local footwear. Gazing at the ceiling and walls, Ethan realized this was not going to work out. The purpose of renting a room was to get out of the elements, not share space with them. He remembered seeing a few boarding houses closer to Bucks Row and the London Hospital on Whitechapel Road. Though he'd be further from Ten Bells and his coffee, he would be more centrally located. Deciding to check out the area once some new shoes were purchased, he'd break them in with a necessary stroll to find a better place to stay in the East End. If memory served, he'd seen a rather nice establishment on his way to meet Clemens, the tailor, while over on Osborn Street. Relieved that his pocket watch had been spared a drenching, tucked safely beneath two layers of dry clothing overnight, Ethan checked the time. It was 8:38 a.m.

Desperate to come up with a plan that would allow him to avoid wearing those scratchy trousers purchased the day before, he had neglected to buy extra underwear when he had the chance. Now he was in a pickle. Itchiness around the leg area was one thing but to have to walk to the tailor with that much chafing was unfathomable. The only thing to do was to compromise. Opening the window to his room, sunlight came beaming through, bursting in with the cooler morning air. Hanging his cotton boxers and undershirt over the curtain rod, it seemed a perfect place to let them dry. In the time it would take to do so, Ethan would suffer the indignity, the torment of going "commando" for his trip to Ten Bells Pub. Coffee was *that* important. Taking one for the team, he hoped Anson would appreciate the humor in it upon his return. He *knew* that Colin would! The clothing would dry. It was only a matter of time. In the interim, he intended to write about this episode in his journal for all to enjoy!

Passing by the innkeeper's window downstairs, Ethan quickly discovered why the man was scowling at him, stopping this tenant dead in his tracks. He had yet to pay his dues for another night's stay in this tribute to the rainforest and was heading out the door. Perhaps part of the mumbling he had heard the night before was meant to remind him of such, but the notice was made quite clear by the man currently on duty. Ethan informed him that he would return shortly to take care of the bill, having no intention of doing so. He was rather rudely informed he had until noon to cover another night or he'd need to find another place. That he understood. No problem. Without saying so before departing, Ethan knew he would be moving on.

Stepping over the threshold, it was brilliant outside with the perfect temperature and breeze to remove almost all the pungent odors that had been holding his nostrils hostage since his arrival. After his marathon walk the night before, this trip to the pub was simply short and sweet except for the scratchiness of the trousers on, well, areas that should not be itchy in public. Arriving at his destination, Ethan found his favorite nook available. It was quiet in the pub; the menagerie from the night before had dispersed and were all likely at home sleeping it off. He was immediately met by the same server from the morning prior. Finding a vacant window seat available, she then introduced him to another cup of coffee. Ethan looked at her as if he was a starving beggar being given a hundred dollar bill. Asking if he could get whatever variation of eggs and potato were available from the kitchen, she knew what he had wanted and went off to place his order. Making the best use of time whilst waiting for breakfast, out came the journal along with the authentic Mordan Arrow pencil donated to the project by a generous collector. Unfortunately, the journal suffered wet edges but the leather cover did its job, protecting the pages. Like his clothing, it too would dry in time, exposed to the morning air and light of day. Staring into the blank page before him, he hardly knew where to begin. Before his arrival, Ethan wondered if it would be a trip interesting enough overall to make a dent in the dense journal. By this time, he was wondering if he'd need to purchase another to record it all!

***

Journal Entry ~ 29 August 1888

Having completed the initial night reconnoiter of the Mary Ann Nichols murder location on Bucks Row, doing so gave me a clearer perspective on the best area to witness this first (collectively agreed upon) murder committed by Jack the Ripper. Unfortunately, the weather did not cooperate. I was flustered to have to cut my time there, shorter than expected. It would seem I will have to risk another night recon, hoping neither the police nor the killer are in the vicinity early Friday morning, at the same time I am choosing my best vantage point.

Before any plans for tonight there are plans for today. You'll all get a laugh out of the stories I'll tell you about the fabric torture I'm already being subjected to in this century, but paramount today is the finding of decent undergarments and a new place to lodge as the one I'm in has running water, literally running down the walls. There are some things no amount of research or rehearsal prepares you for and a flood is one of them. There is a tailor I have met by the name of Clemens who may refer me to a cobbler. That is my first order of business on the very busy day ahead.

There is still a considerable amount of time until the first murder, yet I fear the time will pass too quickly and it will be upon me with sudden impact. I'm ready but "ready" being a relative term in this living history, an era I find myself interacting with in relative ease, all things considered. Keeping my head down and pushing the "fly on the wall" persona to its perfection does not work in a place where everyone seems to depend or prey upon the other. Social interaction is the common place for marketers, racketeers and profiteers which, pretty much, encompasses the vast majority of the population and transients of Whitechapel. Silence seems to denote suspicion. An "eyes front, heads up" image relays to others, power and confidence. Tipping a hat to passing women or saying "no" to barterers on the street integrates me into the background scenery of the land. Perhaps this was what JTR figured out and used in his "cat and mouse" game with the authorities. Perhaps I have seen him and didn't even realize it because I was looking at the ground in front of me, going about it all wrong. Learn and live, even among the dead. In less than forty hours, I will see Jack's face. The question is, will it be the first time or have I already passed him on these streets? I have every advantage over him knowing this case inside and out, knowing everything except for his face. Breakfast is served!

***

XI.
FANCY MEETIN' YOU HERE

With breakfast behind him and a lengthy, itchy, scratchy journey ahead, Ethan was off. The path was not unlike the direction he took back from Bucks Row in the rain the night before. Starting along Commercial Street once again, he walked until reaching the corner of Whitechapel Road then paused to survey this urban terrain, an immersion in history, decidedly different in the bright light of day. Taking a left, he ambled through the center of town passing London Hospital along the way. The torment was mind-bending trying not to scratch, using mind over matter techniques; by any means necessary. Attempting to walk with a wider stance was unflattering, at best. At worst, it looked as if he'd had an *accident*. Lifting his legs in a marching mode made Ethan look just plain crazy! Ultimately, he decided to succumb to this overwhelming urge, freely scratching at his lower extremities, all of them, in public. Anyone witnessing him would assume the man had a personal problem. Adding to his discomfort was the annoyance of having to wear waterlogged shoes and socks, a squishing sound made with every step he took. It was all downright undignified.

Finally reaching Hutton Street he turned right onto the small road until he came to the tailor shop. It was quiet, appearing vacant of customers and proprietor alike. Wondering if it was open, it must have been. The door was unlocked. Much slower this morning, it would, no doubt, gain business throughout the day, at least he hoped so, for Clemens' sake.

"Well, you don't look like a rich man anymore, but at least you don't look like a naked one!" The familiar voice of Clemens was heard from the back room of his shop. Emerging, cane in hand, he slowly made his way around the sewing machine, on his way to his first client of the day. "Glad to see you! I knew you'd be back!"

Until that moment Ethan had not realized his own fixation on the prosthetic leg attached to the old man, remembering his vivid nightmare.

Equally intrigued by the oak cane, he tried hard not to stare at either piece of wood.

"Yes, a bit more fidgety of a man due to the fabric, I'm afraid." Ethan replied, focused on looking into the eyes of the tailor as he stepped farther into the shop.

"I was wondering how you'd fare with the change. I'm not just a garment maker but a prognosticator! I knew you'd be seeking some resolution. Ah, dare I say your upper class attire will be your downfall, *Mr.* Bridgeman." Mocking Ethan in a most jovial way, somehow Clemens also knew he'd get away with it.

Ethan smiled, accepting of the ribbing he received but in his mind he could still see the tailor in his dream laying prone on the ground, bleeding out from the severed leg. So embedded was the vision, he'd caught himself turning around, expecting to see the watchmaker Drakes behind him wielding a knife. Clemens seemed to know exactly who Ethan was and his purpose there. Impossible for anyone to ascertain his point of origin without confession, he quickly dismissed the notion, considering it borderline paranoia based on a bad dream, nothing more. Perhaps the old man's wisdom and experience from so many decades of life enhanced his intuition, simply using the good sense God gave him.

"I was hoping perhaps you could direct me to a local shoemaker you may know, one not your triplet." Ethan said, playing along with the tone set by the shopkeeper.

"And not a moment too soon it would seem!" The old man observed the current condition of Ethan's formerly valuable shoes.

Looking down at his shoes, nodding in agreement, Ethan heaved out a sad sigh. "Yes, as you can see, I had a bout with last night's weather during a roundabout."

"And what, may I ask, would've had you out fighting the conditions that started so late last evening?"

Ethan again looked cockeyed at Clemens, wondering why he'd asked about his activities and how he knew just when the rain began to come down. Not wanting to draw any more attention to the subject, he changed it.

"Do you have undergarments for sale here?"

"Yes sir. Right there in the corner, we have them in stock." Clemens pointed to the back of the store, noting that his customer did not favor the prior topic.

Feeling a little uneasy, a bit pressured, as if there was more to the irritation he felt than just his pants, Ethan needed to make this a short visit. He grabbed the first three pairs of undershorts and shirts he saw in his size, at least close enough to do.

"These will be fine, Mr. Clemens. Thank you, sir."

Placing the garments on the counter, Ethan pulled the billfold from his pocket to make quick work of the transaction. He felt a sudden urgency to be on his way.

Sensing Ethan's mood, the tailor took the money, returning his change without uttering a word. As he wrapped the clothing, Clemens spoke once more as he tied the package with string to secure its contents.

"The cobbler is on the corner of Whitechapel Road just past the hospital, across the street. You'll find him a pleasant chap."

Ethan nodded in appreciation of all the old man's assistance but knew he could only extend the olive branch of familiarity just so far, feeling the necessity to keep his interaction brief and to the point, no prying questions allowed. A nightmare had gotten to him, perceiving it to be an ominous forewarning to keep the tailor at arm's length for his own protection and Clemens, as well. With a wave of the hand, Ethan walked out the door, the bundle tucked beneath his arm.

Making his way back to Whitechapel Road in the direction from whence he'd come, he spotted the cobbler's shop, having missed it passing by the first couple of times when he was either attempting to keep a low profile by looking at the ground or was too distracted, discreetly scratching some embarrassing part of his anatomy. Unlike the watchmaker's shop or the tailor's place, the cobbler shop had a window display of the products available. Ethan attributed that to the store being on one of the major thoroughfares prone to heavy foot traffic, as an enticement to prospective customers. Entering the store front he was met with a wide array of leather footwear to choose from, shelf upon shelf of this cobbler's handiwork. Some shoes polished to perfection, others had a dull finish but he couldn't help but notice the absence of signs denoting "manmade" materials, as was so often the case in his plastic fantastic century. It was a pleasant surprise. Pair after pair of shoes and boots staring at him, some with four or five grommets for men and far more for the women's designs. A simpler style low-heel laced shoe was what he was seeking and, as luck would have it, they were here in abundance.

Within minutes of his entrance, Ethan had chosen two pair, a prompt purchase made as the sales clerk watched amused, bundling one pair of new shoes along with four pairs of heavy woolen socks, another hasty choice made. Utilitarian by nature, Ethan's approach to the purchase was pragmatic, not a shopping spree. These items served a purpose, getting him out of what he was in. Even before leaving the shop he removed his damp footwear, donning a new pair of shoes and socks to match his scratchy suit, secretly longing to quickly slip on a pair of underwear, as well! Ethan examined his "doctor" shoes, concluding that they would need some tender loving care to be salvaged and restored to their former condition. It had occurred to him to leave them with this cobbler for repair but that would create even more interaction, perhaps stirring suspicion, soliciting more prying questions, so he'd decided against it for the time being, pausing to pop open his timepiece. It was just before eleven.

Carrying these articles in a store sack, along with the brown paper package from the tailor, Ethan did appear to be weighed down by the wares he'd bought to wear. Holding his wet shoes in hand, he began to head back in the direction of his lodging. Recalling that he had seen some additional housing along the way on Old Montague Street to be exact, Ethan remembered the place from his research, tenants routinely evicted for the lack of funds to pay the daily rent. He'd surely find a room available there, quite confident he would locate a suitable dormitory with a vacancy.

Ethan carried on, continuing to make his way along Whitechapel Road. Looking up to see a local police constable dead ahead, he was walking directly toward him, looking directly at him. The officer greeted Ethan by blocking his path.

"Morning, sir." The bobby's voice was cold and stern, all business and certainly curious about what business he'd been conducting in the area.

"Good morning, constable." Ethan replied, trying to look nonchalant.

"You're not from around here." It wasn't a question, more so an observation.

Officers were trained to spot suspicious characters on the streets, those who did not appear to fit in. Through experience they learned to deduce an intention as they approached someone, watchful for any reaction. Ethan seemed odd, out of place to the bobby.

"You appear to have your hands full, an armload, in fact." The insinuation was obvious, an implicit accusation.

"I do, indeed!" Ethan tried to play it cheerfully, fighting an urge to scratch his lower extremities the more nervous he became.

"I've not seen you before." Inspecting Ethan from head to toe, he continued on, "Just noticing those shoes you're carrying. I have seen them in a store in the upscale part of London. Odd to see them around here. Strange to see a man dressed like you having those in your possession."

Considerate of the policeman's observation, Ethan attempted to explain.

"Of course, I clearly understand your confusion. I'm a doctor doing research in this area. I have dressed like this so the locals would be less apprehensive about my presence when approaching them and you don't believe a single word I'm saying, do you?"

"You say you're a doctor, sir? May I see your personal identification? Medical documents?" The bobby extended his hand to receive verification of this story.

Ethan put down the one package of underwear and the sack of socks and shoes so his hands would be free to reach into his vest pocket to retrieve then produce the papers that were actually tucked under a pile of clothing on the desk in his boarding room, for the sake of their protection. "Fuck me buggered." He said in a low voice, nearly inaudible but the bobby heard it.

"Pardon me, sir?" The officer asked, assuming a more authoritative stance.

If Ethan didn't know better, he'd think someone gave Colin the remote control to a video game and he was having one over on him! One in a series of unfortunate occurrences, this mishap told him it was not going to be a *walk in the park* research event thanks to this unavoidable human interaction. Dressed like a commoner and holding a pair of expensive shoes did look suspicious, walking with a scratchy groin and no personal identification? Blimey! Standing there for a moment, frozen in fear, lost in thought, Ethan had an epiphany when the building came into view just ahead of him.

"The bank!"

"Beggin' your pardon, sir?"

"Officer, look, I am sure you've heard this story before but truthfully, I've left my credentials at my residence. I can *prove* who I am! They can vouch for me over at the bank." Pointing in the direction of the institution in plain sight, Ethan hoped the constable would be willing to take a short walk with him to resolve this inquiry. "My medical bag is in the vault."

"That bank over there, you say?" The bobby turned to see where he pointed.

"Yes. Look, I understand your position, sir. If I were in your shoes, which look quite comfortable, by the way, I would also wonder why I was carrying *these* shoes. All I'm asking is that you take a brief walk with me to the bank and everything will be explained." He punctuated his plea with the most innocent puppy dog eyes.

The constable stared at Ethan and began tilting, rocking back and forth from his toes onto his heels, squinting skeptically, as if it might cause him to read the man's mind, intuiting true intentions while rubbing his chin with a thumb and forefinger.

"Alright sir, let's go see about your bag at the bank, but no funny business."

"No sir, none. Thank you, officer."

Walking silently beside the constable, feeling like nothing more than a common criminal under arrest, conspicuous in the extreme, embarrassed by the ordeal, he'd do his best to get through it. Sensing the many eyes upon him, this was not the low profile he'd intended to keep in the East End. Far from it. Entering the bank, Ethan hoped the tellers and management were the same, and to his good fortune they were. The manager, Mr. Edgewood stood from his desk seeing the officer in uniform first but as he approached them, recognizing his companion.

"Doctor Bridgeman? Is that you, sir?" The manager inquired, a rather quizzical expression in his eyes. "Well, of course it is!" Extending his hand. "So sorry I didn't recognize you…your attire."

"Doing some historical research in the area, Mr. Edgewood. Trying to blend in with the locals a little better."

"Ah, yes. The suit you wore yesterday was, shall we say, a cut above?"

"Do you know this gentleman, sir?" The officer asked, lightening his tone.

"Why, yes. One of our finest clients, a top physician of impeccable reputation." Mr. Edgewood exaggerated his knowledge of the gent standing beside the officer. After all, money was money. For the Whitechapel district, this client's deposit made the day before was monumental.

"Well, then doctor, this all seems to be a misunderstanding. Good day, sir."

"Perfectly understandable. I thank you for doing your job constable and keeping the peace." Ethan shook his hand and the policeman went on about his beat.

With the lawman beyond earshot, the inquisitive manager drew closer to Ethan.

"Is everything well, sir?" Edgewood asked in a hushed tone.

"Yes, yes. Fine. A misunderstanding, indeed. He thought I stole my own shoes!"

"Why are you dressed in this clothing, sir? What research are you conducting? If you don't mind me asking." Edgewood pried, curiosity getting the better of him.

"Long story." Ethan shook his head. "Long story. I think it would be wiser to keep my medical bag with me at all times. May I close out my safe deposit box?"

"Will you be closing your account with us as well, sir?" Suddenly nervous, the banker cringed at the thought.

"No. I'll still need to keep the account open."

"Of course. Please keep it as long as you wish, Dr. Bridgeman. So glad to be of service. I shall return." Relieved, he went to gather the necessary paperwork.

Retrieving the bag from the banker, withdrawing a modicum of funds to replace what he'd spent shopping, Dr. Bridgeman was on his way once more. Traveling the rest of the way with his fancy shoes hidden inside the bag, Ethan did not expect any further delays in his plan but then he hadn't expected the ones that already occurred. Making his way onto Commercial Street, nearing his current lodging Ethan planned to make a few adjustments to his wardrobe before going shopping for a new roof to place over his head.

"Arthur. Arthur!" A female voice wafted across the street. He failed to respond, not recognizing his own 19th Century name.

"Oh, shit! Is that me?" A shocking thought, he was afraid he'd said it aloud.

Ethan looked back to see Maggie, his server from the Ten Bells Pub, addressing him by his fictitious name. Dodging the horse drawn carriages as they passed, she'd lifted her skirt to keep from dragging any remnants of a filthy street along with her. The gentleman paused, awaiting her arrival as she ran across the road.

"Fancy meetin' you here!" She began, excited to find him out and about.

"And what are you doing out this early?" Ethan inquired.

Her eyes seemed brighter than he remembered, that dark pub obscuring details of the woman he'd rediscovered in the daylight. Maggie had some facial lines and a bit of weight on her, yet there was a young maiden quality about her, as well. Her sparkling eyes appeared to burst forth from her round face as she smiled, obviously happy to make his acquaintance again, quite by chance.

"Just checkin' my work days at the pub. I'm on tonight if yer stoppin' by."

Walking alongside him required two steps to each one of his, as she was only slightly above five feet tall. He slowed his pace to accommodate her own.

"Well, if I get moved in time it's in the cards, yes."

"You're movin'?" Maggie exclaimed with concern and a hint of sorrow.

"Just out of this place. Too many leaks. There are a few places on Old Montague I saw. Hopefully I'll find a vacancy."

"You will. I know most o' the lords who manage 'em...they always have a few open. I can show ya if ya like."

"I really wouldn't want to impose."

"No imposition at all, sir!" Ladylike as could be, Maggie curtsied.

"Well I'm grateful for your assistance, ma'am." Tipping his hat in a reciprocal gesture, he continued, "I just have to collect the rest of my belongings."

"Not *ma'am*. Maggie. I'll come along with ya to help ya then." Delighted to be in his company, happy to help, she'd taken a shine to him.

Ethan couldn't resist cracking a smile at Maggie's energy. She looked up at him in much the same way his 21st Century Maggie did handing him the review forms at The Valley.

"Come on." Ethan gestured with his head. "It's this way."

Walking together through the entrance of his lodging passing by the innkeeper's window, an old man stuck his head out, yelling at the tenant and his guest.

"OY! You can't have any women in your room out of wedlock! Thems the rules or you're gonna have to leave."

Ethan calmly looked at the man then Maggie and finally back to the man.

"Well, I suppose it's a good thing I'll be moving out then."

Ethan continued walking toward the stairwell as Maggie followed, flipping off a rude gesture in the manager's direction. Arriving in his room, he quickly tidied up, embarrassed by the water leakage and disheveled condition he'd left it in, especially self-conscious about undergarments hanging out the window to dry. He snagged them in an instant, tucking them into a coat laying on the desk.

"Oh, no. This won't do. This is no place for a doctor." Maggie said, both hands on her hips. "This won't do, at all."

Ethan looked completely puzzled, knowing he'd never said he was a physician during their chat the night before. Maggie seemed tickled by his little secret.

"How did you know?"

Nodding at the medical bag he had placed aside while scampering around doing clean-up duty, she'd actually noticed it first when running across the street and said nothing at the time.

"Of course." Ethan shook his head. "Gives me away every time."

"I've a few doctors as customers. I recognized it." With that, she pitched in.

"You don't have to do that." Ethan said as she began handling his clothing.

"Ya don't understand women very well, do ya? It's what we do best."

"Folding?" He wrongly guessed the intention of her comment.

"Takin' care of men!" She promptly corrected him.

Grabbing up the rest of his belongings they began the trek over to Old Montague Street to rows of lodgings where Maggie knew several innkeepers. Along the way he told her his research required him to dress down and fit in, though he kept it all quite vague and non-descript. Then he told her the story of his run-in with a bobby, leaving out the money part and his nightmarish experience as it rained in his room. Maggie had never asked him anything personal either during the walk or in the pub the night before. She seemed to respect his privacy or simply did not care to pry.

Ethan asked how everybody learned to walk in the shoes they wore, referencing those nicer shoes he was more accustomed to, the ones that almost got him arrested. They also talked about itchy pants which were, by then, driving him out of his mind. There was not a thing he could do about it in mixed company, particularly in such close proximity. He had to grin and bear it. Maggie suggested he purchase the type of stockings worn over socks up to the knee. Ethan was drinking it all in, absorbing the minutia of local idiosyncrasies and colloquialisms of those who survived these times. So much of what was provided in the written history never really tapped into the experiences he'd already taken in over just the past two days.

Nearing the end of the road at the corners of Old Montague, Hanbury Street and Bakers Row were several lodging houses. Ethan and Maggie walked past a few that were closer, yet she did not even give them a second glance. He decided to trust her judgment. Apparently she had a specific location in mind. Where these three roads met was one particular place along Bakers Row which seemed well kept and freshly painted. There were some floral arrangements in the front, reminding him of ones adorning the façade of his flat in Oxford, the place he missed the most with all the comforts of home.

“Wait here.” Maggie instructed Ethan as she walked to the manager’s window. A stout man who looked to be in his fifties appeared at her beckon call, smiling at her as she’d waved. Although Ethan couldn’t hear their conversation it looked as if it was friendly and familiar. The man peered past Maggie at his potential tenant as he nodded in agreement. Calling him over, she introduced him to the innkeeper as Mr. Arthur Bridgeman, discreetly, not to give him away, preserving his privacy to the title of “Doctor”.

“Nigel here has a perfect room on the second floor for ya, close to the first floor kitchen n’ privy, a wash basin all to y’self in the room, love.”

Ethan was shocked by the powers this woman possessed. It all seemed too easy.

“How much per night, sir?” Ethan inquired.

“The room usually goes for ten but for a friend of, uh, Maggie, you can have it for sixpence a night, long as you like.” Nigel seemed a pleasant enough chap.

“Does it leak?” Ethan had to ask, prompting the confused expression from the man in the window.

Maggie burst into laughter, telling Nigel to ignore the question as Ethan pulled out the coins to cover his first night in a new, less humbling abode.

“Come on. I’ll show ya your room now.” Maggie took charge by taking the key from Nigel, conducting the tour on the way to his private quarters.

Walking into the building, Ethan was astounded by the obvious cleanliness and comfortable furniture in the public sitting area. The kitchen was fully supplied with hanging pots, cutlery and a wood stove along with cups and saucers for coffee and tea. Long wooden benches stretched along a table of the same length in the middle of the room with enough space for all the occupants. By the stairs to the upper floors was the back alley doorway to the privy or outhouse. The stairs to the second floor had lit candles fixed in holders on the walls. Directly ahead was Ethan’s room, just as they said, accessible to everything. The last thing he noticed before entering his room was the absence of an odor he thought he’d never escape in his former digs.

One of Ethan’s favorite classic films was “The Wizard of Oz” and his favorite scene was when Dorothy stepped out of the house after the tornado transported her to a magical world. Opening the door, she stepped from a black and white existence into Technicolor. Crossing the threshold into this room he felt like Dorothy entering Oz. He was met with finely polished wood flooring, a wool rug running the length of the room, an actual dresser to place his clothes in and the wash basin, a beautiful pitcher and bowl resting on top of a fine, fancy lace doily. The bed was an oversized twin with a wooden frame, an ornate oak spiraling corner design rising high at the headboard and slightly above the footboard at the end of the thick mattress, like a four-poster that hadn't yet matured. It rested against the inner wall to the left of the entrance, rather than the outer foundation wall, protected from the elements should a leak occur. The bed cover and pillow were both down feather and the writing desk was beneath the window that faced Bakers Row for best lighting. A generous mirror hung on the wall. He had two candles available, unused, placed in cast iron holders, one located on the dresser, the other on the desk. It was paradise.

"Do ya like it here, love?" Maggie asked expectantly, knowing the answer.

"I am forever in your debt, Maggie." He said. "How did you manage this?"

"I told ya. I 'ave a lot o' customers." She smiled coyly, handing him the key.

"How may I repay your kindness?" Ethan offered without hesitation.

"Will ya be comin' 'round to the pub tonight then?" A leading question.

"The only place I trust to eat, yes." An honest answer.

"Then ya can buy a round or two o' beers at the end o' me shift."

"Done." Ethan reached out to shake her hand. Maggie giggled and winked.

Walking her downstairs to the front door, thanking her profusely until she told him to stop, no need, they bid farewell, parting ways for the time being. Returning to his room to put things away and arrange his schedule for the day, Ethan was sure he was living in the lap of luxury. First things first: off came *all* the itchy clothing! Having locked the door, no need to worry Colin would come knocking (or anyone else for that matter) Ethan had a sudden urge to be naked. A normally modest man, he found the sensation liberating, to say the least, finally out of *that* clothing which had been tormenting its victim all day. Rubbing his hands over every itchy spot, he scratched until the itching subsided, a relief he had longed for and would not forsake for the sake of propriety. No one was watching. Looking in the mirror, he laughed. Ah, to be comfortable again. He decided to do his work then nap in the buff.

Laying out all his possessions on the desk including documents, money, journal and pencil, Ethan sat there for a minute, conducting an inventory of his belongings, another way to organize a cluttered mind. Having replenished his funds, he felt the security that having money at one's disposal brings. He would happily buy Maggie a round or two, or dinner if she liked, with plenty to spare. Good to go to the pub.

This room was blissfully tranquil, a far cry from his former boarding house. Its walls were thick, insulating him from his surroundings. Opening the window, Ethan heard Maggie's voice from a distance. Wondering if she remained on the premises, he gazed down upon the street below, spotting her instantly. She was still speaking with Nigel, the innkeeper, except their formerly cheerful banter was replaced with a tense exchange, the low murmurings of an argument in hushed tones. Maggie was flailing her arms, making a few rude gestures then she stormed off in a huff. Though unfamiliar to Ethan, he guessed it had nothing to do with wishing Nigel a good day. He wondered why she was so angry with the man but let it go, none of his business.

Ethan went back to his inventory once Maggie was out of sight. Within minutes he heard a small voice calling his name over and over again. It was the featherbed, an amazing down comforter and pillow. Last night was far from restful, spent curled up in a ball so to avoid the wet spots on either end of a mattress. He sought a sound and safe slumber wherein he could stretch his frame out fully and recharge before a second night of canvassing Bucks Row. Checking his pocket watch, now 1:42 p.m. it was time to take a nap. The quilt felt heavenly, caressing his exposed skin. In less than two minutes he was out cold.

XII.
IF MEMORY SERVES

Ethan had slept so soundly, when he woke up he absolutely forgot where in the hell he was and jumped up in somewhat of a panic, the kind of sleep when he didn't even remember dreaming. It was dark already. He hadn't lit the candles in his room prior to laying down, assuming he would awaken within a couple of hours. Leaving him to find his way in the dark, in search of the stick matches, once located, he lit his lodging and immediately looked at his timepiece. It was 6:40 p.m. Disoriented, Ethan hoped it was still Wednesday and he hadn't missed his date at Ten Bells Pub. Deciding to run downstairs to the first floor and find someone to verify the date, he had to be discreet about it so no one would think he was insane. Redressing into an acutely uncomfortable outfit, it felt like being imprisoned, again.

Approaching the manager's window he found a night watchman instead. Done for the day, Maggie's friend Nigel had gone.

"Good evening, sir." The man was alert, acknowledging his tenant at once.

"Hello, sir." Ethan said with a nod. "I am a bit curious. For a Wednesday night, the common area downstairs seems very quiet. Is that typical?"

"Well, sir, most stayin' 'ere work ten or twelve hours a day and ain't home yet. Those who are mostly go right to their rooms and right to bed. Usually picks up on the weekends but normally its quiet 'ere."

"I see." Ethan felt relieved knowing he hadn't slept through to Thursday night. Now he needed to get to the pub for dinner, as he'd promised Maggie he would.

Returning to his room, Ethan could now gather an ensemble from an assortment of shirts, pants, socks and shoes plus a few accessories for his evening out. He used the wash basin to clean up, already having been filled with fresh water for the new tenant, a nice touch and much appreciated. Dressed and ready, Ethan found this inn secure enough to leave his medical bag behind as he headed out to Ten Bells Pub.

Travel to the pub was now a longer walk, about ten minutes to eat safe food. He fit right in, tipping his hat to the ladies as he passed, picking up the pace when he passed one he'd presumed to be a lady of the evening, lest she pay him some mind. Arriving at his destination, it was even more crowded than the previous night. There really wasn't much to do for entertainment in the era but to drink, socialize and play cards. Filtering through the crowd, he felt a tap on his shoulder. It was Maggie.

"Beginnin' to wonder if ya was comin'. Missed ya tea. D'ya oversleep?" She'd had to shout to be heard above the rowdy crowd of patrons getting drunk.

"My apologies." Ethan said. "That may be the most comfortable sleep I've had in a *long* time!" His enthusiasm was infectious. She considered it a compliment.

Maggie laughed, taking Ethan by the arm. She held a table for him in the corner away from the drunkards. Seating him, she told him she had a surprise for his dinner then went to the kitchen straightaway, returning only minutes later with a fresh cup of coffee and a glistening game hen surrounded with roasted potatoes, a sumptuous platter prepared just for him.

"You didn't pay for this, I hope." Ethan asked.

"Bloody hell, no!" Maggie laughed as heartily as he was about to eat. I'd o' had to if ya hadn't showed up! Oh no, you're a payin' for this *and* then some! I figured ya was hungrier for somethin' besides rabbit stew. It's been keepin' in the oven."

She was right. He hadn't eaten a thing since breakfast and had worked up quite an appetite, incredibly hungry after his long walk. Diving right into the meal, Ethan began consuming the delicious food with a primal fervor. Maggie stood there at the table for a bit, enjoying him, satisfied that she'd made a good choice on his behalf. Another one. He was so focused on the food, he didn't even notice that she was still there until she spoke again.

"Me shift's almost over. I'll be back with the beer yer buyin' me."

Waving a drumstick her way, he smiled, his mouth too full to speak. He would later feel a pang of regret, realizing he had not thanked her yet, feeling obliged. Her kindness toward him had warmed his belly, a direct route to his heart.

Watching him from a distance, this server took her charge seriously, returning to the table to clear what miniscule scraps remained the moment he was finished.

"Thank you, Maggie, it was wonderful and so are you. Absolutely wonderful." Ethan glowed with gratitude. Wiping his mouth with his hands, his only option, not a napkin in sight, he rubbed them together then laid them on his stomach, a gesture indicating his complete satisfaction with the meal. Sublimely sated, he punctuated his pleasure. "My compliments to the chef…*and* the server."

Maggie glowed with perspiration and a hint of embarrassment. "Tell me, what bloke talks like that, I ask ya? An odd bird, Arthur Bridgeman, that's what y'are." The feisty middle-aged woman talked back, blushing like a schoolgirl.

Paying his bill along with a generous tip for her, Maggie went into the back of the pub to clear the debt then sign off her shift, returning with a pint in hand and a few more colorful stories to tell. Her memory served him well. Receiving quite the education, Ethan soaked it in the same way he'd sopped up the juice from his plate with his last piece of bread. Absorbing every word, committing it to mind, making memories of his own, Ethan was entranced and enchanted by living in the history.

Once again the two of them sat for hours and chatted. This time Maggie had fun pointing out different patrons in the pub and telling Ethan some of the dirty laundry about them she had picked up over time. No names, just the faces and their stories. He found it all quite entertaining to hear about these people, making mental notes, intrigued by how similar the tales were to the people he knew from the 21st Century. Infidelity, corruption, embezzlement, frauds and con artists would stand the test of time. *"The more things change…."* Ethan thought then shook his head, a believer.

Ethan was amazed by the transformation in Maggie from a midday sober, sunny lady to a woman who could adeptly put away four to five real ales without showing any sign of inebriation, although she was a trifle more flirty and sociable than usual. He wondered how much she would have to drink to actually get drunk. They spoke metaphorically of life and death, love and pain. Ethan continued savoring his coffee while Maggie ordered yet another beer. Offering to buy her own after the third pint, he refused to hear of it, knowing she wasn't trying to take advantage of his generous nature. It was simply the way she lived, assimilating alcohol into her system as if it was water, as if immune to the effects.

Monitoring his time on the pocket watch, he needed to be on his way by 10:00 p.m. and it was already ten minutes past the hour. It was time to do one more check of the Bucks Row region of Whitechapel…time to go. Disappointed, Maggie took notice of his need to leave.

"I know." Slurring her words, "You've someplace to be. I wish ya could stay."

Maggie seemed a bit tipsy, sentimental in the way drunks sometimes get before they fall asleep, though he didn't think of her at all that way. In fact, he thought she held her beer remarkably well, better than he ever could. Impressive! However, by sheer volume, the beverage she'd ingested was beginning to take a toll on her senses and her speech. Rising from his chair, Ethan left another tip on the table, thanking his gracious hostess again for all she did for him then bowed out with a reasonable explanation and was soon through the door and down the road.

Looking up into the night sky, he saw nothing but stars above, giving him hope that this night's weather would be more favorable than the last. No need for another drenching. Returning to the street where his lovely newfound quarters were located, at Bakers Row, Ethan was only a street or so away from Bucks Row, where destiny would unfold. He actually liked this arrangement better. A nice walk to and from a meal at the pub, a quick route to and from his first research vicinity, it seemed quite convenient, giving new meaning to the phrase "falling into place".

Taking Whites Row then crossing Thomas Street, passing Court Street and then reaching the old boarding school, he would again find himself at the future murder scene of the distant past. His pocket watch read 10:36 p.m. Ethan knew he had to take his time on this expedition, planning to stay later. He had to see who came and went in the area. Perhaps the killer was surveying it, as well. He would not be able to identify who it was but could certainly tell if somebody else was conducting the same type of surveillance, quickly moving in and out of dark shadows, scoping out the best vantage point from which to observe…or to strike.

As a few commoners passed by or a constable came strolling along on his beat, Ethan would determine if he could remain unseen in the shadows as they passed. If he were to be spotted and questioned he had his credentials at the ready, prepared, a story to tell. His only worry, an incessant itching and scratching, a dead giveaway. No proper doctor would be caught dead looking or acting the way Ethan did. It was an awful distraction at a time when he needed to maintain complete focus on a job unlike any other, stuffed inside an outfit he could not tolerate and a reaction to it he could not control. Though he was becoming more accustomed to the annoyance, it was on his mind; distraction could spell disaster. Deciding to heed Maggie's advice, he'd purchase some protective stockings as soon as possible. With this addition to his wardrobe, he might just survive his trip to the 19th Century, after all. Maggie's presence was a comfort to him in many ways, his only friend. She'd proved a good ally in his battle to adapt to this century's discomforts. Certainly the new room and a steady source of coffee should sustain him for the duration of his stay.

Ethan remained out in the area until 3:40 in the morning, the time around when Mary Ann Nichols' body was found. He was now less than twenty-four hours away from witnessing the actual event as it occurred, the thought of which sending a chill through the man. Needing to head back to his lodging for some rest, his prolonged nap might interfere with that process but he had the utmost confidence in a magical new bed ready and waiting to wrap its arms of comfort and security around him and sing him a lullaby of silence and solitude. Arriving at his new digs, the manager on duty never even peaked out to see who was coming in, probably not as necessary to be quite as diligent at his post as on the busy Commercial Street, or he was just too lazy to look out from the office.

Back in his room, Ethan lit only one candle then disrobed for bed. He peered out the window onto Bakers Row. There were only a few people walking by then, most likely on their way to an early work shift, others staggering home inebriated. Then there were those who had no money for lodging, which was all too common a theme during these times. Far too many homeless souls had no choice but to locate a quiet doorway or a dirty gutter to sleep in, no way to live. The night had its many secrets and just as many tragedies. In the summer or early autumn living in the streets really had no elemental dangers but as days passed and winter approached, the conditions quickly became a far more prolific serial killer than Jack the Ripper, claiming more lives than any murderer in history. Blowing out the candle, Ethan crawled into bed. Though he'd meant to write in his journal, fatigue won in the end.

That night he dreamed of music. *He was a conductor of a symphony orchestra, playing Tchaikovsky's "Waltz of the Flowers". Some of the faces were familiar to him as they followed his direction with clockwork precision. There was Anson on the Tuba, Drakes and Clemens on tympani, Colin on the harp and Sparks on piano. As for the young, 21st Century Maggie, she held the violin as 19th Century Maggie played the flute. Other faces obscured by shadows, their music was sublime, yet he knew and felt the eyes of all the orchestral members directly on him, watching every motion of his hands.* When he awoke at one point in the night, Ethan saw his hands outstretched across the quilt, still conducting as he was coming out of this dream. He laughed, turning onto his side then fell right back into an even deeper slumber, surrendering his subconscious mind to sleep.

Waking to a far less pressing day of activity, Ethan knew it from the start; there could be nothing hectic about it. This was the day to relax and focus: breathe. Today was more of an exercise in psychological preparedness for tonight, or so he thought. He knew it was necessary to walk Bucks Row at least one time in the daylight. He'd truly be meticulous in his search for loose stones or any hazards posed by moving in the dark of night, as footing could cost him an injury or worse, detection. Tonight, he thought, with any luck the risks would be minimal and the observation would go without a hitch. First he was going to check on something that may be a time saver. Once dressed, he went downstairs to the public area on the first floor. There were three people either having a late breakfast or early lunch, the time being 10:33 a.m. There was a pot of coffee one of the men was pouring into a cup.

"Good morning." Ethan approached the stove. "Is the coffee complimentary?"

All three tenants snickered beneath their breath at Ethan's peculiar question.

"The manager's got grounds and tea for sale." The man pouring his own looked at Ethan, assuming his funds were meager. "Here, have some of mine, old chap."

"How very kind, sir. Thank you." Ethan lifted a cup and saucer from the table. The brew had a bit of a bite to it, but then again, the only bad coffee is no coffee so he was happy to have it, thanking the gentleman again as he left.

Feeling brave, he decided to take a stroll over to Whitechapel Road. Perking up his appetite, the coffee got him moving. Ethan had seen a few eateries in his travels, some serving food much closer to where he now resided. Ten Bells Pub would have to wait for dinner. He'd likely see Maggie for a bit while he dined before his Scope work began in earnest. For the time being he'd be content to purchase something to take with him on his trip over to Bucks Row.

There is a trick to finding good food in a new town. Follow the line. Just beyond Turner Street on Whitechapel Road was a place that only had a window. The locals staying at his lodging told Ethan they cook the best bangers and mash in the entire area and the line for orders was always a dozen people deep. It was run by a family; mother and daughter cooked and the father ran the concession window. It took him almost ten minutes to reach the window, almost ten whole seconds to eat it. Another example of all the additives of the future tainting the full flavors of food, he savored the delicacy because he had more than his share of bangers and mash in and around Oxford, yet this was perhaps the most delicious thing he'd ever tasted. Enjoying his meal ever so much, Ethan indulged himself, doing something Colin Bishop would do. He got back in line for a second helping. Asking the proprietor to double wrap it, he bought a bottled lemonade for the journey.

One road down was Corner Street which took him directly back to Bucks Row. Ethan located a secluded spot across from the boarding school and sat on the ground with his back up against the wall of row houses. Nibbling on a second order of food, he washed down the bits with his beverage. All the while Ethan was thinking. Every last detail of the murder engrained in his memory, he visualized the timeline like a calendar leading up to and after the death of Mary Ann "Polly" Nichols. He'd seen the months passing before his mind's eye, coming to this day, 30 August 1888, the day before the night of her death.

Suddenly those bangers and mash were not sitting so well. Ethan dreaded the actual event so much, the thought of it was literally turning his stomach. Before the jump he had been totally detached from the reality of these brutal slayings. Having interacted with Drakes and Clemens and Maggie and other assorted *living* persons from this time, it gave him pause, reconsidering the concept. What he was about to witness tonight was very real. Now, more than ever he needed to apply his logical, disciplined training, the scientific mindset to get through what would be a horrible scenario happening in real time in front of him. He had to remind himself to detach from the reality and objectively watch it unfold. He could not afford to care.

As he sat there, a small boy who was passing by stopped and stared at his food. The lad was all of seven or eight. Big brown eyes and brown hair with bangs draped across his cheeks, pants too short and shoes too large, he licked his lips as he stared, obviously an orphan living on wits alone. Ethan thought of Oliver Twist and could not resist offering the young boy what remained of his meal, a gesture of kindness. Snatching it from Ethan's hands lest the man change his mind, the poor boy ran off yelling "Thank you, sir!" as Ethan thought, *"The guttersnipe I've just fed may have been Tony Blair's great grandfather!"* He smiled sadly, seeing such a desperate act of self-preservation or the epitome of self-service. Either way, it broke his heart to see a child suffering on the streets, the plight of too many children in this dark era. He seemed to Ethan to be a survivor. There but for the grace of God. Who to bless them and keep them safe?

Standing, sipping the last of his lemonade, he intended to walk the area in front of him one more time. Scrutinizing this place was imperative. He had to know each cobblestone in every alleyway, especially along the main drag of Bucks Row where history recorded the location of the body's discovery. There could be no obstacles, no debris visible that may endanger his mission in the early hours of tomorrow. He should be able to slip in and out of the zone with ease. His knowledge of constables on duty and their standard shift routes provided Ethan with an accurate timetable in which to maneuver into place without risk of detection. He'd recalled a memorable moment from his past, serving to remind him of the solitary nature of his work.

Ethan began reminiscing about times when he'd taken Colin to this spot, having him play the role of Jack the Ripper. Colin enjoyed it when Ethan invited him along. He would look for lovely female tourists in the area and tell them he was portraying Jack the Ripper and needed a "victim" for his research while Ethan scoped out the different vantage points from which to observe. He appeared so sweet, so innocent, they would always agree to play along. As the "Bishop" on the chessboard, moving his angular strategy to coerce the pretty players, he was a *caractère naturel* for the part, even the devilish grin Ethan supposed the truly fiendish killer donned during his brutal attacks. At The Valley Colin reprised the role and used the same approach on the young female Flicker trial staff. Sometimes he wished Colin had come back with him, as a second pair of eyes and his lighthearted attitude would go a long way toward easing the gravity of the task, the weight of its inherent responsibilities, but there was no way Colin would ever cope with these trousers or the living conditions. Ethan thought, *"No way Colin would come here!"* Scratch that thought. Scratch that leg. Scratch. Scratch. Scratch. He knew tonight would not be an opportune time to be itchy anywhere. His next stop would have to be on Thomas Street to purchase some undergarment stockings. As the time was fast approaching, Ethan could sense the darkness of it now, no laughing matter.

XIII.
A CHANGE OF PLANS

Journal entry ~ 30 August 1888

The proverbial countdown has begun. In a little over twelve hours I will become immersed in the darkness, witnessing the brutal murder of a woman I've never met, yet know all too intimately. This is my first journal entry from my second flat in this century. Maggie the barmaid is to thank for all of my creature comforts. Her latest witchery, convincing me to buy leg stockings, yet I must confess, no more itching!

I've cleaned and dried my physician's outfit I came through with, as well as my nice high end shoes. I need to be as comfortable as possible in this covert operation. Silent as the grave in my approach and observation. This would be a four day jump if all my research was about one death and one killer, but there are five women that all seemingly fell under the knife of one man, or maybe a woman? Time will tell. If Jack the Ripper is actually the one person committing these five particular murders then I must complete my project fully, down to the last of his victims, returning with definitive proof of who was history's most notorious serial killer and that, indeed, these deeds were done by one. Once I identify the culprit, I will attempt to track this individual, compounding the evidence of my discovery.

All my research, the years spent looking at forensic photos, examining cadavers in the university's medical department, reviewing all the police and medical reports from each of the murders and the numerous Flicker trial reenactments have all led up to this moment in time. My reason for being a Scope in 19th Century London, my life's work, begins with the end of a woman's life. All I have to do is watch history repeat itself and be the proverbial fly on the wall, out of sight, invisible and obscure. I own this night, wings or not.

I'm off to the Ten Bells in about an hour to meet with Maggie, have a couple of cups of coffee and eat something that isn't an animal, a rancorous thought prior to tonight's pending visuals. Only for tonight I hope, because the bangers and mash I got from a window was too delectable to dismiss from the eight additional weeks I will be here. I may be the first Scope too fat to fit through the Flicker doorway upon my attempted return! Colin, do you remember our talk in my cold, gray little room? This is what I meant. I know my research. I know you'll feel as confidant in yours.

***

Ethan waited a little longer than expected before heading off to the pub. Stalling for time, he wanted to avoid the rain. It started pouring outside and although he was wearing a recent acquisition, nothing to write home to mother about, he didn't need to be soaked for dinner or, God forbid, end up with a cold, sneezing in the shadows of Bucks Row in the wee hours of the morning. Though it would be considered cool for a summer evening almost any place else, for England, in August, it actually felt warm and breezy, quite beautiful, if only the rain would pass. The ensemble of vest, tie and a coat kept him comfortable, offering some shelter from the storm. Oh! How he longed for his elegant umbrella, mahogany in his hand, left propped in the corner of his flat. *"A bit inconvenient to retrieve at the moment!"* Ethan smiled at the thought, a subtle reminder of what an incredible journey he had made through time.

Out the door of his room just past 5:30 p.m., steady rain had tapered to a drizzle. With still a ten minute walk ahead coupled with the late start, a change of plans was in order. Ethan thought it best to skip his previously intended trip to the bank, likely closed by this time, no ATM at his disposal to replenish his funds. Maggie had put a serious dent in his wallet the night before...beer, beer and more beer...he laughed at the thought of it, how well the woman could retain fluids! But he still had enough on hand to buy his dinner, as well as hers, along with her beverage of choice, should she join him after her shift for another delightful chat.

Mist rising after the rain, lingering drizzle quickly dissipated. Ethan decided to take a nonchalant journey, the *tourist* route from his time, maneuvering through the streets of Whitechapel undetected, one of the locals on a bustling Thursday afternoon. He had wanted to take his time, absorbing more of the ambiance, the characters of the area, he wanted to breathe the air, albeit stinky. Visually, it was a cornucopia of delights, like the many vintage photographs he'd studied coming to life before his mesmerized eyes. A change of plans with time to spare, this was a selfish endeavor, not particularly pertinent to the tighter rungs of his project other than descriptions he could offer upon his return, notes for his journal. However, as a Scope, this was inherent to the project's design, integral to his overall perceptions of the mission.

Along the way he passed an outdoor flower stand. Although he never had any interest in Maggie from a romantic perspective, nor could he, Ethan was so grateful for her kindness, friendship and generous assistance in making his visit that much more pleasant, helping him adapt, providing him with a level of comfort somewhat closer to his life in another century. To her, what an upper class doctor from London expected and deserved. Aside from the obvious, no electricity and indoor plumbing, he was relatively cozy in his new room. An expression of appreciation in the form any woman most desires and admires, Ethan bought a bouquet of freesia, gardenias and daffodils, a glorious mix for Maggie, made at his request.

He had been walking a while when he noticed something remarkable. With the addition of the stockings he had not felt the least bit of an urge to scratch anyplace on his body. He felt like a local. Surprisingly, it felt good. Checking his timepiece, nearly six o'clock as he approached Ten Bells Pub, as expected, he found the place busier than his previous visits, a crescendo building, rising to a fever pitch attained on the weekends. That is when the fights break out, according to Maggie. Ruffling through the crowd, hoping to find his friend or an open booth in the back, his usual table was occupied and he could not find Maggie. Assuming she was in the kitchen, most likely in the weeds, he searched for a seat.

As Ethan passed through the pub, flowers in hand, all the women smiled at him. Some looked at them longingly, others teasing him, curious to know the true object of his affections. "Are those for me?" He smiled uneasily as he stood out like lilacs in a snowstorm. Making his way to the bar he found a free stool. The bartender was a stocky man with a black moustache, gruff and quick to question a customer.

"What'll it be, mate? Here for some beer and skittles?"

"Is Maggie here, per chance?" Ethan queried.

"Who?" The bartender was unable to hear the name over the rabble-rousers.

"Maggie."

"Don't know any Maggie, mate. Are you orderin' or not?"

"Yes, um, coffee please." Ethan was taken back by his abrasive manner.

The barkeep appeared insulted that the order did not include alcohol, predicting by his expression that Ethan wasn't going to be a big tipper. A Thursday night bust. Never considering the tip, or lack thereof, might be contingent upon his attitude, he instantly prejudged Ethan the most difficult patron in the place, delivering one long, hard stare before delivering the coffee. With its arrival he wrapped his hands around the mug, scanning the pub, trying to find a friendly face among the motley mob.

"Her name's Maggie. She *works* here." Ethan figured the chap must be new and didn't know all the staff by name yet.

"Don't know 'er. Don't care to." With that, he turned and walked away toward a more promising patron. Bloody bloke.

Spotting Maggie's friend, the one who'd served them beer, Ethan reached out to touch her arm as she passed, getting her attention.

"Excuse me, Rose, was it?"

"Love, ya can call me whatever ya want if them flowers be for me!"

"Actually, I was looking for Maggie. Is she here?"

"Maggie?" The woman looked confused then appeared to regain her senses.

"Oh, *Maggie*! Yes! No, sorry love. Sad to say she got fired last night."

"I beg your pardon? Fired! Why in bloody hell was she fired?" Disbelief in his voice, Ethan awaited the answer, searching the barmaid's eyes for the truth of it.

"Uh, stealing, I heard." The bartender yelled for Rose, flipping his hands from the wrist, gesturing for her to move along. "Sorry, love. Customers waitin'."

As she rushed through with her tray to pick up drinks and attend to her tables, Ethan sat there stunned, in mild shock. What the hell happened? Why didn't Maggie come to him for help? He would have at least done something more to reciprocate her kindheartedness other than innocently contributing to her drunken delinquency. Suddenly dispirited, his one true friend made in the new "olde" world was gone but not forgotten. Ethan's heart sank, not knowing how to find her or if he would ever see her again. It was beyond disappointment. He was saddened because she was the one person that could lift his spirits and even make him laugh a bit before a morbid undertaking the wee hours would bring. Staring at his mug, he was not in the mood.

"I've changed my mind. Bring me a pint instead." Ethan spoke emphatically.

"Well, that's the spirit!" The bartender seemed more amenable.

Ethan sat there nearly ninety minutes nursing the beer along then drank his cold coffee, staring off into a void as if he'd lost his security blanket. "Keep the change." As he paid the bill, leaving a generous tip, it immediately changed the barkeeper's disposition. Spotting Maggie's friend clearing off a table, he approached her again.

"Rose? Sorry to trouble you. Might you know where Maggie lives?"

"She was over on Thrawl Street, got evicted last night. Sorry love. I wish I could be more help." Rose seemed genuinely sympathetic to her plight and his, as well.

Ethan handed her a decent tip along with the bundle of flowers then left the pub. Bewildered, his mind still buzzing, he wandered the streets in the vicinity, heading in the general direction of his lodging, though he felt no urgency to return there. It meant sitting alone in his room trying to make sense of something nonsensical. He simply couldn't understand. Was she too proud to ask for help, or just too stubborn? Reluctantly making his way over to Thrawl Street, he knew this was where so many desolate souls congregated, including Miss Mary Ann Nichols. God knows he was not looking for her and he would see her soon enough at the end of her life. Instead, he was searching for his friend Maggie, anxious to help, to return the kindness she'd so graciously extended since their initial meeting.

"Want the business?" Quietly approaching him from behind, a woman proposed with a colloquial expression prostitutes used to solicit clients. Ethan did not respond or even dare to glance back, fearing it might be "Polly" Nichols. Even in his current somber mood, he kept the non-interference protocol paramount in mind at all times. Several other ladies of the evening made the same proposition, an all too common inquiry. Rapidly realizing this was a wrong turn to take, he did not want to go down that road, literally or figuratively, especially tonight. It was time to focus on the job at hand and return to his room and his mission, preparing for what was to come on Bucks Row. Arriving there just past 9:30 p.m., he felt all alone in the world.

Lighting only one candle, placing it on the dresser beside the pitcher and bowl, Ethan allowed his eyes to adjust to the dark. He sat down at the foot of his bed, lost in his thoughts for far too long, perhaps for an eternity. Draping his coat then vest on the corner spiral post, he tried to shake off a defeated spirit that truly had no rational merit. People lose jobs all the time, lose their homes daily. If Maggie stole from the pub it was to keep a roof over her head, nothing more. This was her natural history, her destiny unfolding, nothing he could do nor should do about it. He knew that kind of thing was a common occurrence. This rumination was uncharacteristic. Ethan knew he needed to let it go, at the very least, lay it aside for the time being.

This fascination had gone woefully askew. Engaging with Maggie as he'd done then losing track of her created unsettling sensations in the man, detecting emotions he did not expect to feel. Maggie meant much more to him than being an indigenous specimen of the era, more than a subject of study. Standing, he began pacing around the woolen rug, doing the mental work necessary to reset his priorities for the night. As his pace then his breathing gradually slowed, he reestablished his focus on a set of predetermined goals. Exercising a favorite metaphor, Ethan adopted the mindset of an Olympic skier, a Scope adapting to a slippery slope. Visualizing Bucks Row, navigating the mental maze of paths and exit routes consuming his mind, he paced six steps, turned, then paced six more. Over and over like the cadence to the rhythm of his heart, eyes closed, Ethan refused to open them again until he achieved his *in the zone* status in the veritable time zone in which he now found himself, attaining a confident invisible cloak of knowledge. Once a calmness and certain purpose was again instilled at the core of his being he could then begin preparing for what he'd come here to do…watch. Ethan opened his eyes.

Having laid out all his clothing for the night, the doctor's attire he'd traveled in through the Flicker, he disrobed, shedding his common clothing in lieu of finer fare. Standing naked at the water basin, washing himself in an almost ritualistic manner, Ethan wanted to feel as pure in mind and body as possible prior to what he would have to witness, a fateful hour coming closer with each passing moment. From time to time, he'd glance out the window, gauging the weather conditions, becoming noticeably cooler as the night progressed. Periodically checking his timepiece like an expectant father would, he was awaiting a death instead of a birth.

Back on course, his mindset exactly where it needed to be for the task at hand, at last check it was almost midnight. Intending to wait until the last minute before leaving his room, allowing for the dissipation of street traffic, thinning the chances of any testimonial account of him being seen roaming alleys in the night, he planned his exit for 2:45 a.m. Having factored every possible scenario into this equation, it allowed him a six-to-seven minute window of opportunity to move into the position he'd chosen to observe from well ahead of the arrival of the players…hopefully.

Suddenly Ethan was overcome with a craving for caffeine, his most basic need. Redressing in his commoner clothing, he went downstairs to the night manager to buy coffee grounds for the kitchen kettle. Being so late, unencumbered with duties, the young man volunteered to make the coffee for his tenant. Waiting for it to brew, Ethan propped himself in the doorway, quietly surveying Baker's Row, sensing the chill in the air. Looking up into the clear sky, but for a few soft clouds whisking by, the temperature felt far cooler now, expected to drop further as history recorded on this morbid date destined for the history books, a story from the ages, for the ages. As Ethan patiently waited to watch this event unfold, he considered the facts of the matter, the case that forever remained an unsolved mystery until now. Though some would die sooner than others, the cold truth of it was simple enough to comprehend. Everyone Ethan encountered in the year 1888 already qualified as the "living dead". They were ghosts but tonight was the night a ghost in Whitechapel would bleed.

"Sir?" The lad had not come emptyhanded, the aroma preceding his alert.

Standing behind him holding a hot cup of coffee, he looked at the mug then the man with a smile of gratitude. Well paid for his time and effort, he returned to his nook while his tenant turned to once more stare out the door. The presence of people on the street waning, a few stragglers passed by. Making short order of his first cup, he went to the kitchen, refilling it before turning to go up the stairs. It was then that he noticed something he hadn't seen earlier. In the narrow hallway to the back door leading to the outhouse, just to the left of the stairwell was an alcove, a cubbyhole, really, yet it contained nothing less than the wonders of the world. A small lending library, no more than a dozen books awaiting his detection, John Milton's "Paradise Lost" was included, as was William Blake's "Songs of Innocence and Experience" and one well-worn volume of Alexander Pope's "The Rape of the Lock". The Bible, along with several other books, obscure titles lost to time, he'd discovered a treasure trove of delights. Two books had been placed face down, both considerably frayed. Ethan flipped the first, revealing a copy of Lewis Carroll's "Alice's Adventures in Wonderland" which he instantly tossed back as if plagued by a Universal curse.

"Fuck off!" Ethan said with a smirk, speaking to it as an animated thing.

He turned the second book over and burst into laughter. Daniel Dafoe's classic "Robinson Crusoe" written in 1719. There wasn't a literary work that could parallel Ethan's plight in this new land more than the story of the shipwrecked Englishman and his daunting task of strategy and survival, minus the cannibals. Having read the tale countless times, he'd found it fascinating that it was first published as a fictional biography, as if "Robinson Crusoe" wrote it himself, and second, the actual author, Dafoe, was once a British spy. More astounding was the fact that he had not noticed the bookshelves during trips to the loo. More disturbing, these literary masterpieces were likely used as bathroom reading material. Counting twelve steps to the second floor, Ethan returned to his room, book in hand. A plan made to lose himself in the novel until it was time to go, he delved deeply into a poignant and beloved passage, knowing precisely where in the text to locate it. *"All evils are to be considered with the good that is in them, and with what worse attends them."*

There were certain entitlements to oneself. Indulging in what makes one happy should be a priority but is oftentimes sacrificed. Ethan always loved books. Though in print, he imagined the writer putting paper to pen. As a teacher, he assigned many of these giants of literature to his students. All he did was pass the word, so to speak. It was these authors who had made their imprint and had the honor of being conduits of hopes and dreams, depicting a creative core of life for generations that followed. Ethan browsed the pages, selecting some of his favorite passages to revisit, thinking that he'd like to be remembered one day for this journey, pen to paper, recorded for posterity. Upon his return he would have eventual permission from The Consortium to declassify this mission. He'd write about his experiences in a memoir, something readers would come to know and love in time. Dutifully checking his pocket watch, it was 2:25 a.m. Time to dress the part.

Ethan was beginning to develop a finer appreciation for his fancy vintage duds. Peering in the only looking glass in the room, ALICE came to mind. He took a step back then another, improving the vantage point to accommodate his height. Gazing at the reflection of his image in the mirror mounted just above the basin, from what he could see, he appeared a fine figure of a man, distinguished, a worldly sort. Ethan stood taller, finding this authentic garb more appealing by the moment. Projecting himself back into the future on a lark, he smiled coyly imagining the reaction of his students were he to walk into his seminar in such apparel. Would he be dubbed the new trendsetter on campus or the laughing stock? An icon, a classy counter-cultural influence sporting alternatives to denim jeans and designer shirts students typically wore or would he be someone mocked then directed toward the drama department? Professor Ethan LaPierre: Fashion Guru! Chuckling, relaxing his shoulders enough to realize how tense he'd become straining to maintain a statuesque posture, he bent over, extending his long arms to the floor, lacing his self-restored physician's shoes as the finishing touch to his outfit, one fit for a gentleman and a scholar.

Composing himself, Ethan drew a deep breath where he stood, filling his lungs to capacity while assuming his former upright position. During this pass before the glass, he caught a glimpse of his own expression. Startled, his features exposed an underlying emotion, a hint of a grimace on his lips, dread in his eyes. Naturally, he was nervous. A gentle man would soon witness a historically hideous attack, death resulting. Gazing into his own soul, Ethan lingered with the image, acutely aware he was still holding his breath. Deliberately releasing stored oxygen with his angst, expelling it from his body with an intense rush, drawing another breath in to replace it, by necessity, in an instant it occurred to him, he had adjusted to the putrid stench of the air. He was almost ready to go.

A sudden change of pace, he bustled around the room, making certain all of his documentation was in order, identification required should he be stopped by a local member of the constabulary. There could no pitfalls along the path, making his way into the shadows. Finally, pulling his watch from its pocket, it read 2:39 a.m. Ethan was punctual by nature and this would be the most important appointment he'd ever keep. Leaving with ample time provided him breathing room before arriving at his destination to witness an event which, like a vacuum chamber, would remove every last atom of air from a timeless bubble about to form around Bucks Row.

The *antique* skeleton key in hand, he slipped it into the two-sided lock. Turning the handle, opening the door before grabbing his bag, any semblance of calm he'd achieved prior to his scheduled departure dissipated instantly. Stunned, stilled by a sight, the woman lingering on the other side of the door had her hand raised, balled up in a fist, preparing to knock, perhaps working up the courage to do so. Caught completely off guard, Ethan stepped back. It was poor, pitiful Maggie. Disheveled, a bit unsteady on her feet, before Ethan could speak she launched forward into the room, wrapping her arms securely around his neck, clinging to him for dear life. He caught her by reflex, requiring both of his arms and all his strength to hold her upright. Timing is everything and this qualified as bad timing.

Under the current circumstances, he accounted for her behavior as a wanton act of desperation, a cry for help, perhaps pure emotional exhaustion, considering she'd lost her job and had no place to go. Having endured both a firing and eviction within the past eighteen hours, Maggie was overwrought, vulnerable; a sad state of affairs.

She kissed him, a sloppy and awkward attempt, at best. No question of her being inebriated, the smell of hard liquor heavy on her breath and bitter on her lips, Ethan pulled back, immediately launched into a memory of a similar frat party experience. Quickly peeling the woman off of him, Ethan grasped her firmly by the shoulders, holding her back while holding her up to keep her from falling down drunk.

"Maggie! I was worried for you. I heard what happened at Ten Bells. I'm sorry." Ignoring her advances, Ethan tried to speak rationally to the woman.

"Bloody Bells! Oh love, I *hated* it there. Yer the only good come of it."

"How much have you had to drink?" Ethan asked rhetorically. The answer was obvious…clearly, more than she could handle and it certainly wasn't beer.

"Jus' a nip, doc." She stood at attention, saluting Ethan as one would a military man. That action threw Maggie off balance and she crumpled in place, folding like an accordion, collapsing into his arms again.

Ethan provided support, guiding her further into the room, closing the door with his foot to preserve Maggie's privacy, as well as his own. No need to cause a scene, particularly at such a late hour as well as a critical moment in history, it couldn't be tampered with, regardless of circumstances. Her untimely arrival, her presence was far more than an inconvenience for him, it was potentially disastrous for his project. She'd have to go so he could do the same. Removing his hands from her shoulders, Maggie freed herself then cavorted around the center of the boarding room she'd arranged for him, taking the liberty of making herself at home. Sauntering about as if pretending to be one of the royals at a Grand Ball, she was the belle, twirling her shabby skirt, creating the breeze that lifted it in an overtly flirtatious manner. Ethan noticed Maggie was still wearing the same dress she had worn the other morning while assisting him with his lodging. The only addition to her attire appeared to be a new bonnet. Pointing it out with some pride, she brought it to his attention as an enticement, the article of clothing he would surely want to remove first. Seductively running her fingers along the edge, playfully entangling them in soft satin ribbons, she giggled then dropped one arm, lifting her skirt provocatively higher, throwing her head back and off kilter again. Steadying her gait with the help of the bedpost, she began to lift the hat off her head as an intimate act, an inviting gesture, intending to stay for a time, perhaps for the night. Ethan abruptly stopped her momentum.

"No! Maggie, you must go. Now." Ethan was kind but firm. All of her dancing and prancing came to a halt, her forlorn eyes staring into his own, penetrating him, pleading with him and passing through him on the way to nowhere.

"Ya don't like it, doc? Doctor, don't ya like me? I thought we was friends here." Her effusive demeanor told Ethan this impasse wouldn't be easily resolved.

"Yes! No! I mean, can we please do this tomorrow?" He was getting flustered.

"We can do it?" She expressed with induced excitement. "Well, let's do it now! Won't take *that* long!" Maggie suggested facetiously, with a wink.

"No Maggie, I have to leave now, don't you see?" He tried reasoning with her.

Stepping further away from him, her posture altered in an instant, sizing him up from top hat to the bottom of his shoes. Crossing her arms over her chest, she used her forearms to hoist her bosom higher, a force of habit, no doubt.

"Well, I *do* see! Don't ya look all proper like, all dressed up with somewhere to go and some bloody hour, eh? My! Oh my *Arthur*, ain't you the poshy gentleman?" A smack of sarcasm spoke before the next words could pass her distilled lips. "And I s'pose I ain't the properest kind a *lady* for you, *sir*."

"It's not that. Not at all. Look, you need to leave now. I have someplace else to be and quite soon." More frantic by the moment, Ethan could not afford to be kind but his stern disposition wasn't working either.

"Why? Ya got a *meetin'* at this time o' the mornin'? Someone ya need to go n' *examine,* doc?"

"Maggie! Please!" He begged her to leave, as much with his eyes as his words. "I've something urgent to attend to and I mustn't be late. I'll give you whatever you need for lodging tonight. I'll meet with you tomorrow." Ethan reached for his wallet to retrieve an offering which she promptly refused, rejecting him along with it.

"Don't want your monies, love. That's not who…not why I'm here."

"Please do me this favor, just go. Please." Beads of sweat lined his brow.

"Fine. Fine. I'll be off, then." She said in a whimsical tone, tipping her head to him while curtsying. She stumbled toward the door while Ethan faced away, feeling terribly bad, about to abandon her in a time of need. It was painful to watch. As he turned to make his apologies, he saw her quickly lock the door and remove the key. She spun around, leaning back against it, eyes awash with the glaze of intoxication. Unsteady on her feet, as if the door was holding her up, she grinned as she dropped the key down her blouse, quickly buried in the cleavage of her ample breasts.

"No! No! No! No! No!" He blurted out the word in rapid-fire succession.

"Why go out, love? I've gots the goods ya want right here. I'll stay the night."

"Maggie! What do you think you are doing? Give me that key!" Extending his hand to receive it, she ignored his request, projecting her body off the door.

"C'me on and take it, doc." Another playful reply, she sashayed across the floor to the center of the room, passing him on her way to the bed. Cat and mouse.

"I'm not joking, Maggie. I demand you give me the key!" Insisting she comply with his directive in the most commanding voice a passive man could muster, Ethan was at a loss and clearly at a disadvantage. For someone not in the least bit assertive by nature, the situation made his skin crawl from within, as if the vermin of London had infiltrated him by osmosis. Taking one long stride, shoulders back, spine rigid, Ethan placed himself squarely in front of Maggie, reiterating his clear demand with emphasis. "Maggie! Give me the key!"

"Tells me what ya really want, love." She taunted.

"The fucking key."

Maggie grabbed Ethan by the crotch, giving a spirited squeeze as she giggled.

"Let's trade me key for yours." Ethan leapt backward, nearly losing his balance, shocked that he'd been groped. Rendered breathless, Maggie's next words flushed his face of blood and sent chills down his spine.

"So, d' ya want the business?" He had heard these familiar words before on the streets of London. The reference was specific, no mistaking the intention.

"What? What did you say?" Squinting his eyes as if hoping it would help with his comprehension, Ethan couldn't believe what he'd just heard.

"Come now, love, ya know what I mean." Maggie patted both sides of the bed as she sat, yet another invitation issued.

Ethan's eyes gave away his awareness of what she was *giving* away for a *price*.

"I been playin' a role too, *all this time just...like...you...Arthur.*" She spoke his pseudonym with a deliberately acidic accentuation.

"Maggie, I really don't have time now..." Ethan got that much out of his mouth before she interrupted him.

"That's *not* my name!" She shouted, shocking him into silence. "And *Arthur* is not yer real name...ya didn't know that first...when I yelled *Arthur* 'cross the street that time, ya know." Slurring her words, they were loosely strung together.

"There were people everywhere...and the traffic passing by, I couldn't hear..." Ethan tried to excuse the lapse he remembered before she cut him off again.

"Don't bother bloody lyin' to me, love. I tells ya I know enough about you mens to know when yer lyin'."

Before continuing on with a drunken rant she paused, attempting to fix her hair and dress with a press of her hand here and there.

Ethan was at a loss for words, locked in the surreal lost world of his room. This stranger stood from the bed, extending her hand, wanted to try again with a formal greeting.

"Start over, shall we? M' name ain't Maggie...m' friends calls me Polly."

The floor beneath Ethan's feet suddenly destabilized, shifting in place. Shaking, he began questioning his own existence and hers in an instant of pure panic. Hoping her response to his next query would result in removing the true fear tightening his throat, it was blocking the passage of words needed to ask what he must.

"Polly? Polly...Nichols?" He could barely utter the name, choking it out with a nearly inaudible whisper, but she heard him.

"Yes! Ow'd ya know that?" She asked with a smile, softening haggard features, taking it as a form of flattery, almost relieved to finally drop the façade.

Ethan stepped closer, hoping it was his ears deceiving him and not the cosmos.

"Mary Ann Nichols. Born 26 August 1845 to Edward and Caroline Walker in London, England?" Ethan could no longer chance a coincidence, just as Polly could no longer smile. As though every word he spoke kicked her further away, knocking her off balance, she staggered back, trying to get away from him.

"Oh, bloody hell! Ow'd ya know that? Who, *what* are ya?" Alarm in her voice, she leered at the man who knew too much about her.

The two stared at one another in silence. Ethan had not noticed the resemblance, having only seen her corpse in vintage photographs, the details of her face obscured. This was nothing he'd trained for, nothing he could've anticipated or even remotely prepared for, as a scenario unfolding before his disbelieving eyes never crossed his mind, not as a Scope, scientist, historian or doctor of letters. Dumbfounded, he was a helpless victim of circumstance, as was she, the intended victim still keeping her distance. Time was suspended. Submersed in the fog of conscious thought relating to the current and pending event, he had to quickly reconcile this painful revelation, coming to terms with the truth that the woman about to become the first victim of the notorious "Jack the Ripper" had locked herself inside his room. A woman he'd befriended and felt sorry for because of her losses in life would shortly lose her life as a matter of destiny, becoming a figure in history.

There had been a reason for the hours of non-interference discussions with The Consortium brass and this was precisely it. Unbeknownst to him at the time, Ethan inadvertently invested himself emotionally into someone intricately involved with the historical timeline of events. *Maggie* had no significance. Polly did. According to his perception of things, *Maggie* was irrelevant to these proceedings, a side show; the common barmaid with an equally common side job, to make ends meet. It never occurred to him that Maggie might play such a pivotal role in history. She'd become part of his journey and now he would have to let her go, literally, to her death.

The timeline derailed, getting it back on track was the priority. He had no choice but to detach, no matter how difficult. Likewise for Ethan, a cruel twist of fate but at least it would not cost him *his* life. He had to convince Polly to leave, condemning a friend to death, sending the defenseless, unsuspecting soul out the door alone, into the darkest of nights. This was not a choice. It was history. No time to think, barely time enough to act, Ethan didn't have time to tell another lie. Lifting the watch from his pocket his heart nearly stopped at 2:51 a.m. as the shot of pure adrenaline surged through his veins, a bolt of lightning; the ultimate wake-up call.

"Mary…Polly." Stepping closer, he tried to reason with her as she stepped back. "You do not understand. You really need to give me that key and leave now."

"No! Bloody come clean…who are ya, a bobby? How d' ya know who I am!" The more upset she became, a reaction amplified by abundant alcohol in her system, the farther away the suspicious woman stepped from his tenuous approach.

"No! No! Hell no! I'll explain it all tomorrow." Stepping forward again, Ethan knew there would be no tomorrow for her.

"Who are ya then?" She demanded again, anger raging in her sparse words.

"There's no time! Give me the key!" Ethan demanded, moving closer.

They maneuvered about the room, Polly going backward as Ethan leaned in. He wasn't one to grab at her the way she had done with him, no attempt made to search her bosom. He wouldn't push her around but he needed to push the issue. Her head was spinning in circles, as was the room, a dizziness undoubtedly due to her severe state of inebriation. Disoriented, stumbling over the lip of the rug, tripping, twisting, and turning, unable to catch herself, Ethan reached out to save her but Polly went down too hard and fast, striking her head just below the left ear against the corner of the solid oak bedpost. It knocked her unconscious. Having fallen with such force the impact spun her around to the right, that side of her face slamming to the floor with one dull thud. Mary Ann Nichols, Polly appeared to be dead to the world.

XIV.
BEGGIN' YOUR PARDON, MA'AM

"Is she dead?" He could hear the words rattling around in his skull, words he'd heard carelessly uttered by one youthful, inexperienced member of the FTC team. Ethan froze, mere moments seemed like a millennium. Coming to his senses again, he immediately knelt beside her, checking for her pulse. Polly was alive. However, the combination of excessive drinking and the impact from the fall knocked her out cold. Mary Ann Nichols was right. He wasn't a doctor in the way she'd thought and he did not know the full extent of her injuries but common sense dictated, she most certainly had a concussion. He would have to try to wake her up. She'd merely have to walk with a hell of a headache, that is, if she could walk at all. Propping her back up against the footboard of the bed, Ethan repeatedly called her by name, by ALL of her names! Shaking her by the shoulders he even splashed a little bit of water on her face. She remained entirely unresponsive, no signs of regaining consciousness. Ethan's mind and body moved at light speed. Time was running out.

How could he have allowed this to happen? He was not a religious man per se, but he wondered if God was punishing him for tinkering with the laws of physics, with time itself. Ethan was considering the implications of Mary Ann Nichols being absent, not present for her own historical death. There was no way she would make it on her own to the spot where she was supposed to be murdered. Looking around for resolution, it came to him. He could still salvage the timeline and his research, but he had to get Polly to Bucks Row. Already dressed in his physician's attire with all of his paperwork in the vest pocket, Ethan lifted Polly from the floor and placed her on the bed, laying the medical bag atop her midsection to take along as cover.

After a moment's pause to reflect on this desperate situation, apologizing aloud to an unconscious woman, Ethan reached down into her blouse in search of the key, obtaining it quickly then ending the awkward contact.

"I'm sorry. Sorry. Beggin' your pardon, ma'am." He was a nervous wreck.

Unlocking the door, Ethan lifted Polly and the bag into his arms. Deadweight, he knew she would not be easy to move but it was his only option. As carefully and quietly as possible Ethan maneuvered her body downstairs to the first floor. Nobody visible during the early morning hours, slipping out the back door past the library, Ethan carried her through the rear alley where the outhouse was located. It became apparent that her motionless frame was too heavy for him to manage. This journey would require several stops to reposition her along the way. Adding other variables into this complex equation, he'd calculated her additional weight and the timing to avoid any encounter with police or anybody else out this late. If all went according to a revised plan he'd make it to his intended destination in just under ten minutes.

Ethan had the advantage over the key players in this historical drama. He knew police constable John Neil would be over near the slaughterhouse and he knew that Charles Cross and Robert Paul hadn't yet departed their respective homes. Random encounters were the real variables, the incidents he could not predict. No one knew exactly when Jack the Ripper actually attacked Mary Ann Nichols so he needed to get her to the precise location and do so undetected. Any undue confrontation would chance endangering the timeline further. If stopped by another constable, he would be close enough to London Hospital on Whitechapel Road, just a few streets away, to rightfully demand passage with a patient in tow. No officer of the law would try to keep him from an appointed task, from getting an unconscious woman into a bed. Thankfully, he didn't need to explain anything. It was a struggle but he made it.

Ethan gently placed Polly down near the gate by the boarding school on Bucks Row in the exact spot where her corpse would later be found. Grabbing his medical bag, crossing the street to the north side over to his preplanned vantage point, Ethan hoped the timeline had been unaffected, that Jack the Ripper would come upon her prone body and still perform the murder and mutilation in spite of her incapacitated condition. Checking his pocket watch, it was 3:12 a.m. *"Shit! Shit! Shit!"* Had the killer already come and gone, having no potential victim in sight? Had Ethan made it there in time? His mind plagued with questions, to now have to watch the woman he'd come to know and care for be butchered, to succumb to the hands of a madman was not what he'd expected to experience. Though he never anticipated this sudden turn of events it would've been somewhat less disturbing to see it happen to a virtual stranger. What was even more terrifying for the tenderhearted soul, he'd now have a personal vendetta, a vested interest in hating the demon about to murder his friend. He needed to know who it was so he'd know who to hate.

Remaining crouched in the shadows, trying to regain his mental acuity, a safety zone he'd acquired prior to Polly's arrival at his door, the minute hand on his pocket watch was fast becoming his enemy. It was now 3:17 a.m. Where was this monster? Polly's body was recorded being discovered at 3:40 a.m. Ethan began ringing his moist hands together, rubbing the skin from his knuckles. Muttering a mantra chant, the words in his head escaped his lips as a guttural whisper: "Please show up please show up please show up please show up please show up."

How cruel could a Universe be? How did a humble Scope research project get so fucked up so fast? This wasn't about him or Maggie, Polly, Mary. This was about the discipline of time. This was about an oath taken to The Consortium, those years spent training, learning to comprehend the inherent complexities and complicity of changing an immutable timeline, interfering in history in terms imaginable…or not. A glitch in the minutia could ultimately affect the world on a much grander scale.

It was 3:22 a.m. Time stopped. It ceased to exist, if it ever did. Ethan held his breath while the cosmos conspired against him, turning on him in a blink of God's eye as he realized the killer wasn't coming. He was already there. Now it was up to him to maintain the timeline, come what may. This was the grand scale. It was also a personal crisis. Everything changed in a flicker with the repulsive realization that he, Dr. Ethan LaPierre, in Jack's absence, would have to play the role of the Ripper.

No. No. Ethan was no one's understudy, he hadn't rehearsed for this part. It was all a vicious joke, another hellish nightmare. Maggie was not Polly Nichols and he was not Jack the Ripper. He'd awaken any moment to find "Robinson Crusoe" on the bed beside him, laying open to the chapter that prompted this insane dream. No.

Pacing in place, rubbing his hands raw, Ethan glanced down at his medical bag. Among its contents were surgical knives. No! He'd be incapable of doing what was being asked of him, a demand made in error, no doubt. The monster would round a corner any second just like the black-winged Pegasus had, a harbinger of evil deeds in another nightmare he recalled. No. This could not happen to him. The man hadn't done anything in his life to deserve this, as he'd never hurt another living soul. Not so much as a spider found in his flat, released from its prison into the light of day. He never deliberately killed anything and certainly wasn't going to begin by killing a friend, even if she'd been dead far more than a century by the time they met. No.

Now 3:24. Where was the son of a bitch? Conflict rising like acid from his stomach, it got stuck in his throat, burning him alive from within. He felt ill, as he had coming through the Flicker, ready to vomit again. Breathe. Breathe. *"No time...must make time to spare, even a minute. Give him another minute."* No time.

Now 3:25...3:26...Ethan visualized the culprit rounding a dark corner of Bucks Row, how he would look, what he would do as he practically stumbled over Polly laying on the cold cobblestone. The demon would stand there a moment snickering, the thought of how easy it would be, no fight at all. Leaning over her, deciding she was already as good as dead so he'd do her a favor and finish the job. Ethan was so tempted to yell "About time!" as his brain created a ghost lurking among shadows but there was no one hiding in the fog...no one there but him. 3:27. Out of time.

No! Grabbing the medical bag, Ethan crossed the street, counting every step as he went astray in the night. Off script. Crouching down beside her, looking around once more, it was up to him to maintain the timeline, up to *him* to finish her off. It was an unfathomable task. The bastard must have already come and gone, leaving him to fulfill the dictate of history. His pocket watch would never lie to him. 3:28. Polly did not move. She did not even appear to be breathing. Perhaps she'd already passed. No sign of life, he didn't bother to feel for a pulse. The head injury she had sustained in his room must have been worse than he thought. Thank God she would not feel a thing. Polly was already lost and gone. It would ease the pain of what needed doing, not her pain…but his own. 3:29 a.m.

He sifted through the medical bag to find a knife that he could use to make the identical incisions, lacerations on her body recorded in autopsy photographs. Those medical reports were burned into his memory long ago in a faraway time. His hands slick with sweat, his throat tightening with tension, he couldn't swallow. There was no saliva in his mouth. Barely breathing, he found one surgical knife at the bottom of the bag, sunken by its own weight. Knowing it would be similar to the knife used by the assailant, it was an archaic tool, obsolete, almost violent in appearance, yet it was as sharp as any modern medical instrument in any operating room. Mustering the courage, Ethan knew this was a *no way out* scenario, something he had to do to preserve the timeline. Polly appeared so peaceful, placid in repose, a still life, lying at his feet in the cool night air. The woman seemed an ethereal creature in morning mist, an otherworldly optical illusion sprawled out before him but she was real, as real as the fire pulsing through his veins. Time was of the essence.

"Stop it!" The man was trembling uncontrollably. *"Stop it! You know what you have to do! Do it now!"* Kneeling over her torso, Ethan straddled her, holding the blade to Polly's throat long enough to steady his hand. The angle of the cut had to be precise. Puncturing skin, the first recorded incision was under the left jawline.

"I'm sorry, Maggie." Ethan whispered the mournful words, riddled with regret. Then, attempting to quell the brewing storm in his mind, he silently talked himself through it. *"I've got to do this."* Rationalizing a completely irrational act, the kindly professor transformed into a butcher preparing to all but sever the head from Polly's body with precision technique, knowing he *must* replicate the imagery impaled in his mind. *"I've got to go through with it. This is her destiny, and now mine."* Gazing at the poor, pitiful woman, an equally helpless victim of circumstance, Ethan issued the final prompt that would send him careening over the precipice into the darkest abyss of night. Willing the strength to do what he couldn't possibly do, he chanted a silent incantation. *"You can do it…you can do it…you can do it…."*

Ethan took a deep breath, steadied his hand and began to cut her throat. Slicing several inches in, shocked by the ease with which a knife slid through supple skin, Mary Ann Nichols opened her eyes. Penetrating his soul, he jerked back the knife. Staring at each other, connected for eternity, in that singular moment of recognition, Miss Maggie knew her killer.

"How could you do this to me?" Her bewildered expression stilled the man.

Taking it in as the images appeared in rapid-fire succession, creating permanent postcards for Ethan to take back into the future, he had already sliced clear through her larynx. Polly did try to speak to him, her eyes darting as wildly as his own. The few words she mouthed with blood-spattered lips produced only the slightest moan as gurgling sounds bubbled up through the slit in her throat. He could smell blood, watching incredulously as steam rose from the wound, pouring out and around both sides of her throat, channeled by folds of skin on her neck, gravity tugging it toward cobblestone. As the crimson substance flowed with ease, forming a puddle beneath her shoulder blades, she didn't move. She did not struggle. In shock, as if reconciled to her own demise, a certain fate, she made no attempt to fight for her life. No need to check his pocket watch. He was certain time had stopped. It was irrelevant. They were together in the timeless bubble, suspended in the moment. Consumed with the event he was sharing with his victim, Ethan paused to reconsider the cosmic cousin to the seven stages of grief. He saw this transpiring as it happened. In her eyes he'd seen the seven stages of fear.

<u>The Seven Stages of Fear</u>

Defiance: self-preservation / life embrace / fear of unknown
"I don't want to die."
Shock: disbelief / astonishment / realization of what transpires
"Could this really be happening?"
Confusion: disorientation / chaos / uncertainty
"What is happening to me?"
Denial: rejection / turmoil / renunciation
"This cannot be happening to me."
Betrayal: blame / anger / self-loathing / devastation
"How could you do this to me?"
Despair: grief / inevitability / relinquishing will
"I thought you loved me."
Surrender: acceptance / acquiescence / transcendence
"This is happening to me."

Ethan knew there was no turning back, no running away from the scene of this crime. He had to finish what he started and so, went in for the second cut. He finally found courage, knowing he'd have to perform the mutilation exactly as it occurred, according to the specific details in the autopsy report. This cut had to be from the bottom left jawline down across her entire throat to the right jawline. He had to cut back and forth until it reached Polly's spine, all the while holding his free hand over her mouth to muffle what sounds might come with the pain. He'd hoped the shock of it had a numbing effect. Tipping her head backward, exposing the existing gash, her eyes were locked onto his and Ethan couldn't break the cosmic connection. He could not afford to look away. Instead, he was forced to observe everything he did to exactly recreate these mortal wounds. Trying to soothe her, to comfort his friend, he repeated, "I'm sorry. I'm so sorry. Shhh…shhh. It's all right. It will be all right. I'll make it right, Maggie." Tears were trickling down his face.

Blood expelled through her nose splattering on his right hand, still covering her mouth. He removed his hand, realizing she was incapable of making any accidental or deliberate sounds as the life force left her body. Plucking the handkerchief from his vest pocket, Ethan tenderly cleaned her face. He knew he was not done, yet. He had to complete this morbid task, maintaining the integrity of the timeline. He had gotten her where she belonged, where she needed to be, in time and on time. It was an issue of authenticity, this matter of continuity. Having no choice but to desecrate Polly's body in the most gruesome way imaginable, this was no longer a matter of life and death. Based on what he knew he'd have to do next, he cursed God for his role in history and thanked God that she was already dead.

Lifting her woolen skirt to the neck, his swift action as a single sweeping motion revealed her lower extremities to cold air she could no longer feel against dead skin. Though he'd known of the absence of undergarments, it was nonetheless a shocking sight to see her so exposed. The abdomen and genitalia visible, Ethan firmly seized the handle of the knife, fixating on all the documented details, postmortem findings of the murder and the subsequent disemboweling. He could not close his eyes and plunge right in.

Instead, he had to watch what he was doing, duplicating the details. Choosing a location, he jabbed the blade into the left side of her belly. With a flick of the wrist, a twist of the knife, a nick of the liver, the stand-in for the brutal butcher forever fixed in history, Ethan attempted to fix history. He could feel the spearhead impacting her vital organs. Dragging it down toward the vaginal cavity, he delved deeply inward, straining the sore muscles he had already used to carry his victim to Bucks Row then lay her at death's door. He stopped, retracting the eight-inch blade, assessing the damage inflicted, Ethan took a deep breath then refocused. He noticed how warm her blood was to the touch, how moist flesh clutched at his hand from within her core with each impaling blow as if clinging to life from beyond the grave. Keeping count in the same way he'd always counted the steps of a staircase, Ethan had to be exacting. The clock was ticking. He had no time to check the time.

Deliberate in his approach, the man stabbed repeatedly into Polly's lower torso, penetrating to bone, decimating the pelvic region. Every gouging, ripping, serrating motion kept him preoccupied with getting it right. It was now Ethan's blood racing, pulsing through his closed veins and arteries. He could feel the rush of heat surging inside his body. His hands were no longer trembling. His mind steadied, he watched his own handiwork, horrified and astonished by the amount of blood in one human body. He struck at her flesh with such force, each withdrawal of the weapon exerted pressure enough to lift her corpse from the cobblestone. Polly Nichols felt immortal to him, still alive in some inexplicable way, yet Mary Ann Nichols, Polly, Maggie was dead and, in some way, so was Ethan, as if he'd just cut his own throat. Time would tell but for the moment, he felt like one of two victims, the lone survivor.

During the next few minutes Professor LaPierre continued on, against his will, to play the heinous role of Jack the Ripper. He despised the faceless man who never showed up and put him in such an untenable position. Choosing the spots recorded, he impaled the blade into the right side of her belly. He had no choice. As to what would be historically and accurately chronicled of the murder, the angle of her body allowed for most of the blood to flow underneath her, gradually soaked up by her clothing, leaving only a small pool behind her back. Standing to reason, considering that blood was no longer pumping through her fragile heart, given willingly to the man of her dreams, a ticket out of abject deprivation, Ethan could not bear to think of her as Maggie or Polly or Mary Ann Nichols. She had expired. She was a corpse. Catching his breath on the breeze, he made several more documented cuts, jaggedly slashing across the lower abdomen, opening a fissure that provided visual access to her lower intestines. Duplicating the depraved mutilation was a challenge, the most grotesque kind of reenactment Ethan could conceive.

In went the knife again, this time into the lower right side of her stomach then down deeply into the pelvic region, repeatedly plunging the weapon into her lifeless form while keeping close count. Maintaining his concentration and conformity, just as meticulous with the murder as he was with his research of it, he knew the precise number, the precise locations, depth and breadth of every puncture wound inflicted, recorded for posterity, spending years of his life pouring over every detail. He knew what to do and he was nearly done. Ripping her body cavity wide open with a single slash, he exposed her internal organs. Each strike more severe than one preceding it, according to the coroner's report that's exactly how it happened. The adrenaline racing through his veins bulging with the rapid flow of his own blood, sweat raining from his brow, the aggressor was exhausted, gasping for air in much the same way his friend had only a few minutes earlier.

A quick comparative analysis, Ethan recalled the images of this victim hanging on his office walls, autopsy photographs displaying every lurid breach of her body. Looking down at the gaping wounds he'd duplicated from memory, they matched. Suddenly he wondered, had he acted prematurely? Had the REAL Jack the Ripper been hiding in the shadows all along, watching over Ethan committing the barbaric act in error, the murder of a victim not rightfully his own? A woman HE had been destined for, deprived of because of an overzealous professor? An understandable paranoia developing in his mind, considering even the potential paradox of *another* Ethan from another time lurking in dark alleys, in the shadows of his soul, a fellow Flicker traveler might be watching him at that very moment. No! He could not wrap his otherwise facile mind around the convoluted concept. Self-loathing aside, the work he needed to do was finished. He'd done all he could to preserve the integrity of the crime scene as a historical event, the authenticity of the timeline for the sake of an unknown future. Nothing had changed except him.

Peering once more at her face, into the open eyes of the woman who was once "Maggie" the barmaid to him, until a mere forty minutes before when he had first mouthed the words *"I'm sorry"* Ethan said it again. In hushed tones, expressing his regrets, he was drowning in sorrow, awash in emotions flowing through him as fast as the blood flowed from his victim. Shock. Horror. Grief. Anger. Being plunged into a predicament beyond his control, compelled by the cosmos to take control of a situation not of his making, circumstances he could never have predicted, a flood of remorse burst from his heart, pouring from his eyes while he sobbed.

Disposing of the knife, throwing it back into the bag, he snapped it up with one hand, placing the other over his mouth as he raced across the street to the relative safety of the alleyway. Remaining in a crouched position, his urgency was no longer born of the fear of detection but the visceral sensation that he was about to be sick. Barely making it into the secluded corner he had chosen to observe the proceedings, Ethan covered his mouth to muffle the distinguishable sound as he began to retch, catching the contents of his stomach in the hand drenched with the rusty residue of coagulated blood congealing between his fingers. It came over him in waves as he knelt down near some discarded construction materials. The vomiting was violent, no doubt due to the compelling event, compounded by the knowledge of what he'd done; sickened by this part he played in history. Mind reeling, thoughts fracturing with reasons why he *had* to kill a friend then mutilate her corpse, he was overcome. A human being lost her life to the hands he found himself staring at, reflecting upon what had occurred…and why…and what may come of it.

Did this mean he'd have to murder the other four women he was there to simply observe? Would he become a suspect in their brutal slaying? Never in all of his life, not even during the first three days he had spent here in the Whitechapel district of old London, had anything been quite as *real* as it was in that moment spent peering at his own bloodstained palms. Closing his weary eyes, Ethan's tears escaped from the corners, cascading down, absorbed by his collar. In his mind's eye he could see an image of young Maggie stumbling in the mud, leering back at him with playful disdain, a postcard, the keepsake he had carried with him into the past. It has often been said the *first cut is the deepest* and what he had done cut him to the core, there as a permanent scar. Pulling out his pocket watch, it was 3:32 a.m. In touching it to open the face, blood smeared on his faithful companion, the three-legged horse.

XV.
A VICTIM OF CIRCUMSTANCE

Despair he could not escape, no matter how fast or far he ran from the scene of the crime, Ethan lingered in the shadows. Perceiving himself to be as much a victim as Polly, she'd paid with her life to fulfill her destiny, to satisfy a dictate of history. In playing his part, Ethan might have sacrificed his soul. No exit from this hell, his reality could neither be fully denied nor reconciled. As a mind expanded can never retract, innocence lost is never regained. Tucking the timepiece back in his pocket, he trembled in the corner of the alley like a little boy lost in the dark. Every muscle in his body shaking violently, every pore of his flesh producing perspiration, Ethan was too physically and psychologically exhausted to make his way out of this alley to Bucks Row then back to his room. He'd have to wait out the timeline, go through their gruesome discovery of Mary Ann Nichols' corpse, maintaining his position as the proverbial fly on the wall, wingless, anticipating the arrival of two men who'd find her along with the subsequent constables and the attending physician. This was the way it was all supposed to play out. Ethan imperceptible in the shadows, there to simply watch it transpire, veiled from history itself. The time neared 3:40 a.m.

As if on cue, one man fitting the description of Charles Cross approached from the left. He'd paused, looking in the direction of Polly's lifeless form, moving ever closer until he stood beside her corpse. Like viewing a movie he'd seen a thousand times, Ethan knew the entire script by heart. Cross would notice Robert Paul, also leaving for work, calling him over. With each anticipated movement of what was recorded history following suit, Ethan was painfully assured that the timeline was still intact. The pain he felt was in knowing his actions in killing Mary Ann Nichols may have, in fact, always occurred, yet he was in disbelief, in denial of a potentially unavoidable truth. He appeared to be like a gentleman at Wimbledon, sitting center court, turning his head left then right, looking continuously toward both ends of the street, still hoping to observe the *real* Jack the Ripper running from the shadows as he escaped unscathed. Ethan considered the consequences of his actions. He blamed the real killer for leaving blood on *his* hands when he was but an innocent bystander. Perhaps the true hunter saw Ethan early enough to allow him the kill.

Thus far there was no other motion but the two men looming over Polly's body. Uncertain of her demise or if she was passed out, they pulled her layered skirt back down to cover her out of respect, an act of human decency. These men, on schedule, left to alert the local authorities. The next cued character arriving at 3:45 was police Constable John Neil. Coming upon the corpse, PC Neil used his lamp to inspect the body. As he proceeded to discern her demise Constable John Thain appeared up the street. Neil flagged him down with a wave of his lamp.

"Here's a woman with her throat cut!" Neil shouted to Thain. "Run at once for Dr. Llewellyn."

As the officer continued to initially examine the woman, he walked around and, at one point, shined his lamp on her throat. From his vantage point Ethan could see the result of a carnage he created in the light. The urge to vomit returned. It was too overwhelming to control. He once again put his hand up to his mouth then turned his head to muffle what sound he could, but it projected from his mouth with such force, it sprayed the ground around him. As his throat constricted the uncontrollable guttural choking noises emerged. Looking back toward the street he saw the officer looking his way. PC Neil began walking across Bucks Row toward that sound. As he raised his lamp, Ethan inconspicuously slid further backward into the protective shadows of the alleyway. The range of the lamp he held wasn't considerable but it did offer enough illumination to pose a problem if the constable removed the eerie dark shroud Ethan was using as cover. If the bobby came any closer there would be no shadow left for him to hide in!

When he was halfway across the street someone called out his name. Constable Neil turned to look at whoever was coming up Bucks Row. He walked toward who Ethan could only expect to be Constable Mizen who was alerted by the two workers about the fallen woman. Both men walked back to the body. The cast of characters in the play kept coming onto the stage, from Dr. Llewellyn who examined the lady on site, declaring her dead at 4:00

a.m., all the way through the ancillary characters who hauled her away to the morgue, others who would remain at the scene of the crime to wash away any evidence of it. There was no preserving anything for future reference, a far cry from modern times. In 19th Century London, the intention was to preserve the peace, thereby removing Polly's body then washing down the blood to prevent gathering onlookers from spreading the word, done to avoid panic in the local population. There were no forensics specialists, no "crime scene" tape or any other technique developed, perfected over time. There was no murder investigation in this regard, no official protocol implemented because it did not yet exist.

The event having reached its conclusion, Ethan remained in the alleyway until the murder scene was cleaned up and the police left the area. No one emerged from the other hiding spots around Bucks Row. No REAL killer for whom Ethan did the job, no sign of Colin observing him and no future Ethan observing himself fucking it up. Now well past 6:00 a.m., people were beginning to file out of their homes and into the streets on their way to destinations unknown. It was safe enough for him to step out from the shadows to blend in, bloody hands plunged into his pockets, head down. For the sake of his remaining sanity, Ethan searched every last crevice with his eyes, every potential hiding place he had located on his earlier preemptive scans of Bucks Row. He needed to be absolutely certain, beyond any doubt, there was no one who'd been scoping out the Scope for the entire episode, no one who knew his secret. He did not even know who to look for! Unless he'd encountered either Colin or himself from yet another Flicker jump, he could not be sure the person he would stumble upon was the real Jack the Ripper or just another local seeking shelter from the elements. His only hope, if he did locate someone and they were the real killer, once they locked eyes, (or if he displayed a smile of mocking intent, knowing what Ethan had done *for* him), he could then afford to feel a sense of relief that what had to come no longer need involve him. Unfortunately, there was no one to be found. No one came or went prior to or during the time he was committing a brutal murder. It became painfully clear. IT became real. People walking past the former murder scene were likewise walking right past a murderer.

Time to return to his room, the man did not meander. Maintaining a professional demeanor, the medical bag looped over his forearm, he kept up the pace as if on his way to an appointment. The sunrise muted by cloud cover, Ethan marched on to his intended destination, noticing every single detail of the journey, as though he made a unique transition from a three-dimensional existence to a multidimensional plane of action in which everything leapt out at him. The flower in a window box bending toward the light, the patterns of tracks wagon wheels make in the mud, the rim of a woman's skirt torn loose from its lace fabric, he saw everything with different eyes. Arriving at the back entrance to his lodging, he quickly passed the kitchen area so not to engage with anyone in any way. The imperative was simple, to get his bloody body behind a closed, locked door. He located the key in his pocket.

Entering the room, it had a different air about it, the space in which everything changed. It was time to gather his thoughts and perceptions, to begin processing the event. Sitting on the bed, tears spontaneously burst forth, catching him off guard. It was an explosion of emotion quietly falling from his eyes. He couldn't pretend that it hadn't happened. Privately pondering the consequences of his actions, Ethan had to come to grips with what occurred and why, to justify and sanctify his role. What he had done preserved the historical timeline, nothing more significant than keeping a misalignment of time from changing the world. A glitch in time saved by divine intervention? The nausea returned with the thought of it.

"Why the fuck am I here?"

It all seemed beyond implausible, quite impossible! Maggie *really* being Mary Ann "Polly" Nichols, coming to his room drunk, knocked out before she could even get where she was supposed to be killed. No fiction writer could make this shit up! Ethan still couldn't believe it, in spite of the fact that he had already lived it! To his knowledge, no one saw a thing. No constables knocking at his door, no accusations flying around in print, not yet, he was not a suspect. That one close call was reason enough to remain ever mindful of the inherent risks, keeping an even lower profile, a decided necessity. Ethan had to get naked, burdened by the weight of his clothes.

With the exception of some of Polly's blood and his vomit still on his sleeves, the outfit was stain free. He removed all but his shorts. There was still half a pitcher full of water from his last wash down so he immediately placed the sleeves inside to soak with hopes of removing the stains. He'd once more found himself sitting on the end of his bed. Ethan was in uncharted territory on a cosmic course charted, one he had no part in, no knowledge of, but planned out long before he stepped through the doorway called Flicker, long before he'd opened the door to his flat when Colin told him his fate, long before he'd opened the door to his room one fateful night to find the face of a friend named Maggie staring back at him like a ghost.

To look within himself and try to invoke the wisdom and logic to comprehend what he did, or what he had always done, Ethan LaPierre was forever, if not always, part of this story. But how? He was perhaps one of the gentlest souls there ever was, as tenderhearted as he was level-headed and pragmatic. Even at his most angry, he would simply rationalize it then step away, lessening the momentary emotion until it passed. It was his way. He never had the slightest hint of a violent side, and was, in fact, so likeable, he never faced a confrontation in his adult life. As Ethan sought to make sense of it all, he sat on the soft down comforter on his bed, virtually naked to a world in which he now found himself deeply entrenched. His worry was not in being implicated in Polly's death. He knew virtually every move that the police and Scotland Yard would be making in pursuit of the culprit. He knew all of the suspects they would be focusing on and clearly had the advantage if the cat and mouse game was ever presented for him to play. No, his concern, his foreboding dread was with the non-interference directive he'd breached, flipping itself around on him, the twist of the knife. He had always perceived it to mean he was tasked with an observation *only* without taking moral justice into his hands, harming the culprit nor saving the victims. Now the term "non-interference" meant he must do everything in his power to preserve, not disrupt the events that were recorded in the timeline of history.

"NO! I am **not** Jack the Ripper." Ethan spoke emphatically, if under his breath, so not to be overheard by a passerby in the hallway. He said it to himself hoping to will away the events which had already transpired. "I am not Jack the Ripper." He said it again. "No. I'm not Jack the Ripper. I am Dr. Ethan LaPierre of St. Leonards and Oxford University, born in 1978 to François and Anne LaPierre. I can't be **him**! Jack the Ripper. No!" He'd spoken the name with utter contempt, its implication as the historical connection to pure loathing and abject terror. He was the farthest thing from terrifying. The gentle professor was, at most, tall.

Ethan changed, dressing back into his local attire. He needed to get more water and some soap from the kitchen to wash off the blood from the knife and anyplace else he might find reminders of the carnage he created in the wee small hours of the morning. Exiting his room with the pitcher in hand, he went down to the common area where he came upon several other tenants including the man who'd generously shared his coffee. Ethan avoided eye contact with anyone in the room as he slipped out the back door nearest to the privy, heading for the adjacent well pump. He felt a sudden social paranoia, a phobic sense of each pair of eyes scrutinizing him. Even though the news of the murder of Mary Ann Nichols had not yet reached the public, he felt as though his façade was tainted by an overwhelming, uncontrollably guilty look he carried in his eyes. It was mere minutes before he would return to his room, and the false sense of security it provided. He could not finish that chore fast enough for his liking then get back upstairs, away from prying eyes.

Once again behind his locked door, off came all the clothing. Ethan produced some busy work to occupy his troubled mind, devoting his hands to scrubbing everything he'd gotten blood on, including his watch. As if in an attempt to wash away his sins from the hours prior, he cleaned the surface of the case then softly buffed it with a towel in a sacred, circular motion, the way he had witnessed the watchmaker do it. Hypnotic, almost ritualistic, he slowly and gently wiped encrusted blood from deep within the crevices of its intricate embossing. Everything he did felt so meaningless, a futile act, yet the work was necessary, a requirement for him to reestablish some semblance of normalcy, no matter the century. His quantum leap in consciousness had occurred, a leap far surpassing his jump through Flicker as he realized *nothing* would ever be the same again. Indeed, Ethan had forever changed. For the duration of the next twelve hours he remained sequestered, refusing to leave his room.

Logical thought was temporarily suspended while he sat at the desk staring out the window at passing clouds, flashes of sunlight bursting between them. *Thoughts of a sane man expecting to get caught or turn himself over to authorities for a crime committed.* Had he done this unthinkable, unspeakable act in 21st Century London, by now he would have been apprehended, taken into custody considering all of the sophisticated scientific methods and equipment at the disposal of law enforcement. He would not have made it to another sunset as a free man in the year 2020. In the 19th Century things ran a bit behind the times. It was no surprise the Keystone Cops never caught Jack the Ripper. He smiled at the thought of it but didn't know why.

Ethan was pondering his responsibility, his possible destiny. It looked like there might not have been a serial killer in the 19th Century, at least not of these women, all documented as victims of the same predator. Looks can be deceiving. Based on the available evidence there had been a general consensus reached by many experts on the subject. The same predator. The same blade. Discarding all other possibilities as cosmic conspiracy theories, only one concern remained. Call it predestination or divine planning, a philosophical dictate or historical mandate, he probably was the infamous Jack the Ripper.

"This can't possibly be the truth of it! No! This isn't what I'm destined for here. No! God damn it! No! This is not my fault and this is not my job!"

It *was* personal. His goal for this project and The Consortium's approval of it, was contingent upon him being prepared to identify a killer, not become one. Based on his keen powers of observation, he could definitely see how it would appear that this had already been scripted more than one hundred and thirty years in the future, set up like some bad practical joke gone terribly wrong. An Oxford professor could be the greatest, most infamous uncaptured murderer in recorded history? "No!"

Ethan moved from the chair to his bed. Darkness had fallen across the window and he did not want anyone to see him in the candlelight. He held the pillow like a security blanket as he lay on his side, pondering events that may still come. He was only eight days away from meeting the next, or *his* next victim, Annie Chapman. He could not turn himself in nor could he get caught if, for no other reason, to be sure. The prime directive: do not interfere with the timeline. Anything Ethan did beyond what was already seared into memory over years of preparation would immediately and irrevocably change the future. The ripple effect would spread, the impact made by tossing one little pebble into the river of time would create repercussions felt far and wide, no way to stem the tide. This wasn't a pebble. It was a boulder.

During the preceding twelve hours he remained completely aware of what was happening regarding the case. He knew all the players and their placement, meeting their marks on the stage in this grand drama unfolding. Robert Anderson, appointed Assistant Commissioner for Crime had chosen Donald Swanson to take charge of the case. Tomorrow William Nichols would identify the body of his estranged wife. Ethan had the upper hand, knowing every action taken during this investigation by those involved in law enforcement and journalism. For a killer it would be bliss. For Ethan, it was an assurance that he could maintain the historical timeline and if need be, if no killer miraculously appeared to intercede, he would have to conduct the ruthless, vicious attacks in commitment to continuity.

Were he to break protocol and return through the Flicker prematurely, it would have no bearing. Once Ethan had divulged this precarious twist of fate or historical absolution of his involvement, The Consortium brass, including Anson Van Ruden, would immediately insist upon his return to complete the task at hand, whether as a Scope or an assassin in a morbid quest to maintain those recorded events as they occurred. Even Colin would also, in his own way, admonish Ethan. "Fuck me mate. Better you than me, but you'd bloody well better get back there and figure this shit out." He couldn't even suggest, if necessary, sending a convicted murderer back to finish off the job as the FTC would never allow it, expecting a coldblooded killer would not have enough mental stability or discipline to wait patiently for only those victims chosen by time to lose their lives, nor would they ever trust anyone else to perform the mutilations to those exact specifications corresponding precisely to the medical and police reports. He was screwed. If this were to go in the worst possible direction, there would be no reconciling his internal conflict. No way out. "No."

No one at The Consortium, not one military strategist, not one psychologist nor any single Scope could have foreseen this scenario. No one could have envisioned this complication. Dozens of trial runs at The Valley and not one model portraying this event happening because it wasn't within the Scope's criteria to be involved in even the most miniscule of roles. Ethan tossed and turned in bed, bouncing around from one emotion to the next, one moment crying over Maggie then laughing at the insanity of it all. Wailing like a child over what he may need to do next. He had not eaten a thing but had no appetite. The nausea was incessant. He arose from the bed just to drink some water, but the basin was pink in color from the washing of bloodstained garments and a medical instrument he did not want to touch, let alone clean for yet another vile use. Clutching his hair in clumps, Ethan's frustration was with himself. Nothing was going right. Pacing the room as he'd done prior to the fateful night's event, when seeking to center his focus, this brooding did not have the same underlying intent. As he walked six steps to the window facing Bakers Row and six steps back to the foot of the bed, the man began violently whipping his left fist then pounding the right side of his chest with his fist in a blatant act of self-attrition. No. Nothing alleviated the angst he endured, not even self-inflicted pain could distract him from the pain he felt in his soul. It was an immense dilemma, an overwhelming torment taking a hold of a man who always, *always* held it together.

Recalling his years at Oxford, Ethan had met some wonderful men and women from the local police department. He remembered speaking with some of them who, either while serving in the military or out on the beat had no choice but to shoot and kill a person. He recalled some of their poignant remarks, never forgetting the event or the face of who they'd killed. He understood what they meant now. He couldn't get the image out of his head. Maggie laying there with her throat cut, her dead eyes staring back at his in disbelief. He remembered asking those officers how they dealt with these everlasting images, receiving a uniform response. They all said they had to simply keep reminding themselves that it was their job.

The job. That was it! Like a sledgehammer to the softest, most vulnerable part of his skull, it hit him hard. Ethan was tasked with a job. Had he not done so, had he neglected to do whatever was necessary at the required moment the implications would have been catastrophic. Truth be told, even in a dire, desperate situation such as this, the training took over. Rational thought compelled him to act in accordance with his directive, preservation of the timeline. Period. Beyond his own emotional and mental anguish, everything was going right! In that moment of clarity, Ethan's conviction regarding what *could* happen became steadfast. Of course, a realization did not in any way lessen the obvious traumatic anticipation of having to go through it four more times, having to do the job for a delinquent Jack the Ripper. Well aware it wouldn't be anything but torturous to once again stand upon the precipice, poised at the edge of reason, there to fathom the depths of depravity, Ethan made an inner pact. With a smile, he thought he could hear Colin saying a few choice words.

"If this bastard shows up to kill Annie Chapman and the lot of 'em, for what he put you through, before you bloody leave here you should kill that little shit then hide his fucking body and *that's* why the sonofabitch never got caught!" The mental manifestation of his best friend was an effort to sell a bad bill of good comedy to his own aching conscience. Ethan's mindset was, for the moment, one of relative calm, convincing himself to believe this was another thing entirely. Centered in the eye of the storm, gauging by a peripheral swirling barrage of emotions he had been swept up by in the preceding hours, though it had subsided, turmoil would certainly resurface. No CLEAR & RESET order available, this wasn't a reenactment. In eight days he would potentially have to obey the immutable laws of history and kill again. "No. Please. No." In the next chapter of the saga, this next pivotal scene of the drama yet to unfold on a stage he also occupied, Annie Chapman had the spotlight and her presence would tell all.

"She'd better not be Maggie's friend, Rose!" In jest, trying to muster up his dry wit, a lame effort made to recover some fragment of his former self, it did not seem to have the effect he hoped for, after all.

Ethan ran his hands through his hair as he drew a deep breath through his nose, expelling a heavy sigh through his mouth. His mind reeling with imagery, he never recognized this Maggie as Mary Ann Nichols until she was lying dead beneath him, carved by the blade from his bag. The all too familiar vision of Polly staring blankly into his face became excruciatingly real, identical to the postmortem photographs. It was not too far-fetched a notion to think he had already passed Annie Chapman on the streets. He could have literally run into her passing through the crowd at Ten Bells and been none the wiser. According to his research, the only historical images available of her were those of the disfigured corpse after her death. No portrait, not a single photograph of her alive and well. More's the pity.

There is a discernable missing character once a life has left its body. That factor cannot be labeled, it merely exists. A person asleep might appear similar to a person expired on the surface but, once photographed, there are specific nuances apparent that definitively differentiate them somehow. Having memorized all of the graphic postmortem pictures of all five women he was supposed to watch getting murdered, he had been unable to recognize the first of them alive and well. So, for this purpose, these images were meaningless in real life. Yet, it became critically important that he recall every detail if he had to perform these acts alone on the world stage. After the debacle with Mary Ann Nichols and her simple façade as Maggie the barmaid, Ethan knew there was a distinct possibility he could run into any of the remaining four victims without making the connection. Prone to repeating itself in a mocking manner, history was now an adversary. Deciding to deliberately isolate himself, he would avoid contact with humanity for the remaining time he had to be there to fulfill the historical design. The man learned his lesson. If ever there was a time to write in his journal, this was it, the pencil trembling in his grasp. "*Write it down.*"

***

Journal Entry ~ 31 August 1888

Assuming this is expected to be turned in along with all the other items provided for my jump, this entry may fall under the category of a written confession. In the early morning hours of this historical date I, Dr. Ethan LaPierre, in an attempt to preserve the timeline regarding the Jack the Ripper case, had no other alternative but to take the life of Mary Ann Nichols in the manner and procedure indicative of her demise for the sake of maintaining accuracy in historical record. There was an inadvertent meeting of the two of us a few days prior to her fateful destiny unfolding which I will explain further in my debriefing. I am convinced that no other person arrived before or after the recorded time of the murder, leaving me no alternative but to kill Polly Nichols in precisely the method Jack the Ripper did. This was my interpretation of non-interference. If no one else shows up in eight days less myself and Miss Chapman, maybe the simplest confession should be that I am the Ripper.

You, as the Consortium have a decision to make upon surrendering this journal to you and following debriefing to decide if I am to be convicted or commended for the acts I have done and maybe am about to do. Since my return through the Flicker is not until November 9th it could be my sole burden and responsibility to maintain what history recorded. Therefore, in eight nights I might be compelled to continue the work of Jack the Ripper by murdering Annie Chapman. Sequentially, I'll need to take another leap of faith in my logical approach and actions should it become necessary to take yet another life for the sake of continuity. I might have to murder three more women prior to my return on the morning of the last victim's demise. I hope you can appreciate my dilemma, not one of my own making, I assure you.

Remembering well the hours of Flicker Scope conferences on the matter of non-interference, the importance of never causing a ripple in the fabric of time, this was drummed into us to such a degree that it became part of our psyche. Never was this conundrum discussed. I will accept whatever judgments are passed upon my return. However, regarding the instructions I'd received, I have acted in good faith and in accordance with my comprehension of it as the Scope-apparent.

Divulging the reasons for my actions I hope allows you to empathize should the next Flicker project necessitate a Scope to intervene. Would he or she be judged in turn should the act be illegal or praised for saving the timeline of history? It is the dilemma I will unfortunately bring back to you at the end of this project. Genius is the mind that sees the way through impossibility. If my decision is likewise my crime then I am ready to face the consequences of my actions upon returning to the future. I did what I had to do and will complete my mission, come what may.

***

In Ethan's tired eyes, the world filled with shades of gray was gone. Like a still life shot in black and white, the image was never sharper. A personal conviction to the deepest well of his core, he questioned his existence, his part in the play, yet he never questioned the necessity to do what must be done, the honorable thing to do. Assuming he'd have time to reflect after any act he might be forced to commit, he was committed to what he perceived to be a right ending to a wrongful journey. To surrender his purpose along with logic meant he could let go of everything his head was polluted with up to this point, simply follow the blueprints the great architect of history gave him to build the most haunted house of all time, riddled with ghosts.

XVI.
THE TASK AT HAND

Ethan woke the next morning with a song lingering in his head, namely "Rude" by the pop group Magic, recorded in 2014, one hundred and twenty-six years in the future. *"Saturday morning jumped out of bed and put on my best suit...."* Causing him to smile, it surprised him. The ambivalence had subsided with sleep, as well as the all-consuming remorse. He had not thought of music of *any* era since arriving in this one, his mind possessed with other matters. Yes, he'd passed by a few street vendors with a musician nearby them on a sidewalk and there were bawdy, raucous beer songs flying about Ten Bells. It was entertaining enough, but for Ethan, it was not *real* music, ethereal compositions that had moved him someplace deep within his soul. In that instant, Ethan longed to visit the symphony orchestra, aching for a concerto. Although not overly fond of a song still stuck in his mind, burned into his memory bank in 2014, it made him smile because he felt weight being lifted from his psyche. It made him feel lighter, as if floating on a feather in a cloud.

A profound relationship existed between Ethan and his muse, as music was his truest love, the one who would never leave him. That subtle yet sublime connection occurred between him and melodies, sometimes just the poetic lyrics. Their union, a communion between the spirit of the composer and listener was something sacred. Whether it was his favorite classical station turned down low in his office while he worked, jazz when conducting tutorials, it was omnipresent, providing the pleasant backdrop he needed but his flat was his sanctuary. He owned the best sound system known to mankind, redefining the phrase state-of-the-art and worth the investment. Music played an integral role in Ethan's life. It was a part of him, the missing piece in this puzzling leap of faith he'd taken into the past. In a flicker came the epiphany. There was nothing and no one to stop him from fulfilling his heartfelt desire.

The Consortium had provided him with enough currency to stay a year. Perhaps a trip to central London was in order while he was here, to attend a concert and take in a show. It was perfect, just what the doctor ordered for himself! Yes! An inspired idea. If only briefly, for an evening, Ethan needed to escape the horrors of what he had done and cope with the possibilities of what was to come, events he had to plan for and execute, if need be. His entire Scope schedule would have to be revamped. Should Jack fail to show up again, he had to be prepared for the worst case scenario. Annie Chapman. That night, an event destined to occur in the not too distant future here in the past, *that* night would clarify history. Truth be told, the characters who'd be present at the scene of that crime would tell all, revealing everything Ethan had a desperate need to know. He had little more than a week to prepare for the worst. The rub? The *best* case scenario involved watching "Jack the Ripper" decimate the body of a woman after claiming her life. In comparison to the alternative, it did not seem so horrible anymore. Ethan would welcome the *hands off* approach.

Rising from his bed stark naked, he found it rather liberating to sleep in the buff. Sometime during the night he'd shed his shorts like a snake sheds its skin and there they were, laying in a wad on the floor at the foot of the bed. Ethan began dancing around them in ballet fashion, manifesting a favorite piece from Brahms to replace the "Rude" intruder still humming along in his head. Not thinking whether he was forcing this change in emotion to occur or if he really felt an actual release from the burden of what he had done and what was still to come, Ethan was taking a moment to live in the moment, present and accounted for in 1888, doing his own version of the "Bishop Bounce".

Yes. He would have to manage the anxiety. It would not be an easy week ahead, undoubtedly riddled with trepidation. Last night Ethan had all but accepted the role, relinquishing the right of refusal but this morning it seemed only right he should be free to turn it down, but it wasn't that kind of role. This morning he saw it, *all* of it in a new light. Blessed sleep had swept the cobwebs from his mind. This was not a foregone conclusion, far from it. Any number of variables could enter into play as whatever kept Jack from his appointed rounds was an equally unknown variable in a complicated equation. This first incident, a case in point. Ethan screwed it up by befriending Maggie, so history placed him there to fill in the gap.

It was as viable a theory as any other but Ethan did not want to think. He wanted to dance and dance he did! Like no one was watching (because no one was), Ethan let his hair down and let his bits bob in the wind. Dangling free, naked as a jaybird, he laughed as he suddenly realized the window was open. The cold air had impacted his warm skin. The subsequent shrinkage caught his attention but not in a big way.

"Gigglemug!" He was true to his word, giggling like a naughty school boy, just dancing and prancing to his heart's content. A decided chill in the air, he found it a refreshing sensation as he worked up one hell of a sweat doing pirouettes. "All work and no play makes Jack a dull boy!"

He leapt back beneath the blanket, making sounds indicative of the Daffy Duck cartoons he had watched as a child. He was acting childish considering his situation and surroundings, as if trying to find an appropriate personality to match conditions and directions currently presented to him. Sufficiently warm, he rose again, walking to the window. Having draped the blanket around him, Ethan peered outside. It was overcast and he couldn't tell what time of day it was so he looked on the desk before him to find his watch, which was resting, open, on the cover of "Robinson Crusoe". The irony was too much to take. Out of character, Ethan swept the watch aside then furiously grabbed the novel, flinging it across the room as if the story intentionally mocked him. Another minute, another emotion. He was all over the place, literally and figuratively, acting like he was losing his mind.

Reflecting as he wandered the room, he resented the fact that he'd have to get dressed to go down to the loo but he needed some coffee anyway. Ethan considered his own volatile emotions, wondering if he should rightfully keep strictly to himself for the sake of others during this tumultuous transition. There was so much to think about, plan for and prepare in the interim between this morning and the forthcoming demise of Annie Chapman. Ethan would take his father's sage advice. He'd always said to plan for the worst and hope for the best. With that, he got dressed.

The trip downstairs involved little interaction, as the common kitchen was void of tenants upon his arrival. He'd had the presence of mind to bring his wallet and so, in purchasing coffee grounds from the manager, he also paid his rent in advance for the next several days. Brewing a strong pot, he drank two cups downstairs and brought the rest back to his room. One more trip down to refresh his basin water, it was all he needed. Having barely spoken a word during the brief excursion, Ethan felt safest when cloistered in his own little world, separated from humanity. Perhaps he should take another day before showing up in public, he thought. Uncomfortable in a crowd by nature, the idea of being surrounded by others at this time seemed a lot more disconcerting than it ever had, as if people would know what he'd done by being in his presence. The concept of interacting with anyone was anathema to him. When the time came for him to reemerge into society for a few hours, he would go listen to an orchestra serenade him for one night. It would come in time but not yet.

One day turned into three days of Ethan confining himself like Lon Chaney Jr., fearing he would manifest into the werewolf upon the next full moon. It was not all egregious to the cause. He did manage to finally remove every last drop of sanguine fluid from his clothing and the blade, no trace evidence remaining. He also finished "Robinson Crusoe" again, apologizing to Mr. Dafoe for tossing it across the room in a fit of anger, reminding him that no one likes to be mocked. Slowly but surely, the spell was subsiding and Ethan was returning to a staid, pragmatic state of mind, transforming back into the good doctor, Professor LaPierre. He was enjoying more and more staring out of the window, as if viewing a moving picture in an old theatre house, safe from altercation, from the element-apparent of this time. The events he knew almost in oracle form were transpiring around him. Leaving him untouched, a drama unfolding beyond his window on the world, leaving him further unstained from an ongoing investigation. While waiting for his coffee to brew, Ethan read the city newspaper someone had discarded in the public sitting area, all about the local authority's earliest considered suspects. They had nothing, in keeping with the tune they'd sung of the earlier unsolved murders of Emma Smith and Martha Tabram.

"...these gangs, who make their appearance during the early hours of the morning, are in the habit of blackmailing these poor unfortunate creatures, and when their demands are refused, violence follows, and in order to avoid their deeds being brought

to light they put away their victims. They have been under the observation of the police for some time past, and it is believed that with the prospect of a reward and a free pardon, some of them might be persuaded to turn Queen's evidence, when some startling revelations might be expected...."

Ethan scoffed at their initial research, what little was done by the Metropolitan and City of London police dating back to the death of Miss Fairy Fay in December of 1887. His cynical side wondered if they'd really put their hearts into it or were these women just disposable members of society, not worth the effort? In total, the collective department named thirty-one suspects as the murderers of some eighteen women between December of 1887 and April of 1891. During his research phase, conducted in earnest, Ethan never took an adversarial stance toward the police and their investigation, yet now he chuckled, looking at this offset count of victims-to-suspects ratio, imagining the rationale of the police thinking that maybe men were working in pairs during the murders! He facetiously uttered "Come on! Really?" as he read where they were going with this and they were going nowhere fast. They'd reminded him of a movie he once saw called "The Dark Knight" wherein Gotham's police were trying to ascertain the true identity of Batman and on their "suspects" corkboard were posted the photos of Abraham Lincoln, Bigfoot and Elvis Presley. They were guessing! Local authorities were drawing conclusions that were clearly inconclusive as none of the thirty-one men under suspicion were ever charged, tried or convicted. If all of Ethan's fears were realized, then the closest anyone ever came to the true Jack the Ripper was by happenstance, approached by a bobby on patrol, curious about a man carrying a pair of expensive shoes on Whitechapel Road.

From time to time over his three days of isolation and reflection, Ethan thought of Maggie, a name synonymous with two women he'd known and cared for in his life. His first thoughts led to the most recent of introductions in the form of Mary Ann "Polly" Nichols, his server, his confidante, his guide and ultimately, his victim. She really was a sweet lady, very generous of spirit and kind of heart. She just could not find her way out of the bottle. Who knows how she might have wound up were it not for her being a drunk? Under different circumstances, had she not been Mary Ann Nichols incognito, he might have taken the two months he was tasked here and on his down time, effort to help her sober up and make something of herself in life. Unfortunately, she was a historical figure, one victim of Jack the Ripper. Therefore, she had to die.

Now, as far as young Maggie back at Oxford, there was a true paradox. If Ethan had listened to Colin's advice (which he wisely never, ever did) and looked into the possible romantic avenues with this bright, nubile face and facile mind, all of these circumstances occurring perhaps would not be. If they had fallen in love he might have chosen to stay in the future, settle down, have a peck of kids and continue to teach. Who was he fucking kidding, himself? He had to ask! Ethan was completely terrified that *this*, all of it was all planned by the universal playbook millennia ago. Only one thing he knew for certain, when he returned home through the Flicker, if not condemned by the law for his actions, he would ask Maggie out on that date. He would ask her forgiveness and beg her comprehension of his circumstances, should she not understand that he, too, was a victim. He'd convince her to make a life with him, even after claiming one, even if he'd be compelled by an unforgiving history to take four more before departing the 19th Century. If anyone could, she would be the one to understand. Young Maggie was his link to a guilt-free common life.

Ethan put the paper down. He didn't need to read or listen to anything redundant to his research, having experienced the raw expression of emotion from individuals he encountered like Nigel, the manager at his lodge who originally checked him in based on Miss Maggie's referral. He had been the first as word spread of her killing. He'd known precisely who Mary Ann Nichols was, Polly to him, telling his tenant Arthur of her untimely demise a few nights earlier. Ethan made the connection over the past three days to the strange way Nigel had said the name "Maggie" upon their first meeting. He remembered that she'd whispered something to the manager, who truly was her friend and a customer from time to time. "Call me Maggie" likely her directive because it was how this man Arthur knew her, not as Polly the prostitute. When Ethan saw the two of them arguing below his window, he expected Maggie was scolding her friend about almost blowing her cover by mocking the fake name, a name she reserved for Ethan alone. Dressed as the physician, he would never have been seen keeping company with thieves, beggars or prostitutes and she was keen to know it. There was (and would be again) a strategic advantage to his upper-crust society wardrobe beyond the defensive posture assumed by investigative personnel approaching him. It could make him quite a prized mark to the other prostitutes he may need to possibly lure in, using his appearance as bait to continue the task.

The task. It took the death of a woman and his acceptance of the task at hand to pull Ethan out of this seventy-plus-hour long anguish of emotions he did not even know were part of his psyche. The woman was gone. Now there was only "the job". Focused more than ever prior or post Flicker jump, Ethan became slowly but surely accustomed to the real possibility that Jack may remain in absentia for the duration. No longer languishing in the murky waters of the ocean tide of time, instead, Ethan found his directive and purpose in a clear, lucid stream of consciousness. The clarity was such that, in preparation for the next scheduled victim, Annie Chapman, focus *was* the directive, complete concentration on his memory embedded knowledge of every nuance in the case. The timeframe for the next historical murder was tight. It required precision, attention to detail with single-minded purpose. Emphasis placed on the thirty minute window, maybe forty-five, it was not much time either way for opportunity to strike. The time frame depended on witness testimonies and medical evaluations documented in police reports. Ethan knew he needed to fully utilize the next few days leading up to a duty plagued encounter. Either from a distance or up close and personal, fate with extreme intent, Annie Chapman was destined to die.

Of course, he would have to go over all the routes again, city sidewalks leading to the back yard of 29 Hanbury Street. Unlike the method he utilized for Maggie, it was different now. This time only working the scene during the busiest hours of the day, there would be no shadow seeking from this point on. He'd need only play the part of the horny medical professional out for an early morning romp, a bit of fun. The only shadowing to be done by Ethan would be in stalking fashion, knowing his next femme fatale's movements more than twelve hours in advance of their destiny-driven meeting. By the time their fateful moment arrived he would have memorized every hair on her head. It had to be, as there could be no mistakes. He had surmised over recent days that this was a necessary element of his preparation, to know how she walks and talks and dresses, to know how she speaks, to *know* Annie Chapman. Compelled by a self-discipline to purge his personal emotions from "the job" ethics played no part in it as he came to reason that it wasn't under the guise of decision making or moral judgment or fearing for his immortal soul. These five women were already dead and this had already happened. It was going to happen again.

Naturally, he'd prefer to wait in the wings but as the understudy, he had to know the lines, just in case the star got a flat tire on the way to the theatre, again. Yes! Of course he'd rather sit back, not to enjoy the show but to fulfill his original purpose in making this trip, to identify the real culprit. Nothing would please him more than to relinquish the task to the master. He'd never have to hold that bloody blade again! However, if he had to, he would. There was no higher purpose than preserving the timeline. Ethan knew he would have to be prepared to walk out on that stage again. Either way, it was his "job".

He stepped out of his quarters and into the streets for the first time in over three days. Dressed in his clean physician attire, hat and polished shoes, he strolled hands in his pockets like he had not a care in the world. As Ethan worked his way toward Commercial Street, he purchased a common walking cane from a vendor who had a stand over on Old Montague Street. He whistled and twirled the cane, tipping his hat to the ladies passing by on a busy avenue. Ethan was not acting. In fact, it was the possible newfound role forcing the man's confidence in the mission to realign, as he knew the control was his and his alone.

Turning north onto Commercial Street he heard a young paperboy bellowing headlines from the day's newsprint.

"Read all about it! Extra! Extra! Man only known as LEATHER APRON suspect in Whitechapel murders. Read all about it! Paper, sir?"

Pulling the proper coinage from his pocket, Ethan gave it to the boy in exchange for that print. It was of nostalgic fascination to hold this particular paper physically in his hands, headlines he only read copies of online in a library during his research. "Leather Apron" as this man was known, would be publicly identified as John Pizer the day before Annie Chapman's death. He'd been extorting money, strong-arming prostitutes at knife point over the past year. It had recently come to light, backed up by corroborating stories from several of the women he threatened. This tied into the anti-Semitic sentiment in Whitechapel. John Pizer would be arrested on the 10th of September and subsequently released when he provided alibis for the prior murders. Ethan knew what was coming before the police did, or anyone else for that matter. He continued walking as he read an article he'd already committed to memory, yet it seemed different from this unique visual perspective. As he came upon the name Mary Ann "Polly" Nichols, Ethan abruptly stopped.

"Mind yourself, mate!" A passerby dodged him as he blocked sidewalk traffic.

Ethan stood aside, watching the man pass. As he made his way in front of him, he looked up to see where he'd stopped. There he stood, outside the Ten Bells Pub.

"Fuck!" Ethan said to himself, lowering his head and quickly facing away from the patrons inside, fearing he may be recognized or the ghost of Maggie might step through the doors and identify him as her murderer. If she were still alive he'd kill her just for fucking with his head so much. He stepped up his pace, making it to the next corner and discarding the paper. He didn't need to read what he already knew. He needed to just get "the job" done. Reaching Hanbury Street he turned right onto the road to his next meeting with destiny until he came upon the backyard entrance to #29, the place he might be leaving Annie Chapman's body in four nights.

For the next three days, Ethan would take his strolls in a visibly cocky manner, as if he owned the streets of Whitechapel. He could feel his confidence building as he held the pocket watch open in his right hand while timing the different routes to and from his lodging and the next kill zone on Hanbury. During the last day of the survey, he'd finalized his choice of a route, selecting the one from which he could assess the traffic most efficiently as well as have prime accessibility through to the back yard on Hanbury. He wore local attire for this day to appear more unassuming for this delicate and clandestine task. He then had the day to get some of his bangers and mash on Whitechapel Road and eat as he sat on a window ledge and watched the traffic pass. The air was a bit brisk and a hot and delicious meal was the perfect remedy to warm him up. Ethan was treating this day like the last hours of a holiday. He was completely relaxed, having a picnic. He did not know if he was fooling the crowds or just fooling himself. He surrendered to the calm in the same way a patient with a terminal diagnosis eventually accepts the inevitable. Worrying or crying over it was not going to change the sequence of required actions and necessary outcome. No amount of panic ever resolved anything. He accepted his terminal case. Not his, but that of these women. Over the past several days Ethan had taken the perspective that the victims were already dead and fulfilling their prophetic ending, if needed, was merely a formality of great expectation.

His visibility paramount to maintaining his mental state, being forced by proxy to appear psychologically intact in public, inside the confines of his room was quite another story. As the first of several site checks on Annie Chapman's whereabouts and movements rapidly approached, based in no small part on the testimony of her friend, Amelia Palmer, Ethan was overcome with violent tremors from adrenaline. He stood naked in front of the mirror, dowsing himself with basin water, what now seemed ritualistic in manner. The cold fluid combined with the chilling air intruding through his perpetually open window added to this uncontrollable quivering. There was no fear in his mind; performance anxiety might be a more appropriate diagnosis of his trembling. He could visualize the entire act he was designated to carry out in due course, should the real killer again neglect to attend an event slated for the early hours of the following morning. He could also reason with himself how the process would come about and conclude. However, there were unknown variables within a troubled soul. He was not sure which Ethan would surface at the actual moment he needed to muster the cold, sterile, rational scientist. The indulgence of doubt wasn't an affordable commodity on a budget based of necessity.

He thought about it in the privacy of his room, agreeing to allow what gripped him have its way, as this too shall pass. Let the trembling occur, let it have its way with him as long as necessary to get this out of his system, just as long as it subsides before his scheduled departure to scope out the 5:00 p.m. whereabouts of one Annie Chapman. It did not matter. He was sure of one thing, above all. Once out in public his façade of stoic demeanor would naturally return. The tremors could have their way with him for the moment but he still had yet to shave. This was going to suck. If he could only avoid drawing his own blood, he'd consider it a successful effort.

Ethan was mastering the straight razor. Not a single nick from his shave, the fine razor provided in his medical bag by The Consortium. They thought about hygiene. Too bad they hadn't thought of everything! He still felt himself to be the proverbial stranger in a strange land, a Connecticut Yankee in King Arthur's Court, living akin to the classic 1889 publication, cosmic forces providing the paradox, happening the year before Mark Twain's story would come to life in the pages of a novel.

"Hells bells!" Ethan thought to himself, *"Maybe Twain is here on holiday, here in England penning the tale whilst this is happening. Perhaps he is a Scope, too!"* In a spontaneous fit of laughter, he said aloud, "Never the Twain shall meet!"

Switching his outfit to another of local design, his shirt, trousers, shoes and coat, undergarments and hosiery worn the way Maggie told him to avoid itching, he felt another twinge of remorse thinking of how helpful she'd been to him then how he'd repaid her kindness. Nothing to be done for it. Nothing. He was going to walk over to Dorset Street then loiter in the vicinity just before five o'clock, when and where he expected to find Annie Chapman in an ill state, conversing with Amelia Palmer as they discussed plans for Saturday night. His expected time was almost identical to his walks from his flat on Dorset Street over to Bucks Row during his first few days in this era, only a little over a week before and yet it seemed like eons ago. He always timed it on his *new* pocket watch, anywhere from thirteen to fifteen minutes. For this trip he was once again taking the more casual route, portraying the man not on a mission of any sort. Estimating he'd have to leave in roughly twenty minutes to make it to Dorset just before five in the evening, seeking his visual confirmation, surveillance imperative to definitively identify this woman with his own two eyes, off he went for a stroll.

Ethan was, of course, familiar with Dorset Street as the site of the first room let to him upon his arrival, the room with indoor plumbing every time it rained. While the main road, Commercial Street was churning with activity, Dorset was dimly lit, mostly accessed by those staying in its run down lodgings along the passage. In the few minutes he leaned against a lesser lit section of one of the buildings, as history recorded and he expected, he spied a woman who fit Annie Chapman's description exiting one of the lodgings across the alley. If he was on point with his research and this was actually her, she would be approached in the next few minutes by another woman by the name of Amelia Palmer. Two minutes passed. *"Here she comes!"* It was in his research he discovered Amelia's testimony about these transpiring events leading up to Annie Chapman's death. *"Brilliant!"* So far Amelia was damn precise in her tale recounting their encounter. If all the testimonials were expected to be as on point as hers, this should go smoothly and without incident. Of course it would.

"I was never caught." He mumbled beneath his breath.

Amelia departed the alley. Knowing the history, she would be returning shortly to Annie. He chose this time to cross the street diagonally to get as close as he could possibly come to Jack the Ripper's next victim without drawing attention to himself so that he could get a better view of her face and clothing. She was short and stout in physique. Pale in complexion with brown hair and blue eyes, she was half bent over and unobservant of his passing. Ethan was satisfied with his assignment and was now comfortably assured he would later identify her in the early morning hours on Hanbury Street. As he exited the alley, Amelia Palmer was rounding the corner returning to Annie Chapman's side. As Ethan in turn entered Commercial Street he found himself stopping in a shadowy corner across from Ten Bells Pub. He stared at the entrance, imagining Maggie walking out of the front door and waving at him as he waited for her. He had hoped the whole incident in his room was a bad dream instead of a wide awake nightmare, hoping it was a case of mistaken identity. Polly Nichols was dead but Maggie was still there to help him get through the madness. Were it only the truth. With a heavy sigh meant to unburden him, Ethan shoved his hands in his pockets and traveled back to his place, stopping at a few vendors to get what necessities he might need for the night.

Returning to his lodging, he stopped in the kitchen, buying some coffee to bring into his room. There would be no meal before the upcoming task.

Should Ethan feel an urge to purge, hopefully it would only manifest as dry heaves. He had it fixed in his mind. This event was going to be easier *yet* more difficult than his experience on Bucks Row. The task was as complex as the emotion wrapped around it, feelings he was working diligently to dismiss. He had made every effort to harness all of his focus on the historical facts and his blueprint for the evening. Well aware he was a human being, better at empathy than apathy, he did not *want* to kill this woman, but if that low life bastard Jack was a no show, he would *have* to do it for him. Fucker!

This pending incident had deeper impact than historical preservation. Through Ethan's unprecedented access to the future, as well as the past, knowing the victims was not a side show but an added attraction, an eventual benefit to the victim. Annie Chapman was sickly, not from the recent physical altercation she had with one Eliza Copper (who was competing for the affections of a customer) but sick beyond the black eye and bruised chest she'd received in the tussle with her nemesis. Medical records indicated she was suffering from disease of both the lungs and brain. It was suggested she was dying of either tuberculosis or syphilis. Ethan impaled in mind that this would be a mercy killing, if he had to kill her, sparing the woman from a long agonizing death spiral downward, much akin to Anson Van Ruden ending the life of one Japanese soldier. He wished he could sit her down and explain things to her wherein at the conclusion of their conversation and his big reveal, she would hug Ethan and thank him for his heartfelt actions taken on her behalf to end her suffering. If only it were that simple.

Having once more disrobed, laying naked on the bed, staring blankly up at the ceiling, Ethan could not decide if the absence of permeating odors in the air was no longer apparent due to becoming desensitized to it or if colder night temperatures had diminished what was often carried on the breeze. It had rained slightly between six and seven that evening but it had completely subsided by 10:30 p.m. He tried to imagine the cold air swirling about the room somehow empowering him with icy veins, invigorating him for the night's required task. The man had a job to do.

XVII.
COMING INTO HIS OWN

He needed to focus all his attention on the upcoming scheduled whereabouts of Annie Chapman. Her next recorded activities would be in about an hour, returning to Crossingham's lodging house where she would ask permission to enter the public kitchen area. There she'd linger for another hour, seen by a few people drinking the brew she concocted, taking the pills she'd picked up at the casual ward apothecary. Stating it was for her ailments, she then told a tenant she was going to her room to lay down. When she arrived, Annie informed the manager she did not have enough money for her room yet but asked that it not be given away, as she'd soon be going out to get the needed pence for the rent. She was reported heading in the direction of Spitalfield's Market between 1:35 and 2:00 a.m. on 8 September 1888.

Ethan's fateful encounter with Annie Chapman wasn't to be much later, around five in the morning over on Hanbury Street. Reclined onto his bed, he recalled some fictional suspense classics he'd read when he was a boy in school at St. Leonards, stories such as H.G. Well's "The Invisible Man" and Robert Louis Stephenson's "Dr. Jekyll and Mr. Hyde". His power of knowing the future before anyone else did along with the cloaking effect of night gave him the fascia of invisibility, allowing him to move stealth-like through the streets of the East End of London. His likeness to Jekyll and Hyde was evolving, growing more complex with each passing day. It was a fascinating tale of two men in one. As Ethan always deciphered the story akin to a tale of an alcoholic run amuck, the potion which transformed the physician into a raving lunatic killer was simply too good a vintage. For Ethan, his knowledge was intoxicating, not in the sense of being drunk with power but the voracious thirst for it, drinking in the thoughts and ideas of those before him. He found irony in the fact his identity for the jump was as a physician, but he didn't fancy himself comparative to Mr. Hyde. He knew the physical disguise as well as the guise he had to mentally portray during the gruesome process, should he be forced to undertake it with Annie Chapman. Though he'd much prefer to watch from a distance as a voyeur in the night, he still found solace in the dizzying inebriation of knowing everything occurring and what was still to come. Without this omnipotent power, Ethan would be another mere mortal murderer in a nomadic existence. There was only one missing piece to the puzzle, not knowing for certain the role he would be asked to play tonight.

Finishing up his now cold coffee and ritualistic *in the zone* meditation practice of pacing, it was time for him to get ready. He once again dressed in his upper social class attire with the knowledge, hope and acceptance that he'd stand out enough to be a tempting approach for Annie Chapman who needed to make time to make rent. Placing his earlier purchases from the street vendors inside his medical bag, he had bought a thick leather satchel along with a bunch of rags which would, if need be, do the job of soaking up the blood when he removed the uterus from her inert body.

It was about 4:30 a.m. when he departed for his destination, Hanbury Street. He would take Osborn Street straight up to Hanbury, arriving near the historic location, number 29 just before five in the morning. He need only wait for Annie to arrive in the next half hour or so. Ethan knew that John Anderson, a tenant at 29 Hanbury, had been reported sitting on the backyard steps around 4:45 a.m. adjusting his shoe, seeing and hearing nothing odd in the yard. There was always some speculation as to Elizabeth Long's testimony to the authorities as to when she saw Annie Chapman speaking to a man on the street. During her interview she reported hearing the Black Eagle Brewery clock on Brick Lane chiming on the half hour, marking the time as 5:30 a.m. when she saw the man and woman speaking, but some researchers believe she could have been mistaken, having heard the quarter past chime of the clock. It mattered not. He was already there. This was why he needed to be prompt, on time, if not early to cover opposing opinions contradicting Long's statement to police.

The air was chilly again, reminiscent of eight days prior, as if the elements were conspiring to set the scene. There were a few people passing along the way, coming and going from work or a late Friday night or early Saturday morning rendezvous, only a few stragglers around. As if on cue, she appeared. He recognized Annie right away from her attire, still half a road from him. Ethan had to play the odds now. If everything was by design in the Universe any plan he had was already decided long before he made the jump through Flicker. He'd chosen to play the part coyly, some unsuspecting gentleman, allowing Annie Chapman to approach him. Removing his pocket watch, he stared at the time, 5:09 a.m. As he did in the alley shadows before and after Polly Nichols' passing, Ethan waited and prayed that he was wrong about himself and his destiny, begging to be released from this awful obligation, hoping that before Annie could spot him she would be approached by his salvation, the true mad murderer. He'd hoped to be spared the continuing role. He prayed to be saved. It is always darkest before the dawn and it had not yet dawned on Ethan that he was a player in this drama for a reason. No more doubt. No more excuses. No time.

From the corner of his eye he could see Annie sizing him up, deciding whether or not to solicit him. This was going to happen…it was inevitable. As it was written, so it would be done. Surrender was in his heart. It was his destiny. To prompt her, he peered up for a moment then offered a friendly smile. She walked up to him now considering the gesture an invitation.

"Evenin' gov'ner." Annie began cheerfully. "Bit of a nip in the air tonight."

Ethan realized one certain thing. He was not an actor. However, neither was he concerned that his lack of thespian training would alter a supreme plan, one cosmic in nature. He just did not want to hear his own bad performance stink up the air any more than it already was, but his momentary pause was a sign to Annie of rejecting her advance. She began to step behind him and continue on her way. Ethan had to act fast to correct the issue. He turned around, facing her directly. For a moment he just looked at her with his mouth agape, shocked by his own lack of social skills.

"Yes." He muttered. "It is, quite cold, out here, in the air, tonight, I mean."

Annie laughed at the man, not to be insulting but rather charmed by an awkward response she wasn't used to and didn't expect, not one typical of her usual clientele. She actually had quite a nice smile, much better teeth than Polly. Ethan rolled his eyes and shook his head at his performance, judging himself harshly.

"Well, aren't you the gigglemug?" He tried to make light of the darkness.

"Well, perhaps I can warm ya up a bit if ya fancy the business?" Annie was not shy, though her flirtatious manner was far more subtle than Maggie's approach.

Ethan's expression changed for a moment as he reflected back to Maggie saying almost exactly the same phrase in his room the night his whole world turned upside down. It unfortunately humanized Annie that much more. He would have to expect that phrase from each of the Ripper's victims, discarding the connection as his link to a fictitious character Mary Ann Nichols had concocted. Annie began to step away again, thinking she struck out based on Ethan's demeanor.

"Wait. Please." Ethan implored her. "I'm sorry, I'm just not used to... this."

"Ah, yer first time then, love?" Annie asked with genuine interest.

"Second, actually." His prophetically ominous statement had another meaning, a more insidious content than she could ever imagine.

Ethan did not hear her response, as another woman walked past them. He made every effort to obscure his visual identity from her while interrupting Annie.

"So, will you then?"

"Yes." She replied, caught off guard by his abruptness.

Just as the woman turned the corner at the end of the street Ethan heard a clock chime. It was a quarter past five. The woman must have been Elizabeth Long, right on cue. She'd been mistaken about the time, as some of the historical records stated. It was not 5:30 a.m. when she saw Chapman, but instead, the alternate assumption, that it was 5:15. From his vantage point Ethan could see clearly in every direction. There was nobody else in sight, no hardhearted criminal lurking in the shadows of a dark alley, just softhearted Professor LaPierre thrust down the gullet of the beast, as the beast. As an integral part played, as history in the making, the time had come for him to abandon the role of understudy and take the lead, time to commit history.

Because of the varying schedules of local workers, most of the lodging's main access halls to each room were always unlocked, most of the time merely left wide open. Number 29 Hanbury was no exception to the rule. They walked the few doors down from where they met, stopping to chat then continuing on as Annie Chapman held onto the arm of her momentary suitor.

"I see the bag you're carryin'. Yer a doctor?" she inquired.

"Yes, I'm here for a speaking engagement at the hospital."

"Oh! An out-of-towner! A rich doctor then, are ya?" Hoping to make her rent.

"Far from rich. I'm comfortable enough."

"Comfortable sounds nice." She snuggled up closer wrapping both arms around his left elbow. Without missing a step in her pace or looking up at him, Annie asked one last question. "Yer not the Whitechapel killer, are ya now?"

More surprising to Ethan than the question was his instant response.

"Heaven's no! Why do you think I give speeches? I hate the sight of blood!"

A trigger was pulled in his psyche. A defensive trigger cocked and ready to fire away for survival purposes. A clever corner of his mind accessed to protect himself from becoming detected for his true intention. Annie Chapman laughed with relief, deciding a killer would not possess wealth and wit accompanied by purely irrational violence. A girl had to be careful nowadays. She took him at his word then laughed again, squeezing his arm a bit more tightly. It was the last time she would laugh.

In gentlemanly style he allowed her the lead into the hall access to 29 Hanbury.

"Are you staying here?" Another question, she wished he would say yes.

"God, no. I've a flat let to me on Bakers Row nearer the hospital."

"Then why the stroll so far? There are ladies workin' those streets." Seemingly suspicious all of a sudden, her companion had a quick retort to ease her mind.

"Well, too close to the hospital, someone coming on or off shift might recognize me out at this hour in the company of a lady." Ethan came prepared with an answer for every question. He was fucking brilliant, he thought, clever as hell.

Stepping out the rear door of the hallway into a fenced back yard, Ethan closed the door behind them. The two of them moved to the left, nearer the fence dividing them from 27 Hanbury Street. Ethan surveyed the yard. As expected, no bystanders within view. As he walked and scanned the perimeter he wound up standing in front of Annie, her back to the lodging through which they'd just passed. They stood for a moment not speaking. Annie placed her hands on his chest and moved in closer as Ethan froze, as nervous as if he were on a first date. This was the unknown factor he was trying to shake, the uncertainty of whether or not he was able to do what he must do. He had to quickly choose which of the different emotions he experienced over the past week he needed to do the job.

"The job."

"Beg ya pardon?" Annie said, appearing confused.

Ethan zoned. He dropped the bag where he stood and lunged at the throat of his much shorter victim with both hands. She managed to get out a weak audible "no" before he cut off her air. With his leverage, he pushed her backwards to the ground as he continued to squeeze with all his strength, restricting the access of blood and oxygen to her brain. He needed her to pass out. Either Annie Chapman was stronger than she appeared or Ethan LaPierre was a weakling or doing it all wrong, but Annie was fighting back, kicking, trying hard to beat him off but his arms were too long, her legs flailing, her hands trying to pry his loose. Losing this battle, he had no other option but to win the war. Freeing his left hand, Ethan reached into his medical bag. The knife, deliberately placed atop the rags and the satchel bag was easily removed. Metamorphosis occurred as he came into his own painstaking self-awareness.

Remembering every detail of this slaughter, Ethan made no mistake in the cuts. The first was reportedly to be along her throat. He repositioned his right hand, using the butt of it to drive her lower jaw upward, forcing her to expose her neck fully to his blade. He went for the deep cut first, slicing across her throat from left to right. The sharpness of this eight-inch-long surgical steel blade was mesmerizing. It slid easily and deeply through the skin, muscle and tendons of the left side of her neck, causing an explosive rush of adrenaline drenched blood to spray, painting the fence to her left, nearly fourteen inches from the cold ground Annie laid upon.

His first cut continued, sawing as he went, the butcher taking an order for a slice of filet from a fresh side of beef. Ethan tried not to, he truly tried, but he could not stop looking into Annie's eyes as he completed the almost full severing of her head with one cut. Any fight she had remaining left with her life. She may not have died right away. Shock may have set in prior to the last few beats of her heart, the sound of one life marching off into the past. To repeat the patterns, he'd duplicate details in the reports from Dr. George Bagster Phillips who documented every wound to precise measurements. Arriving around 6:30 a.m., he conducted a thorough examination on site before Annie was taken to the mortuary. Based on his knowledge of its facts, he'd have to make two additional incisions, both entries on the left side of her neck. With precision he plunged the blade in facing her spine then pushed it in a carving motion, pulling white tendons and red muscle up with every swipe of the blade as it hit bone, the vertebra protecting her spinal cord. Blood sprayed then oozed from the wounds. Ethan had to replicate the last incision a half inch lower just as deep, up to the spine again, according to the job description.

Annie was finished but Ethan had more to do and now he was racing the clock. He removed his blood-splattered hand from her blood-drenched chin, as well as the ornate white, red lined handkerchief that she had tied securely around her neck. Her tongue had been pinched between her teeth and appeared swollen. Ethan hopped to the left side of her body next to the fence and pulled the leather satchel and rags out quickly, stuffing half of the rags inside the bottom of it then placing it next to the bag past her feet. Lifting up her two petticoats to expose the lower half of her body, he had a much better angle for opening up her stomach, puncturing and slicing fatty tissue, gaining access to other internal organs simultaneously.

There was a specific incident in Ethan's childhood where, in one primary school science class, he was expected to dissect a living frog, which he promptly refused to do to the poor, defenseless creature. His actions or lack thereof found him going to the Principal's office for some discipline, disobeying an order, in so many words. He stood his ground and elected to receive punishment in a conscientious objection to killing the frog. Ethan couldn't reject this dissection. Principals of the time would not allow it but for Ethan, it was a matter of principle. The Immutable laws of the Universe would have none of it. He was bound by history, by duty to follow through with this far greater desecration. Maybe his science teacher would pass him now.

Again, he plunged the blade into the far right side of her abdomen then began slicing a half circle down and past her vaginal region then fully around to his side of her hips, following every detail learned in an anatomy class he had been privy to attend at Oxford Medical College. Based upon Ethan's autopsy practice on cadavers, he began peeling back the skin, fatty tissue and muscle from her midsection like a page in a large book, slicing through any superficial connections that he missed on the first cut and then resting it on her thorax region. From the case research, photos, reports and cadaver training, he carefully severed the intestines from the mesenteric attachments. Laying the knife at the opening edge of the incision, with his two free hands, he lifted the intestines from her body, placing the mass up on the right hand side of her chest. In doing so he lost his balance, slipping in the blood then falling back toward the fence. Quickly reaching out with his right hand to support himself against it, his hand landed where the blood from Annie's neck had sprayed and slid off the spot, causing Ethan's full weight and measure of a man to strike fully against the fence. Repositioning himself to the left side of his victim, determined to finish what he started, with a surgical precision and acute memory of the actions recorded, he cut out her uterus, cleanly removing it along with all the connecting appendages, slicing away the upper portion of her vagina and posterior two-thirds of her bladder. He took these parts of Annie and placed them in the leather satchel.

Then he grabbed the second pile of rags with the exception of two of them and stuffed them on top of the uterus and other internal organs before shoving it all into his medical bag along with the weapon. Ethan took the other two rags, using them to wipe off his hands, sleeves and shoes as completely as possible then threw those into the bag before closing it. He repositioned Annie's legs exactly as she was found by resident John Davis, scheduled to occur in less than fifteen minutes. He wanted to wipe his brow of sweat but did not dare, not knowing if he had wiped his hands clean enough in this dark foreboding yard that he wouldn't stain his face. If he were apprehended, he'd have to talk up a blue streak to explain away the red streak across his forehead. The cold air should evaporate the perspiration within minutes anyway, he thought. Ethan gently kissed Annie on the forehead, turning her head to the right, as reported, speaking to her one last time.

"It's a far, far better place you go to, Miss Annie Chapman." Ethan whispered a few kind words into her dead ears. Arising from her corpse, he calmly crossed to the back door then stepped through the hall, exiting out the front door onto Hanbury Street. The slightest hint of daylight rising with its gray hue bathing the horizon, as Ethan checked his pocket watch, he discovered he was right on time. 5:43 a.m.

XVIII.
ALL IN GOOD TIME

The cadence Ethan established would be considered a hurried pace but not one as conspicuous as to draw attention to himself. The trek back to his lodging was the most dangerous because of the spoils he'd claimed during his interlude with Annie. He held the medical bag close to his chest with both hands, rolled up in his coat for safekeeping, embracing the bundle to absorb any leakage from the organs he hoped were sufficiently covered by rags wrapped within the leather satchel. He never even checked his pocket watch. No need. Time was on his side. He need only get where he was going without detection and it was prime time to make the journey, early on Saturday morning. Although foot traffic was light, he chose to take a more discreet route, back alleyways to lessen the possibility of chance encounters. Many a worker coming home from local slaughterhouses traveled with bloodstained clothes. Still, given the prior murders and subsequent uptick in foot patrols in the area, he did not want to risk suspicion and testimonials from anyone curious about his appearance who could report him to authorities. Along his path there were several times when he felt someone was approaching too closely. He would slip into a doorway or slide down a wall into the fetal position with his head tucked down trying to look like a vagrant or street vermin, one of "the untouchables". Ethan went so far as to scratch and cough to offend those travelers, thus informing them without a word to keep their distance. He was but a few roads away from his 19th Century sanctuary, a room with a new world view.

Coming upon a chimneysweep in his travels, Ethan stared at the man all covered in ashes and soot. What a clever disguise! With the vision planted in his brain, what next came to him was a favorite moment from "Mary Poppins". *"Winds in the east, mist coming in, like somethin' is brewin' and bout to begin. Can't put me finger on what lies in store, but I fear what's to happen all happened before."* He could hear the innocence of his childhood in the words, a comforting memory.

The rising sun still hidden below the horizon shot perforations of light through morning clouds as upward rays. Legend was these upward rays indicated someone passing to Heaven, perhaps not just a silly superstition. Ethan felt vindicated by this action, best serving Annie her own slice of Heaven by removing the burden of her decaying human form, releasing her to the light and life above and beyond. Mercy. It was a mercy killing in every sense of the word, a deliverance, a kindness extended in her own best interest. Convincing himself he had done this vile thing on Annie's behalf eased the burden he carried. What he likewise carried in the bag he clutched would get him the death penalty. There was much to consider. Ethan walked alone in half light, finding his way through his darkest thoughts.

At the corners where Old Montague, Hanbury Street and Bucks Row intersect, he slipped around where a recreational area was located, moving past it, behind the row of houses. Taking longer than usual strides, Ethan arrived at the rear entrance of his lodging. Moving quickly and quietly past the kitchen he heard voices of other occupants. Though he never glanced up to make eye contact, hoping no one would bother to note his presence, he was alerted to the contrary by one who'd taken notice of him in passing. He knew he'd been seen when he heard the man speak.

"Looks like *someone* had a good Friday night!" Other men laughed along.

If they only knew. Ethan never reacted or even turned around. Taking the stairs two steps at a time, he opened the door to his room, disappeared from sight. Closed and locked, he leaned back against it in relief and sheer exhaustion. Physically and mentally spent, for a fleeting moment he smiled and looked up to the heavens, well, toward the ceiling. Feeling grateful for whatever assistance he received to get him through it, he likewise felt the supreme satisfaction of a job well done on his end of the cosmic conspiracy. It happened, across the board, down to the last detail, exactly as it was written in the history books and medical records, it happened. Everything he knew, every image he studied or word he memorized was brought to bear in his endeavors to keep the timeline continuity intact and he did it! Could it be that all of this had happened before? Time would tell.

Ethan moved with heavy legs into the room. His arms aching from carrying the overweight medical bag, he placed it down on the dresser and poured himself some water. Loosening his tie and first three buttons of his shirt, he emptied his cup then sat down on the bed to remove his shoes, pausing to reflect and laugh once again.

"Perfect!" Ethan said to himself. His mind was reeling with details swirling all around the pitch perfect timing of the event, a lone witness Elizabeth Long passing them at the precise time the clock chimed. His elaborate knife work and extraction of the uterus was textbook, as if a murderer was gloating from within the professor. He had to admit the positioning of her body and head was precise, no differences from images taken at the crime scene, right down to the removal of her rings.

"Fuck!" Ethan threw himself back on the bed. "Bloody Fucking hell! The rings! The bloody fucking rings!" How could he have forgotten her rings? In the mortuary reports and subsequent police investigation, it was noted that Annie Chapman was in possession of three brass rings that were chronicled as 'missing' after the murder. He had forgotten to remove them from her corpse. Ethan saw them! They were on her fingers! He saw them while she struggled, fighting for her life, trying to pry his hands from her throat. In his mad rush to exit in time he neglected to repeat history and take the rings. "Fuck!" He repeated again and again, not knowing the depth of significance this tiny error would have, as there was no margin for error. What kind of ripples would be created by tossing *this* pebble in the river of time? It hit him as a bomb, a nuclear explosion in his brain. Having no immediate knowledge of these implications prompted him to pace. Ethan knew, even the slightest of changes was significant to the timeline of events; how significant was yet to be determined. Only time would tell the tale altered by his neglectful failure to complete the task.

Ethan wasn't going to let himself off the hook. He began his animalistic pacing to and from the window and bed, all the while removing more and more layers of clothing until he was again stark naked. Every raw human emotion ran through his body. Coupled with cold morning air, it chilled him to the bone. Fear, rage, doubt and sadness among many other sensations arose in his psyche then subsided, only to return with a vengeance moments later. Each thought there to taunt and torture him. No one! Not Colin or Anson or the ghosts of Polly and Annie could beat him up any more than he was doing to himself. He was too smart to be that stupid, too in control to lose it over such an oversight. Gripping the edge of the desk under the window with both hands, he hung his head low, shaking it in denial. It was not the brutal murder of one sick, helpless woman committed by his own hands that ripped him apart. He'd already reconciled himself to the task. The fact that he did not fully accomplish the task tore him asunder. Mr. Meticulous. Mr. No Stone Left Unturned. According to Ethan, the self-proclaimed king of due diligence, in an ongoing fit of self-deprecation, he had to admit he'd fucked it up royally.

Then suddenly, Ethan realized he still had one chance to fix what he broke! Oh! Joy! An opportunity right under his nose, a perfect opportunity to right this wrong, to put the timeline back on track. Up until this time he had only used his physician's façade in a limited capacity, to be an easy mark for Annie, somebody lacking street sense. Mostly it got in his way. This time it would pave the way into the morgue. It was time to use his credentials and proper attire as his part in a power play, to obtain access to the mortuary and get those fucking brass rings back.

"Grab the brass rings!" Ethan chuckled at his wittiness, especially under duress. He turned from the desk, crossing to the dresser to refill his cup of water. His mind so preoccupied, he did not notice the wet spot and stepped right in it. Ethan slipped, almost falling. He caught himself by bracing the top of the saturated dresser.

"No, no, no, no, no. Fuck me. No!"

Blood. Seemingly everywhere, it had seeped down the sides of the dresser onto the floor, oozing from the internal organs he removed from Annie Chapman's body just an hour before. It had soaked through the rags and satchel and began leaking from the corners of his medical bag. He was revisiting the carnage as he'd harvested her organs so quickly, they didn't have the chance to bleed out before being ragged and bagged. Ethan grabbed up his physician's attire from the floor, placing it on the bed out of harm's way then took one of the outfits he bought to wipe up the splatters. What a mess! He turned the soaked clothes over, opened the medical bag and placed the sopping satchel of organs on top of them. Placing all of it back into the medical bag, Ethan knew he had to dispose of this and fast. He also knew exactly where to do it. Within the next twenty-four hours Ethan would discard the bloody organs he cut from a woman then proceed to make his way nonchalantly over to what was left of the same woman's body to dispose her of the rings. He'd use his fine physician's attire to get his foot in the door at the mortuary or in hospital, wherever he needed to go, all of this done for the greater good, for the sake of maintaining the timeline. Professor Ethan LaPierre, poster child for the Flicker Project.

Washing and wiping his hands dry before peering at his pocket watch, he didn't want to smudge it with blood again. It was 7:16 a.m. Although he was exhausted, he still had so much to do before he could rest. This was the second time he'd have to work diligently removing both the visible blood stains on the lighter fabric of his tailored shirt and any remnants left on the darker fabrics of his coat and trousers. It all had to be clean and dry by sunset as Ethan would need to be out in public again, accomplishing what remained to be done.

For the moment, he had a grip on his emotions. Settling into a more purposeful mindset, his first order of business was to bathe in a basin of water. Residual blood notwithstanding, what he didn't wipe off at the murder scene, it was the event itself Ethan hoped to wash away, to cleanse his soul along with his body. To be rid of the smell, the sweat, the stain on his memory, all of it to be wiped away with the stroke of a washcloth. For Ethan this was an exercise in psychological cleansing that was fast becoming regimental in this post-murder purge ritual, redemptive in nature. He wanted the Universe to know what a sacrifice it was for him, as well as his victims. Bathing revived the man, for the time being, at least. Ethan put on his contemporary period outfit and went downstairs to replenish his pitcher with fresh water, dumping its pinkish, blood-tainted contents down the outhouse hole. Returning promptly, he bought some soap from the manager and more coffee grounds for the kitchen kettle. Ethan needed to call in the reinforcements. Caffeine…and more caffeine.

For the next two hours Ethan spent his time washing out all stains he could from his physician's outfit, placing them in position near the window to dry unwrinkled. As much use as this suit already had, it went far beyond normal wear and tear. He knew he would have to visit downtown London and have another one tailor-made, perhaps a fine suit from Savile Row, the best of the best. After all he'd been through to this point, Ethan thought he deserved some pampering, especially considering he was apparently going to wear the original down to bare threads all too fast. Sooner than that he would need to purchase another set of "local" attire since one was now a blood barrier stuffed inside his medical bag. Once his current suit had sufficiently dried, he planned to change into it and again assume the corresponding personality. Then he'd make his first attempt to access London Hospital on Whitechapel Road. It was where the most available incinerator for *doctors* would be, the place to dispose of Annie Chapman's innards discreetly. Amputations and exploratory surgeries on cadavers were common practice in 19th Century medicine and, by necessity, a need for all remains to be destroyed properly so as not to create an environment ripe with disease. Confident in his newly acquired persona, Ethan knew he'd get it done.

As the long day passed into night, Ethan could hear murmuring beneath his own window as word spread on the street of the gruesome death of Annie Chapman. He gazed down upon them knowingly, watching the vendors gossiping, ladies gasping in disbelief. Feeling almost omnipotent, observing from a higher plain of existence, untouchable and undetectable, the drama continued to play out on the stage below. It could have been titled "Whitechapel" with bit actors scrambling around, making absurd assumptions and jumping to conclusions that, after all the players had taken their last curtain call, would leave the case with a starring cast of thirty-one suspects including three doctors, claims of a royal conspiracy and even one female suspect. Thirty-one suspects, minimally, for a total of eighteen murders. Truth be told, they didn't have a clue.

During a period early in the 21st Century several authors claimed that they had definitive DNA evidence that proved who Jack the Ripper was, yet, unfortunately, they had different players in the same game, including Aaron Kosminski and Walter Sickert, another coinciding book release on the horizon. Author Patricia Cornwell who discerned Sickert to be the real Jack the Ripper stated, "The biggest challenge in very old cases is chain of evidence and contamination." Her erudite observations came before another author, Russell Edwards, claimed the same of Kosminski. So, even though forensic science vastly improved over the centuries the fact is, just like the people gathering below Ethan's second floor lodging, it was sheer speculation, anybody's guess who the real killer was, but Ethan knew. He was tasked to Scope five specific women from eighteen murders committed. All had the same patterns of mutilation, leading the police to determine they were all falling victim under the same knife, same style: same killer. It left thirteen women whose attacker(s) were also never caught and punished. Still, the thrill seekers of empirical evidence in the most infamous unsolved case in history throw statements of "fact" against the wall of acceptance to see what sticks. Ethan knew the truth. He was stuck with the role.

He assumed either clothing he wrapped Annie's uterus in was holding back the blood or cooler temperatures already caused coagulation in the medical bag. Either way, Ethan could not and did not want to hold onto it any longer. He began dressing the part once again, donning his fanciest duds. Ready but waiting for darkness, his old friend, to fall upon the town, it was after 9:00 p.m. when he left his lodging, the medical bag tucked discreetly beneath his arm. Making certain not to draw attention of the gossip brigades clambering along Bakers Row, he once again exited through the back door of the lodging and took the back alley, made a left onto Whites Row then a right onto Thomas Street until he reached Whitechapel Road. Directly across the street was London Hospital. Slip out the back, Jack.

It's funny. Ethan, on his Flicker trial walkthroughs of Whitechapel had passed the hospital dozens of times but never had reason to go into the historical building. The street activity wasn't much different on the outside even with over a century of time separating his visits. The same vendor stands lined Whitechapel Road on the north side, selling a variety of merchandise from fruits and vegetables to clothing, accessories and rugs. The marketplace was bustling on a Saturday evening, a chorus of voices bartering, children displaying every energetic, emotionally charged noise they could get away with before being scolded, told to hush by their mother, if they had one. Orphans running the streets were reputed to be at an epidemic level during this time. Although they were children by adult standards, they learned quickly how to survive the elements and conditions just as well as their grown up counterparts.

The face of the hospital leered over Whitechapel Road. The five tall archways leading patients and visitors into the front entranceway of one of the world's most advanced medical education and research centers of its time, England had taken the lead, even in these darker times, as the beacon of civilization and progress. Barbaric compared to modern standards, where Ethan had come from, yet where the rest of the world was in comparison on the dusk of the 19th Century, the English character of sophistication became a driving force behind accomplishing many of the world's advances before their global counterparts in science, medicine and social structure.

Ethan sat down on a bench to rest on the far side of the street, taking in the view. Laying the bag beside him, he suddenly felt it begin to move! Startled, he looked behind him at a vagrant mutt who obviously had no master, licking away dried and lightly seeping blood lining the outer edges of the leather. In uncharacteristic form, he stood up then kicked at his ribs to ward off the poor pup. Other than his love of horses, he had no use for animals since his youth but never would he be so cruel as to harm a helpless, hungry stray. Never before now. The dog yelped and ran away.

Ethan waited for a moment for the horse and carriage traffic to diminish in order to cross Whitechapel Road, then he entered the side door on the west wall, past the tall wrought iron fencing where the medical staff arrived at start of shift. There was always an understood aristocracy associated with British physicians and never was the case when anyone questioned their validity or status in the hierarchy of authority and importance. Ethan's research in taking on this persona was, again, playing out to his advantage. He was greeted by several hospital staff recognizing the standard medical bag. Addressing him as *doctor* in passing, they went about their business. He accessed his memory of the hospital's layout and reaffirmed his destination via the posted signs until he arrived at the incinerators. Their evening shifts had already begun, a virtual skeleton crew compared to the day shift, far thinner in attendance, leaving Ethan to enter some of the lesser trafficked halls of the non-patient wards. As expected, he located the incinerator room where the boiler was already running, indicating someone was using is to discard hospital waste material and would return soon. He needed to be exacting in his disposal, yet prudent with the time provided. Annie Chapman's organs wrapped in rags inside his local attire, the weight of the bundle felt like a small pot roast as it was lifted and placed into an oven for dinner. He wasn't measuring in cannibalistic terms, rather, in comparative serving portions. Ethan smiled with that thought for no reason clear to him, yet his motive for smiling next was in satisfaction, completing the task of tossing his victim's remains into the fire, watching them transform to ash before his eyes. He could've tossed his bloody bag and medical instruments but he thought it would be too suspicious right now to purchase new equipment during an ongoing police investigation of the Whitechapel murders. No need to draw the spotlight. He would merely wash and dry everything, including the bag.

"Waste not. Want not." Ethan spoke softly to himself, making sure not to alert anyone in the vicinity to his reason for being there. Without incident or interference he exited the incinerator room and began his journey back through the corridors to the original entrance point. As he crossed through one of the large reception areas he looked up, spotting a familiar face, not someone he'd been properly introduced to but rather, a character from his research. Standing at the receiving table was none other than Inspector Frederick Abberline. He was interacting with some of the staff, no doubt, now in hot pursuit of clues following the death of Mary Ann Nichols and Annie Chapman. They never made eye contact and Abberline never even saw Ethan pass by. Once again, it made him smile knowing he was just as invisible physically as he was historically. Before exiting Ethan approached a clerical office attendee at her desk, seeking some information of his own, a clue or two about his next stop.

"Would you be ever so kind as to tell me who is on schedule at the mortuary on Old Montague Street at this hour?" Ethan spoke with confidence as Dr. Bridgeman.

"The Death House?" The young lady was startled by the handsome doctor, the mysterious stranger, someone she'd not seen before but oh, a welcome addition. He could see it in her eyes. Of course, Ethan knew it was a bold move to direct attention to where he was going, but he was growing ever assertive in his "time" advantages, knowing that historically, the two locations were linked.

The young woman dutifully opened the logbook resting on the desk beside her, nervously sifting through the calendar to find the current date and related schedule.

"Yes, Doctor. It seems Miles and Rogueford are on duty until midnight."

"Miles and….?"

"Rogueford, sir."

"Thank you, kindly. And what is your name, may I ask?"

"Certainly, doctor. My name is Alice."

Ethan closed his eyes and shook his head.

"Of course it is."

Ignoring her quizzical expression along with the blush on her cheeks, he smiled, winking at the lass as he left. He didn't introduce himself, merely turned and walked away with the arrogance of an aristocrat, playing a part and relishing it. Ethan was toying with "time", just testing the cosmic configurations as his stars aligned.

He continued through the lobby, out the front door, onto streets lit by gaslight, illuminating the main route to the mortuary on Old Montague Street. The constant, repetitive brainwashing techniques imposed on him by The Consortium's military brass was tactical training he saw the value of as it kicked in automatically. Never take the same route twice. He headed west, passing his favorite establishment, the home of the best bangers and mash in the city. Giving his bank a cursory glance as he passed before turning north on Commercial Street, from there he would double back east on Old Montague Street until he came upon the mortuary. He checked his watch in transit. It was 9:58 p.m., still plenty of time to grab the brass rings.

Smirking a bit, he knew he need only arrive there and depart before shift change prior to the incoming midnight graveyard shift. The less eyes and ears on him, the better it was for his timeline reset. Approaching five steps, he'd counted them while ascending to his proper position. Catching a glimpse of two men through the lighted window, both were sitting at a table, apparently engaged in a card game. Knocking on the door, Ethan heard one of the chairs slide across the hardwood floor.

"Don't look at me bloody cards, y' tart." One man chided the other as if it had happened before. Upon opening the door the man smoking a carved pipe looked at Ethan with marked disdain, obviously put out by his presence.

"Who the bloody hell are you?" Asking rather abruptly, he made no effort to be pleasant or welcoming in any way.

"Dr. Arthur Bridgeman. I was directed by the hospital to assess any unclaimed and unidentified corpses for use in autopsy studies for my medical students." Ethan knew this to be a common practice within the community, still continued in modern times with the benefit of refrigeration.

"At this hour?" The attendant was annoyed, his game interrupted for another.

"I beg your pardon, sir. I was woefully detained in hospital with a patient. I *do* give precedence to the living over the dead. I can't help *them* anymore." Tilting his head toward the adjacent room where bodies were stored, Ethan's posture staunch, his demeanor spoke in a tone which was as polite but as firm as his words.

"I will need to see some identification then." The man spoke rudely, obviously not educated enough to respect the title of the gentleman standing before him.

"Yes. Of course." Ethan responded, reaching into his pocket for the credentials. He realized he needed to establish his credibility through authority.

"Good man. Doing your job well. We would not want any unsavory characters, curiosity seekers poking around now would we? Which would you be, sir, Miles or Rogueford? You're both thought well of in hospital." Ethan made a clever move to personalize their meeting. Likewise, complimenting his host was one bloody good idea that came quickly, thinking on his feet.

Barely looking at the documents in his hands, instead the man passed them back to Ethan as he replied, "Yes, Dr. Bridgeman, the name's Miles."

"Well, Miles, the sooner I get done, the sooner you can get back to winning that game of cards." Nodding toward Rogueford, acknowledging him, as well, he said, "A worthy opponent? So good you have each other for company, as the occupants of this building don't seem too keen on small talk anymore."

"Yeah, right." Miles grinned knowingly, inviting the doctor inside the reception area. Approaching the doors to the mortuary's main examining room, Miles paused to look at Rogueford still waiting at the card table.

"Who the hell is he? No more players allowed." Roquefort was equally put out.

"Look at me bloody cards and it'll be the end o' ya!" Miles had lightheartedly threatened his workfellow as he acquired the keys to the locked door from a hook.

Opening the room, he stepped in first to light two lanterns set atop a small table near the entrance. As Miles did so, Ethan stepped in from behind him, spotting four covered corpses lying on different slabs around the autopsy table, fixed in position at the center of the room. Made of wood with drainage holes for their bodies to be washed, it likewise received any other fluids passing from the corpses. To Ethan, it looked like something from The Dark Ages. Miles placed one of the lanterns on a writing table then handed the second to his guest, leaning in toward Ethan until his face began to glow in the lamplight.

"Call me when yer done then. I'm off to win me a hand if the bloke didn't cheat me none."

"Right. Will do." Ethan replied as the attendant exited, leaving the door slightly ajar so to hear the good doctor should he be called upon.

As proper procedure would have it, each body brought into the mortuary would have every last possession removed, cataloged for inventory, at times, for evidence. The written list would accompany the autopsy report, laid near the top of the table at the head of the deceased for any needed review. Ethan need only pull the covering from the face of the prone bodies to identify Annie and the corresponding manifest. Knowing that he needed to manage this time well, he began to pull back the sheets on each of the corpses one by one. The first revealed an elderly man who'd probably died from old age, disease or exposure to the elements. The smell of death reminded him of his first aromatic encounter with this era upon stepping through the Flicker, an odor both pungent and putrid. The second body was uncovered to reveal a second man. Exposing his face revealed brutal open wounds to the head.

Either the victim of a mugging or some other form of attack with a sharp object, it appeared he might have suffered a painful end.

As Ethan approached the third table with a covered body he was running out of corpses. An irrational fear instantly swept over him. What if Annie's body had been removed already? What if she'd been transferred to the morgue near Scotland Yard due to the severity and related nature of the cases and crimes committed? What if? The Whitechapel murders got the attention of the public, in spite of the profession of the victims. What if the authorities felt it prudent to isolate the corpses, moving them from the mortuary to a more secure location? Nothing in Ethan's recollection of his research noted the body's location between its initial delivery to the mortuary and its final resting place. If this were true then there would be no way for Ethan to retrieve the three brass rings and realign the historical record, reaffirming that these rings were no longer on her person by the time Annie was examined then autopsied. Mortified by the thought of it, he knew there would be no going back to an untainted future. This was his ultimate moment of truth.

Pulling back the sheet from the head of the third corpse, Ethan stared at possibly the most beautiful face he'd ever seen, that of Miss Annie Chapman. With one huge sigh of relief, he dropped his head then shook it as if disappointed in himself for his lack of trust in the Universe. Once again, he gazed upon the ephemeral seductress.

"Fancy meetin' you here." He arranged the words to counter the conditions and circumstances of their fateful reunion. Reaching for the folder beside Annie's head, Ethan flipped through the coroner's report and the police records, in search of only one document until he reached the personal property manifest that logged all items found on the deceased when brought in. Examining it closely, Ethan was shocked.

- Long black figured coat that came down to her knees
- Black skirt
- Brown bodice
- Another bodice
- 2 petticoats

- A large pocket worn under the skirt and tied about the waist with strings (empty when found)
- Lace up boots
- Red and white striped woolen stockings
- Neckerchief, white with a wide red border (folded tri-corner and knotted at the front of her neck
- Scrap of muslin
- One small tooth comb
- One comb in a paper case
- Scrap of envelope containing two pills. It bears the seal of the Sussex Regiment. It is postal stamped "London, 28 Aug., 1888" inscribed is a partial address consisting of the letter M, the number 2 as if the beginning of an address and an S.

"Where are the rings?" Ethan asked himself silently as he placed the file down, yanking Annie's hand out from under the sheet, the hand where he'd seen the three rings during their early morning encounter. There was nothing on her fingers. Ethan pulled the sheet completely off, exposing her naked body to the light, revealing the results of his handiwork that he was oblivious to while he frantically searched the area around the body only to discover they were nowhere near her. They were gone. Sometime between when her body was discovered and its arrival at the mortuary, some desperate and greedy bastard lifted the brass rings and pocketed them. Ethan closed his eyes, standing there anchored to the floor as if his feet were cemented to the foundation, then, as if he had no control over his own body, he began to dance.

Ethan realized and finally accepted one certainty he would not make the mistake to doubt again. The Cosmos, the Universe, Divine influence, no matter the driving force, it would not let the course of history be corrupted or interrupted. Perhaps the rings had always been removed in this manner, part of a storyline never told in the history books because it was always assumed Jack the Ripper took them. He was never in danger of creating a new timeline. He never could. As he danced, he softly sang the lyrics to the Rolling Stones song, "Time Is On My Side". Yes, it was.

"Time is on my side...oh yes it is." Swaying in rhythm with the tune, he bent over, singing it softly to the lifeless face of Annie Chapman, as her swan song.

"Time is on my side, Maggie. Yes it is!" He knew it wasn't her, but she too was due a celebration, Annie, her stand-in. "Time is on my...." Ethan stopped mid-lyric and stared harder at his victim's face. Then, without a thought, leaned in and kissed her tenderly on her cold, dead lips. It was partly a gesture of appreciation for playing her historical role, for being ring free, partially because he needed to say goodbye. Then there was a piece of that kiss he did not understand nor cared to consider, the strongest urge of all. He then retrieved the cadaver sheet from the floor and draped it again over her body, laying the accompanying file beside her. He did not bother to speak to the two men playing cards as he passed them exiting the mortuary. There was an impervious power that had come over him. He was now reassured by destiny that there was no possible way to fuck this up because the immutable laws of living history would not and could not allow it. He walked the streets of Whitechapel in 1888 gleefully singing a song written in 1963. Ethan was a rolling stone and would gather no moss on this journey through time.

"Time is on my side, yes it is." Over and over again. To the onlookers he passed, they could've only thought an improper gentleman was either intoxicated or insane. Little did they know who they were passing by, their street side diagnosis far more accurate than they truly knew. As Ethan continued singing, tipping his hat to pretty ladies, some giggled, amused by his crazy antics, while others were rightfully wary of him, attempting to avoid the man altogether, crossing the street as he drew near. Who could blame them? Ethan was quite the sight.

Arriving back at his lodging just before midnight to a dark room, he opted not to light the candle as he disrobed, enough ambient streetlight to navigate around his living space. He considered "destiny" his new companion, laughing aloud as he had the notion to waltz on down to the privy naked. It was all so bizarre, contrary to his character and demeanor in every conceivable way, yet Ethan seemed to be allowing these thoughts and urges to enter his mind, deliberately inviting them in, allowing himself to experience subsequent feelings as deeply, trying to process and label it.

Otherwise, how could he possibly understand it? Regardless, he was going through a tumultuous evolution, emotional upheaval. Things he had seen and done, what he was doing would not make sense to the 21st Century man named Dr. Ethan LaPierre, but for the "time traveler" caught up in events unfolding, these unspeakable actions taken, in time, would become historical if not legendary. Not a thought or emotion, however bizarre, would be unexpected. Would it consume him? He had to wonder.

There he stood at the dresser again, staring at his own reflection, asking a mirror for answers, trying to comprehend what was going on behind the eyes peering back at him. *"Mirror, mirror on the wall."* Wishing it would speak aloud he initiated the conversation, withholding some questions he was just too fearful to ask. Ethan had to have faith that the answers would come, all in good time. Breaking away because of the deafening silence, looking instead at the medical bag he had placed onto the dresser, in the morning he would take a journey over to the tailor shop and purchase another set of clothing to replace the set he'd wrapped hemorrhaging organs in with haste. Oh yes, the bag needed to be cleansed along with its contents. The bag. That room was dark and the black leather of his medical bag seemed almost void of color with the exception of a few shiny blotches on its corners where the blood had dried. Ethan remembered the mutt in the street and its fixation on his leather bag. He lifted it above his head to examine it more closely, to observe how much dried blood was actually covering the base that drew the animal to it. Well. It was considerable. He brought it right up to his nose to inspect it as if he, too, had developed an enhanced sense of smell. He sniffed for the bloody aroma but really did not detect much until the tip of his nose touched the leather. The sudden urge took over, an overwhelming urge. Why did the dog lick the bag? Was there a mysterious potency to *coagulated* blood? Why was the substance so enticing to him? Whenever Ethan had cut himself on occasion, mostly paper cuts, as anyone does he'd lick the wound, tasting his own blood while searching for a bandage. A basic human instinct, he'd thought, but does another person's blood possess a different taste or possess magical qualities? Ethan sniffed around the bottom of the bag a few times before sticking out his tongue. He mimicked the lapping motion of a dog's tongue as he drew the bloody leather closer to his mouth. For a moment, he caught a glimpse of his own reflection in the mirror. It was too disturbing. Retracting his tongue, he lowered the bag, never breaking eye contact with the insane doppelganger staring back at him.

What was it? What was this "thing" gazing back at him, contemplating him and scrutinizing his existence so severely? Was he witnessing a monster in the making? Was this conversion to perversion permanent or a temporary malady? The man had to ask but there was no answer forthcoming. Ethan placed the bag down and backed away from the image until he was concealed by shadows, to see those eyes no more. He slid along an inner wall, scraping his bare back against exposed nails, taking no apparent notice of the pain. Once out of direct sight of its reflection he climbed into bed and lay face down on top of the covers. No one came to call that night, no poets or prophets graced him with their presence, no songs sung to lull him to sleep. Ethan was abandoned by his nearest and dearest, as he laid there alone in the world, only daring to hope that morning light would make things right in his mind. Hoping the blame would fall on fatigue and not fate. It took him almost two hours to fall asleep.

XIX.
THE PLAY'S THE THING

Chilled air filled the room. Ethan finally opened his eyes to the morning light. With a purposeful agenda ahead for the day, he rose from the warmth of his blankets and walked to the window. Passing the mirror, he noticed it seemed as if the demon had disappeared and only his mortal reflection remained. Looking out onto Bakers Row once more he watched the bustling crowds of men and women scurrying along to their various destinations and duties. Drawing one deep breath of tainted morning air, Ethan welcomed the malodorous lingering scent of what he could only describe as the "life" of Whitechapel. Even the grim category of "death", be it the expiration of a person, dog or rat, added to the fragrance of the street's presence and aromatic personality. If Ethan were to travel out to the open countryside and lush green fields of England right now he wondered if these horrendous missing smells would linger in salacious appetite, awaiting their return to his nasal passages.

Dressing the part for the day as a *local* instead of the doctor, Ethan then decided the first order of business was seeking out a sense of normalcy in the form of coffee. He finally had some down time between events and intended to use the next twenty-one days to fullest advantage. Three weeks until the next victims of Jack the Ripper were murdered, this was his time to prepare, to relax. He still needed to cleanse his medical bag and surgical tools this morning then make another trip to the tailor but those priorities aside, he had to make sure he had no contumacious encounters with local authorities. In just another day George Lusk would be elected as President of the Whitechapel Vigilance Committee and soon after there would be patrols of local shop owners roaming the streets in the evening hoping to become a visible deterrent to the Ripper's agenda. Ethan knew he would be contacting George Lusk later, yet, once again, had a unique advantage over the committee, police and Scotland Yard, knowing every move they would make long before anyone ever conceived of which direction to take with this baffling case. He knew everything before they did.

All dressed for success, Ethan made his way downstairs to purchase his grounds for that first delicious cup, taking it with him to the public water well just down the road to replenish his pitcher. Stopping in the common kitchen, he poured the water into a hot pot to boil then went back to the well for more. Back in the kitchen again, he refilled his cup then took it upstairs with him, returning to his room. It was wise to multitask, to use his time as well as it used him. Heading back down the stairs to retrieve the boiling water, he transferred it into the bucket, what he'd use to cleanse his instruments and medical bag. Once in his room again, he soaped up then soaked the surgical steel. Cleaning off the leather exterior with wet towels, setting it to dry on the windowsill, he allowed his tools to soak, giving him some free time to write in his journal. A stitch in time, so to speak.

***

Journal Entry ~ 9 September 1888

One day past my second non-interference directive to maintain the timeline as history recorded it. In the early morning hours of yesterday I proceeded with the murder of Jack the Ripper's second victim, Annie Chapman. Well, my victim as fate would have it. All of my fears relayed to you previously have now manifested.

There was no last minute rescue of my new role by a demon of this era claiming the title of serial killer. My deepest fears now fully realized, this task must be fully, correctly performed. The recorded manner of this second murder, like the first, was carried out with exactness according to my knowledge through research down to the blade cuts and organ extraction. To my fear, there was an assumed error in my procedure, in failing to remove some possessions of the victim, but as it turned out the action was never mine to take. I have been struggling with conflicting thoughts and emotions over the past week. I now feel with this down time I can regroup and hold fast to the purpose of my actions and intent honoring the laws of physics.

I might take in a concert in London next weekend when I go shopping for new physician's suits. God knows I need a little pampering right about now. There is an ethereal comfort knowing now more than ever that history was not only my ally but a supportive friend, lately letting me know everything will be alright and no worry needed. While my opponents are busy arresting John Pizer, also known as Leather Apron, busy forming vigilante parties, I'll be in downtown London dining in fashion before attending a classical performance surrounded by England's upper class. It will be a pleasant change of pace from my work, exiting if even for a weekend the doldrums of the streets of this impoverished section of the greatest city in the world. Oh! And I want to pick up some decent tea while I am there along with some tasty pastries! At last! Something to get all excited about. It will be a little boring for this week as it is best to limit my outside activities. The news of Annie Chapman's death, her murder is spreading through Whitechapel and is kicking up the emotions of the townspeople. Well, at least the view from my window will be interesting!

I will still have to go see my friend Clemens at the tailor shop and pick up some replacement garments. There is nothing worse than wearing the same clothes over and over. Any sense of purity and purging of the filth of this inheritance helps me.

***

There was enough emotional conflagration going on in Whitechapel for anyone to get burned who looked or acted suspiciously. Ethan needed to lay low for a week. Yes, time was definitely on his side but there was no need to take unnecessary risks of chance encounters of the wrong sort. In broad daylight he could easily blend into the traffic of crowds along the main roads, to get some errands at the bank and tailor completed by nightfall. It wasn't that he was a marked target or had been identified, but why make himself conspicuous? He'd been foolish to parade through the streets the night before singing a song that didn't yet exist. He was not about to rationalize his irrational actions following perhaps the strangest series of events in Ethan's life. He simply needed to play it smarter, adding a hint of slyness into his daily routine. It was a process and Ethan was a transformational work in progress. There was still an unknown factor at play, as he was yet to determine if the timeline was fragile or firm. This aspect of the conversion remained to be seen.

By necessity, Ethan had to finish cleansing and drying his medical bag, satchel, rags and equipment. Soaking in the pitcher for some time, he began to wipe down these formerly stained instruments. Having purchased a loaf of bread in the kitchen, he knew it was used in history to absorb congealed blood during wartime and other conflicts. Using it on all of the tools in his bag, he made blood sandwiches, a variety of blades and other devices as the 'meat' of the meal. Astonishingly, it did the trick. Sopping up fragments of Annie Chapman, the carnage was no longer detectable on the leather or the steel. He inspected them, laying each object out, spaced apart on the dresser, there to air dry. He then placed the bag on the desk near the window to catch some of the sunlight and hoped it wouldn't shrivel and pucker the way leather sometimes does when wet.

The morning was cool, crisp and clear. Ethan was eager to get out and complete the tasks planned for the day. He drank the last of his coffee and departed the room, stopping at the back alley toilet to pee. He had probably used it dozens of times by then, convinced he would never become accustomed to that unbearable stench. A quick trip to the pisser then he'd be on his way to the bank on Whitechapel Road, he was on a roll. Intending to make a considerable withdrawal in preparation of his "vacation" in Central London over the next weekend, he would need provisions as his sequential plans included becoming a recluse until then, quarantined in his room for as long as necessary leading up to the next event, two murders set in time on the thirtieth of September. His previous interactions with the branch manager bordered on awkward, an *'at your service in your face'* approach Ethan found disconcerting. He feared on one of his visits the man may attempt to kiss him, judging by the royal treatment he received during his past encounters, including the last one with a local constable in tow. Picking up the pace, Ethan intended to make this trip to the bank expeditious and uneventful. Then he would head to the tailor for additional trousers, jacket, a new shirt and tie to compensate for the items he'd had to incinerate. Able to complete both ventures with no trouble, he returned to the room where he would remain for the balance of the day. Choosing yet another book from the little library, reading freed his mind from boredom, literary escapism in its purity.

With the exception of the necessities of meal and drink, Ethan took his advice and did his best impression of '*finals week*' back at Oxford where he'd bunkered in his dorm room, hunkering down to read for hours. Later in life, it is what he'd do *during* finals, reviewing papers from students, making painful corrections to the grammar and spelling, not to mention historical errors. Ethan wondered still, should his story ever be declassified and released to the public, would his students admire and respect his decisions? Would they appreciate *how* he used his own retention of historical data to maintain an advantage in the midst of newly designated priorities? Might they be fascinated by the gruesome nature of his necessary acts or would the campus grow silent and watchful as he passed. Only time would tell his tale of woe.

Having polished off four borrowed books in four days, Ethan stayed true to his vow and laid low, trying to keep his mind busy during his otherwise tedious hiatus. The end of the week approaching, he'd paid the rent in advance so that his absence would not be noted. Management knew, even if he'd overlooked the payment, this tenant was good for the money, so there was no fear of eviction. However, Ethan's plan was to take care of any loose ends prior to his departure. Returning to the bank once again, he reestablished his safe deposit box so he'd have a place to secure the medical bag and its contents. Just the thought of leaving his room unattended for a couple of days made him feel vulnerable, in some odd way, exposed, not trusting the innkeeper or his fellow tenants. It was something he would not risk so, on his way for a serving of bangers and mash, he stashed the bag in the vault, safe from thieves and prying eyes and the manager did not even try to service him with a kiss! Only Colin could "give us a kiss"!

The time had come to take his jaunt, to steep himself in the delights of London. Taking his time to dress the part of an "English Gentleman" he'd be heading for a side of town he knew well and loved dearly. To visit downtown, Ethan would hire a carriage off of Whitechapel Road, deciding to experience the fullest ambiance of an elegant era. Reminding himself it was just for the weekend, to indulge his senses, it was something sorely lacking in his 19th Century experience and he desired to see both sides of London. A first endeavor into what was familiar real estate in his own time, color-lined streets of the capital were cluttered with vendors and entertainers, making the atmosphere electrical and alluring for the locals and visitors alike. Ethan instructed the carriage driver to chauffer him to Savile Row where there were shops stocked with the finest in men's fashion to be found anywhere. Hard-pressed to add two new suits to his wardrobe, this current high fashion had literally been through the wringer over the past two murders. He wanted to be presentable for the women he had yet to encounter so, a bit begrudgingly, made the investment.

Checking into a lovely, understated inn, the linens in his room felt like satin on his bare skin. Rolling around on the bed, he let the fine fabric caress him, a pillow embrace his head, having almost forgotten the feel of real quality beneath him. He donned one of his new suits, the less understated of the two, perfect for a night out on the town. Primped and prepared, Ethan was off to the concert hall a few streets away, strolling with an air of confidence, a tip of the hat to the ladies as he passed. An evening spent immersed in culture and classical compositions, filling his heart and mind with some of the world's greatest musical creations in history was a pure pleasure. He went to Gilbert and Sullivan's operetta "The Yeoman of the Guard". Ethan sat silently through most of the musical, even during the moments of brevity, in complete awe of his surroundings. The audience was refined, the cast as sublime, whether or not they were ghosts performing in his presence. But it was the play that captured his imagination, overwhelmed as he was to actually bear witness to it and in its own time, an astounding privilege. According to Ethan, the play *was* the thing! It pulsed through him, feeding his soul, expanding his mind. To be able to sit in an audience with many of London's richest, most influential men helped him to purge his psyche of the filth and grime of the East End, daily encounters surrounding his meager dwelling not thirty minutes away by carriage. It was as if he was living in a different world, not just a different time in history.

During intermission he kept to himself, listening to those around him engaged in conversation. Men of leisure, Ethan truly enjoyed their refined, proper use of the English language. In polite discussion, he heard no mention made of the murders, as if what was happening had no bearing on their world. No matter. If they knew at all, and they must have known, this was all occurring in a far off land to a far lesser class of people who didn't really matter at all, or so it would seem. Ethan shook his head, wondering how they would react if they knew who was in their midst. Back to the play, the finale was grand!

Ethan deliberately spoiled himself for two days, riding in fancy carriages, taking in the sights, dining in fine establishments, immersing himself in the culture, all but bathing in the experience. Luxury accommodations, the best of everything, Ethan was convinced he deserved it for the sacrifices he had made and would continue to, on behalf of history. Indeed, Doctor LaPierre fit into this realm far better than where his ongoing work was located, by necessity. No one stared or cared as his demeanor and character was, by nature, indigenous to this region of London.

Ethan took in as much of his weekend *away* as possible, to realign his mind and purpose before the tedious carriage ride back to Whitechapel Road, from where he would disappear into an alley leading back to Bakers Row and his humble domicile. Arriving just after nightfall on Sunday the 16th of September at the door to his room, Ethan never felt the place so heavy and dark, as if in his absence the spirits of Polly and Annie moved in and waited for his return. Every thread of his weekend escape unraveled with the first footstep through the door, absorbed by its darkest shadows, no light in sight. He felt it right down to his last fiber of consciousness, sucked back into the abysmal void of duty and despicable acts towards two more women in two more weeks. Placing his new attire on the bed, Ethan began to undress, removing a familiar ensemble, the original fancy threads he'd worn upon arrival and chose to wear for his journey back to Whitechapel. The cuffs of the jacket, shirt and bottoms of the trousers were beginning to appear threadbare, well worn, having to scrub the bloodstains clean. He compared it to new ones on the bed and knew it was a prudent move not to wear either back to the filth of Whitechapel yet when he glanced back at his new suits, he noticed they'd already begun to take on the dingy pallor of the East End, a shame. The area certainly had an influence on everyone and apparently, everything. He missed London proper and already longed to return.

"Perils of the job at hand." Ethan uttered, an attempt to recenter his psyche for what had transpired and the actions to come. It was a typical

Sunday night, nothing much to do on this side of town. He curled up on the bed and fell asleep reading.

The next morning Ethan returned to the bank on Whitechapel Road to retrieve his medical bag, knowing its contents would soon be needed. In addition, he would stock up on sundry supplies from Spitalfields Market and return home for a spot of tea, delicious tea he bought over the weekend while he was in London Central. He thought he'd wear one of his new suits for the brief quest, just to break it in. He had also purchased a new pair of shoes even though the ones provided for him from The Consortium were top notch, durable as well as broken in, really quite comfortable. Finishing his tea, Ethan once again exited his room and entered onto Baker's Row where a Monday seemed no different than any other day in the realm of possibilities of encounters both welcome and not. His destination unplanned and unimportant, he merely wanted to try his legs in preparation for the double murder.

Perhaps the anonymity of downtown London restored some sense of wonder he had for the historical era he found himself in at this point in time. Ethan wanted his eyes and mind to drink in more than just those four walls of his room. Amongst the hordes of people rushing by hurriedly with purpose along the streets were men in work overalls and heavy boots, gentlemen in coat and top hats and ladies in custom fashions from skirt to bonnet. He fell more so into the latter category of gentlemen. On this stroll, as he had sensed earlier, Ethan was aware of a subtle yet a consistent change. Navigating passages between buildings he noticed far fewer faces, seeing more so the tops of hats and bonnets. Most of the people were seemingly avoiding eye contact, opting instead to keep their heads down with the mood.

Annie Chapman's murder was certainly fresh on the minds of the townspeople and palpable fear was overcoming the other stenches in the air. The women seemed hesitant to draw any man's attention from a simple courteous smile and nod to more forward suggestions. It was best, safest to focus on the road ahead, arriving at one's destination in mind in one piece without bringing any unsolicited approach by some stranger. Many of the local men hung their heads low, as well, but in their cases, it could have been to avoid eye contact due to the increased police presence on main streets.

They weren't guilty of being Jack the Ripper but it was apparent some were responsible for other crimes, perhaps crimes that had gone unpunished. As scrutiny intensified it became as thick as the air they breathed. It was obvious to Ethan, who knew about the increased presence in law enforcement from historical record that this was more of a visible deterrent and social assurance that local authorities were on the case, even though behind the scenes, they still didn't have a clue, no concrete leads to go on as to whom this monster, this murderer could conceivably be.

Ethan's casual saunter guided him onto the familiar Commercial Street. At the corner of Hanbury Street near the marketplace the crowd began to bottleneck, being filtered through several officers randomly questioning some of the men passing by. Instinctively, Ethan felt the urge to turn around in an attempt to withdraw from this otherwise unavoidable encounter. Instead, he thought in terms of what experienced lawmen would do, how they'd react should any of them see him fleeing the scene. It would undoubtedly spark more interest than pushing through the crowd in hopes of being one of the men allowed to pass. Ethan also felt his good friend *Time* was on his side, by his side, still accompanying him. It would never allow history to be altered, so forward he pushed.

There's something that happens to a person when in the presence of the police. Even the guiltless have a hard time attempting to act innocent. One does not know if, whether looking down at the ground or up in the air will create suspicion in the eyes of the constables. Ethan's eyes were fixated on the direction of his path, chin up, the proper posture for a man worthy of the fine gentlemen's suit he wore. It was certainly apparent as Ethan approached closer to a half a dozen uniformed officers, this was definitely a casual yet visible presence in an effort to make the public feel more comfortable and secure in knowing they were on the beat, always on the job. The questions the officers posed to randomly selected men passing along the street, from his vantage point, certainly seemed to focus on the killings as they asked about their whereabouts, employment and residence. As the questions were answered the constables jotted down the responses in report pads, which is precisely what Ethan had to avoid. His full access to all of the reports logged by the local municipality, Scotland Yard, as well as every news article, private case journal and file authored by anyone involved in the case, his research showed no record of his fictitious name being logged. He'd figured as he came closer to the police they would wave him on through due to his professional, upper class appearance. He may be right that *Time* was his companion on his journey but Ethan did not realize *Time* also had one sick and twisted sense of humor.

"Afternoon, sir. Would you mind answering a few questions?"

"Well." Ethan scrambled for an excuse. "I'm actually late for an appointment."

"I understand that, sir. Won't take but a minute then you can be on your way."

The officer politely insisted, taking Ethan by the upper arm, guiding him out of the conveyer line of people moving through the marketplace. Rather nervous, this detainee was trying to quickly decide how to avoid being asked to identify himself by name, only to become cataloged in the officer's book. He feared returning to the 21st Century only to discover the fictitious name The Consortium (and he) came up with was now a part of the Jack the Ripper case file. It would be nothing compared to whatever ripple effect it would otherwise cause. He thought perhaps he should play the authoritative role, barking at the officer as if to reflect having a position of power that could make the bobby's life a living hell by just talking to his superiors. As he rapidly plotted his strategy, he asked for the man's name to which he replied.

"Police Constable William Smith, sir, and might I ask yours?"

Ethan recognized the uniform insignia identifying the officer's division and the three-digit personal I.D. number. He had just been dealt a huge cosmic poker hand equivalent to four aces. His years of background research on everyone involved in this case included the personnel files of one Constable William Smith.

"Smith? My God, man! What's happened to you?"

"Excuse me, sir?" The officer looked confused and taken back by the question.

"Don't tell me you don't remember me now, my good man. Arthur Bridgeman. I knew your parents Richard and Eliza when I lived at Milton under Wychwood in Oxfordshire. I came over for tea on occasion when you were just a lad."

The officer was visibly struggling with his memory so to place the gentleman's face. Ethan knew he had to seal the façade with a little more detail.

"Oh dear. How dreadfully forgetful of me. If memory serves, then I owe you a belated 'Happy Birthday!' young man. I remember attending a lovely party for you around this time of year, if I'm not mistaken. I believe it was your fifth, as I recall. What are you, twenty-four now?" Ethan was conducting the interview.

"Twenty-six, just past the quarter century." The bobby seemed a bit shaken by his failure to recollect this charming man, extending his hand in friendship yet still unable to hide a shade of embarrassment, not remembering a friend of his parents.

"Twenty-six is it then? My word you're actually making me feel quite Neolithic at the moment. My apologies, you said you needed to see my papers?"

"That won't be necessary Mr. Bridgeman."

"Doctor Bridgeman, if you please." Ethan boasted in jest, casting his gleaming grin down upon the bobby. There it was. The smugness returned to Ethan, knowing his good friend *Time* was once again right there beside him. He could have ended this interaction sooner but was just beginning to have fun.

"Doctor then, sorry sir." The officer continued. "You workin' in hospital then?"

"Actually, I'm here to deliver a seminar. In fact, I've arrived from my office in northern London." Ethan's smile was broad, warm and inviting. The bobby lowered what defenses he possessed instantly.

"Brilliant! Has anyone on staff there told you about the murders locally?"

"They have." Ethan responded. "Absolutely tragic, Smith. Any leads?"

"Honestly, several. None of them worth a pence if you ask me." Smith said.

"Well, London's finest is on it. I'm sure something will surface."

PC Smith lowered his report log book as Ethan had hoped without recording this encounter and discussion and once again extended his hand for Ethan to shake.

"Well, I won't keep you sir, seeing as you said you had an appointment."

"Yes, I'd best be off." Turning to leave, Ethan looked back once more. "A real pleasure to see you, lad…all grown up! Give my best to your parents." He turned, walking away from the officer.

"They both died in a fire, two years back." Smith spoke woefully, in a somber, quiet tone, his words lost in the ether but Ethan heard them, though he did not turn to react or respond to the news of their horrible demise. He could not turn around because he was forcing back laughter. Not only in the admiration of his cleverness, but in the cleverness of his good old friend *Time* who was, more than at any other point before now, on his side. *Time* had murdered Constable Smith's parents only for Ethan, in case Smith decided to bring up the name Arthur Bridgeman to which they would have no knowledge and things could have become complicated for him. He waited until he was out of sight and rounding the corner of a tobacco shop to let it fly, an outburst that left him in tears. Ethan peeked around the corner several more times to make sure he did not draw the attention of officers, but as far as those who were walking past, the men and women judging with disdain. Both their trepidation in step and their facial expression caused him to point at them and laugh harder. It was time for a good, hearty laugh.

Eventually Ethan made his return to the room. His route was unencumbered nor remembered as he was totally in the clouds for the entire walk back. Upon closing the door Ethan collapsed to his knees, exhausted from his fits of laughter and pure euphoria. The encounter with P C William Smith and Ethan's false affiliation was indeed entertaining, but what had him in hysterics, now rolling around on the floor, was his sudden enlightened acceptance that his close companion had even played one on him. *Time* was manipulating everything as it had always done. It has been said that "time" is a manmade concept but then so is "divinity" and "the cosmos" and anything else his species and his species alone manifested to explain why things happen the way they do. Ethan chose "time" as the designation from all the other variables because it was all-encompassing to thought and deed.

Ethan laid on his back on the rug, still chuckling, finding the elusive answer in front of him. *Time* had always been the true killer. Ethan glared at the ceiling, yet, did not see wood and paint and nails. He saw the awe of his companion. *Time* was the greatest serial killer in the history of, well, time. Cunning and masterful, no one could ever see it coming or when it would target them. No mere mortal ever knew what weapon it would use, when or whether its attack would be slow and torturous or quick and painless. *Time* had no mercy or forgiveness, pushing on with macabre intent to eventually take the life of everything within reach.

Suddenly Ethan began to cry, weeping like a newborn baby. Rolling on his side into a fetal position, surrendering to the fact he was as controlled by *Time* as anyone or anything else. He was not guilty of these despicable acts he had committed and would still commit. He was the instrument of *Time*. To make sure he would fulfill his assigned tasks in history, it had murdered that policeman's parents by burning them to death two years earlier, so his fictitious identity would never be divulged. Pulling his knees close to his chest, surrendering to an infinite power and persuasion of his friend, to the degree of being fully submissive to its control, as long as Ethan was obedient to what was already laid out in front of him he would preserve history as it was and return home unblemished from his venture. Tears rolled off his face as he brought his clenched hand up to his mouth, biting down on his knuckles in an effort to suppress anguished cries. It seemed to have no effect so he sought another alternative method of muting himself and promptly stuck his thumb in his mouth. Before he was aware of the action he was sucking it like an infant, cooing in lieu of crying, remaining in this position until he fell asleep in the middle of the floor.

He awoke somewhat lost in his day as there was still light outside. Had he slept through the night and it was Tuesday? Pulling his pocket watch, checking the time, it was 4:55 in the afternoon and probably still Monday. Ethan rose from the floor, walked over to the desk then sat in the chair by the window. The tears had dried on his face as he slept and the cool air penetrating his room breezed along his skin. He looked down upon the audience a floor below as he had done countless times prior but this time he heard a murmur of anti-Semitism rising from the chorus of voices, a circulating opinion, the view was such that "an Englishman" would never commit such heinous crimes, but a dirty immigrant with a sordid past could've been capable of it. From within the four walls of his own room, Ethan worked feverishly within his mind to understand what was happening to him.

If he was to be an instrument in the hands of *Time* he needed to comprehend the complexities of his role. His sudden awareness of surrender was the signal from his ally that the next two victims of Jack the Ripper were all about time and timing. In the span of forty-five minutes he would have to murder two women in two separate locations. He was already growing in his moustache for the plan he'd put in place, knowing every detail about a night in the past that was to come. The theatre curtain for the next act would be raised in less than two weeks and it was rehearsal time for Ethan regarding his role in the play. This was the third act and one of the trickiest. Two performances, back-to-back, the "Double Event", as it was titled by the press. Ethan would have to become the master of *Time*, not subject to its whims. It was more than one mile between Berner Street and Mitre Street, far closer to the City of London. There would have to be time trials, walkthroughs during the middle of daytime traffic to gauge just how much of a pace he would need to maintain going from point "A" to point "B" in this short timeframe allotted between victims, only forty minutes total from one murder to the next murder. Other variables were taken care of by history, from precisely where the two women would be when it was time to strike, to the players and witnesses involved up to and after his performance and perfunctory bow. It was also the first time he needed to leave clues for the clueless, graffiti on a wall, streets away from the second woman's body, a message written in chalk which he'd borrow from the public kitchen's chalkboard downstairs. The clue he'd leave behind did not reflect his opinion nor was it a personal indictment or statement. It was merely of historical significance and a part of the timeline so it had to be written because his friend *Time* said so.

Over the next two weeks Ethan would begin his rehearsal and run-throughs on Berner Street just off Commercial Road which was south of Whitechapel Road. In local attire, he would work in broad daylight during the busiest point of the day so not to draw attention, blending into the masses of traffic between Whitechapel and the main part of London. Between the 16th and the 29th of September, Ethan went through the paces with the accompaniment of his pocket watch, hoping to pin down a set time frame to proceed from start to finish. He even made runs during the rain on several occasions, as it was recorded that it had rained earlier on the night of the "Double Event". Ethan walked the streets a dozen times or more, pacing himself at different speeds, searching for the path of least resistance as the most direct route, assuring his arrival at Mitre Street was not too early nor too late. Over twenty miles of round trip walks allowed Ethan to condition his legs, developing several painful blisters in the process. Ah, what actors will sacrifice and endure for the love of the craft, so to nurture the artist at heart!

XX.
AS A MATTER OF FACT

Ethan claimed the day of September 29th to rest and relax, refocusing his mind and memory on files, the facts of the case. He had once again, if only for a moment, obtained the will to do "the job", what he'd been tasked with, destined for in history. Lying prone on his bed, eyes closed, he visualized every nuance of a planned attack and route to and from each location. Accessing his memory for witness statements and historical accounts of what was to happen, he had masterfully planned how his role would play out later this evening and with a whimsical thought of himself being Dickens' character the artful dodger, *Time* being his mentor, the elderly Fagin from "Oliver Twist", he began to get ready.

There was not much left to chance and Ethan was not one for superstition where the facts were concerned, especially when laid out ahead of time by *Time* itself. His actions were based solely on historical accounts of the case. Deciding what to wear, he felt far more comfortable in his physician's proper attire, what he wore for Polly Nichols' and Annie Chapman. Earlier in the week, after a completion of one of his practice runs, Ethan had bought the pipe which he knew had relevance later on that evening. His moustache had also grown out considerably. Completing his ensemble for his night out, including preparing his medical bag appropriately for what was to come, he was ready, waiting for the play to begin, anticipating the opening act.

Knowing he would need to be more careful during his evening departures now, even though *Time* would never betray him, he would still have to remain vigilant, be pragmatic about intangibles, what role the unknown plays in history. Ethan had to be a sleuth, stealthy. If he were spotted leaving the lodging someone in the future might mention it to the local authorities in a bout of suspicion and fear for what was happening in Whitechapel. Prior to his departure, Ethan paced the room, returning to the mirror to revisit those eyes, someone he used to know. He gave himself the once over in his lucky suit but luck had nothing to do with it.

Slipping out the back exit near the outhouse, once more he made his way in the direction of the busy Whitechapel Road. It still was raining, wind bustling, causing the pedestrians to grab hold of their head covers so to protect them from lifting off into the air. Turning west on Whitechapel, journeying to Plumbers Row, he turned south then continued until he reached Commercial Road. His destination was just across the road on Berner Street. He opened his pocket watch while under the cover of a market canopy. It was 11:41 p.m. on a Saturday night. He was aware from his case study, Elizabeth Stride and Catherine Eddowes had already been busy *working* several men that night. Miss Stride had been seen exiting with a man from a public house just down from him about forty minutes before. She had also been seen with a well-dressed man exiting the Bricklayer's Arms, embracing and kissing. She was seen soon thereafter on Berner Street with a man wearing a sailor's hat, kissing and caressing each other. The rain had stopped. Drawing the curtain….

Ethan would be standing under a canopy between these two encounters, seeing the events play out in his mind. Even in his research he had always questioned the testimonies of witnesses to Elizabeth Stride's whereabouts until just past midnight. On a Saturday night in the Whitechapel district one could throw a stone in virtually any direction and hit a woman working the streets, the majority of them dressed in very similar attire. Also, he had wondered how many of those making reports to the police or the local newspaper were simply seeking some attention in their otherwise monotonous lives or hoping some reward would be in order. If they were all correct in their testimonies, then either Elizabeth Stride had rejected these first two men or she was damn good, proficient in her profession. Either way, her proclivities prior to 12:30 a.m. really had no bearing on the case nor Ethan's dutiful acts to come. He knew there were conflicting reports of the description of the man Elizabeth was last seen with; different heights, hats and details of attire were divulged by eyewitnesses including the officer Ethan met earlier, Police Constable William Smith. One report had the man holding an elongated package, another stated he was holding nothing. Only one testimony gave Ethan all the facts, information he needed to know.

Based on this eyewitness account, Ethan knew precisely where to stand, lying in wait, since this particular witness would likewise witness him. Casually strolling down Berner Street in an attempt to appear as if he was going on a nonchalant walk late in the evening, he'd found his way to the spot where he'd watch it all transpire, reminiscent of being a Scope instead of a murderer. Ah, the good old days. Standing in a small alcove across the street from where he spotted Elizabeth Stride poised in her proper position, it is where he saw a shorter man approaching her. He need only wait for the director, *Time* to set the stage for his grand entrance in the opening act. His performance would follow that of the next character in the play who was now walking down the alley towards center stage and into his important supporting role.

Israel Schwartz was a Jewish immigrant who had no idea he was walking into a passion play, that obscure part in strolling down Berner Street, he would become a part of history, a part of the play. Ethan had the perfect stage cue to enter the act from the wings. In Schwartz's testimony to the police (through a translator because he spoke no English), he stated that he walked up upon Elizabeth Stride and a man who was trying to pull her into the street from the alley. As she struggled and turned away the man grabbed her from behind with his hands on her shoulders and pushed her down forcefully onto the cobblestone street at the entrance to the alley. Hearing the woman make three soft outcries, he crossed the street to avoid the altercation. Not knowing the relationship, not wanting to get involved, Schwartz made his exit. As he did so, he was spotted by the brute who was accosting Stride. Pointing at Mr. Schwartz from across the road, he yelled one word:

"Lipski!"

That was it, Ethan's stage cue. Having looked at every single perspective of this particular event, he came down on the side of Inspector Abberline who believed the man shouted "Lipski" in epithet towards Schwartz, a man with pronounced Jewish features. A year before, a Polish Jew named Israel Lipski murdered a neighboring woman in a lodging there on Berner Street by pouring nitric acid down her throat. The assailant was captured and hanged for his crime but the act outraged the local residents, inflaming anti-Semitism towards the Jewish immigrants. Londoners were known to create phrases from events, thus *Lipski* was used to identify an unsavory or unwelcome person of a certain appearance. Ultimately, Abberline's investigation concluded there was no one by that name living in the area during the Whitechapel murders, leading once again to a logical deduction: the man who threw Miss Stride to the ground was using that name as an indictment, most likely to chase him away. A safe enough assumption to make, Ethan had drawn his own conclusions. The way he saw it, when the man was observed accosting Stride, he yelled out the infamous epithet in an attempt to blame Schwartz for his own sinister assault.

Right on cue, the name Lipski called out, Ethan lit the pipe he'd bought just for this special occasion. He knew that Schwartz, in a panic hearing *that* name shouted at him, would walk right past Ethan which he promptly did. Perfect stage directions. Schwartz gazed at Ethan who brazenly stared right back at him as he passed. Israel reported the man he had seen as five-foot-eleven in height. Ethan was six feet tall, only a slight miscalculation on the part of the witness present at the scene of a crime. Schwartz broke the gaze first, obviously thinking Ethan and the man who yelled at him were together. He kept on walking, picking up his pace. As Ethan had expected, the attacker disappeared into the alleyway behind where he'd beaten Miss Stride to the ground then blended into the shadows, never to return or be heard from again. Once word got out that she'd been murdered, obviously not wanting to be punished as, at least, an accomplice, the less than gentlemanly sort probably left the country.

On cue, Ethan hit his mark. After Schwartz passed him, he immediately crossed the road, heading over toward Elizabeth Stride, knocked out cold. She looked dead already. Without breaking his stride he arrived beside her. Crouching down, Ethan opened the medical bag, retrieving the familiar blade. Though he had his timepiece in his possession, it was not a stopwatch he could click to gauge his pace from there to Mitre Street for his next appointment with destiny. Instead, his start time would have to be the completion of the killing of this helpless woman. In an instant, *Time* took the lead.

Grabbing Elizabeth Stride by the hair, he pulled her head back as she lay there, face down, unresponsive to the tug. Ethan began to slice back and forth across her throat, severing the left carotid artery and continuing the sawing motion until he hit bone. As he held her hair firmly in his grasp, her neck bent back more and more as the muscle and tissue were severely separated by the piercing blade, exposing bone. The crunching sound of the knife against her spine told him he'd completed the job in a timely manner, what was required of him by his taskmaster. Though he couldn't see her enchanting light gray eyes, the color of storm clouds brewing, releasing her beautiful curly brown hair signified the start of the race like a gun going off. Placing the knife in the bag, hastily gathering himself, Ethan began his trip to the outskirts of the city of London, over a mile away. His encounter with Elizabeth Stride took a total of thirty seconds. 12:46 a.m.

One, two, three, four, five, six. Ethan counted his steps as he quickly exited this stage for the next, in route to another victim. Wanting to smile, knowing Schwartz's statement that the "taller" man had followed him for a bit, then stopped, obviously Israel mistook Ethan's pace along the same route as somehow connected with him, when in fact, he was not being pursued by a stranger because of what he witnessed. In fact, it was a mere coincidence. Their paths crossed, that was all. Ethan tried to find the humor in it but he could not smile. There was a sick feeling in the pit of his stomach, an emptiness. A lack of fulfillment. He had an emotional reaction to the murder of Elizabeth Stride, a woman who he did not get to see before he'd claimed her life. Other than the police postmortem photographs, he never truly saw her face, just a glimpse of her profile as blood spurted from her neck. No! He was angry at his accomplice! Not at the man who took her down but at *Time* for not arranging the history in such a way he could have completed a full mutilation of this victim. Ethan took pride in his precision technique replicating the autopsy reports, the facts of the case, doing so to exact specifications. He could not linger at the first body. Time did not allow it and history never recorded it. He felt robbed.

Thirty-two, thirty-three, thirty-four, thirty-five. His pace had quickened, not because he was late or falling behind, but due specifically to his increasing angst. Ethan not only felt *Time* kept him from proving his devotion to the cause by having him perfect another mutilation down to the last nick of the blade but he also thought of Elizabeth Stride's plight.

Time never gave her the just recognition she deserved because she wasn't torn apart like the others. She would always be the appetizer as opposed to the main course that night, namely Catherine Eddowes. How fair was it that this woman had her life taken and was a bit player in this theatre, second even to Israel Schwartz because he was the only living person who witnessed the alleged attack on her? There was nothing fair about it. She paid the same price and should have been *immortalized* just like all the rest. But they weren't, really, and he knew it. Sure, *he* knew all their names but how many mortal souls never bothered to know them? They were the victims of Jack the Ripper, tossed in a file, into a pile together; tossed out with the trash of history. Lost to time and a character who upstaged them from the start. Nobody knew who he really was but everyone knew *his* name! "Pace yourself, mate." Ethan spoke to himself, alone in the dark.

Eighty-seven, eighty-eight, eighty-nine, ninety, ninety-one, he kept on moving. Pulling his pocket watch out and opening it, he measured the checkpoints along the way from his rehearsals so to time it perfectly for his arrival in Mitre Square. Too soon or too late and he could run into one of the roving policemen such as Constable Edward Watkins who'd been conducting a fifteen minute patrol of the area and who would also be the one to come upon Miss Eddowes' body quite soon. Ethan knew his judgment on timing was probably predestined and would really have no bearing on any fluctuation in his arrival. *Time* would not allow him to be apprehended, not before, during or after the killing. Everything happening as it always had was both liberating and confining for Ethan. His practiced pace brought him to the edge of Mitre Street in nineteen minutes, well within the estimated times from rehearsals. In fact, a little early as he walked with a huff for a time along the more than a mile trip. Who would have thought he'd have to come back to the 19th Century to really get in shape?

He would enter Mitre Square through Duke Street via the dark narrow Church Passage. Due to time constraints, Ethan was being pushed harder than ever before. The precision *timing* over the next thirty minutes would be as crucial, if not more so considering precision *cutting* he'd have to perform. Assuming that the reports of encounters were accurate from the three men seeing Eddowes with a shorter man around 1:35 a.m., her body being discovered by PC William Smith at 1:45 a.m. meant his work had to be exact and swift. *Time* was really fucking with him in more ways than one. The really bizarre twist was that Catherine Eddowes was released from the local drunk tank at Bishopsgate Police Station less than twenty minutes before her date with destiny. When she signed out, she used a fake name: Mary Ann Kelly. Jack the Ripper's last (agreed) victim and Ethan's last task before returning through the Flicker was Mary Jane Kelly. He didn't believe in coincidences to begin with but since his jump into the 19th Century and this unexpected role, he was sure that *Time* had a human quality with a wicked sense of humor.

Ethan moved further into the poorly lit Mitre Square and out of Church Passage where, in the minute or two after his entrance, the first scheduled appearance would be that of Police Constable William Smith who reported entering the Square at half past one. In fact, he arrived at 1:20 a.m. and left in less than a minute. Irrelevant as it seems, Ethan perceived it to be close enough. One milestone met, one historical part of the event now down on the schedule. Ethan then heard a female voice from the end of Church Passage near Duke Street. Staying in the shadows he could see a man and woman stopping at the entrance. She leaned back against a warehouse wall and faced the man leaning in closer to her. Ethan had no doubt, this was Catherine Eddowes and her customer, the man spotted by Joseph Lawende who was with two other men who were exiting the Imperial Club, a local social favorite, around 1:35 a.m. according to reports, but according to Ethan's pocket watch it was 1:27 a.m.

Ethan need only hope that his friend *Time* was trying to make up for not letting him eviscerate Elizabeth Stride earlier and force this man to leave at an earlier time in order to give him a wider gap to work with than the reports had given him from the case, which was only about fifteen minutes. Ethan assumed the man or Eddowes didn't like the arrangement of price and he walked off earlier than 1:30 a.m. causing Ethan to close his pocket watch and kiss the three-legged horse on the case. He then tucked it away in his coat pocket and opened the medical bag, extracting the knife he used earlier on Elizabeth Stride, sticky blood still hugging the blade for dear life.

Ethan saw Catherine Eddowes. After a hard night she appeared dead on her feet. If she only knew. For all intents and purposes, it was an apt description of the poor woman. She began to walk down Church Passage towards him. He moved over to the dark corner where her body would eventually be found and he waited for her to come into the square. Eddowes popped out of the passage onto Mitre Square, head down as she was fiddling with something in her hands. Ethan really wanted to find out just how *Time* was on his side. Instead of calling out to her or approaching her, he waited in the dark corner to see if she was scripted by fate to turn right and walk right into him. His patience paid with dividends. Catherine Eddowes indeed walked directly towards him, never looking up as she was still tinkering with whatever she had in her hands. Ethan had the blade hidden behind his left forearm, concealing the butt of the knife with his hand, rhythmically tapping on the handle against his pocket watch buried in his coat as if to relay Morse code to his friend to say "thank you". Intermission had been stressful but now he could settle into the role. Time for the second act.

From the moment Ethan struck there wasn't a word. The work ahead for him to do "the job" precisely required he begin as soon as possible and swift in completion. Ethan lunged for the considerably shorter Eddowes, grabbing her lush, auburn hair with his right hand, spinning her around backwards then to the ground, landing on top of her in a squatted position, leaning with all his weight forward with his left hand holding the knife and pushed it onto her throat with such weight and pressure it began breaking the skin and cutting into her larynx before he even began slicing back and forth. Although Ethan's eyes adjusted to the extremely dark corner of the square, he couldn't make out Catherine's eyes while he continued to hold her down, sawing through her neck. Cutting from behind her left ear, through the left carotid artery, across to her other ear, not nearly as deep on the right where he started, he forced the knife all the way back to her intervertebral cartilage. Catherine Eddowes never had time to utter a noise before she died. The still canvas now before him was the gift, his chance to make up for his rush job with Elizabeth Stride and fulfill the heinous performance his role demanded to this point. Ethan was convinced that everything he did was under the auspices of *Time*, pulling his strings as a puppeteer. Ethan knew he was being manipulated and choreographed. He was the marionette, dancing to *Time's* tune.

He couldn't screw this up if he wanted to because he would not be allowed. He need only conduct the intricate cuts and slices to her body and history would record it as such, the same as before. It was dark and he had to dive in, literally with both hands. Feeling the form of her face, he located her eyes which were still open. He'd read they were a deep shade of hazel but he just could not see them. Softly shushing an already silent woman, with two fingers he closed both of her eyes. This allowed him to take the point of the sharp surgical steel knife and cut into her eyelids, slicing top and bottom of both eyes about a quarter to a half an inch out from the nose and all the way through the membrane. The angle forced an unavoidable collateral cut to the bridge of her nose which Ethan enhanced by pushing the blade point deeper into her face on the right side of her nose bridge and ripping downward towards her mouth, severing all the muscle and tissue along her cheekbone. His blade reversed course and dug into her gums then upper lip before he angled the blade in such a way as to slice through her nose from the nostrils to the bridge again, sawing back and forth until only the superficial skin was all that was left to hold the nose on the face. He made another cut near the nose bridge and yet another from the right side of the mouth, all looking like random jabs at her face but were, in fact, all precisely where they needed to be. Like slicing sandwich meats, he turned the blade sideways and carved up the woman's right cheek, leaving the skin flapped back in a triangular shape. He obliquely cut through the lobe and auricle of the right ear.

He was performing surgery in the dark using a mental stopwatch, as if trying to set a world record. Hurriedly, he moved from atop Eddowes' chest and kneeled on her right side, yanking apart Catherine's buttoned coat and man's shirt she wore so he could more easily pull the multiple layers of skirts she wore to keep warm well above her sternum region, fully exposing her midsection. The first two jabs and the cut in the dark missed their mark, hitting the inner left groin separating the labium and leaving a flap of skin on the groin. He'd attempted to readjust but stabbed and cut into her right inner thigh. Feeling around her pelvic region to get his bearings, Ethan realigned, driving the blade straight in and down above Catherine's pubic region then began a steady slicing of the abdominal muscles. At the naval, he cut around to the right and under to the left before continuing to the breast bone, leaving her belly button supported only by tendrils of the rectum muscle on the left side of the abdomen. Making oblique cuts at the top and bottom of that long opening, he separated her midsection, exposing her internal organs. He'd already made several stabs and cuts into her liver. Ethan had to remove her intestines, covered mostly in feculent matter, placing them on her right upper chest and shoulder. Not letting go of the knife, a two-foot long section was then cut away from the intestine, which he methodically placed between her left arm and side. He was now unobstructed and able to cut away other appendages and remove both her left kidney and Elizabeth's womb without disturbing the vagina and cervix. He opened his medical bag which he'd pre-lined earlier in the day to avoid leakage issues he had suffered harvesting Annie Chapman's organs. Placing both her kidney and her womb inside the medical bag, he then cut away a section of her apron and placed it within, as well.

Before he could clean up, he heard the unmistakable hard soles of a constable on patrol by the name of James Harvey who came to a halt inside Church Passage before entering Mitre Square then turned back down the passage away from Ethan and his victim. Officer Harvey's appearance was a warning signal to move his arse! In only four or five minutes PC Edward Watkins would discover the remains of Catherine Eddowes. It was time to go on to the third and final act in tonight's play, taking an alternative route. He'd traveled through Church Passage via Mitre Street to King Street then past Duke Street. Knowing not to take the identical route twice, Ethan traveled Stone Lane, crossing Middlesex Street into a small alley called New Goulston Street. Where this intersected with its original namesake, Ethan stopped. Goulston Street was quiet and empty. Pausing, not to reflect but merely to clean off the remnants of the murder, he wiped his knife of the blood, tissue and fecal matter, using the piece of torn apron. This was where he would replicate history, leaving the cloth on the ground inside of the frame of an archway of this soon to be busy boulevard just below where he would write in the chalk he had borrowed, words Police Constable Edward Long would soon discover scrawled on a wall about 2:55 a.m., which stirred up more confusion in the case. There was controversy as to what exactly was written on a wall, as well as its meaning. PC Long reported one version and Detective Halse, yet another description and no photographs were taken of the location because the order was issued by Sir Charles Warren, head of the London Metropolitan Police to wash the wall down before the nearby marketplace became filled with immigrant vendors. Ethan chose the words Sir Warren put in his report:

"The Jews are the men that will not be blamed for nothing"

Unlike Ethan's role surrounding Mary Ann Nichols or Annie Chapman's death, he never really struggled in his mind whether he did everything exactly as history recorded it. He was now in the hands of *Time*. Working in near pitch black darkness, for him to try to meticulously duplicate the injuries presented by Dr. Gordon Brown in the postmortem report would have taken a miracle (or more time than he had) to perform. He had to trust his colleague and logic that whatever he did to both of the women he'd murdered tonight he had already done historically the exact same way. The curtain was closing on this final act and the man at center stage in the lead role was taking his final bow. Ethan went home.

Arriving back at his lodging at 3:19 a.m., Ethan considered everything that had transpired outside of his room window was exactly as history recorded. Now, with the "Double Event" completed, he need only wait to see if his theory was right and all was as it had always been. Ethan had avoided as many gaslight streetlamps as possible, any exposure or human contact while returning home because he had no idea how much blood and other fluids from the women he'd victimized had gotten on his clothes. Once inside his sanctuary he locked the door and lit the two candles in his room, one on the desk and the other from the dresser. Before disrobing he'd briefly glanced over his outfit for signs of that early morning carnage. His sleeves expectedly received the worst of it, blood staining both coat and shirt. He avoided stepping in any blood but several drops were on the topside of his shoes, most likely from when he was inside Eddowes' abdominal cavity. Splatter was also present on his trousers, though not apparently so while he was walking through the dark alleys. In fact, it was his wise decision not to wear one of his fancy new suits for the task. Ethan disrobed, once again becoming what was more and more comfortably naked. Distant police whistles had died down from earlier when he heard them as he moved further and further from the murder scenes. Everything playing out as it should. He was down to the last assignment of this mission. The last woman. The last murder. In thirty-nine days, Mary Jane Kelly would die.

There was something wrong. Ethan lay naked, sprawling out on the bed, staring at the ceiling above, hands behind his head. He tried to label his emotions but could not. From the point he surrendered to *Time's* construct he'd felt cheated, dissatisfied with his role, as if being guided like a small child needing to have his hand held to cross the street or the stage, insulting his intelligence. He was given a script which he'd memorized, no improvisation necessary, no alteration to the construct already provided for him. Were he offered artistic license he would have written his part in the play with a more generous timeframe in which to work. There was no time to interact and to meet his co-stars, Elizabeth Stride and Catherine Eddowes, before cutting into their throats to the point of almost decapitating them. Ethan was not a coldblooded killer. He was an artist. His script would've included some interaction, maybe a dinner or a romantic run through the rain before he took his blade to their bodies, some kind of meaningful interlude. He would have loved to see their eyes, transforming from an expression of pure adoration to abject terror then ultimately, to a lifeless stare. He'd found himself agitated, indignant as he rested his sore body and sulked, his self-perception under attack from within.

Successive emotions building upon previous feelings as he laid there, he had to wonder why, how could *Time* betray him after he'd done everything asked of him? There would never be another opportunity to not only observe history but become a major character within its story. Upon the conclusion of his debriefing, he knew The Consortium would never again allow a risk of interaction in any future Flicker / Scope project approvals, no matter how descriptive Ethan would be in explaining how it would not affect the time continuum. Anson would be too paranoid to listen to him. This experience would be studied and analyzed for decades to come.

Wouldn't it have been something to have a few amazing personal characteristics of himself added to the story by getting to know and perhaps even love these women prior to the moment he killed them? Ethan began pounding his fists into the mattress on each side of him in, exasperated. In such a sweet spot, to be robbed of time, he resented being slighted, not factored into the equation. Stiffening his body in primal rage, he appeared to be having a child-like temper tantrum, acting out for not getting his way, angry at *Time* playing a parental role, telling him he couldn't have his toys. In fact, just like a spoiled little brat.

"I hate you. I hate you. I fucking hate you." Repeating it through gritting teeth, his jaw clenched, tears of frustration formed in Ethan's eyes. His emotions directed towards his only friend in this strange land, *Time* had abandoned him, too. The huge "Double Event" was over and there was nothing to do about it but fret, acting out in the privacy of his room until the tantrum passed and he finally fell asleep with a blood-covered thumb tucked in the corner of his mouth.

XXI.
OFF THE GRID

Ethan awoke mid-morning around half past ten to a cool, cloudless sky. He had recovered from his childish outburst just six hours earlier, resuming his "mission" mentality immediately. First walking over to the dresser and washing himself down of the stains and vestiges of the night before, he stared at the remains of one of the two candles he had not extinguished during the night, burning itself out sometime earlier that morning. He knew the feeling. Not wanting to gaze in the looking glass, not just yet, he was worried what would be gazing back at him and thought it best to focus on things to be accomplished for the day. Once he had cleansed the crimson color from his hands and arms he dressed into one of his local outfits simply to hit the loo, visit the kitchen for some hot coffee then replenish his pitcher with fresh water. It was becoming a routine. The next task at hand would be the labor required to remove bloodstains from his clothing, a formidable task.

The buzz of the tenants still sitting in the kitchen was two-fold. First, the word had already gotten out about the two women murdered. Second, as the Daily News had been printed, the paper on the table, all of the talk was about the text of the first "Dear Boss" letter which was signed with the *nom de plume* "Jack the Ripper". As Ethan walked past the table he stopped to sit on a bench and hold it in his hands, to read the words the first time they were printed. With his weary eyes transfixed upon the page, Ethan read the name of someone he knew in the paper. Soon everyone in the world would know the infamous name, the legendary Jack. He'd caught himself smiling at the thought *"You don't know Jack"* then covered his mouth until the urge subsided. If anyone saw his face they'd think it an expression of shock, appalled by what he was reading. The letter was of course, fictitious, subsequent letters, as well. He need not concern himself with having to write anything to maintain the timeline. Too many researchers over the centuries were in complete agreement that this series of letters were fraudulent, conjured up for hype by someone within the press to sell more papers, maybe make a name for himself down the road. This was undoubtedly the nefarious work of a roving reporter willing to exploit these victims again for his own ill-gotten gains.

It was surreal for Ethan, holding *this* newspaper, seeing his pseudonym glaring back on the day it was conceived, concocted by another hand, another mind. Truth be told, Jack the Ripper was not born this very day but he'd certainly been adopted on it. As a historian, to touch and read *the* newspaper was fascinating. He snickered, relishing an important moment in time, proof enough that the "real" Ripper did not write them. Ethan had not lifted a finger or a pen to contribute to the growing frenzy, essentially victimizing these women twice, perceiving himself to be above that sort of thing. No mercy bestowed, whoever wrote them owned no moral compass. Ethan found it rather humorous. The name "Jack the Ripper" was invented for the sake of publicity, a name synonymous with carnage and depravity. No one ever dared come forward to claim credit for what was to become one of the most infamous names in recorded history. A cynical, heartless marketing strategy worked as the first printed letter and successive "Saucy Jacky" postcard, (both of which allegedly fabricated), drove people in Whitechapel into mass panic. His only "personal" correspondence would come in fifteen days when he would send tangible evidence to George Lusk, as President of the Whitechapel Vigilance Committee. The recipient of the package would receive something of substance, an actual clue significant to the case.

All the more reason for Ethan to remain in his room. Cast as the lead in the play, he was a horrible actor. He was afraid the conversations he'd engage in with anyone would surely turn towards these murders and he did not know if he could fake being shocked and mortified quite enough to suit his purposes or to cover his arse! Even though it seemed no matter what he did *Time* would fix it for him, he still had that scientific logic telling him not to tinker with the Universe. It was a tumultuous day in Whitechapel. At the minute he was reading the letter, proposals for reward offers were being discussed all the way up the food chain to the Queen's desk, yet the case would soon become more convoluted, riddled with speculation. The suggestion had been made by Doctor Frederick Gordon Brown (who'd conducted the postmortem examination of Catherine Eddowes), that the murderer could possibly have had the occupation of a butcher, referring to the jagged cuts. Anti-Semitism was dividing the townspeople, adding to the case's convolution. With Eddowes' death bringing the City of London police into the fold, it contributed a jurisdictional conflict to the mucked up calamity of a notoriously failed investigation, going nowhere fast.

Ethan returned to his room, coffee and fresh water in hand. He'd have plenty of work to keep him preoccupied until he had to return to the hospital incinerator later at night under cover of darkness. As his clothes soaked he sat at his desk and opened his journal. No matter how morbid, he needed to document the "Double Event" and chronicle his personal take on it for posterity, taking his role in history seriously.

***

Journal entry ~ 1 October 1888

Woke to a beautiful morning. There was a variety of late season finches singing outside my window. Started the day with a refreshing cup of coffee as I am soaking bloodstains from my soiled sleeves. Second "local" attire has been put on. Either I am becoming accustomed to the rough tweed or this was made better than the ones before. Once I am finished with fabric restoration, washing the medical bag then cleaning the instruments, I'll be ready for more coffee and an in-house meal from the kitchen. Not going out anytime soon except to the loo again.

Oh, Anson! Once I'm back in the 21st Century I would like to talk with you about possible future Flicker projects and the fact that, well, it does not matter what they do. If the Princess Diana proposal is approved, then let the bloody Scope be on the motorcycle that drives the Mercedes off the road. It really won't matter. TIME will reformat the storyline immediately and succinctly so that everything transpires as it should. Not saying he should get off the bike and shoot Diana in the head or strip naked proclaiming he did it! However, through my experience and involvement I have concluded that I was meant to be here. I was always here. This becoming more obvious with each execution of the job it is now my determination that the Flicker anomaly was always designated by fate to exist so events of the past could manifest as designed by Time. Pray to the time gods! They made the door that may allow us from the future to fulfill all of our roles in the past!

Upon my return you may have an ethical dilemma with what I've had to do to preserve history as it was recorded but I believe, in retrospect, you and the entire Consortium will thank me for what I've done and perhaps erect a statue in my name honoring my dedication to deciphering and keeping the non-interference directive paramount in my mind considering the sacrifices I needed to make emotionally and ethically so that we all may continue to exist in the only future we know.

Enough of my pontifications. I am 39 days away from my homecoming and have several requirements left to prepare for, then execute. Sorry for the 'execute' play on words. I've got a lot of down time but it wouldn't be prudent to take another trip to the city of London for yet another concert or shopping spree. I think I will simply immerse myself in a few more books for entertainment and passing of time until my rendezvous with Mary Kelly on the 9th of November. Honestly, I cannot wait until I meet my final victim. The work I will do on her body is intricate and specific; artistic design. It should be fun. I can take my time with that canvas. Although I could not see their eyes, the texture of their blood, particularly Eddowes' open abdomen was arousing, having to use only my sense of touch to find my hidden treasures. If I must say so myself, I'm getting very good at this!

***

Around midday, Ethan surrendered his coffee, celebrating an early tea time as he was on his third bowl of fresh water. Still washing instruments, or rather, soaking them then sterilizing them once more, he had slipped downstairs to boil a pot in the kitchen once it emptied of tenants, so not to draw any suspicion. After all, everyone in Whitechapel was wary of everybody else. There was nothing less than a palpable paranoia in the air. As he sipped the tea, he thought it best to load up on more items to keep in his room in order to reduce his time in public while he waited to do these recorded acts of Jack the Ripper to keep the timeline rolling along. To the detriment of his plan to hide, Ethan would take one of a few remaining excursions out amongst the crowds, avoiding reward seekers or police inquiry. Going out by early afternoon on a Sunday, the streets would be heavily trafficked with carriages and pedestrians, allowing him to blend in, little or no effort required.

Being British and looking the part eliminated him from being profiled by those suspicious of immigrants of one certain ethnic background. The recent suspicion of Jack the Ripper being a local butcher also diminished the odds of drawing attention, as typically their clothing and overall appearance was indicative of their profession. The suspect's description was becoming more comedic and variable by the hour as just about every official on the case had a difference of opinion regarding a culprit, who committed these brutal slayings. Sailor, butcher, doctor, policeman, immigrant and even royalty! All would become targets of the investigation. Ethan didn't worry about the man he'd seen with Catherine Eddowes moments before he killed her in Mitre Square. He wouldn't be coming forward. If he fit any of these aforementioned categories or was perhaps an unfaithful husband, bringing attention to his encounter with Eddowes would result in nothing beneficial for him in the matter.

For Ethan, to be the sycophant to local authorities would no longer benefit him. Instead, it would cause suspicion as he might otherwise be ignored. He entertained the thought of returning to Spitalfields Market near Commercial and Hanbury Street where his "family friend" PC William Smith worked a beat, just in case he was to be stopped again. Smith would vouch for him. It was a beautiful day for a walk.

The chattering outside his lodging along Bakers Row had gradually turned into a whisper. Everyone was afraid and no one knew who to trust. The warmth of smiles and greetings from a passerby was nowhere to be found. The women were terrified and the men were paranoid. Sheep. Up and across Hanbury, he arrived at the market to find no policeman present, something he found rather odd. Then he remembered from his research, they were cloistered in preparation for the hunt. In two more days the officers would begin a door-to-door search, covering a two-hundred yard radius of Dorset Street, the area authorities concluded must have been where the murderer was hold up. Indeed, Ethan's placement was fortuitous. Whether it be Polly Nichols or that good old chap *Time* helping him along his mission, either way, relocation to Bakers Row had put him outside of the search grid. The conspicuous police absence meant they were already at their respective stations receiving instructions for their Tuesday kickoff of a comprehensive search that would require over two weeks to finish, yielding absolutely no dividends. Over 100,000 flyers were to be distributed during the same period of time to the apprehensive residents of Whitechapel.

On the mornings of Friday 31st August, Saturday 8th and Sunday 30th September 1888 women were murdered in or near Whitechapel supposed by someone residing in the immediate neighbourhood. Should you know of any person to whom suspicion is attached you are earnestly requested to communicate at once with the nearest police station.

Spitalfields was a busy place on any given Sunday, no different than any other marketplace from any era, the one day of the week people got out and about. Ethan strolled around the market in a leisurely manner. As if on holiday, he was absorbing it, taking his time, still taking snapshots in his mind. Stopping at each vendor to see if there was something which caught his wandering eye, he had purchased two large boxes of fruits and vegetables, one tin can and lid as well as a cheap bundle of rags to wrap a few bloody organs in, by necessity. Spending most of the bright afternoon there, Ethan noticed the interesting juxtaposition between the blissful day and the solemn air of those suspect and suspicious alike around him. Having only one more important stop to make, it was to purchase a bottle of wine of common vintage for an uncommon usage. All errands completed, he continued along the way, returning home without incident.

Eager for the late hours of the evening to approach, Ethan was already changing into his upper class wardrobe. The inside of his medical bag was securely lined with fresh rags. The object to be transported was neatly wrapped as a butcher would do prior to delivering an order of meat. Although he'd planned ahead for this late night trek to pay a visit to the hospital incinerator, anticipating minimal staffing, he chose to do so only as an extra precaution. It probably would have had no bearing on the outcome regarding when to go, as *Time* would manipulate events to accommodate Ethan's necessary movements. It was merely a good time to do the deed, as he had no previous plans for the evening.

Street traffic was lighter than usual, and yet, for an outer section of London, the population dictated that the odds of people still out at all hours was not uncommon. During this particular period in history local authorities estimated there were more than twelve-hundred prostitutes working in Whitechapel on any given night. It was surely a busy district of the city. In light of the recent murders, he was certain that number dropped somewhat but for most of these women the necessary risk of going out to earn a living meant the risk of death while the killer was on the loose. It was a necessary evil, food and shelter paramount over safety. The women had no choice but to rely upon their own keen observations so to keep their wits about them and likewise, keep their heads. In tandem, customers during this time had to convince the prostitutes they were not cold-blooded killers before any agreement to have sex was struck. It certainly seemed everyone was on the defensive. Most working girls, from an overabundance of caution, would stick to regular male faces and attached appendages with which they were familiar.

As he continued his walk, there were those coming and going to and from work and of course, there was a police presence, as if they were guarding the fair maidens rather than pursuing them for arrest. He spotted a small cluster of police along the way to the hospital and fortunately, positioned at such a fair distance, there would be no definitive encounter. Except for the few ignored proposals from vendors and vermin his arrival was swift and unencumbered. As expected, London Hospital was staffed by a skeleton crew at this time of night. As long as he'd dressed the part and carried his medical bag, he felt safe from discovery. Not one staff member lifted a head or a finger from paperwork duties or patient care rounds. It was as if he had become invisible, free to carry out "the job" in the incinerator room. Ethan tossed the human remains he was carrying into the intense flames and kept vigilant watch until the rags and contents were all engulfed by the inferno. Time brief, job done, time to go.

Although the mortuary on Old Montague Street had been the stopping point for the last two victims, those who expired (not under criminal circumstances) while in hospital would be brought to the basement morgue until processing was completed. The corridor taking him to and from the incinerator passed by two access doors to the morgue. As Ethan was walking along he was drawn to the sign like a child with a sweet tooth spying a big glass display in the window of a candy shop. He entered the morgue which, of course, was void of the living, but had six covered bodies on wooden slabs in various stages of preparation before autopsy then release for burial. He'd noticed one corpse was a young woman, in her late teens or early twenties, he surmised. Removing the sheet covering her to the shoulders, she did not have any indication on her body identifying a cause of death so she must have succumbed to some kind of internal injuries or disease. The lass was beautiful, appearing to be in perfect condition. Flawless skin, her long auburn hair drew him closer to her side, an enticement to touch without threat of retribution. Stepping closer, Ethan leisurely observed her form, taking in every detail with rapacious eyes. He began caressing her silky hair, daring to continue running his fingers tenderly across her cheeks then slowly, delicately down the center of her chest between her breasts to the middle of her abdomen, as if seducing a lover. He wondered if she had died a virgin or knew the pleasures of the flesh before expiring.

"Fancy a dance with an older chap?" Ethan asked, almost expecting a response.

How pale she was from head to toe. Fully exposed, she was no more than five feet in height. Lifting the body off of its slab, when he swept her up in his arms, in spite of her being unresponsive, dead weight, she felt like a toy doll, albeit one with rigor mortis setting in.

"Honey, you're a little stiff tonight." Ethan improperly joked, but who was there to judge him? The girl in his arms? He felt free, knowing *Time* would protect him. He laughed aloud, quickly wedging his face into the nape of her neck, muffling his ode to joy. Her feet dangled free as he began waltzing around the room with her in tow, moving as gracefully as possible between the autopsy tables. His partner was not being cooperative.

Their intimate dance had a soundtrack. Ethan suddenly heard a song in his head, humming along to a favorite tune by Tom Petty, an American singer he'd admired since youth. *"Last dance with Maryjane, one more time to kill the pain."* Yes! This morbid mannequin's name must have been Maryjane or he wouldn't have thought of the song! A mind whirling with their bodies, Ethan thought himself quite mad for a moment but only one shard of a second. Then he thought himself brilliant. In light of his current fluid feelings, a madman was awash, feeling everything. Every human emotion balled up in a fist. Ethan took it like a man, one strike after another, but the pain of the emptiness came in his unfulfilling liaison with Maryjane. She was as cold as ice.

Returning the girl to her resting place on the table, he repositioned then covered her precisely as he'd found her. Realizing his actions were hovering on the brink of insanity, it *was* crazy for him to think he could enjoy a dance with a body no longer alive. Had he felt the life leaving her, it may have been more satisfying but the lass he held so closely was long gone, dead to him, no attachment formed by the union. It was then he realized the most intimate and personal aspect he could ever imagine experiencing had already happened. He had felt human life slip away and craved it, a sensation unlike any other. It was his consolation prize for these last two victims, as he was deprived of peering into their eyes. His vindication came in taking from these women the flow of life's blood. Considering the personal sacrifices he'd made for the sake of *Time* and its demanding schedule, he had fulfilled his obligations to date and wanted to know what was in it for him. It wouldn't be asking too much.

It took Ethan no time to return to his lodgings. He could not undress fast enough, taking a moment to pose nude before his mirror image with narcissistic intention, a true reflection of himself. From the top drawer of his dresser he retrieved Catherine Eddowes' kidney, still wrapped in rags. He didn't bring it to the incinerator because he was not done with it yet. Gently unwrapping the vital organ she no longer needed, he carefully placed it in a small tin can he had bought at the market earlier. Stepping over to the desk Ethan grabbed the generic bottle of wine and opened it, poured just enough into the tin to completely cover the kidney before placing the lid on the can. Masking the smell of decay, wine also inhibited the degrading process. Replacing it back in the top dresser drawer, he carried the remaining bottle of wine over to the desk and sat there drinking it as he stared out the window. He was wide awake.

Something of a transition in Ethan's biological chronometer had occurred, as it was becoming more and more apparent to him. A seismic shift in routine, he'd been going to bed later and waking up barely before noon, a drastic contrast to his Oxford schedule just over a month earlier. He'd always realized he would be having many late nights on the job but never expected to become a true night owl. There seemed to be a shift to his inner clock. Laying naked in bed before one in the morning, he found himself once again staring up at the ceiling. He laid there for over two hours then finally fell asleep from sheer boredom.

For the next four days, with the exception of trips to the outhouse and kitchen for coffee and a book from the library shelf, Ethan never left his room. In that time he ate and read and drove himself crazier. Once awakening, he'd sit at the desk later and later, watching activities in the street from his window. The door-to-door search had begun nearer to Dorset Street and he could see all of the flyers being distributed on the road. Somewhere in the district were some busy men trying to piece together a puzzle, each and every fact thrown at them over the month plus of carnage added to the enigma now known as Jack the Ripper. They'd eventually seek out a psychic who was deemed a damn fool. Even dogs did not seem up to the task at snout.

Adding background music from a silent film to this whimsical ballet now being performed, it had great entertainment value. The dog and pony show. Police officers raced around Whitechapel, quickly getting nothing done but appearing busy doing it. Tomorrow would be the same, identical to this day and so on, monotonous in the extreme. Ethan felt like he was at Heathrow and his plane was delayed, forever. In hindsight, if he could have and would have known his true destiny in this story, he would have used Flicker after every murder to return to the 21st Century for the hot showers and a chance to sleep in his own soft bed, perhaps stock up on the delicious local bangers and mash he loved so much before making the leap. Everybody back at CERN would certainly enjoy the authentic meal, especially Colin. That would have been the ticket to ride! Jump in, do the deed and get out, quite like having sex as he recalled from his youth as a student. It was a vague recollection, at best.

Ethan had not thought of sex in an eternity. He romanticized all the time, even to the point of arousal, imagining a rendezvous with a beautiful 17th Century French maiden, perhaps a World War II British nurse. His thoughts being drawn to the act, the physical satisfaction, Ethan pondered his circumstances. Having been inside of three women from the perspective of pain in the last month, he thought it might be nice to be inside one for pure pleasure. His brief dance date with the corpse of a girl in the morgue was the closest he had been to a woman without cutting her head off since his junior year at Oxford. It was similar though not exactly as he remembered, feeling the weight of a woman in his arms. Perhaps it was precisely what he'd been needing, a little affection. *Hell's Belles*, there were over a thousand women working the streets of Whitechapel. He was bound to find at least one with some modicum of conversational skills and basic intellect, someone quite like Maggie the barmaid. Maybe Anson had sent him on with so much money precisely for this reason, almost as a dare, to go make a little mischief during his down time. As this titillating, rather salacious idea occurred to him, Ethan suddenly felt a distinct life force entering his body again, causing him to tingle in unmentionable ways, in some places more than others, liberating him to fantasize about keeping company with a lovely lady.

The grudge match ensued between his fear and his libido. Hormones prevailed. To the victor (or rather, to the Ethan) go the spoils. Excited, filled with anticipation, Ethan began to prepare just after eight in the evening as if he was going to his prom. Shaving for the first time in more than a week, including the moustache he'd grown for the "Double Event", his effort presented a smooth, clean appearance. He washed down twice then chose the second fancy outfit from his trip into the city of London to wear for his night out on the town. In desperate need of a haircut, he would have to attend to that in the days to come, though he'd assessed the growth as manageable once wet down and slicked back a bit. Ethan then took the time to organize and put away or hide all of his identifying items such as the medical bag and his documents, should he have the opportunity to entertain a guest in his private quarters.

It took three hours to prepare for this excursion, two devoted to his appearance then another sixty minutes to muster up the courage. Stepping out "out of character" was terrifying. Ethan had flown on autopilot since Annie Chapman's ring epiphany, relinquishing all decision-making to destiny, but this was not a recorded event. This was about making choices on his own behalf, frightening and exhilarating in equal measure. He needed a little risk and some female companionship and it may just be what the doctor ordered to feel some semblance of normalcy again, if possible. He wondered if he would ever feel normal again. With one final personal inspection in the mirror he looked like a proper English gentleman of means; all dressed up with someplace to go. Ethan thought he looked pretty damn good by candlelight.

Money tucked inside the breast pocket of his jacket, his timepiece attached to its fob and his trousers, he pulled it out to check. Nearly 11:30 p.m., it was, indeed, a good time for a chance encounter with a lady of the evening. As Ethan exited the room he locked the door behind him then went downstairs, out the front door onto Bakers Row. For the first time since his arrival he did not have a direction to follow, no research to do or obligation to meet according to the dictates of his master *Time*. Ethan was free to wander the streets of Whitechapel in search of a nameless woman with whom to share some shameless time. It was only a matter of time before he'd find what he was searching for on the streets of London.

XXII.
GRAVEYARD SHIFT

Heading south, after several steps Ethan turned north, pivoting in place, with an abrupt change of mind and direction. It occurred to him he'd best avoid the bustling Whitechapel Road. At the intersection of Hanbury, Old Montague and Bakers Row, he stopped. As these streets had relevance to "the job" past and present he chose to bypass them and continue north along Bakers Row. A few streets up, the pedestrian traffic had slowed, only workmen coming and going from shifts. He would have to ignore the pertinence of the other avenues and stroll back toward the intersection. Ethan decided to loiter a bit on Hanbury Street, as there were less vendors and more public housing, so anybody out at that time of night was obviously looking for only one thing. Women of the streets could readily distinguish between those who were walking with purpose to a destination and the others waiting for an invitation. Ethan was utterly shocked by the immediate barrage of women approaching, considering the brutal murders of Elizabeth Stride and Catherine Eddowes were less than a week past. Some of the ladies must've known the dead women and yet, were still out and about. Ethan guessed correctly. The necessity to make money took precedence over safety and it appeared, by the sheer number of them, most had the same idea. They were literally risking death to earn a living.

They all appeared to respect the time required for each to take her turn in asking any of the potential customers, "Do you want the business?" If the man agreed then the deal was set and off they went to some secluded corner. If he showed no interest then he was open game for the next girl. Ethan had no idea of what he was looking for, he only knew what was approaching him wasn't it, forties and up with missing teeth, unkempt and unbathed, actually, not unlike his unfortunate victims. One after another, he responded in the negative as kindly as he could.

"Thank you, no." A mild shake of the head shook them off his trail.

He must have repeated those words twelve times or more as he crossed the road on Hanbury and returned toward Bakers Row. Ethan wanted to get off of this street as soon as possible, not only because of the caliber of the women he was seeing but also his manner of dress was now drawing the attention of some of the street vermin. Pickpockets or gang members, he didn't want to overstay his welcome there to learn their intentions toward him. Once back on Bakers Row, Ethan felt safer and decided to continue south, only up to Whitechapel Road where, if he saw no one of interest, he would give up and try his luck again another night.

Just past Whites Row, near the rear end of the Pavilion Theatre off Whitechapel, one lady caught his eye from some distance. There was something so familiar about her, though she was facing away from him at the time, speaking with another young woman, one of her own kind, no doubt. Ethan played coy, passing the two women, stopping a few lampposts down, as if reading the notice posted on the theatre wall. He then scanned back where they stood, only to notice them both looking his way. In their profession, that line of work required knowing when the shy ones had no idea how to approach. Ethan was far too easy to read. Moving directly into his line of sight so to ascertain his interest, the one woman he fancied smiled at him as she lifted her hand, a modest wave, so sweetly, innocently acknowledging her admirer. Ethan was suddenly stunned. He could not stop himself from staring at her as he held his breath. The resemblance was remarkable! Either *Time* had toyed with him or this was one excellent argument for the concept of reincarnation but she was the spitting image of a young understudy from the Flicker trials down in The Valley, Ms. Maggie Daley, apparently alive and well in Victorian England.

Ethan felt a flicker of light in his dark heart as he reminisced for a few moments, thinking back or forward to the last time he'd seen her, covered from head to toe in mud, falling to her knees as she hurriedly brought him his field reports. This woman had a soiled face, as well, but not from mud. Street grime, he suspected, as she spent many a night walking the route he was on in the Whitechapel district. She possessed the same gigantic green eyes filled with wonder, blonde hair and a cute button nose, Disney-like features, characteristics creating the fairy tale air of her presence. If he dared to stare, it was nothing he could control nor did he wish to break his gaze. As he peered in her direction, the two young ladies began giggling, as they'd whispered a few words to each other. Obviously Ethan was the focus of the humor but he had no idea what he'd done until he realized his slack-jawed mouth was hanging wide open. Perhaps, he thought, he should close it as he became aware of his expression, a singular moment of recognition showing on his face. Swaying to the left then back right, as if pondering her next move rather than his own, he strained to see her more clearly in the dim light without appearing rude. The woman gestured once with her index finger, indicating that he should come to where they were standing. Actually looking behind him to be reassured her invitation was meant for him, not someone else, she laughed when he did a double take. Yes! Indeed, it *was* Ethan, her potential client all alone, feeling like twenty-plus years had just been stolen from his maturity and experience and he was but a mere schoolboy lost on the street. He took a deep swallow to remove the lump in his throat but it didn't do the trick. He was a nervous wreck as he walked toward her, drawn moth-to-flame to the lovely lass. The nearer he approached the more Ethan recognized a resemblance so striking it was uncanny, right down to her height and petite frame.

"'Ello, gov'ner." She opened their discourse with her melodic voice, the sound a songbird would envy.

Ethan did not speak at first. Rather, he tipped his hat to both women, who once more looked at each other and tittered in reaction, responding with a curtsey.

"My name's Eth…Arthur Br...Arthur." Though a nervous man hadn't stumbled over his feet going closer to her, he was certainly stumbling over his words.

"Well, 'ello Mr. Eth-Arthur. Was ya lookin' for the business tonight?"

Ethan cringed inside. He hated that phrase. It reminded him of all the desperate women he'd already been accosted by along his journey, the same words uttered by Polly Nichols in his room on that fateful evening which changed everything.

"I'd like some company, if that's alright?" He offered a more subtle approach.

"Sure. Do ya want to go up the alley over there?" She seemed more than willing.

"No. No. I have a place, just down the street." He pointed north on Bakers Row.

Smiling, yet, with a rather peculiar, cockeyed expression, the girl stepped closer to inspect Ethan, scrutinizing him more thoroughly beneath the lamplight overhead, all the while well aware that looks can be deceiving.

"Ya ain't the Ripper now, is ya?"

"How could you even ask such a thing?" Slightly indignant, Ethan was a really bad actor. He was amazed that she seemed to accept his disclaimer with such ease.

"A girl's gotta be careful nowadays." She said, turning to her friend. "Used to be we'd ask if ya had any money. Now we gots to ask if yer a murd'rer. Sorry, sir."

Ethan needed to lighten up to meet the more cheerful mood of this young lady.

"Well, to answer your question, miss, no. I am not. I'm off this week, in fact."

"Well, d' ya mind if me friend 'ere watches where ya bring me, then? After all, we got hard times here and a girl's gotta be careful." A bit redundant, with reason, no truer words were ever spoken on the streets of Whitechapel.

Ethan agreed and off the three went, which he actually preferred. Walking with one woman looks like an arrangement but two looks like three friends or associates. Threesomes were something quite uncommon in a city so impoverished, regardless of the competitively low rates these women were charging, just not done at the time. Arriving at his lodging house, the women waved at one another as Ethan escorted the Maggie doppelganger inside. He wasn't concerned about the other girl knowing where he resided, as there was no Whitechapel girl murdered on this day in history.

They walked through the kitchen area and up to his room. Some lodgings would object, charging more for an additional person or rejecting the visitation out of hand but Ethan had been such a good, quiet client, the best kind of guest, always paying in advance, the innkeeper did not dare utter a word as they passed his window. Once entering his private space, upon further inspection, she circled around it as if she'd consider buying the place! Checking out the small desk then crossing to the dresser, her movements were graceful, her air, light and breezy. It was so obvious she didn't often frequent such nice digs and Ethan's was one of the nicer she'd ever seen, quite comfortable. He watched as she surveyed the landscape, running her slender fingers along the surface of the wood. There was something whimsical, magical about her. If he did not know what she did for a living he would think of this fresh-faced lass as the personification of purity, the essence of youthful elegance as she sashayed to the center of the rug, spinning in place to take it all in once again. So clean and tidy, the bed made up with nice linens, she'd fallen into the lap of luxury. His preparation prior to departure had paid off based on her impression of the place.

Ethan closed the door behind them. He stood there observing her every nuance, still peering in amazement at the lovely creature before his eyes, a vision. Though he had left one candle ablaze inside its cast iron cauldron, he lit the other atop the dresser, merely to shed more light on the subject, wanting to witness every facet of this diamond in the rough as she sparkled by candlelight. Setting the dreamy mood, one more conducive to romance, he was the one burning inside. Neither had spoken since entering the room.

"You're…beautiful." Ethan's anxiety was belied by his honest babble.

The young woman was awed by his candor, smiling again, approaching her host. He was much taller, gazing down into her eyes from a bit of a distance. She'd looked away only for a moment to the top of the dresser where she spotted a few of the rags Ethan had purchased. Taking one, dipping it fully into the water basin, she wrung it out then repositioned the candle on the dresser closer to where Ethan stood, allowing her face to be in better light for him to see.

"Didn't get a chance to clean up for ya. Would ya mind?" Offering up the moist rag for him to assist her.

Ethan surrendered to her eyes as he took the rag from her. He began to wipe her face clean of the day's remains, never breaking from the locked gaze they shared, wiping away the grime of time, hoping to find his apprentice beneath the soot.

"Uh, what is your name?" In his bewilderment he had forgotten to ask.

"Who d'ya want me t' be?" She offered as a courtesy…or a fantasy.

"Maggie." He couldn't believe he'd blurted it out. "May I call you Maggie?"

"O' course, love." She then grabbed Ethan's hand, shaking it too hard. "Name's Maggie, then. Nice to meet you, um, Arthur was it?"

Amicably shaking his hand to no end, he grasped hers firmly in his own to slow the momentum, then leaned over, dropping his lips below her wrist.

"M'lady." This time he glanced up into her eyes.

Looking toward the pending rendezvous, she found her way to the bed without him. Sitting, she'd bounced around a bit, testing the firmness of the mattress before testing his, enticing him to join her. Sensing no threat from his presence, she'd felt free to be playful with Ethan. Growing more comfortable by the moment, Maggie decided to dive right into the center of the bed as if it were the deep end of the pool, laughing all the way. Clean her up and put her in a linen business suit from the 21st Century, the woman was absolutely Maggie. Ethan still could not believe his eyes. Spreading out, she laid on her side in his bed. He brought one of the candles closer for examination. Noticing her one and only flaw, by comparison to Ms. Daley, and undoubtedly due to her poor diet and equally poor dental practices of the time, her smile was not as bright as her twin from the future but it was still as infectious.

"Are ya comin'?" A leading question, she motioned for him to take the plunge.

"Yes." Amenable to the suggestion, Ethan laughed in embarrassment, realizing his intense nervousness was obvious to both of them.

Maggie was trying to loosen him up, ready to help him out of his clothing.

"So, what's yer pleasure, love? What can I do to warm yer toes, aye?"

Ethan had no answer. He hadn't thought this through.

Yes. The ultimate goal was to have sex, but he did not even know how to begin. This was going to be more awkward than he remembered. Ethan cleared his throat.

"To be honest, I was hoping you could decide."

She looked at him first with pity but then adoration. Most men she encountered locally were filthy, disgusting pigs with no manners, uncouth in the extreme. Ethan was a breath of fresh air, a revelation. She felt empowered in his presence, in a way she rarely had before. The seductress-in-chief, by necessity, as he would never take the lead role in this scenario, it was up to her to make it happen. She wanted to have some fun with it, to enjoy her work for a change.

"C'mere, lover." *Maggie* beckoned.

Kneeling on the bed, she leaned over, snagging Ethan's trousers at the waistline, pulling him in closer. She started taking off his fancy clothes, beginning with layers covering his chest and back. Peeling the jacket, it fell to the floor revealing his shirt. He watched as pretty fingers fumbled with the buttons, deliberately taking her time, she viewed his bare chest. He wasn't a hairy man. She was fascinated by its absence, running her hands up inside the fabric along his soft, smooth upper body then over his shoulders, around to his back. Her hands were all over his torso, a tender touch. He craved more, desired more. Removing his shirt, she kissed what she could reach from her position on the bed, leaning into his midsection, sliding her moistened lips across his chest so gently it tickled. Ethan couldn't even remember the last time he had been touched this way, if ever. *Maggie* was, indeed, a seductress, tempting him to lay his hands on her but he suppressed the urge, his palms as sweaty as his brow, and on such a cool night. The temperature outside his open window had nothing to do with it. This heat was emanating from within, a fire so intense he feared he might burst into flames. As her lips caressed his chest he studied her glistening hair, how it draped over her shoulders. Oh, how he ached to reach down and stroke her locks. Ethan was barely breathing yet his heart was pounding. *Maggie* placed an ear to it, hugging him around the waist, listening to what she had done and she had only just begun to arouse the man compared with what she intended to do to get his attention.

As she continued her oral exploration of his quivering torso, *Maggie* reached in then down, unbuttoning the top of his fine trousers. He quickly pulled away to stop her before she could go any further. He was a modest man. When it came to matters of intimacy, the shy nature he had as a boy was still very much intact. Interpreting his action correctly, not as rejection, her reaction to Ethan's anxiety was sweet.

"I don't bite, love." She spoke lightheartedly to ease his tension. "That's extra."

Ethan didn't mean to withhold his affections. He was lost, in uncharted territory, wandering into No Man's Land. He blew out the candle nearest to the bed, allowing the other to remain as ambient light in the room, except for the soft glow of gaslight lamps shining through his window from below. Regaining his courage, Ethan stood directly in front of her, ready to take it like a man. Placing his palms upon her rather diminutive shoulders, there was room to spare. Feeling free to do so, he traced her hairline with his fingertips then sunk them into thick strands where they too got lost as did Ethan, his thoughts wandering with his hands. She pulled him down onto the bed with one solid tug, flipping him over in such a way that his legs dangled loosely off the side of the mattress. If it'd seemed a surreal trip to Wonderland prior to that instant, it was about to get real. This woman knew precisely what she was doing, a practiced methodology, multitasking even before it was a concept, let alone a word in the Oxford English Dictionary. She had it down to a science, a form of fine art.

Removing his shoes so to streamline her confiscation of his trousers, Ethan laid very still, allowing her to work her magic. With each button undone came a kiss as he languished in her care. Leaving behind wet marks wherever she went, her supple tongue teasing him along, his skin tingled where damp as the cold night air intruded on a private interlude, though neither of them felt chilly as it swept through an open window. *Maggie* found the air as refreshing as her newfound client, Arthur. Slowly, but surely, his trouser buttons undone, one by one, she pulled them off, leaving him with just his not very sexy wool socks and stockings. Pausing to stare at what fabric remained, *Maggie* muffled the urge to burst into a girlish giggle once again. Trying to contain herself, Ethan quickly explained his predicament.

"The fabric of the pants is itchy. These help keep the scratching under control."

His Maggie clone continued staring at the leggings as Ethan hurried, awkwardly removing them himself. She raised her eyebrows, nodding in approval overall.

"Ya know? That's good common sense." She complimented his sense of utility if not his sense of style.

She had him lay back once again as she straddled him. It took a few minutes for her to unbutton and remove her top layers, albeit slowly for his enjoyment, but once she did, *Maggie* waited patiently, allowing his eyes to linger, letting him absorb the exposed top half of her body. Ethan's shyness returned with his embarrassment, as if he was staring at the beautiful bare shoulders, neck and breasts of the real Maggie, though he could not bring himself to look away, gazing submissively.

She lifted his hands, pulling them toward her bosom, embracing the back of his head as he tenderly kissed her breasts. As he suckled, her breathing kept increasing in depth and pace. She latched onto a handful of his hair then pulled his head back, looking into his eyes as she continued to breathe through her mouth then she smiled at him. He leaned back once more while she reached up beneath layers of skirts and moved aside any obstruction to their joining with one another. She began moving back and forth, attempting to work him up a bit before entering her. He continued watching her eyes as she threw her head backward, moaning and breathing heavily. Leaning forward, *Maggie* rested her hand on his bare chest, letting her silken locks drape across her face, swaying over his as she thrust her hips forward and backward, harder and faster but then she suddenly stopped. Ethan was not becoming aroused. His subconscious mind wouldn't allow him pleasure as it kept repeating in his head: *"This isn't real. She's acting. None of this is truly her. No. She's not my Maggie."*

"Ya alright, love?" Awkwardly inquiring, she felt nothing down there from him. In spite of her effort, no sign of life.

"Yes, I'm sorry. I don't know what's wrong." Indeed, he did know what was wrong.

"Not to worry, love. Happens to the best of 'em now and then." She countered, hearing of these stories from other working girls. It never happened to her before.

"Wanna give it another go? Try again?" Kind and sympathetic to his plight, the young lady wanted to complete the task for her client. It was her job, after all.

"Perhaps another night?" Ethan responded as he rose and sat on the edge of the bed, hurriedly putting his pants back on. He was lost in thought, thinking too much.

"Yeah, anytime love." Taking her cue from him, she began to get dressed again. "Th' girls know me as Abby. If ya ask 'round they'll know where t' find me."

Ethan asked what he owed her without looking in her eyes, his head down. She told him the meager amount, a pittance for her, which he immediately remitted, five times what Abby expected. She briefly objected, politely so, noting his refusal of a refund promptly issued. In gentlemanly custom, with very little said between them, Ethan walked her back downstairs. A hug goodbye, he closed the door behind her. Off she went, disappearing into a foggy night. The itching had returned everywhere. He'd put on his trousers without the protective stockings. Scratch. Scratch. Scratch.

XXIII.
COMING AND GOING

Two more times over the next six days Ethan heard an impromptu knock on his door during the late night or early morning hours. Abigail would return. Ethan knew it was for nothing more than money. He was likely the most generous customer she ever had. In spite of it, he was delighting in her companionship. After trying again to arouse his loins with no success, they'd talked. The second return visit she stayed the night and they slept together, just slept until late in the morning, wrapped in one another's arms. Ethan enjoyed bringing her coffee. They sipped their morning brew as he told her of his college days, a few adjustments to the era so as not to divulge any secrets. Abby told her untrue stories too, speaking of her intentions to someday go to school, improve her circumstances in life; they both knew it wouldn't happen. For a brief time she exited the room, returning with a pair of kitchen scissors, shears for Ethan, explaining how she'd fancied herself a decent barber in earlier days when she routinely cut her two brother's hair. It was Ethan's first haircut since his arrival. An intimate liaison, she circled him over and over, leaning into him as he remained poised quite still in the desk chair centered in the room. Supple breasts mere inches from his face as Abby kept snipping away, allowing them to stroke his cheeks from time to time, the common haircut transformed into an alluring interlude playing out in slow motion, a scene he memorized and would never forget. Whether it was her intoxicating presence, her body so close to his own, or perhaps because Abigail was holding something so sharp in her hand, so close to his face and neck, Ethan found it sensual, erotic, a thrillingly dangerous moment for the of both of them, had Abby known whose hair she was cutting.

After her third paid visit with Ethan when he tried eel pie for the very first time, Abby's treat, as he'd done before, he walked her to the front door then said goodbye before returning to his room. Once behind the door, he crossed over to the window facing Bakers Row. From there he could clearly see Abigail talking to a man across the street, no doubt an interested midday customer or perhaps she was making plans for an evening rendezvous. Ethan felt no possessive tendencies toward Abby. What he saw had no effect on him it that way. In fact, as the man talking to this *imposter Maggie* felt some entitlement to grasp her by the waist, pulling her closer into him, Abby showed her reluctance to oblige him. Ethan felt a sensation long absent from his loins; a visceral stimulation he had not felt in quite some time. He was achieving arousal by watching the controlling way in which that brute was manhandling her, testing the water to see how deep he could go. Their encounter appeared to be more of a power play by the man, not the woman. He might well be one of the local gang members attempting an extortion. Indeed, she was younger than most on the streets but she was a clever lass and a manipulative woman, as well. She knew these streets and how to handle herself. He felt no sense of impending doom, of her being in any sort of danger but his imagination hoped differently. Besides, he'd have to abide by the non-interference directive. Abigail's knight in shining armor couldn't intervene on her behalf if he'd wanted to help. Smirking, he thought, "I'm off the time clock."

It was crystalline clear, painfully so, yet another moment of epiphany for Ethan LaPierre in his ongoing process of illumination. He was a voyeur. It shouldn't have come as a surprise to him. For the last several years he'd been training to be exactly that, a Scope. His duties in the respective Flicker projects primarily included these proclivities, an ability to watch events in history unfold. In the case of Ethan's task, it was to watch murders being committed, to spy on tragedy porn in its rawest form. Trained in this, he'd wound up participating instead of watching from the shadows, a safe distance, undetected. It became immediately obvious why he had an arousal, looking down at the scene below. It explained his flaccid dysfunction with Abigail. Calling her *Maggie* by name did not help nor would anything else because his only interaction with women since being here was violent by his own actions. He started rubbing himself harder against an edge of the desk through his trousers, looking on. The feeling faded too quickly because the encounter below had abruptly ended with Abigail shoving away from the bloke then storming off down the street. Ethan had an intimate internal glimpse of who and what he had become and it wasn't what he expected to see in the metaphorical looking glass. Perverse thoughts he entertained were paramount in his mind to the exclusion of all else, savoring the self-reflection.

Over the next few days Abigail did not visit him. Ethan kept silent vigil, peering out the window through most of each passing day to see if he could spot her on the street. When he wasn't reading or in the kitchen preparing his food or drink, he was watching for her with every glance, a peripheral turn of the head, certain she would return to him eventually, likely due to reemerge once she had run out of funds. He wanted to see her but Ethan was not deluding himself, either. Theirs was a business arrangement, first and foremost. He longed to talk with her, to explain his dilemma, this newly acquired and very specific taste of pleasure. She had been so patient with him their first three times together when he failed to perform. Of course, the money helped with any impatience she struggled with, as it was surely her main motivation for returning again and again. He was certain they could find an amicable solution, a proper price to compensate her for his unusual request, a fee for service rendered elsewhere, in the arms of another man. Ethan's discovery of his unique inclinations and appetite, a penchant for voyeurism was a tendency he simply could not ignore.

The very next night Abby did indeed return to his room, as predicted. A familiar knock on the door sent a surge of adrenaline pulsing through his veins as he leapt up from his desk to answer the call. The poor darling was sporting a blackened eye, a battle scar from yet another dangerous liaison on the streets of Whitechapel.

"Please don't ask." Abby interrupted before he could begin an inquisition.

"Wasn't going to mention it." He responded, easing tension in the air. He knew the badge of defiance most likely came from a thug on the street, a sign of the times and the tough life she lead.

Abigail walked in then over to the desk to lay a few items down as she rambled on about her day like she had just returned home from work. In the meantime, Ethan went to lay down on the bed. Turning to face him, she let out a remark of shock.

"Bloody hell, Arthur! Yer socks are filthy! Looks like ya been walkin' 'round without any shoes on fer days!" In fact, her assessment was correct.

Taking the initiative to pull them off his feet before he could resist, he laughed. Ethan could imagine his 21st Century Maggie doing the same thing in his apartment at Oxford. She balled them up and threw them near the pitcher on the dresser to be washed later on, then opened the top drawer, searching for a fresh pair.

"I'm not paying you for changing my socks, you know!" Ethan joked.

"On the contrary, sir, I should be the one payin' for the honor!" Abby's rebuttal was adorable. She sifted through his underwear, looking for a matching pair.

"What's this?" she said, still sifting and searching.

"What's what?" Ethan asked curiously.

"This." Abby repeated, holding up the tin can in which the wrapped, preserved kidney of Catherine Eddowes was contained, saturated in cheap red wine.

Ethan felt a jolt of electricity fly through his entire body, a high-voltage call to attention. He'd known it was still in there, destined to make its historical debut quite soon, just forgotten about in the moment as his mind was elsewhere, lost in thought, consumed with another fixation. Any story concocted would lead to more curiosity, which could lead to horrible consequences for both. He decided to rely on his ever present friend, *Time* to bail him out of this oversight.

"It's a preserved heart. Open it!" Ethan boldly asserted his claim, offering Abby access with a facetious grin. He was too clever by half, going the way of half-truth. He was playing his part flawlessly. To have said a *kidney* was stored in the container might trigger a memory for her when the "From hell" letter went public. Thinking quickly on his feet, even when lying flat on his back, practice makes perfect and he played her perfectly.

"Ugh. Stuff that, love." She placed it back inside the drawer. "Pro'bly the other socks y'ave yet to wash. At least in there, they won't stink." Finally matching two socks, she closed the drawer. Instead of sliding them on his feet she balled each one up and threw them at him, laughing as she did. Abigail jumped on the bed then kept jumping all around Ethan chanting in a girlish tease: "Dirty sock man. Dirty, dirty sock man. Yer feet stink. Yer a stinker!" She dropped, straddling his hips, ready to give it another go, more than willing to try again.

"Ya wanna?" Knowing she'd be paid regardless of whether or not she asked, it was her suggestion, secretly hoping he would agree. Having grown quite fond of a rather shy, odd gentleman, her inquisitive nature was about to be sated. Ethan was ready, too...ready to tell her what he needed, what he desired from his new mistress. Breathing deeply, attempting to calm his angst before making an indecent proposal, Ethan had spent several days preparing for this unique request of Abigail.

"I have to ask a favor of you." He began tentatively, a slight tremor in his voice. "Please understand, you are free to deny me, no hard feelings. Say 'no' if you want. I'll completely understand." Speaking the words aloud was as foreign to him as the appeal he was making of her.

Sensing the seriousness in his demeanor, Abby sat straight up, looking down on Ethan with wide-eyed wonder, perplexed and enticed in equal measure. Most of the men she serviced were quite predictable in their sexual interests and pleasures. She knew this was something "different" by the expression on his face. The price *they'd* pay kept a roof over her head. The price *she* paid was monotony, bored to death by the same old tricks night in and night out. For her, it was all an act. For him, it was as well, but the role he wanted her to play for him on the stage below, on the street outside his window, well, it may prove to be too difficult, a bit too bizarre for her.

"What's ya pleasure? What'ya have in mind?" Awaiting his answer, Abigail's anticipation made her playful. Open to suggestion, she was excited by the prospect.

Gazing up into her eyes, Ethan mustered the courage by drawing a deep breath then blowing it out, puffing up his cheeks with the force exerted.

"I'd appreciate it if you would return to the street in front of my window, across the way where I can see you from here and allow the next man who approaches you to rough you up a bit." He said it all in one single, solitary breath.

"What d' ya mean by 'rough'?" Abby didn't skip a beat. She'd been around and had heard of, if not experienced the depravity of men firsthand, backhanded from time to time. Though she didn't really expect it of Ethan,

Abby wasn't shocked by very much anymore. Most women in the profession have a history of abusive men in their lives from the start, many relating violence with affection. "Normalcy" was assessed on a case-by-case basis, factoring in the complexities of human emotions and experience. This request wasn't so far off the grid.

"Nothing you'd be uncomfortable with, I assure you." Ethan explained further, making his case based on an assumption that she had endured such behavior in the past and may be willing to again, if the price was right. "I will reward your efforts, I promise you that, lass. It's the only way I can, well, you know."

"And are ya gonna come to me rescue and save me from the bloke then?" She asked with a *'damsel in distress'* expectation of some drama in her life.

"Um, not exactly. No."

"Well, then where might ya be?"

"Uh, watching from my window." Ethan asked more than suggested.

She fell silent, staring at him for a moment before she got up, sliding off of him. Ethan thought he'd blown it, that he went too far. He stood from the bed in his bare feet and followed her over to the desk, thinking Abby was about to gather up all her belongings and leave his residence before this sordid discussion went any further. There she stood, staring out the window. His intention was to apologize for the lurid suggestion and ask her to forgive and forget what he'd said but before he could, she spoke quite candidly regarding the proposition.

"This is gonna cost ya more, love." She stated her position matter-of-factly, still peering out the window to determine the best possible vantage point for his viewing pleasure. Abigail sighed heavily then turned to look at him. "Right, then." Holding out her hand, an expectation of payment in advance, he gladly obliged her request, finding her honesty refreshing, almost innocent if not for the seasoned response.

Ethan went into his pocket and gave her a generous sum for the impending task. There wasn't a word or gesture of disapproval from her, as she could not turn down her best client. This was a business transaction, after all, nothing personal. Abigail knew if she held onto him long enough she could dare hope to escape the street life and invest the money wisely for her future.

The amount he handed her could sustain her for nearly two weeks, or more. Looking at Ethan once again without judgment, she collected her belongings from the desk before exiting his room in silence.

Standing motionless for a few minutes, wondering if he'd exposed too much of himself in the process, he pondered his decision to divulge his most intimate needs. If the girl were to take the money and run, well, Ethan really couldn't blame her. It was a lot to ask of anyone. He took a huge risk revealing his deepest, darkest desires to her, sharing a secret. Having developed this obsession seemingly overnight, with a chance of watching his fantasy being played out before his eyes from above, the man was barely breathing. His initial voyeuristic role, the one he'd been mentally prepared for by the psychology department of The Consortium (in false expectation of his role here in this century), his fixation had turned perverse and self-gratifying. At this point, his selfishness may have driven off his Maggie replacement, never to see her again. It mirrored images he had kept as postcards from The Valley of a fair maiden walking away across the soggy soil path. Recalling her soft, sweet voice as she fell once more, he had come to her aid. A knight in shining armor. A damsel in distress. It had all been so romantic in his mind. This role had expanded beyond the limited boundaries of propriety. To say he'd gone off-script was an understatement. This kind of improvisation could prove dangerous for everyone involved.

Ethan heard Abby's voice rising as sweetly from beyond his window. He leaned over the desk, straining to see who her words were directed toward. It was another working girl doing her job on the graveyard shift. The ladies of the night had to be so cautious walking the streets, as it was potentially a path to the Death House then the cemetery. The two of them standing in the middle of Bakers Row, he could not make out the conversation between them but suddenly they both looked up at his window. Ethan quickly backed up into the shadows, acting like a child caught with his hand in the cookie jar. Wetting his thumb and index finger, he doused the candle on the desk, shrouding the room in darkness. Feeling safely cloaked, he leaned back over the desk to survey the scene. When he looked out again he saw Abigail's friend walking off and Abby herself walking over and standing across the street, her back against a wall. The gaslight lamps were positioned fortuitously to his vantage point. He could clearly see the area where his female friend patiently awaited an approach from a suitor. It wouldn't take long for the lass to get noticed, he presumed.

Shortly into his scoping out session, Abigail's friend appeared with a burly man of average age and height. She walked him up to Abby, initiating what appeared to be a proper introduction destined to result in some improper behavior. Pressing the flesh, they shook hands as the other woman departed, continuing on down the street. They spoke for several minutes as Ethan stared at them, waiting with bated breath. He could see Abby's face and part of the right side of her body but the man's girth obstructed the rest of his view of the vision he recognized as Maggie Daley's clone. It was too far a distance to hear conversation between them but he assumed she was following the directives issued.

He grabbed her by the waist, pulling her into his body with ease, as she was an incredibly delicate creature. His available hand began groping her breasts while he pushed her up against the wall. Until that moment, Ethan hadn't realized he already had an initial stirring, a swelling in his trousers. Reaching down to greet it, a warm welcome, he began rubbing himself in anticipation of what he was about to witness. Abigail pushed the man away, provoking him to get rougher, to have his way with her. Ethan was becoming more excited by the moment, excited in mind but not yet a full physical erection. Relishing the encounter unfolding before his anxious eyes, hungry for more, he was enticed, drawn to the events. Still, he was not getting truly hard. Something was not right, something he couldn't put his finger on. As Abigail clutched the man's massive forearms, he seized her by the wrists, lifting her hands above her head, pressing her arms against the wall behind her as he planted his face into her bosom. Alarmed, Ethan noticed something was wrong with this scenario. Abigail wasn't struggling. In fact, she was fighting back her laughter which got the best of her. His "aggression" was causing her to giggle, enough to cause Ethan to abruptly deflate, feeling defeated by the charade of a performance. It appeared there was no shortage of bad actors in Whitechapel. Suddenly it all made sense. Abigail's girlfriend had brought in a ringer, a man known to them. He was there to role play with the con-woman who took his money under false pretenses. The "couple" down below on the street were unaware they'd been exposed as frauds, so they continued. Ethan was livid, furious that he was being mocked by her and two accomplices, the one being played while they were laughing at him! They were both having fun and at his expense, playing with each other, putting on an act. Playing like children, but he was their toy. Ethan stepped away from the window, retreating into the shadows.

Hands on his lips, Ethan stared down at the floor, feeling an incredible hatred for someone he'd really begun to like. Duped and deceived, Abby had made a fool of him as much as he'd made a fool of himself. "I trusted that whore." As he began pacing the room, rounding the rug, his emotions brewing in a cauldron of contempt, they bubbled to the surface as he spoke aloud. "Doesn't that bitch know who she's fucking with? I will kill her for this!" Those words came so naturally to his lips, the logical thing to say if one was a serial killer. An apoplectic rage rose in him to such an extent, he felt nauseated by his dizzying trip around the room. Stopping abruptly, regaining his equilibrium did nothing to decrease his agitation or ease a humiliation he was suffering. It felt as if his blood was literally boiling in his veins. It occurred to Ethan that he had never understood this phrase before now because he had never been this angry in his life.

The sense of betrayal was palpable, the desire for vengeance, undeniable. Abby had not respected his wishes nor issues. She displayed no regard for the trust placed in her to guard his secret. Her willingness to help him was duplicitous. "You bloody fucking whore. Fucking bloody whore. You sick, twisted bitch." Becoming more furious by the minute, something warped inside him, something had changed. It felt surreal. "Bloody fucking whore, Maggie, you'll pay for this."

Closing the curtain, the room faded to black. He was blind with rage. Fumbling with the matches, he lit the candle on the dresser with trembling fingers then crossed to the window again, peering out through the corner, disguised behind the curtain. They were gone. Their play was over. Ethan turned, glancing toward the bed. Then he walked over, kneeling beside it, reaching beneath the frame, retrieving his bag containing the infamous surgical knife. Cleansed of the flesh of its recent victims, it appeared shiny and sharper than ever, hungry for blood. He began pacing again, slicing the air in front of him as if wildly searching for an invisible target. If Abby had been with him in the room, the knife might have found its natural purpose, the slicing of human flesh. Ethan may have been lashing out, slashing at thin air but he knew he couldn't truly follow through with his immediate impulses, no matter how intense the desire. She wasn't listed among the Whitechapel murder victims, at least not as one of his timeline requirements. To her benefit for the moment, she was out of reach. Paid in advance, she didn't return to his room and he did not expect to see her again. Ethan curled up on the bed beside his knife as his rage began to subside. Though it took some time, he calmed down enough to eventually fall asleep. In the days to come he had things to do of far greater consequence than offing a common tramp, or so he'd finally convinced himself. Too much time on his hands, too much *Time* on his mind, only sleep offered him any escape from the pain.

XXIV. LOST IN THOUGHT

Ethan's rage should have grown exponentially leading up to the fateful date of 16 October 1888, yet a certain serenity rooted instead, an almost divine calm within him. To a logical mind there would have been no blame for a behavioral pattern of intense emotions including anger, betrayal and guilt. Ethan remained tranquil in the midst of his turmoil, too calm to react. He had never been trained, his psyche never prepared for concealing or suppressing such an extreme change of character in the middle of the play, cast as Jekyll and Hyde, performing both roles simultaneously. Even during military preparation, he was not instructed how to be two men at once. He was on his own and should have been scared. In spite of it, he was calm. Though incapable of masking his pain Ethan was capable of internalizing it, playing the part to perfection. He got quiet inside, still. Peaceful. Even in anguish he remained calm. It occurred to him with a grin, if he were currently evaluated by the Flicker medical staff and told the truth, he would immediately be admitted to the psych ward where he would live out his days. No coming back from this leap. Yet again, he was calm. They'd instantly detect definitive signs of mental instability, even in his completely composed rendition of a story, alerting them to signs of his time spent slipping into insanity. Of course, doctors would feel the need to label it specifically: sociopathic behavior. Ethan smiled broadly at the thought.

The enabling methodology he'd developed over these many weeks, suppressing a personal angst, allowed Ethan to clutch the important details of the case still to be fulfilled by his alter ego. Later that day, George Lusk would receive the only "true" correspondence from the notoriously named "Jack the Ripper". The letter would be sent along with a gift through a meticulous array of deceptive routes designed to be entirely untraceable back to Ethan. It would come to be known as the "From hell" letter. Mr. Lusk, as President of the Whitechapel Vigilance Committee, would have the unfortunate task before him upon delivery of a package, contents within telling their own gruesome tale. He would discover the letter along with a decanter which contained a portion of Catherine Eddowes' kidney, a keepsake Ethan coveted, kept hidden in his dresser drawer, pickling in red wine. For two weeks he had hung onto it, waiting out the clock...and the calendar. Everything in its right and proper time. A patient man when need be, he relished the thought of watching Lusk open it up, a fantasy, as he would've had to hand deliver it to bear witness to the event. Medical science of the era had not yet dreamed of forensic advancements which would lead to identification through the DNA matching of victims. However, it had progressed enough to assess the sample as human and female, obvious circumstantial evidence notwithstanding. A fact that this last victim had her kidney removed resulted in the eventual press reports he read, leading Lusk to assume the section delivered to him was that of Miss Eddowes. Ethan knew the letter by heart, yet he never understood why it was written as such, with its glaring errors and misspellings, nor did he enjoy writing it the way it was, so contrary to his language usage, always meticulous. Just another one of *Time's* little jokes and pokes at Ethan. He reminded himself it wasn't personal and not to take it that way, as Colin once said. More food for thought.

From hell,
Mr. Lusk,
Sor,
I send you half the
Kidne I took from one woman
and prasarved it for you
Tother piece I fried and ate is was very nise,
I may send you the bloody knif that took it out
if you only wate a whil longer
Signed
Catch me when you can
Mishtar Lusk

Illiteracy ran rampant in impoverished Whitechapel. Its glaring errors, the mistakes were deplorable to a fault, deliberate, in a mocking manner to those of the times. If Ethan had concocted it from his own imagination, it might not have been too far off from the original. The *perfectly* written letter "From hell" would have tipped off the police that the culprit they sought was a highly educated man. Let the mind games begin.

***

Journal Entry ~ 16 October 1888

I have come to terms with the fact that I will most likely not return this journal to The Consortium authorities upon my arrival into the 21st Century. Not one single person, not Anson, Colin or Maggie could comprehend the necessity of my actions. Not even myself. I just know the actions and not the intent would be judged. I began this as a spectator but soon became the focal point of the research. I was, no, I AM the project. I may have had some inner struggle with what I've done and still need to do before leaving this place, but I am reconciled to the role I play, resolved with these events as I should be, providing the ends to a means and the means to an end.

Still, I log these events for my own posterity. In packaging the parcel to George Lusk, I had to slice away a piece of Annie Chapman's kidney to accompany a letter which I had memorized every word of during my project research. The "From hell" letter was the only one Jack th…I wrote. All the others were fakes and propaganda. Before disposing of the remaining kidney part via the hospital incinerator, I held it in my hand with a primal urge to slice it up and eat it for dinner. I stared at it with a knife and fork in hand for what seemed like eternity, thinking of the character of Hannibal Lecter and his mention of fava beans and a nice Chianti. That was with a man's liver, not a woman's kidney. I'm not insane nor am I a cannibal. I'm having to deal with all the pressures of the job and its Time requirements while all along, dealing with liars and betrayers pretending to be my Maggie. I'm closing in on my encore performance with regards to my final victim, Mary Kelly. Wish me luck! Oh, hell, I don't need it. Time is on my side.

***

The days following the delivery of the "From hell" letter to Mr. Lusk were, for Ethan, like walking in his sleep. His excursion to the hospital incinerator to dispose of the kidney's remains then subsequent trips to the market and his favorite bangers and mash place on Whitechapel Road were without any incident. Relinquishing his will to the fact he would never be caught left him feeling somewhat empty and all but invisible. Ethan was genuinely frustrated that his dedication to duty, masterful duplication of historical events would never be fully appreciated, nor would he be commended or even recognized for these sacrifices and effort extended in the name of continuity. Only Ethan and the eyes of *Time* would ever truly know the lengths he had gone on behalf of every individual who existed past these events. If history recorded that the culprit responsible for the Whitechapel murders had always been someone from this era then Ethan could never divulge his main role. He would have to give credit for these five brutal slayings to one of the dozens of suspects compiled over the decades of research and evidentiary analysis. Ethan would have to lie about the true identity of the infamous killer never named, never caught. He would forever remain silent as to the truth about what transpired during his Scope project. He was not happy about giving credit to another man but it could not be helped. He couldn't trust the authorities in power to understand the sacrifices he had made in protecting the timeline. Instead, they'd lock him away for the rest of his life for doing exactly what would have been expected of him if they had known about it.

Ethan continued wrestling with his darkest thoughts over the next few days, as images of his victims still fresh in his mind plagued him. He felt so robbed, cheated of the intimacy he'd savored with his first two victims, denied him with the last two women. Pacing those six steps to the open window, six steps back to the foot of his bed, talking to himself about this option of possibly murdering other women during the two and a half weeks of uneventful time leading up to the murder of Mary Kelly on the ninth of November, he had developed a killer instinct. It was an increasingly strong desire to see the pleading eyes of another woman as his knife sliced through her skin, releasing the warmth of her lifeblood from her throat, as practice. He was a perfectionist, after all. Imagining himself close enough to her face that, in another scenario, it would be a prelude to a kiss, perhaps he might seal it with one while her life drains away, marking her departure from the world with one gentle, affectionate final pressing of his lips to hers. How sensual, he thought. How utterly romantic.

With each passing day it became more of a struggle for him to listen to the logic and structure of his duties in keeping with the historical events laid out before him, to mind his own business. But what if? He couldn't keep his mind from wandering. Could he be at enough of an advantage over those hunting for him to pull off a few collateral murders? He could be more discreet, properly disposing of bodies rather than leaving them out for display on the streets of Whitechapel. What if he was so protected by recorded history that if he'd butchered a few more women to appease his urges it would not and could not be linked back to him? Didn't it stand to reason that if he went ahead and did it then it would have already been done? After all, he thought, there were women missing all over London. In fact, the torso of a woman had been found in an abandoned building during this time, nothing more of her ever discovered, though she had been there for quite a long period of time, certainly prior to his arrival. Besieged with thoughts of murder and mayhem, this temptation was becoming overwhelming. Recreating scenarios, thinking of myriad ways for him to fulfill his destiny, Ethan envisioned acts of carnage, of murders never attributed to Jack the Ripper but actually not committed by him. He even considered the obvious disposal of the bodies in the basement incinerator of the hospital, a piece at a time, whatever he could stuff into his medical bag. The malignant concept crept into his insidious mind. What were a few more missing prostitutes in this chaotic time?

One, two, three, four, five, six. He would pace to the window arguing one side. One, two, three, four, five, six. He argued the counterpoint night after restless night. It never left his consciousness, even when asleep, claiming its place as an obsession at the forefront of his mind, a perpetual fantasy unfolding. Between meals, over hot coffee, at tea time, even while squatting over the disgusting shithole in the outhouse he considered the concept, dismissing it over and over again. Then, late one evening came a familiar knock at his door by an unexpected visitor. It was Abigail. Startled,

Ethan crossed from the desk then paused, deciding whether or not to allow her into his room. She knew he was there if she had seen the light through his window from Bakers Row. After a moment, he opened it. The two of them just stood there peering at one another. Ethan did not just stare at her, he glared through her, hard and cold. He knew she was back for more money and she knew he knew the truth of it.

"Fuck it." He thought as he turned away then went back into the room, leaving the door open for her to enter. Perhaps he'd wanted to be entertained by her excuses or just a good lie disguised as a story. He figured any vituperation toward her would abruptly end with her immediate departure and a return to his endless isolation.

"How've ya been, Arthur?" Abigail asked as she hesitantly entered his room. It occurred to her, gathering from his disdainful expression, what she had done several nights before by staging a false attack had been off-putting to him, beyond reproach.

"Fine. I'm fine." Ethan responded, if for no other reason than the fact that he'd always been a gentleman. He retained his civility with the lady in this uncivil realm, though he was far from being in a conversational mood.

"What 'ave ya been up to?" She fished for dialogue to gauge just how mad she had made him with her antics.

"Just killing time." Ethan quipped, his tone of voice terse. Briefly looking her way before turning his back on her, he faced out the window, hands in his pockets.

Abigail felt the awkwardness in the air. Causing her to be even more ill at ease, she'd have to find the words to approach him, to beseech him, an entreaty regarding her need for more money. Was he still willing to be generous after what she'd done? Minutes passed before either of them spoke. Ethan turned around and looked at her. She was adorned in new clothing, a bonnet and handbag. He smiled apathetically.

"Back for more money, I assume?" he said callously, indifferent to her plight.

"Don't go as far as it used to, ya know." Abby replied with a flirtatious grin.

A common tactic having no effect on Ethan, it was not her only tool in the shed. Promenading toward him, prancing playfully, he stood fast and stared down at her, only a pace or two away as she looked up at him with green puppy dog eyes. Again, little impact made, if any, his disinterest in Abigail's circumstances duly noted, he was far more absorbed in his contempt for her, attentive to his own need to tell her what he thought of this travesty, taking his money under false pretenses. He could feel the rage rising with the memory of his shame when the blame for it was surely on her, having suffered an indignity due to her insensitivity.

"You staged a play for me down there last time like I was some simpleton." His condescending disregard for her was evident in abundance.

"I did what ya asked. Ya wanted to *watch* me get roughed up by a customer and that's what he did." Rationalizing the scenario, absolving herself of responsibility, Ethan didn't want to hear it.

"It was not *real*." He brushed past her, crossing to the foot of the bed. "You and your friend either knew him or let him in on the joke and I was the joke. You were bloody well laughing at me. I heard you." Ethan tried to speak calmly but the anger was swelling inside. He knelt down, reaching underneath the bed.

"I was laughin', love, but not at you! I was laughin' 'cause I was stronger than 'e was!" She began giggling again. Ethan was having none of it. Quickly muffling herself, seeing that he was not amused, Abby realized this man who had been most generous had particular tastes in mind. She could feel him despising her.

Abigail had left the door open and this was nobody's business but their own, so Ethan walked over to close it, concealing whatever he had retrieved. Continuing to plead her case, he heard every word, refusing to respond.

"Look, Arthur, I may not o' really got in mind what ya wanted. Ya been kinder to me than anyone I ever known in the city since bein' here. Last thing I'd ever do is to laugh at ya and risk a good thing I got with ya."

Ethan's position remained apathetic, his body becoming more rigid as he stood his ground, his back to her. Knowing most of what was being said was the prelude to a request for more money, he was in no mood to extend his usual noblesse oblige. Instead, Ethan became increasingly stern in demeanor. It didn't matter that this was a business arrangement. She was a prostitute, by and by. His issue was being made a fool of and yes, her actions were partially to blame but Ethan was embarrassed by his lack of social education pertaining to women, professional or otherwise. He was angrier with himself than he was with her.

"Arthur?" Abby moved up right behind him, reaching up to touch his shoulder. "How can I make it right? "

Ethan spun around, verbally exploding as if she pulled a pin from an emotional grenade. "I want you out of my bloody room! Keep my money but go, now please!" He pointed toward the door, his directional hand clinging to his physician's shoes.

Abigail stepped back, more in surprise than fear. The time they'd spent together he had never shown any aggression toward her. She realized just how much she had hurt him with the mock attack staged in the street below. Ethan turned back around facing away from her again. Not another word was spoken between them. After a few moments, Abby walked past him and left. Hearing her footsteps echoing in the hallway, as she descended the stairs he began feeling as if he'd been too harsh with her, considering he was as much to blame by asking her to do something so extreme and dangerous. His lack of sexual prowess, his literal dysfunction with her led to a desperate conclusion and uncharacteristic scenario just to satisfy his newly acquired perverse appetite. Ethan had surely chased her off for good.

He was alone again. It was something he was quite accustomed to, as if isolation was a tangible thing, a companion he'd shared his apartment with at Oxford, as well as the room he now inhabited. Communing with his loneliness, together once again, Colin seemed to be the only one who could trespass in his domicile and not disrupt or corrupt the solitude and sanctity he wore like a comfortable suit. Abigail deemed qualified to trespass as Colin did only because, to Ethan, her resemblance to young Maggie reminded him of home and a comfort he had longed for, she betrayed him. He placed his shoes on the dresser to polish them later.

Feeling somewhat upset with his outburst, he began to undress for the evening, draping his trousers over the desk chair. Sticking his head out the window to gauge the temperature then decide how much of an opening to leave for fresh air, well, as fresh as Whitechapel could provide, it was getting colder toward the end of October. Intending to keep the window closed, leaving only a small gap to allow ventilation, as he reached up to shut it, Ethan spotted a familiar figure across the street. It was her. Abigail. *Maggie*. She was looking up at him peering through the second floor window. Ethan withdrew his hands from the windowpane and stared back down at the girl, wondering why she was standing there. Was she hoping he would ask her to come back up, in from the cold night air? Did she return to him because she had spent all he'd given her and was now without lodging? Before he could resolve his questions they were answered for him simply by watching what transpired. Abigail was approached by a man walking down Bakers Row. It was not the same man she put an act on with the last time. This man was shorter and thinner. He couldn't hear the dialogue exchanged between them but he immediately became aware that Abby was going through with his original deviant request, in spite of having walked away empty-handed from his dwelling only moments before this encounter.

The stranger looked around, seeing the street was empty for the moment during the early morning hour. Removing his gloves, he began to freely fondle Abigail. It wasn't welcome. The expression on her face belied the offense as he randomly and roughly ran his hands all over her. For a moment, Ethan looked away, partially due to his embarrassment for her and the equivalent shame in himself. Those reactions quickly subsided, however, vanishing as Ethan's urges took ahold of him the same way this brute had taken ahold of her. He continued watching, the compulsion too strong, too primal to ignore. The gaslight lamps and their proximity to his window allowed Ethan to see her countenance as the man continued to accost her, having free reign over her body. She was grimacing from the manhandling and obviously, his uncaring departure from civility. The savage then spun her around, pressing her face against the wall as she cried out in pain, yelping like a wounded dog. Running his tongue along her left cheek and ear, she grunted from the pressure as he pushed against her then whimpered as he reached up underneath her skirt with his left hand, probing deeply inside her. He was violating her, hurting her, penetrating her, raping her by hand on a public street.

Ethan could not look away from the event he orchestrated. He was experiencing the role he was initially tasked to complete during his time in this century in its pure form and intent. He was a Scope. A spectator. A voyeur. The curious thing, though, was his profoundly unattached reaction to her plight, the incongruity of a response he could not control. Ethan was so fixated on the visual experience of watching this woman being assaulted, he was not even aware of the physical effects taking place within him. Ethan suddenly became aware that he'd begun rubbing himself over his undershorts, bringing him to the point of a full and fruitful erection, something he'd not been able to achieve for quite some time. While ecstatic knowing his impotent condition was not permanent, he questioned the circumstances, wondering whether or not the incidents occurring during his time here were the cause of his deviance. What if it had not transpired as such? What if he had only been relegated to the role of observer, as initially scripted? Would his undiscovered eroticism have emerged as he watched the Ripper murder the women or was it made manifest by his role in the play? The stipulations of arousal, requirements were less than conventional and not something he'd ever had an appetite for in any capacity. Ethan could feel it. He was changing, becoming someone else, something more. His thoughts fractured in his mind, splintering into hundreds of fragments.

Maneuvering his left hand underneath the waistband of his shorts to make better contact with himself, Ethan's pleasure was short-lived as Abigail suddenly pushed away from the wall, causing her assailant to stumble backwards, almost falling. The pitiful woman standing on Bucks Row burst into tears, sobbing audibly enough for Ethan to hear from his window. She was not able to go through with it. His erection quickly ended, as did his fleeting excitement but he was not upset with her. Abigail had helped him restore his sense of sexual worth, for however brief the attempt was, reassuring him that, in spite of appearances to the contrary, all was well. As Ethan continued to watch, the man adjusted his clothing and looked around for witnesses. There were none except for Ethan, from a distance, from above, looking down upon her like a guardian angel who refused to intervene. He briskly exited the area. As it became quiet and still again, Abigail gathered herself then walked away.

Ethan abandoned his vantage point, falling back onto his bed, visualizing over and over the images from his window, hoping to recreate his illustrious arousal, to no avail. He thought kindly of his young Maggie replacement somewhere out there on the streets, crying, undoubtedly confused. What she did must have been difficult. What she did, she did for him. Abigail obviously loved him to make such a sacrifice, or so he thought. As much as he knew the truth of it, he'd hoped the man who was molesting little Abby was the *real* Jack the Ripper. To have the chance to finally watch the brutal slaying of this helpless young victim right there below his window would have been satisfying beyond measure but to observe it from the safety of his own room would have been even better than witnessing it from the shadows of an alley, as it was always supposed to be in all its rage: splendorous carnage. However, as his mind wandered, he imagined being down there in place of that thin stranger, completing the task, unlike his lame replacement who had let Abigail get away. *If you want a job done right...*

In the privacy of his mind he could do anything and not worry about betraying the timeline. The things he could imagine eventually entered into his dreams as he dozed off. Any other person would awaken screaming then label it as a nightmare. He had now become accustomed to it and almost felt it necessary to adopt a mental preparedness, awake or asleep, for all he had seen and done and still was tasked to do. No one in *this* time or the era he would return to would ever comprehend these sacrifices made for the good of the future, yet, there was no denying his enjoyment of it. Ethan slept deeply, peacefully, with a smile on his face.

XXV.
EXIT WOUNDS

Journal Entry ~ 22 October 1888

I'm the man that time forgot. Nearly a week now of living in a void. There was no reason to feed the pages of this journal with the doldrums of the last week. I've had no visitors of any sort. Not that any were expected, although from time to time I'm sure I hear voices in the walls of my room saying HELP or MURDER. Maybe I'm getting visitors of a unique sort and sound. I often talk to them with no response. Earlier today, being a Saturday, I browsed the marketplace and a man directed me toward the local butcher shop where I purchased two decent-sized cuts of a pig. I want to keep my wits and my knife sharp for my next historical event. I plan to do some curvature work on the meat and bone, as this next event is to be most creative carving with the blade of all five of these women. Mary Kelly has to be Jack th.....I mean MY best work! I need to practice my filet work and deep cuts, which is always hardest, cutting through tough tendons and muscles to perfection so that what will be discovered later as the last true victim of JTR is exactly what history recorded. I've decided to remain naked in my room most of the time to preserve my attire and just because I'm beginning to like it. Before this entry I placed the meat on my chest and belly. It was cold and slimy but had such a cooling effect to it. Later I will place the two pieces on the bed and sleep beside it then when I wake I will lay them lengthwise as Mary Kelly would be laying and begin my carving practice. Once complete, I will roll my body over it naked, then, bring it to the public kitchen downstairs and make a feast for all the tenants of the lodge. Food of the gods.

***

To Ethan's credit, if nothing more so, he was a man of his word. When applying himself, putting his mind to the task, he was meticulous in word and deed, to a fault. Everything he planned to do he followed through with including a generous banquet of *seasoned* pork for the tenants dining in at their lodging's kitchen. Everybody was gracious, grateful for his magnanimity and cooking skills. Not a morsel remained. Before leaving them to their devices Ethan uttered a favorite phrase: "Bon appétit!"

Retiring back to his room after a round of appreciative gestures, he carried a hot cup of tea in hand to cut the chill on a particularly cold night. Becoming relatively comfortable with his fellow tenants, Ethan felt secure enough with his surroundings to leave his door unlocked whilst he went downstairs, so he did not have to fumble with a key when he came back up. Ethan found his room occupied. There she was: Abigail. He had not seen her since she ran off in tears down Bakers Row that intense night nearly one week before. Having taken it upon herself to freely enter his room while he was in the kitchen, she was poised near the window.

As he stepped into the room closing the door behind him, Abby turned around, glancing his way then returning her attention to the panes of glass.

"What's it like?"

"I beg your pardon?" Ethan asked, walking close enough to discover she'd been drinking, detecting the telltale essence of liquor in the air.

"Watchin' me. What's it like t' look out this window and watch me?" Abigail faced him directly, her question as pointed. "Can ya see me looking at ya?"

"Yes." Ethan was cautious in his response, sparse, not knowing her demeanor.

Lost in thought, Abigail peered out the window as waning rays of evening light washed across her shoulders, illuminating her eyes with the golden glow of sunset. She appeared in silhouette like a fallen angel Heaven sent, a celestial vision.

"I wanted t' do it for ya, I really did but I got scared. We talk, ya know, all the girls, 'bout the killin's. They call 'im Jack the Ripper, ya know."

"Yes." Ethan answered again in brief.

Abby stared at him with desperate eyes, her penetrating gaze speaking volumes. He almost dropped his tea cup as she wrapped her arms around his body. Squeezing him tightly, tears welling up, she continued.

"I thought long and hard, I did, and it came t' me that havin' ya watch me, if it was him, the Ripper, ya'd come an' save me, ya know, before 'e done me in." Abigail was quivering like a scared little girl lost in the dark. "Even if ya didn't make it in time ya'd catch the bloody bastard an' end 'im for killin' me and scarin' me friends, too." Wishful thinking on her part.

"Yes." Ethan uttered, this time with a vacant smile, an expression Abby wanted to believe meant she'd be safe from harm in his charge. Ironically, to Ethan it meant it could not happen to her because there was no possibility Jack the Ripper would be *down there* on Bakers Row while he was *up here* observing her. Abigail was in the arms of a madman and because of it, was probably the safest girl in town.

Embracing him as if she'd taken a lover, like a child would her security blanket, an overt insinuation of never letting go, Ethan reciprocated only mildly, resting his free hand on her shoulder while taking another sip of his tea. Gazing out the window behind her, a gloating smirk on his face, his apathy toward her was evident only to him.

"Can we, ya know, for old time's sake, lay in bed a while and hold each other? I wanna try again, go back out there for ya tonight. I do. I just wanna be close to ya for a bit, love." She was pleading for his attention and most assuredly, his money.

"Yes." His redundant response void of emotion, he led her over to the bed while she clung onto him as if for dear life itself.

It was still early in the evening when Abigail laid down next to Ethan, the night as young as she was, fresh and full of promise. She on her left side facing him, he on his back staring at the ceiling, Abby rambled on about her struggles with money. The past few weeks had been hard on her friends, other prostitutes in the area whose business was down due to an abundance of caution from both sides of transactions. She spoke of the few times the two of them had done just this in the past, lying next to each other, holding each other and talking but Ethan wasn't doing much talking at all. He continued to stare at the ceiling with a smirk on his face. In his mind he was a god, the aloof, virtually untouchable deity with unmatched powers to predict the future with a worshipper of his omnipotent presence right by his side, believing him to be her protector from any harm, mainly the infamous Whitechapel murderer. As he laid there faintly listening to Abigail he began drifting off to sleep, imagining the emergence of these voices he'd been hearing within the walls being more of his admirers, worshippers come to call. He knew they were there to pay homage to his supreme existence. Their hands reaching through the walls, bloodied and serrated, it was obvious to him that they were trying to make contact with his holiness. They needed to connect, if only for a brief instant with his divine presence. Though Ethan adored this attention, he felt no more compassion for them than he did for the mere mortal lying beside him. Despondent and disinterested, Ethan closed his eyes.

Nodding off with Abigail's voice drowned out by the cheering hordes en masse, the swarm of devotees swelled. In his fantasy, they transformed into the welcoming committee upon his return to the 21st Century. Stepping through the Flicker into the awaiting arms of young Maggie, his reward, he imagined a parade being held in his honor through the center of Oxford University, there to be hailed as "A Hero". He dreamed of being the recipient of the Nobel Peace Prize, creating just for him a new category of award to acknowledge his incredible contribution to humanity for: ***"Sacrifices beyond personal interest in preservation of historical continuity".*** *They had welded the surgical blade he'd used to the golden plaque: "Doctor Ethan LaPierre" in relief, boldly rising from the surface to stand out for gathering crowds of aficionados,* "In recognition of his plight and dedication to duty." *Cameras were flashing, accolades coming from every direction. Standing center stage beneath the white hot spotlight of fame, Ethan was in his glory.*

He'd written a full, detailed, fictional report, an extensive analysis of historical adventures, ending his treatise with a compelling, thought-provoking commentary: "Five women who have spent eternity being overshadowed by an evil man named Jack the Ripper have now had their voices heard from beyond the grave." It was hauntingly perfect. The Consortium was so appreciative, his peers rewarded him. Anson, with the highest level of trust bestowed, decided to relocate the Flicker to his apartment on the university grounds. Whenever he fancied, whatever he desired, Ethan could walk through that doorway without fear of contaminating recorded history because he was a god and just that damn bloody good! With full control of Flicker, he could adjust the coordinates so he'd need only stick his head through to be back at the window in his room, peering onto Bakers Row, watching Abby doing her job over and over again.

Perhaps he could persuade young Maggie to dress in period attire to walk through the holy time portal then go stand on the street corner opposite his window, into the dark corner of history, allowing him to watch her get attacked. Would she do that for him? He wondered then concluded: "Of course she would! Maggie loves me. She would do anything for me, no matter what I asked." He knew she had always hoped to become a Scope. Being a god, he could make it a reality for her, a dream come true, albeit an alternate reality. It was only a dream, bizarre at best, depraved at worst.

Ethan awoke from his narcissistic fantasy wearing an ear-to-ear grin. It had only seemed like seconds since he was out, but it must have been much longer. He awoke alone in his room. Abigail had left. By the silent atmosphere echoing from the street below, it was much later in the night. Wondering if she'd been put off by his lack of dialogue before and after they had gone to bed or how quickly he'd fallen asleep, he wasn't being rude; his dream was simply more interesting than her words. Still, the girl was the only true physical contact he had anymore and it was rare to have his worshipper present, alive, flesh and blood succumbing to his every whim.

He stood from the bed and walked over to the dresser to retrieve his watch from the top drawer. Before he could do so, he heard a familiar voice coming through the window. Even though he never lit the candle at the desk he knew Abigail was aware of his presence from the shadow play. Ethan, or Arthur to her, stood beyond range, out of sight, the man behind the curtain. She was speaking with some false bravado to another working girl passing, complimenting each other's dresses and hair, just another night on the streets of Whitechapel spent among friends. Ethan had stepped away just briefly to recover his now ice cold cup of tea, so to quench his dry palate. Covertly returning to his vantage point, cup in hand, he sat at the desk peering out on the activity below. Though the hour was later, the Saturday night traffic was still bustling with the sights and sounds of typical characters he had become accustomed to during his visit.

Abigail may have been small in stature but she had powerful lungs. Her voice pierced the ambient noise around her. He could almost make out her conversations with various people seemingly familiar and unfamiliar to her. Both Ethan and Abby knew it would still be some time before all the street attendance subsided. Once the audience was gone the play could proceed. Plenty of time remained for another cup of tea. Slipping downstairs for some refreshments before the start of the show, his anticipation was building.

Returning to his room, fresh cup of hot tea in hand, Ethan went to the desk chair to peer at impromptu performances by the ghosts of the 19th Century milling around below. In his mind he heard Mozart's "Marriage of Figaro" loud and clear. Peeking out from behind the curtain, he observed the ballet of street performers entering and exiting, stage left, stage right, as each end of Bakers Row was draped with shadows functioning as theatre curtains. Gradually the supporting actors disappeared into the ether, penetrating the dark vapor of night, making it all the more mysterious as they walked off stage. More and more of those with smaller roles, bit parts, finished their scenes with little fanfare, never to be seen or heard from again. And so it went until, eventually, only the star of the show remained.

There she was, center stage, following her cues, improvising as she always had. Standing on her mark beneath the gaslight lamp, it illuminated Abby like the vision of a ghostly apparition. Mesmerized, almost breathless, he watched and waited right along with Abigail from his unique perspective, the window on his own little world. Abby was as anxious as Ethan for an entirely different reason. She could sense the time approaching for her duet with the stranger. Then she'd put on the performance previously scheduled for an audience of one, namely Arthur.

An old vendor's cart had become a makeshift trash heap left on the street, just enough of an obstruction from anyone passing along Bakers Row to see her. It gave her a bit of privacy. Even from street level the view was prohibitive. The innkeeper below was prevented from seeing Abby while he occupied his office window. Only Ethan had a direct line of sight from HIS Mount Olympus.

After a time, his cup of tea finished, Ethan stood from the desk chair to recover his timepiece to determine how late or early the hour was at the moment. Before he took two steps he heard Abby's prominent voice rising up from the street. Leaning back over the desk to look out in time to see a man approaching her, the gentleman was wearing a long black coat and short brimmed hat. Ethan wasn't watching when the man first entered the lit area so he never saw his face, the only clear view being of his back as he spoke to Abby. He seemed about five-foot-ten with a stocky build, maybe late thirties or early forties. Obviously inebriated, judging by his inability to hold a steady stance, his animated behavior another telltale sign of his condition. In an attempt to hear their conversation, Ethan leaned over the desk, propping himself on the windowsill. Hoping and expecting that this was not just another trick, another con, he didn't have that sense of it this time, considering the amount of time Abigail had spent alone in the cold, on a corner, waiting for the right time and man to come along. It certainly appeared spontaneous, unrehearsed, possessing the hint of danger he'd craved as peril for the woman. Ethan found it exciting to be the sole spectator. A sudden surge of virility swept over him, primal to the core. He removed his shirt to feel the cold night air bathe his body.

To deny Ethan's trueness to himself regarding what this visual stimulation did for him would be more damaging than to simply accept the fact. His body and mind were telling him he had a Schadenfreude extremist's appetite for the macabre. Yes. He liked watching her squirm in discomfort as the drunkard moved in closer to her. He imagined the man's alcohol laden, spirited breath in her face, refusing to allow her any escape from its pungent aroma, trapped as she was against his hefty frame. No exit from his intoxicated binge, the unwelcome, intermittent spray from his lips spattered her cheeks, remnants of his overindulgence as he spoke. He took pleasure in seeing her languish over this physical advance, not too unlike the man a week ago who also began taking liberties with her body by use of his hands, rough in manner, in drunken abandon. Ethan took some amusement in analytical comparison, noting that there was not much imagination in most men, or so it seemed by their fumbling and feeble attempts to explore the female form, something far beyond the awkward clumsiness of a creature with no opposable thumbs trying to dine with silverware.

"Look into her eyes, dammit. Her eyes!" He spoke emphatically, if softly.

Willing the man to do his bidding, to help the bloke enjoy their encounter more, he'd make it a memorable scene if he would only follow his stage directions! With his god-like powers of persuasion, Ethan wanted to direct him from a safe distance but it wasn't working. He wanted to pull the man's strings like a puppeteer as *Time* had been doing to him, so both might have a better experience with the same girl. A hundred men could show up, line up to take their turn with her, one after another, groping feverishly, grabbing at her breasts and bottom, yet to grab her heart through her eyes would be the masterful manipulation. The reaction was the same. Whether the bi-product of the connection made was through love, fear or in anger, she would ultimately surrender her control to anybody. Not that literal anatomical muscle but the proverbial heart was the door to supreme power over her and the key to unlock it was the locking of their eyes. Ethan had acquired that knowledge and power with his first two victims, Polly and Annie, and was deprived of that with Elizabeth and Catherine. If the man accosting her possessed this rarified knowledge, his own level of intoxication would rise considerably. He would become drunk with power over her, far exceeding the potency of any liquid libation.

Ethan was jolted out of his attempted mental assertions on the man when, quite unexpectedly, the dark stranger reached up for her throat with both of his hands. The look in her eyes was priceless, worth every pence he had spent on her. Abject terror. It was beautiful. He wondered if he'd truly guided the man with his will. Had he tapped into his mind? His dirty fingernails gouging into her supple neck, choking her larynx, she was overcome with the fear of death. So many women had known this sensation but Abby was having her first turn with it and finally understood what she had heard described. The tightness in her throat and the inability to breathe, the clutching grasp of this brute cutting her free from life, she committed an act of self-preservation. It was over in mere seconds, as she'd managed to dissuade this assault with a target rich knee to the man's crotch, yet Ethan knew Abby would, no doubt, remember that sensation for all the rest of her days. All three parties involved were frozen in time, remaining motionless for what seemed an eternity, enough time for Ethan to take notice of what was happening to his own body. There was a growing, stirring stimulation as he felt himself becoming aroused.

Though the candle on the desk wasn't lit there was residual light from the candle on the dresser. Gaslight lamps glowing from the street below provided Abigail with enough light to look up to see Ethan leaning over the desk. As they locked eyes, he nodded with approval, not of her defensive knee jerk reflex to a man's genitalia but to the allowed victimization. She nodded in understanding, a nonverbal agreement struck to provide him with the visual pleasure he was seeking. Knowing what was to come but not taking her eyes off of her Arthur, she braced herself for the drunk's own reflex reaction from receiving a knee to the groin. He raised back up from his buckled position and, in one sweeping motion, backhanded her in the mouth. She froze in shock as she turned her attention and her eyes toward the stranger's eyes. Just as Ethan hoped, finally, they both had absolute power over her. Only then did Abby take notice that the combination of excessive drinking and ramming a knee hard into his crotch caused him to wretch all around the ground between them. The splatter was clinging onto his unshaven chin as he began attacking her verbally, the odor of cheap liquor and vomit nearly suffocating her. Abby almost welcomed his hands around her throat again if only to avoid inhaling the unbearable stench.

It was unclear to the voyeur whether it was his witnessing a man's control over Abby or his deity-like power or just fulfilling his role as a Scope but something had aroused Ethan, exciting him in a way he'd never felt before. During that time spent viewing them he'd undone his trousers, dropping them with his undershorts, though he did not even remember undressing. Masturbating with primal abandon, erection firmly in hand, he stroked himself into a frenzy just off the edge of the desk. Fully extended, his torso bent over the surface, resting his stomach and chest on the desk, his free hand bracing the bottom frame of the windowsill for balance and leverage, Ethan was delirious with pleasure. Chills running through his extremities as electric shocks pulsed through his veins, he momentarily closed his eyes. Faster…faster his hand moved of its own volition as the performance continued on a sidewalk below. Ethan opened his eyes again, staring down as the drunkard ripped open her blouse, tearing off the buttons. He spun Abigail around like a top, as if he had read the same playbook as the man a week ago, pressing her up against the cold, moist stone wall.

One hand reaching in from behind over her shoulder then down her blouse, crudely pulling at her tender breasts, pinching her nipples, his other hand was firmly around her throat in a threatening posture. He let her know. If Abby screamed or struggled, if she tried to defend herself, his attack would be the last. She had no choice but to remain submissive to his will or possibly pay the ultimate price. He'd snap her neck.

Ethan continued to pleasure himself at the sight of it. Breathing became labored. Sucking the air in more deeply, from sheer exertion, beads of sweat began forming on his forehead, making immediate contact with outside air rushing in on a breeze. Droplets of perspiration flinging off the tips of his hair, it dripped from his scalp to his shoulders then down the small of his back. His body was on fire, fully engulfed in the flames of his passionate solitude, alive with delightful sensations. Juxtaposed with the stark contrast of cold night air, it was rather striking, an unexpected feature of a surreal experience. It was a sensation he welcomed, serving to heighten Ethan's awareness of all things sensual in or around him. He wasn't trying to imagine being down there in the assailant's place. He was not proficient imagining scenarios, not adept at fantasy role play. It was a live action visualization that had him turned on. Scope trained and safely shrouded by the cover of night, in the shadows, it was the fulfillment he'd always anticipated.

The bloke pressing against her body appeared right-handed as all of the difficult actions taken were with that extremity. Groping at her breasts, he kept his left hand securely on her throat as he withdrew the right, using it to pull up her layers of skirts from behind. Kicking her legs wide apart, he violently thrust his fingers inside her, releasing his grasp on her throat, using the same hand to cover her mouth, muffling the guttural outcry of pain, silencing her alarm. In a drunken stupor, enraged by his own lack of balance, the man shoved her head into the stone then attempted to enter Abigail from behind in a remarkably unskilled manner. Bracing herself against the wall, preparing for an unwelcome and painful penetration, her head was twisted to the left, her right cheek forced against the stone but she could still see Ethan out of the corner of her eye. There was her Arthur, gazing down upon them. He could see her struggling to turn her head enough to watch him watching her feel the pain. And then he noticed his own. The sweat had run down his arm to his hand clenching the full erection, throbbing between his fingers. That moisture was value added, a much needed lubricant for the chafing repetitiveness of his rapid strokes but the agonizing ache in his forearm was becoming unbearable, more than mere muscle strain.

Lifting his upper body from the desk to determine why the throbbing in his arm was so excruciating, Ethan discovered that, in his lustful rampage, while he stroked himself in pleasure, he had blistered his arm. Unaware that he was likewise rubbing it against the desk's edge over and over to well past the point of the blisters bursting, blood was freely flowing from the ruptured skin. It wasn't sweat lubricating his full blown erection, it was his own blood. Possessed by the stunning visualization of an open wound, the crimson stream combined with an impending climax in his role as the voyeur, elevating him to new heights. Nearly collapsing with the realization, he leaned back over the desk to continue observing the rape of his little Maggie clone. The pain did not subside. He didn't dismiss it nor did he attempt to put it out of his mind. Instead, Ethan embraced it, accepting pain as part of the pleasure, part of the plan, awakening him to a whole new comprehension of masochistic stimulation. It was sublime, twisting and turning in his head, transforming into some visceral bond between himself and the beleaguered girl below sharing in his sordid pain-pleasure experience. He was one with her from the shadows.

Convinced that this had been his only role from the start, Ethan knew if he never met any of these women and Jack the Ripper truly was one of the suspects the police considered, he most surely would have been hiding in the shadows, watching it all transpire while masturbating wildly as they were ripped apart by a maniac. He knew this perverted, deep-seeded sexual deviation must have always been hidden within him, the need to perform and receive satisfaction from both, sexually and mentally. His stroking only lasted a mere few seconds more as the compounded gift of visual and physical pain stimulation felt too intense to maintain control. The anguish was mindboggling. He climaxed on the floor beneath the desk, the ejaculation dropping between his feet, semen covering the blood splatter from his wound that had already stained his clothing and much of the wood floor. All he let out was a muffled grunt before collapsing, his body weight hitting the desk. Oh, the pleasure. Oh, the pain.

Down on the street the drunken attacker was still trying to stab Abigail with his own vapid erection, only to fail time and time again in the effort. Either due to his intoxication or her earlier defensive knee to the groin, he couldn't get it up and was so embarrassed, he gave up. Taking his frustration out on her, regardless of whether it was her fault or not, he spun her back around to face him. She stood in defiance, or in surrender in tribute to Ethan. Either way, she didn't fight back. The man reeled back his right hand and with a clenched fist, punched Abigail in the mouth, causing her to crumble to the ground. He then knelt down and grabbed her blouse with both hands, pulling her half off the cobblestone to verbally castigate her for his inability to properly rape her. Tossing the girl back to the ground he stood over her and drove his foot into her stomach, causing him to lose his balance. Falling backwards from the force of the blow, he almost crashed into the old cart. Either from exhaustion or feeling defeated and deflated, or the sobering thought he might get caught, the man pulled himself up from the ground and staggered out of view, leaving behind some of his vomit, pride and his balls. Abigail was still on the ground, softly whimpering, holding her blouse together with one hand, grasping her stomach with the other. He was gone and Ethan figured she would soon vanish into the night, as well.

Rising from the desk, he saw that he left an imprint from the sweat of his body, steam rising from the surface as the cold outside air swept across the same flat wood he had just been lying on. With his frenzied sexual urges satisfied, his wits quickly returned, as did his fuller awareness of the pain in his arm. As Ethan turned to walk to the dresser where the candle was lit, he almost tumbled from the pants and shorts still tangled around his ankles. Neither were spared the mixture of blood, sweat and semen. Leaning onto the desk, he stepped out of both, leaving them bunched up on the floor. Inspecting his wound by candlelight, from the wrist bone to halfway up his forearm, he had pulled back the top layers of skin which looked like crinkled bloody tissue at the top and bottom of the open tear. Ethan dipped his entire arm in the wide mouth water pitcher and began washing off the surrounding blood as the sting worsened. He'd cleansed the arm, rubbing his right hand up and down his left forearm, gritting his teeth from the unbearable throbbing sensation becoming more painfully apparent by the moment. He took a deep breath then yanked off the folded skin at the ends like ripping off a bandage, thus creating two deep caverns, a bloody mess on either end. Washing the wound, removing it from the water twice more to inspect it before he was satisfied with his attentive cleaning, he wrapped one of several rags around it to help clot the blood. As Ethan finished tying the knot with his right hand and his teeth, he heard a knock at the door. It could only be one person.

Opening the door, concealing his naked lower extremities behind it, Ethan was right. It was indeed Abigail, standing there with one hand holding her torn blouse together. She stared at him with those enormous green eyes, her hair messed up and tangled in her bonnet. The left corner of her mouth was bruised, the blood dripping slowly from the corner of her lip where she'd been brutally struck. Ethan, now out of his perverse sexual trance was feeling exposed in more ways than one.

"Are you alright?" He asked in an innocent tone, expressing his false interest. It was the gentlemanly thing to do.

Abby did not reply. She just stared at him. Then suddenly she held out her hand, palm up, in a gesture of required payment.

"Oh, right. Yes." He said as he realized what she was suggesting. "Can you…" Ethan paused. "Can you wait here a moment? Just a moment."

She numbly stared without saying a word as he closed the door, too embarrassed to let her inside with the current condition of the room, bodily fluids mingling with his clothing in a pile on the floor. Kicking the trousers beneath the desk to cover up the blood and semen, Ethan then drew a clean pair of pants and an undershirt from the bottom dresser drawer and quickly put them on. Then, from the inside of one of his shoes, he withdrew his wallet. Removing a generous payment for her, more than she would make in any normal month, he returned to the door, this time opening it fully to her. There they stood peering at one another, Abby wearing the same blank expression and Ethan without a clue of what to say. He held out the money in front of her as an offering.

"This is for you. Sure you're alright, then?"

She took the money from his hand without breaking eye contact to count it then dropped her hand from the blouse, allowing the fabric to open, exposing her breasts. Covered in scrapes and bruises, red marks, literal fingerprints had been left behind from the monstrous man who had squeezed them so tightly. Stepping toward Ethan, she reached up behind his neck, pulling him down to her face. She kissed him, one long, passionate kiss on the lips. Just one kiss. Then she let him go, her eye contact never wavering, her expression never altering. Suddenly, Abigail turned away from him and walked down the stairs, disappearing from view.

Ethan closed the door and stood there in a state of bewilderment. He'd put her through a hellish torment to satisfy his own kinky obsession yet she returned to kiss him tenderly, graciously. Watching her exit the building from behind the curtain, he felt soiled. As he crossed to the dresser, Ethan wondered what possessed Abigail to do his bidding that night. Peering into the mirror, he noticed the blood smudged on his face, a telltale sign of her affection. It had been transferred from her mouth to his as she'd kissed him with abandon. Smeared over his lips, streaked across his cheek, it appeared to be the work of an artist, a broad stroke of genius dashed across his blank expression canvas.

"She loves me." Ethan said to himself, reflecting on the kiss. Rationalizing her return as coming from love, not for money, she'd done what he had asked to please her man and make him happy in any way she could. He surmised that Abby saw him as he saw himself, as a god. She worshipped him. She loved him and he repaid her love with what, money? She didn't want money from someone she adored, she desired only love in return. Ethan did not oblige. He stared at his reflection in the mirror but could bear it no longer, turning away from the painfully telling image. Feeling more battered than Abby, though her body bore the brunt of the encounter, his wounds were much, much deeper.

As he looked down, his gaze fell into the pitcher swirling with the mixture of blood, semen and water. It symbolized his selfishness, revealing his insincere and uncontrollable self-gratifying urges. He'd used her to his advantage, allowing Abby to be ravaged for his pleasure. She loved him enough to do it. Revisiting the looking glass again, a mirror told the truth. Ethan was disgusted with himself. The eyes of a sadistic voyeur gazing back at him, the man was sickened by the sight, knowing what those eyes witnessed in the street below just minutes before. The memories of the heinous act now in full perspective, it caused Ethan to spontaneously vomit into the vase, as if purging his system of an evil demon which had held him spellbound at a window, exit wounds born of self-loathing. Coughing, retching, he spit out the residue remaining in his mouth, heaving it into the mouth of the pitcher. Gazing up again, he hoped not to see the malevolent eyes gazing back but there they were, still attached to his soul. He then refocused once more on the smeared bloodstains on his lips from Abigail's passionate kiss. It looked so beautiful before, innocent and pristine but now it was spoiled and soiled, mixed with vomit and malice. He began wiping it away with his fingers, watching while his hands touched his face. In that moment of sheer madness, Ethan beheld himself spreading the spew out around his lips, stroking his skin with the substance. Suddenly he began laughing maniacally.

"You're fucking losing it mate!" Hysterical, he mustered the words through his uncontrollable fit of cachinnation. In one moment he thought with reason, the next with madness and confusion. He saw himself as a god yet in his reflection, a demon. Ethan knew he was coming unglued, becoming insane. He'd felt rational enough to wipe the blood and vomit from his face, a natural inclination. In the process, some unnatural tendency took control of his psyche. Dipping both hands into the pitcher, he cupped them together, creating a makeshift basin. Staring into the lurid solution, Ethan inexplicably leaned over, splashing the outlandish liquid substance over his forehead, eyes, nose, cheeks and chin, making sure to cover every inch of his face. The oral spew that was captured inside the pitcher along with the blood and semen had found a destination on his features but nothing could disguise the monster lying beneath the assemblage of fluids he was using to *cleanse* himself with that night. The odor, texture and uncommon warmth of that polluted water jolted Ethan back to the present, causing him to glance into the mirror to view his revolting reflection, in search of himself. He started to gag again from the vile, vulgar image and smell of profuse fluids caked on his grimacing visage. Conceding to a stronger opponent, Ethan surrendered his will. He had lost all sense of normalcy and was, if not totally, at least on the outer fringes of insanity, a stark realization causing him to burst into laughter. Unwilling or unable to break the stare down with his alter ego, he watched himself slipping into the depths of depravity. Holding his hands up he began posing, making hideous, distorted facial expressions like someone trying to frighten a child senseless on Halloween as bizarre noises emanated from within the reflection of a mouth he didn't recognize, entertaining only the irrational man staring back at him. His actions were that of a raving lunatic.

The gradual spiral, a descent into madness still incomplete, Ethan felt the need, a compulsion, to remove the clothing he had just dressed in to receive Abigail into a room cluttered with his wanton disregard for her. Hurriedly stripping down to see himself naked and exposed, a more faithful depiction of the monster gazing back at him, Ethan grabbed the entire pitcher in both of his hands and lifted it over his head, tilting it, dowsing himself with the remaining concoction of grotesque waste water. Placing the empty vessel back on the dresser, it freed his hands to begin the typical roaming motions one would normally do during a shower but this was not the clean water he began with for the cleansing of a body. This was the baptism of a newborn lunatic. In a ritualistic manner, he rubbed the fluids all over his body. Touching his own skin with pleasure, he welcomed the irrational, sick and twisted new persona to inhabit his body, giving him free reign. If there were any remnants of the original Ethan remaining, the brilliant professor who stepped into the 19th Century through a doorway opened by an experiment, he was now being washed away, seeping into the wood floor and large area rug below his bare feet.

The imbalanced, disturbed and demented person now solely occupying Ethan's room began dancing around to a tune booming inside his mind, fancying himself to be Natalie Wood playing Maria in "West Side Story". He spun in circles through a dark room, dancing with the shadows, softly singing "I feel pretty, oh so pretty!" in his best falsetto. Spinning and spiraling downward, as a boy Ethan used to be afraid of ghosts but now the ghosts of the 19th Century needed to be frightened of him. He considered, *"If I am indeed, an unhinged madman then time will tell the sordid tale or, better yet, will keep my secret for eternity."* Ethan reclined in his saturated state. Lying on his bed, he reminisced, recalling the perverted erotic visual images he had seen and felt earlier. There he laid, allowing his fingertips to wander about his body as dark, disturbing thoughts occupied his mind, finally falling asleep just before the sun rose outside his now infamous window on the world.

XXVI.
ANGELS HEAVEN SENT

Ethan awoke midday in excruciating pain. It felt like each and every bone in his body was going through some merciless metamorphosis akin to growing pains. He was shivering uncontrollably, nauseated and sweating profusely, severe symptoms indicative of fever. During this period of hibernation the elements conspired to take him down for the count. He was certain his soaked, naked body exposed to the cold morning air had combined to invite a debilitating illness. Climbing under the covers he cocooned himself up to the neck and could sense his body temperature rising. It felt like fire, as if his blood was boiling oil. Ethan knew he had to remain underneath the blankets and sweat it out. The dreadful fever needed to break and do so quickly. It took a toll but didn't take long before he became unconscious. Ethan did not open his eyes again until nightfall. Infection setting in, some insidious disease had made him delirious, staking its claim, fever spiking to a new high.

When he next opened his eyes, Ethan did not know how long he had been gone, if it had been hours or days and he couldn't have cared less. Happy to be alive, he'd been aware enough to know how close he had come to death at the height of it. Far from out of the woods, he was awakened by his own violent coughing, on the verge of choking, the illness still deeply embedded within his core. Barely able to muster enough energy to lift his head and look through the window before fainting again, *"Physician, heal thyself"* came to mind. There was no one to help Ethan, no one to do it for him, no appearance made from his friend *Time* as they had apparently lost track of each other on the journey, parting ways for the time being. During this state of confusion he could not determine how long he had been rendered bedridden and if he received visitors, he never noticed. Ethan was living (and perhaps even dying) in an Olde World where proper medical treatment was unavailable, a time in history when vaccines and antidotes were virtually nonexistent by modern standards. It was an era when it was not uncommon for people to perish from illness readily remedied in the not-so-distant future. He knew from the inception of this project, should such a happenstance occur, it would be a matter of self-preservation. There never was an option to visit that medieval place called a hospital. Not only did he lack the strength to make it over to Whitechapel Road, he would not allow these Neolithic barbarians to touch his body. His trepidation was well-founded. He could go in with influenza and come out as an amputee. There was only one option available to him. Stay put. *"No one touches the body of a god, no one but my Maggie."* With that final thought, Ethan again slipped away.

During one of his rare, lucid moments when regaining consciousness, he awoke frighteningly dehydrated. He'd had nothing to drink, no water since falling sick and he had no idea how long that had been. If he didn't replenish his fluids immediately Ethan knew he could slip further into an illness that may debilitate him to the point of no return. He knew what he had to do. It was either early morning or just before dusk judging by the color of the sky outside his open window. Hoisting up his weak body, he had to force himself to eat and drink something or he'd surely succumb to what ailed him. The closest well was too far for him to manage. Pulling out money from the pocket of the trousers laying at the end of the bed, he struggled to dress in fresh pants and an undershirt then wrapped himself in the blanket to leave the room. He could hear the murmuring of voices downstairs, assessing it was late afternoon or early evening. As Ethan entered the kitchen he found six people dining together.

"Good Lord! You look like death!" One man's harsh remarks caused the others to look in his direction. "Ya reek, mate…spoilin' our meal here. Ya need a bath and a doctor…or a trip to the Death House. Be off with you, then."

Like a pitiful little boy in desperate need of assistance, not knowing who to ask, Ethan held out the money in his trembling hands for all to see.

"I'm willing to pay if someone would be so kind as to fetch me some well water and perhaps a spot of tea and whatever food from the kitchen I can barter. I haven't eaten for some time and have had nothing to drink." Forcing his words through the coughing spell those present surely found downright toxic, he wiped his face with the blanket. No one responded to his plea for help. It was obvious they did not want to be contaminated by him and would've likely preferred he leave the room entirely. Overcome with weakness, Ethan said nothing more as he dragged a chair out from beneath the table then sat down alone near the hot stove, pulling the blanket around his hunched shoulders. An older woman was sitting with her son. She stood up from the bench, approaching what appeared to be a dejected, decrepit old man.

"Of course, sir. Best you get some food and drink in you. Let me follow you to your room so I may fetch your pitcher."

"My pitcher?" Ethan knew it was still morbidly stained with the putrid mixture of fluids he could not yet dispose of or expose to anyone else. "Oh, I've broken it, I'm afraid, retrieving it from my bedside." He cunningly covered his tracks as well as he could while in the midst of a raging fever.

"Best not confess that to the manager. The bloke'll charge ya double the worth." Apparently the gruff gentleman at the table felt a twinge of guilt for his earlier nasty comments, offering a softened, more sympathetic tone along with his sage advice.

Laying her hands upon his shoulders, Ethan appreciated her gentle touch though the simplest contact pained his skin. Kindness extended by this woman (when most would keep a safe distance) humbled him. He didn't know her. He didn't know why she was willing to do this for him and he did not know how close he was to death. Looking up at her face he truly felt her soul through her eyes. Perhaps he was dying, being aided by an angel of mercy coming to take him home. He felt safer than ever before. A calmness came over him in an instant. As his trembling began to subside, Ethan was overcome by an outpouring of tears. He surrendered to her in every way, succumbing to her generosity of spirit. Suddenly, no longer feeling scared or alone, instead, Ethan felt comforted, cared for to such an extent, tears of gratitude poured from his bloodshot eyes.

"I'll take care of you, sir. We had best get you to your room and back into bed."

Helping him stand, she tucked her body up into his to stabilize him, holding on tight as they made their way to the stairwell, assisting him every step of the way.

"I'm at the top of the stairs, first room." Ethan could barely utter the words.

In his weak and vulnerable condition, he possessed the presence of mind to hand her enough to cover any material cost plus a generous compensation for her efforts on his behalf. Once at the door, he motioned for her to allow him to continue alone into his room while she attended to the errands. He could not allow her to enter.

Once inside the door Ethan fought the urge to immediately return to his bed. If the woman was to bring water, tea and food to his room then he needed to take care of the mess of clothing and stains all about the rented space. First order of business was obvious. He'd have to quietly break the porcelain pitcher to validate his excuse. There was no time to clean up dried blood and semen smeared on the floor near the desk underneath the window or spillage from his makeshift bath beside the dresser. With no clean water at his disposal to do so, Ethan's best and only maneuver in this current condition was to disguise the evidence, placing towels and clothing over the areas, making it appear as if he was a disorganized individual rather than one deeply disturbed. Though aching, staggering, he managed to complete the cover-up though he forgot to break the pitcher before collapsing into bed. The vile stench in the room smelled of death, no covering that up.

Not knowing how long it took the older woman to return, if she had knocked at the door Ethan hadn't heard it as he once again fell unconscious. He was alerted to her presence only when she attempted to shake him awake, shouting "Sir! Sir!" He was in such bad shape, she feared perhaps he'd passed away in his deathbed.

Ethan opened his eyes. Still in a fog, uncertain of his whereabouts and who the woman was standing over him, once she saw he was conscious, she walked over to the desk, pulling the chair closer to his bed.

"Here we go, sir. Ups-a-daisy." She spoke as she pulled Ethan upright, guiding him out of bed, propping him upright in the chair. "Sir, we've got to get you out of these clothes. I have bartered for some food and have requested new bed coverings from the innkeeper."

"Thank you, mum." Ethan could barely articulate the simple statement.

Insipidly struggling with the woman, not in modesty but knowing his body was still laden with the remnants of his deplorable soaking sometime in the recent past, Ethan couldn't remember how long it had been. Regardless, he'd been embarrassed but wasn't strong enough to resist her actions as she unbuttoned his shirt.

"Mercy, Lord in Heaven! You've gotten sick all over yourself." Smelling then seeing the residual relics of an illness she'd presumed was physical, she'd likewise presumed he had retched repeatedly in his sleep. Seemingly not in the least repulsed by the fragments of vomit and other assorted bodily fluids, the lady did her job. She continued undressing him then bathed Ethan head-to-toe with care and tenderness, clothing him lightly in clean undergarments when she finished.

"How….I mean what…?" Ethan was coming in and going out of consciousness, lapsing into delirium, crying out for his *Maggie*. He was burning alive from within. The fever was claiming him but he could not die. Who would kill Mary Kelly? He'd have to fight to stay alive if for no other reason than to fulfill his assigned mission.

"Now, don't you worry yourself none, sir, I'm a nurse from Greenwich here for some classes in hospital. I've seen things that'd make this a day in the sunshine."

Explaining who she was, the woman never said her name and Ethan did not ask. Had she told him her name he probably would not have remembered. Wrapping his body in the clean blanket helped with the shivering which finally began to subside.

Handing him a cup of fresh water, the man sucked it down instantly. Once he'd finished, the nurse reclaimed the cup, filling it with hot broth, suggesting he take it in slowly so not to upset his dreadfully empty stomach. As Ethan sipped at the lip of the cup the nurse turned her attention to soiled sheets, stripping the bed in much the same way she had done with her patient. Switching out the sweat-soaked linens with a fresh set, she tossed all of the contaminated fabric in a corner by the door for removal then redressed the bed as Ethan sat silently drinking the delicious broth.

Once she'd finished with the task at hand she refilled the cup, this time with tea. Ethan raised his head and though he did not speak, his eyes were filled with genuine gratitude as she carefully redressed the injury to his arm. She did not ask questions. Once the bandage was secured, she lifted him from the chair and laid him back onto the bed. Tucking him in like a mother would her child, she gathered up soiled linens, wrapping them in a blanket then placing the bundle outside the door. Crossing back to his bed, she placed her hand on his forehead then closed her eyes. He could see her lips moving while she stood quite still. This nurse was praying for her patient. Touched by the gesture, Ethan began weeping again, tears seeping from the corners of his eyes. Kneeling at death's door, he trusted that she wouldn't let him die alone.

"There's bread on the desk when you're ready to eat. I will be back later tonight. Keep your spirits up." With that, his angel of mercy quietly departed.

Languishing beneath the covers, Ethan stared at the ceiling for a few moments, restless thoughts rambling through his mind, awash with emotions. He felt pathetic, disgraceful. Why had she been so kind and sympathetic? She prayed for him! Had she cured him? Do gods look after one another? Had one worked his magic through her healing hands, giving him a new lease on life, sending him an angel from above? Had she been a savior sent to him just in time? She loved him. She must want him to complete his task so she saved his life. The fever spiked. Ethan passed out cold.

No way of knowing how many more times the nurse checked in on him, it could have been three, maybe four visits before Ethan regained consciousness. She would bring more water in a pail and food to help him restore his strength. Those were the times he was conscious so she may have come more frequently. He didn't know. It came to his notice on one such occasion as he rose from the bed, relieving himself in the empty bucket. She'd discovered the pitcher intact, cleaning it out thoroughly before adding fresh water for his use. Yes, she knew he'd lied but understood why.

As Ethan slept he dreamed of the room he was in: *The nurse was speaking too softly for him to understand what she was saying while she was mopping the floor. It was covered in blood and she was using the mop to drain it into a crimson bucket, already full to brimming with blood. Suddenly she halted the chore, scrutinizing it. Peering down into the vessel it came to her attention that it was occupied. Leaning in more closely she detected something bobbing slightly near the surface. The nurse plunged her bare hands into the murky mix, tangling her fingers in saturated hair, struggling to confiscate the severed head of Polly Nichols. "Well, what have we got here?" She twisted the head, facing her toward Ethan. "Say hello, Polly." It opened its eyes, staring directly at him. Ethan had that moment many have described in a sleep state when they try to scream and nothing came out. He was frozen in fear as, to him, this was real. Those eyes had not changed a bit since her death. They were immortal. The rest of the head was dripping with bloody scum water but those eyes were perfectly clear. The severed head of Polly Nichols began to speak. "So, feelin' a bit under the weather, are we? Well, physician, heal thyself, Doctor Bridgeman. Ya look like hell, ya do."*

It seemed to him that his own eyes were open. Ethan was alert in his mind, wide awake yet he could not reconcile what he was observing. It had to be hallucinations:

As the nurse stood there holding Polly's talking head, two arms reached through a nearby wall, taking it from her hands, the remainder of a decapitated torso stepping through the adjacent wall. Clutching the head, grasping it firmly; the arms held it up as it spoke again. "Oh! There I am!" Placing the head upon the neck, the hands adjusted it, completing their reunion. "There…I've pulled myself together, I 'ave!" The arms were attached to a body fully visible. Indeed, this was Miss Polly Nichols. The exposed abdominal cavity was still seeping through the white buttoned blouse, blood steadily dripping on the floor. The nurse was not impressed by the presence. "Oh, for Heaven's sake! I just cleaned that part of the floor! Step aside now, lass. I've work to do." Polly obliged the nurse who continued with her chores while Polly took the opportunity to make herself more presentable, smoothing out the wrinkles on her skirts with her newfound hands. "Yes that's much better." She exclaimed in delight. Blood dripping from the hem of her skirt, she crossed the room toward him, dragging a trail, streaking the floor behind her. The nurse paused for a moment to place both hands on her hips, shaking her head in disgust. A body bleeding out on the rug, it would be impossible to remove the stains. She kept on scrubbing in spite of the futility of a thankless task. Polly approached Ethan slowly and deliberately.

Ethan simply laid there in bed wrestling with the uncertainty of their encounter. Was it a dream sequence? A delusion? He wondered as he watched her come closer. Was he dangling on the edge of insanity or the precipice of death? Was Polly the Angel of Death encroaching, coming to claim him? Ethan was not mortified by the vision. In fact, he welcomed the company but he was quite astonished by the image of his victim seemingly reassembling herself without a begrudging notion toward her murderer. It was gracious of Polly. She was always so congenial and courteous.

Then, yet another vision: *A familiar apparition emerged from the wall. It was Annie Chapman, head intact. She, too, bore the wounds of her attack with a blood-covered exterior, her disheveled clothing doused in her own bodily fluids. A gaping opening at her throat did not seem to hinder her ability for speech. Actually, as uninhibited as usual, her first remark said it all. "Bloody hell, I need a drink." Saying the words as she noticed Ethan on the bed, Polly interjected. "Cor, now yer speakin' me language, Annie." Miss Chapman's next comment was directed at Ethan. "There you are. Been meanin' to ask ya, I cannot seem to find me rings. Ya wouldn't happened to have taken them off when ya butchered me, now did ya, sir?" Ethan stuttered out his response: "No…I…no, ma'am." He was in shock, he presumed, unable to begin to articulate. Annie interrupted. "I expected not. The way you slit me throat? Well, it didn't seem like a robbery, not that I'm favorin' one over the other, mind ya." An incredible scene in this act currently playing out either in his room or in his mind, it left him dumbfounded, speechless, breathless. He watched while the helpful nurse kept moving around the periphery of the room behind the apparitions, frantically trying to keep up with the clean up behind them, the bloody mess emanating from their necks and torsos, pouring down their thighs through the open wounds beneath their skirts. They seemed fine in spite of it. As they both moved to opposite sides of the bed, two more sets of arms emerged from the wall. They were extended with more purpose, both blindly feeling their way into the room. It became so clear, the reason why they were grasping at air. When the two figures attached to these arms breached the wall entering his quarters neither of them had retained facial features. Only in the ill-logic of his fever and the parade of players already on stage standing in front of him did Ethan discern these faceless women to be Elizabeth Stride and Catherine Eddowes. Apparently they had been traveling together since the "Double Event". It appeared as if, because Ethan never saw their faces, they were condemned to roam the netherworld for eternity without the benefit of eyes, a nose or a mouth. Their visible wounds were also the identifying marks of his handiwork as murders committed under duress during a time-restricted evening when he mutilated both without ever seeing their faces, looking into their eyes.*

It was still a disappointment. Crossing the room in tandem, settling at the foot of his bed, they surely intended to coldly stare at him, had they possessed eyes with which to do so. The wounds of his work on both women seemingly fresh, they'd been bleeding down onto the wooden footboard and onto the bottom of the fresh sheets the nurse had recently redressed the bed with, so it was no real surprise when the kind older woman became visibly perturbed. "This won't do. You will all have to move." As stern as any schoolmarm, they followed her directions. Four ladies of the evening backed away from Ethan's bed as she approached him. "This is all your doing, sir. Don't think I can't see it." The nurse, in frustration, was remarking more of the extra work he'd made for her and far less about the women he killed visiting him. Ethan responded to her, hoping to calm down his only helper as he pleadingly asked: "But how is it even possible?" He began to question the lack of logic and reason regarding what he was witnessing when, in unison, all of the women in the room turned their attention to the door, the only entrance. Even the two women with no eyes were instinctively facing whoever was entering. As if flames from a raging fire were consuming the entryway, all of them began to back away, cowering into the farthest corner of the room. The light emitting from the open door was not orange or red, nor was there any heat or the smell of smoke. It was a cool bluish hue growing ever brighter. Ethan could slowly make out from his peripheral vision the two figures entering from within the light, floating alongside his bed. At first their images were blurred, unfocused but rapidly it became clear that they had the blindingly white wings of angels. Both forms were adorned in white and had an essence of the divine, the Almighty. Still unclear as to their identity as the light surrounding them obscured his eyesight, one of the two glided along the footboard of the bed then around to his left. As they repositioned themselves on each side of him, they hovered overhead, revealing themselves to be young Maggie and Abigail, both appearing to be ambassadors from the next life, having come to escort Ethan from his inevitable flu-driven demise to a place of pure love, forgiveness and soulful fortune. "Are….are you here to take me to Heaven?" Ethan meekly queried of the angelic apparitions, the ethereal creatures he knew by name. "Heaven?" Abigail asked him with a puzzled expression, cocking her head. "You're already in Heaven, darling." Maggie clarified. "You have us now, both of us, to do with as you please, whatever you wish…no matter how much it hurts us."

Both of the winged women climbed into bed with Ethan and laid down on each side of him, climbing into his arms which he wrapped securely around soft shoulders as they both nuzzled their faces into each side of his neck. He must've been dying and this was his Heaven, both of these women worshipping him for eternity. He felt one of each of their hands maneuvering onto his chest when he looked down to see them unbuttoning his shirt. He didn't recall having a dress shirt on, only the undershirt the nurse had put him in but maybe, in Heaven there's a dress code. It didn't matter. He closed his eyes and simply felt the adoration of the two loving, angelic bookends.

His eyes closed, Ethan felt a third presence mounting him over the hips and groin. It was not either of the women lying beside him, as they were firmly weighing down his arms. Opening his eyes, he saw a third worshipper straddling him while holding his medical bag. It was Mary Kelly. Although his only contact with her to date was in historical records, her autopsy photographs, he knew instantly who she was and why she was there. "Hello, Doctor." Mary said, smiling coyly as she rested the bag on his lower abdomen. The leather was dripping with blood. Not the worshipper he was hoping for, Ethan sensed a threat. Attempting to wiggle free, both arms beneath the angels lying beside him, the man could not move. He looked to the left then right of him to discover that both had transformed into albino serpents, boa constrictors who were coiled from his shoulders to his wrists, tightening their grip while holding them down to the bed. He was pinned, immobilized and helpless, no one coming to his assistance as he saw the nurse continuing to scour the floor in the background, seemingly oblivious to his plight. The last one on the list, the only victim yet to make his acquaintance was now poised below his belly. Wearing an evil grin, apparently amused by the terrified expression on his face, Mary began cackling as she reached into the medical bag, retrieving the knife, the infamous weapon of choice for Ethan, the one and only Jack the Ripper. She held the eight-inch-long surgical blade with both hands, examining the fresh blood and remnants of skin, inspecting the entrails and tendons and muscle still clinging to its metal serrations, as if admiring all those tendrils obviously belonging to four prior women who had fallen under its evil spell. In that moment she held tightly to the brunt of a handle once wielded by him. Then, speaking her piece, shaking the knife at him in a scolding manner, Mary made her intentions known. "No, sir. You'll not be havin' it with me the way you did with the others, love. I'm to make sure of that right now." Mary Kelly spoke in a convincing tone as she took the knife by the handle with both hands. Raising it above her head, taking dead aim for Ethan's chest and abdomen, he cried out for mercy. "No, please wait! Let me explain!" His pleading fell on deaf ears as Mary applied all her weight to the first thrust of the knife, gouging it into his stomach. Over and over again, she plunged the blade deeply into his exposed torso, making a series of cutting motions after each stab, laughing hysterically as the brutal attack became yet more frenzied. He looked down to see the blade tearing him apart, ripping back flesh as a sequence of his organs began spilling out through the sprays of blood, drenching the bed, the white serpents and Miss Mary Kelly. He could not eradicate the image of what was happening to him, along with the anguished pain caused by grave wounds inflicted with forethought and malice. "Heaven? So you think you're in Heaven?" The blade went into his sternum, penetrating the bone to his heart. He could feel the life blood pouring into his rib cage, warm, softly flowing through the wound, creating a pond on the bed. "Heaven? I condemn you to hell. I condemn you to live! ***Live!*** *" As Mary sunk the blade into his stomach with the force of a man, Ethan screamed in agony. Hurling her thoughts through the cosmos, she ranted and raved while decimating his body. "I want ya t' live out ya days knowin' what ya done, who ya hurt. Killer!" Gutting him like a lifeless fish on a dock, he could no longer feel any pain. Using the tip of the shiny steel blade, Mary smeared his blood around her mouth as if she was applying lipstick. Blood bubbled in his mouth, causing him to gurgle the fluid.*

Turning on his side, Ethan began vomiting violently which, in turn, woke him up abruptly. The fever had broken, his body purging whatever remained of the illness on the floor beside his bed. He was weak, shaking, stirred to the core from a nightmare but he knew he had made it through and was going to live. As Ethan laid prone, bathed in sweat, struggling to breathe the putrid stench in the air, he opened his eyes. He was alone. All alone but alive.

XXVII.
NEEDLE IN A HAYSTACK

It took Ethan the better part of a week to fully recuperate. No question about it, he had knocked on death's door. Remaining diligent in his recovery he took care of himself, continuing to nourish and rehydrate his depleted body. During his first trip to the kitchen since his rescue by a kindly woman, he asked the other tenants about the nurse, wanting to thank her and compensate her further for many selfless, caring acts if she would accept it from him but she'd already finished with her classes and had returned to Greenwich. Told by one of the boarders that he'd been leveled, laid waste for a week by that insidious fever, as he regained his strength, any remaining signs of sickness dissipated. Saturday afternoon moved into night, Ethan spent this time returning his focus and efforts to his mission, back on the job again.

The first priority was to regain his chronological bearings. Not having a clue as to what time of the evening it was, he looked to retrieve his pocket watch from the top dresser drawer so to help reset his internal clock by seeing that familiar face, a loyal timepiece that worked in collaboration with his schedule. It was not where he had placed it. He began searching the entire room, each and every crevice where he might have relocated or hidden it during his delirium, no memory of where it went. His money, identification papers, clothing, shoes and medical equipment were still in his room, every possession accounted for, all but his pocket watch. Someone had claimed his precious timepiece. Ethan considered the possibilities. It could not have been the nurse. She could have sold the medical instruments for a far greater profit. If her son had been with her, while his mother's patient slept, he might have swiped some clothing, as winter was approaching, less likely the watch. No, no. The culprit seemed obvious. Only one person would have taken it.

A week prior, while Ethan was downstairs in the kitchen feeding an ill-prepared pork dinner to the tenants, Abigail had plenty of time to rummage around the room in his absence. She may have always had it in mind to liberate the timepiece from Ethan, seeing him glancing at it from time to time during their earlier liaisons. He figured she took it to sell or she made it a keepsake of their short-lived relationship, albeit one purchased, paid in full. To roam these streets of Whitechapel looking for her would be nothing less than an exercise in futility. Hoping she would first admit to the theft and second, return the watch was sheer folly and he knew he didn't need to have that much exposure and /or visibility so close to the completion of his work. Reconciled to its loss, he had no choice but to seek a replacement. Everything done in life was contingent upon those three hands and twelve numerals keeping Ethan on a tight leash, in sync with the world around him. There was just no way he could continue, no way to complete his mission without a proper pocket watch. Based on his innate dependency, a need for his companion, Ethan required a reliable, ongoing communication with his punctual partner in crime. Imperative that he maintain the means of a direct correspondence with his accomplice *Time*, it would be impossible to fulfill his mission without an *accessory* to the murders. Ethan realized Abby was the likeliest suspect and felt he'd fallen victim to a thief in the night, a con woman, duped by a mere mortal. After all he'd done for her, that ingrate had kidnapped his best friend, no ransom note left in her wake. He felt naked, exposed and vulnerable without it and wanted to punish Abby, to take it back from her but he could not. It was gone with her. Looking all around the room, shaking his head in disgust, Ethan spoke aloud in his quiet space, no tick tock to keep him company.

"More's the pity." It was the last trace of humanity, a final expression of caring about anything. He spoke the words softly into raw, damp air he'd breathed with a sigh of regret. Choosing to take both Saturday and Sunday to rest and fully recover, he decided to begin the planning phase on Monday for the final victim. This was a time to reflect. Ethan knew he had to shed stress as its presence would inevitably prolong his recuperative process. No. He refused to perseverate about it. He had to regain his strength, reset his internal bearings. Come Monday, he would refocus all his energy and attention on the mission, his curtain call, the final murder.

***

Journal Entry ~ 30 October 1888

It's the day before All Hallows' Eve. Back at Oxford, I'll bet there will be some wild weekend costume parties with female students barely dressed and the drunken debauchery of the boys at the school running amuck. But not here. These Christians are afraid of their own shadows nowadays and celebrations in Ireland and Scotland before All Saint's Day are considered Pagan rituals to most Brits. I am the horror show, the monster they fear more than demons, because I am real. What I've done and have yet to do will be more legendary than any creature manifested in the night by religion or writer alike. I exist as fear buried in their hearts, the plague on their minds. I am the story they were told as children, the beast who would come for them if their wicked ways were exposed. My story will be told forever. I am immortal.

I'm only noting this for my own recollection as this entry is on the tail end of a week of terrible fever. I say only for me because I've thought it through and realized my journal cannot return with me. Nothing can. The embodiment of my experiences during my time here will be returning only as memories. Once I've stepped through the portal my account of these events will be presented during the debriefing, given from a very different perspective, an account misrepresented as need be. Everything must be replaced with authentic duplicates of proper vintage. All I brought with me must be destroyed. Any and all remaining evidence will be properly disposed of in due course, as what would never be discovered in this time would certainly become exposed in the future, including this journal, covered in contaminants. There is not enough soap and water in the world to wash it all away.

For two months my knowledge of the past has helped me to save the future. Now it is my knowledge of the future which will aid me in covering my tracks in the past. To fail to do so would mean my own future would be jeopardized, left resting in the hands of others who may not see or might not want to admit that what I have done, what I've given of myself is a godly gift, mankind touched by the divine intervention of one wise enough to foresee the outcome without it. There are those who couldn't possibly fathom the sacrifice I have made, those so jealous and suspicious of a deity they'd sooner lock me away or, I forbid, burn me at the stake as a heretic. Powerful people, woefully misguided souls would be disrespectful of a decision made to carry on, consequently preserving the precious timeline with my unwavering commitment to the Flicker program. Would they rather have me committed to an insane asylum? Could they ever accept that I did this for them? Would they ever accept my sacred role as a humanitarian or would they instead sentence me to death for my perceived infractions as crimes against humanity?

No. I must and will discard every remnant of myself before returning, including this journal and a corresponding persona making these entries, what would be read as a flagrant admission of guilt. They can't be trusted with the truth, an urgent need to irrevocably alter the project to satisfy the demands of Time. Poor, ignorant souls, those lowly mortals. They know not what they do -- or would do if given the chance. No. I cannot risk my work and I will not sacrifice my life to a lack of comprehension.

***

Over the next week Ethan had to have closure on his trails, starting with a few final necessary purchases. His health restored, he embarked on foot then took a few carriage rides in search of an identical medical bag. In addition, he also required a complete duplicate ensemble of the physician's attire he wore as he stepped through the doorway into the past. Because those donated items were vintage, any forensic examination of the replacements would verify the authenticity. There would be an inspection of all his effects simply to identify and categorize all the microbes of the era that might have hitched a ride, those escaping or immune to the chamber. From those forensic tests The Consortium could possibly document what was truly in the air of old England at that time and compare it with samples of other elements from that period that had been collected and stored for this very purpose. With this kind of expected oversight and dissection of these materials, there had not ever been any consideration by Ethan to return with all the contaminants in his possession. Stains on his clothing and the medical bag would be detected immediately. Although there was no way to identify Ethan as the killer he would be hard-pressed to explain why those body fluids did not match his DNA. Oh sure, he could masterfully manipulate and manifest a story, saying that after every slaying he approached the bodies where he'd knelt down or placed his bag carelessly in the blood but to him it was ludicrous. He was perceived as being too intelligent to make such a novice error in judgment. It was smarter to walk back through the portal untainted, clean as a whistle.

Frustrating as it was, Ethan was finally able to locate and purchase the clothing, journal and doctor's bag he needed to replace the incriminating evidence he'd worn and used for the duration of his stay. It was necessary to procure a few additions to his attire in preparation for the next act in this play: a soft felt hat, a long coat with an astrakhan collar and sleeves, a red handkerchief, dark spats and light button-over boots. While he was out shopping, his mind wandered as he watched the many men around him, an endless supply of suspects for Scotland Yard to scrutinize in search of a killer. He marveled at how easily he passed among them, how simple it was to hide his identity, to steal the trust of others in an instant. The women of Whitechapel knew it could be any one of these otherwise innocuous men but those who worked the streets knew they may be next, yet they risked life and limb every night to make a living. He reflected on the irony of it while scanning the crowd as he passed them by in a carriage that took him to the front door of a jewelry shop. While inside, he'd located a horse pin tie clip and also acquired a replacement pocket watch. A tad bit gaudy with a big gold chain which had a large seal and a red stone hanging from it, something about the garish timepiece appealed to him. *"Ah, Abigail."* Ethan shook his head as he thought about all that had transpired between them. There were parts of history he was absolutely sure were of such a bizarre nature, it was *Time* setting up the scene, setting the tone, just sitting back in a lawn chair with popcorn saying: *"Let's see if I can get him to wear this!"* At times it felt like *he* was being played.

It was Monday, November 5th when Ethan finally had everything needed for his encounter with Mary Kelly, a woman who seemed to have the world at one point. Only twenty-five years of age, she was considered to be an attractive woman with blonde hair. By this time her relationship with Joseph Barnett was on the rocks and another prostitute, Maria Harvey was staying with Mary in a small room she rented at 13 Millers Court, or 26 Dorset Street, depending on the research. Regardless, it was the same room, the same physical address, through a small alcove off of Dorset Street overlooking Miller's Court. It merely depended upon the perspective of the witness statements and records. Ethan would wait until the following night to travel to that section of Whitechapel again to hopefully get a glimpse of a living, breathing Mary Jane Kelly. To try and pluck her from the street would be all but impossible, the proverbial needle in a haystack. Ethan had never seen any other photographs of her besides crime scene images which would not help him, as the mutilation done, what would be done to her left no identifying facial features. In that bizarre dream he had as his fever broke he had recognized the woman straddling him then stabbing him to be Mary Kelly only by intuition, a self-manifestation of appearance, a stand-in for the role. By positioning himself near her current residence he might possibly capture a glimpse of her to insure the timeline would succeed beyond theory in the early hours of November 9th. Of course it would. It must. *Time* was still on his side.

For over two weeks Ethan had not shaved. His hair, moustache and beard were fairly well-developed. It was not laziness or even illness that kept him from keeping up with it. Instead, it was part of the plan, part of the character role based on witness descriptions surrounding the death of Mary Kelly. All that hair was itchy and Ethan was unaccustomed to being ungroomed. Once again standing before his reflection, the mirror belied his actual persona. He appeared as someone or something else. As he peered into the looking glass, he suddenly felt an irrational anger toward Mary. Perhaps it was the dream. He was not pleased with her actions, gutting him during an unconscious event when he was most vulnerable. What had he ever done to her? This was not supposed to be personal. He was only preserving history. Why should she attack him when he had never provoked her? It was selfish on her part, a blatant attempt to corrupt his work. For that reason alone she made him angry. He wouldn't make his work personal as far as what was to be done but that did not guarantee he would not take some measure of personal pleasure in what he needed to do to her. Would his mission transform into an act of divine retribution? Time would tell. He scratched his itchy cheeks and chin then abandoned the mirror for the time being.

Monday night was the first night in weeks Ethan laid his head down on the bed without feeling exhausted. Tasked to play catch up, having lost almost a full week to fever, instead he stared at the ceiling for most of the night but he wasn't thinking of coming events, nothing about what he was going to say or portray himself as to Mary Jane Kelly during their forthcoming encounter, undoubtedly the hardest, most intricate "job" he had to do. All Ethan focused on was listening to the voices outside his window on the street below, listening intently for the voice of Abigail. For the life of him he had no expectations of reacquiring his watch, but still, he wanted to see her, his Whitechapel Maggie. If in the middle of the night he was awakened by a knock at the door he'd probably tumble onto the floor from shock and excitement. Abby was the embodiment of young Maggie (if young Maggie had been into his sexual perversions) yet, only Abigail knew them and still loved him in spite of it, kissing him, though bruised and battered due to his proclivities. Stealing his pocket watch was akin to claiming him as her territory. Her remembrance, the treasure she would hold onto and cherish for the rest of her days. That knock at the door never came and he never heard her voice again.

It was critical for the next two days for Ethan to scout the area of Mary Kelly's residence, to finally get a firsthand sighting, a visual recognition of what she looked like alive. His research had only provided a written description of her appearance. The autopsy photographs were useless. Without question, he'd need to identify her in person before Friday morning arrived. A long, heavy coat would be a necessity for their fateful early morning encounter as the temperatures would plummet, near freezing. He would dress warmly for tonight and tomorrow's surveillance certainly, as Ethan could risk wearing the heaviest of overcoats, even though it was far more easily identifiable than most garments of its kind. After all, there were never any witnesses describing a man in a long coat prior to the morning of the ninth. He felt safe enough, shrouded in the secrecy of *Time's* protective covering. However, there was the testimony of one Mr. Thomas Bowyer who saw Mary with a man of dressier appearance resembling the one seen with Elizabeth Stride, no doubt the shorter man who shouted anti-Semitic remarks before disappearing into the night. There were several testimonies transcribed, witnesses who reported seeing different men with the victims near the time of death, of various degrees of height and dress, many of them in the five and a half foot range. It seemed he would need to play the waiting game and make his first introduction to her at the time history had recorded.

Dressing the part, preparing to meet the elements head on, Ethan left his room just past midnight, now Tuesday. The air was cool. It rained earlier in the evening, kicking up a plethora of odors, the damp atmosphere absorbing them like a sponge. The stench of the city traveled through his nasal passages, something he'd become so accustomed to it wasn't much of a hindrance anymore. Activity on the city streets of Whitechapel seemed fairly light, as many might have expected the precipitation to continue through the night, right into morning. For the moment there was a break. Ethan was hoping for his own break as he hung around Dorset Street, nearby the archway leading into Millers Court. Mary Harvey was rooming with his next target but would move out tomorrow, finding new lodgings. Ethan would be observant of two women exiting that small archway together. Still not having any way other than her hair color and Irish accent to identify who, if any woman emerging from that dark passageway, might be Mary Kelly.

Ethan thought he had made a poor judgment call, having taken an unavoidable but necessary calculated risk. As the night wore on he began to tremble, shaking from a decided chill in the air. At least he was counting on this mitigating factor and not a relapse. Perhaps *Time* was letting him know he was wasting it along with precious energy. No one matching her description had appeared in the night. He checked his gaudy pocket watch. Pushing two in the morning, it was a fifteen minute hike back to his lodging on Bakers Row. He thought better of his decision to linger in the cold air any longer. It was time to give up the ghost. Best to make a fresh start of it again tomorrow night, Wednesday night. As Ethan journeyed back toward his room, he'd been solicited a half a dozen times by the women of ill repute working his route of return, expecting one of those faces approaching him would belong to Abigail. No. Finally arriving, sniffles and a mild cough told him he'd made the right decision to rest before relapsing, yet, as he got undressed he threw each item of clothing on the bed in a fit of disgust, frustrated that his body hadn't yet accepted (as his mind had) that he was a true deity. The God of Fate, still plagued by a mortal shell. Climbing in bed, relief came as his chills subsided, a comforting notion as he fell asleep.

His body was not failing him again, just letting him know it was cold. As Ethan drifted off his mind laid out the plan for the next day, knowing from his research he'd stand a good chance of seeing Mary Kelly in person, finally acquiring positive identity of the last woman the "job" required him to kill.

Morning came quickly with a sound sleep and no nightmares to disturb it. There was an air of amusement for Ethan about this entire experience. Had he not become the main focus of these murders and the history, legends and folklore that followed, this may have been quite boring. If, in the shadows of that alleyway on Bucks Row he had never come to the conclusion of his true role, or the role was indeed played by someone else of this era, the entire nearly ten weeks of his stay would have been nothing more than that of a stealthy sleuth working from the vantage point of dark corners, laboriously logging in the lurid details of his eyewitness accounts into his journal. He would have spent the majority of his time here in the solemn, redundant recounting of the adventures of another man from an objective perspective. Instead, it was entirely subjective and HE was the subject! Being the focus of this research far exceeded any imaginable scenario or expectation he and The Consortium could have ever conceived. His insight into how a serial murderer thinks would have been a tremendous asset in debriefing, used for the purpose of future study in sociopathic reasoning and actions, possessing intrinsic value beyond measure. Ethan had gone above and beyond the call of duty albeit for the betterment of recorded history with true and accurate firsthand testimony.

"Firsthand." Ethan chuckled as his thoughts this Tuesday morning directed toward the end of his mission, the foreseeable future, when he would return from whence he came. He was working diligently to keep the mindset that he remained disconnected to the work needing to be done for the "job". There were men even in the 21st Century who were paid to slaughter countless defenseless creatures for the creature comforts of mankind providing food, clothing and many other needs of his species. It was expected of them to perform their jobs without regard to the morality of it, disallowing any sympathy for the living beings that needed to perish.

Ethan killed four women so far and had only one more to go. The question was, could he be held accountable for enjoying his work? Didn't the saying: "Always do what you love" apply to him just as well? He was torn about what gave him a greater pleasure. The stalking? Looking into their eyes as life left them or the accuracy and detail required in the mutilation to the exact specifications of history. He took pride in his work, in the discipline, following through with his own version of perversion, executing the non-interference directive with precision. He took joy in it. Ethan had the sense of great accomplishment. Pondering the fate of slaughtered animals made him hungry. He began thinking of having bangers and mash, one more time, before heading back to his lodging. Soon after the skies opened and the night was drenched by heavy rainfall. Though dismal was the weather, Ethan's spirits were high, energy returning, excitement brewing, the day dragged on into the night. Ethan chose wisdom over bravery. He thought it best to stay in and continue concocting adventures in mockery he would scribe in the new journal, telling a tall tale. It did not take long for him to begin fancying himself a famous fiction writer. By the fifth hour, he was engrossed with his fabrication, losing both time and himself in the pages. He suddenly realized the lateness of the hour and pulled himself away from the journal and into bed. Ethan's morning alarm came by way of some quarrel in the street below his window. His late to bed, late to rise new motto remained intact as, checking his timepiece, it was almost noon. Returning to the journal, he wanted to complete the thought he'd abandoned in the early morning hours due to fatigue. The one thought soon became ten more and before he realized it, over three hours had passed. He hadn't eaten a thing or even had a cup of coffee, something he needed to do to keep his strength up for tonight's excursion.

Setting out a little earlier that Wednesday night for his walk back over to Dorset Street, this time he extracted from his memory the recorded events of this day as to Mary's whereabouts including a nighttime rendezvous with a man with bright white sleeves and an oversized white collar. Ethan needed only to position himself nearby the local candle shop where she'd been seen, there to purchase a half penny candle. Once acquiring a visual of her he could return to his room before the night air grew any chillier. To his advantage, strategy paid off with dividends yet unknown to him. Arriving outside the candle shop he discovered a woman who appeared to be in her twenties with light-colored hair. She was already inside speaking to the shopkeeper. He could not be completely sure it was her. From his vantage point, the shelves full of candles were obstructions, his view obscured. He'd have to patiently wait for her to leave and hopefully affirm that it was, indeed, Mary Jane Kelly. By walking close enough to discern the Irish accent indicative of her origins, she need only speak for him to know. She shopped for a few minutes before returning to Dorset Street.

Stepping over the threshold, not paying any attention to the muddy cobblestone, she slipped and fell to the ground. Ethan instantly stepped forward to take her arm, assisting the lady to her feet. It was then, the moment when Ethan truly believed he had become a part of some elaborate hoax at the hands of *Time* or the Universe. As she stood then turned to Ethan, he shuddered in disbelief, as yet another immediate shock wave from the cosmos struck him. A fresh face splattered and speckled with mud, she was also identical to young Maggie. It was as if they were coming off an assembly line, first Abigail and now Mary Kelly, both passing for replicates of Ms. Daley. It was a stunning revelation. That expression of disgust with her plight took Ethan back to The Valley and time trials fit for a princess, to the night he and Colin watched in amusement as Maggie failed miserably to navigate the mucky quagmire that left her in much the same condition as the woman Ethan was holding onto while she, too, regained her balance.

"Oh, manky!" She spouted. "Thank you, kind sir." She spoke with a distinctly Irish accent as she began wiping off her coat and skirt with now dirty hands, making matters worse. Looking up into Ethan's eyes, the man stared at her in astonishment, apparently in the midst of a powerful flashback.

"You may let go of me now, sir. I'm fine." Mary directed, glancing at his hand cupped around her delicate elbow.

Ethan followed her focus then realized he was still holding onto her arm. As he released her from his grasp, he continued staring at the lass. She peered at him with curiosity because his gaze spoke of recognition from somewhere. What Mary didn't know and couldn't know, their cosmic connection was Ethan's secret alone. The "look" wasn't about some place but rather, from some "time". He smiled knowingly as he thought: *"It's like plucking a needle from a haystack! Time, you are such a prick!"*

Embarrassed, she brushed off her hands on her skirt then smiled at Ethan before turning to walk away from him, heading toward Commercial Street. Astounded, he could barely wrap his facile mind around the notion. To find her at all was amazing but then to find her with such ease, to discover that she was young Maggie's second clone was at least mindboggling. He had no choice but to pause and reflect upon a cosmos capable of mockery and manipulation. Perhaps a little taller and a bit more buxom, according to her facial features she was none other than the sweet, innocent intern he had grown to love and miss in his absence. He watched as she plucked an inside pocket for a handkerchief to swab her face clean.

Keeping his distance, Ethan followed her. She walked along speaking to others on the street in passing. There was an immediate knowledge that she was Mary Jane Kelly. His curiosity sated, he could've confidently returned to his lodging and done so long before the cold night set into his bones, yet he found himself fixated on the impossibility of another identical vision. Ethan felt so connected with her he had to follow her, as if he had no choice in the matter because she was towing him along. Blending into the crowd, she returned to her small room just off the narrow passage on Dorset Street leading to Millers Court then she reemerged after a few minutes, apparently stopping in only to drop off the candle. Then, entering the courtyard, she was approached by a man of decent tailored clothing whom she spoke to for a long time, giving Ethan a chance to hear more of her lovely, lilting Irish accent. He must have been the man Thomas Bowyer witnessed Mary talking with at this time. Ethan scanned the yard to see if there was anybody else focused on the couple chatting. It reminded him once more of a play. Standing there and looking on, right on cue was the obvious character of Thomas Bowyer. He had paused in passing to watch Mary Kelly converse with the man for a trice before crossing through the courtyard.

Ethan's main fixation most certainly remained on Mary Kelly. He was no longer listening to the accent. He simply couldn't stop looking at her. The first four women he'd killed were in their forties, drunken and haggard, beaten down by a rough life on the streets. Mary still possessed a certain innocent quality in her life, the life that now belonged to him, a life and subsequent death he'd known of in the 21st Century. The grand finale of this play had him revisiting imagery that would make something which was not supposed to be personal, very personal. For Ethan, it would become the *pièce de résistance* of the closing scene, his curtain call.

Returning just past midnight, it was a cold, light rain beginning to fall. As Ethan stepped inside he removed his hat and coat, shaking them vigorously to rid them of any residual moisture then he laid them aside, peeling off other layers of clothing. Down to pants and undershirt, Ethan had to stop for a moment. He'd felt something building inside, a feeling he could not label as anger or hatred or even nervousness. It was an anxiety-based emotion with no defining origins. Something primal, it kept crawling beneath his skin. He felt the oppressive weight of what clothing remained on his body and couldn't wait to shed it but stood there instead, wondering if it was the anticipation of killing his next victim, Mary Kelly. Was this emotion filled with a fear that *Time* kept toying with him, constantly sending him reminders of Maggie Daley? Fear that he was going to have to cross that fine line to murder the one thing in his future / past that he clung to for sheer sanity? Or was he angry at the girl who, through no fault of her own, so remarkably resembled the Flicker intern?

Ethan once again sought answers from the reflection in the mirror, staring at the unshaved, unkempt face directly in front of him. He grasped the edge of the dresser top tightly, bracing for the one time that son of a bitch spoke back and told him all the answers to his questions regarding his actions, regarding his feelings. It became, for a while, nothing less than a bona fide stare down. Who would blink first? Ethan won the competition as the man looking at him cracked a crooked smile.

"What are *you* laughing at?" Ethan asked as the spirit mocked him by mouthing the same words, no sound. "You're the one causing me these emotions, aren't you?" A broad smile returned to the face opposite Ethan's in confirmation of the question posed. A demon in the looking glass was a true reflection of himself, of the demon within him, planting thoughts and visions, placing ideas in his mind to keep Ethan unbalanced regarding his reasoning for any actions taken during the most important mission of his life.

There was an incessant whispering in his head, a voice trying to persuade him to listen to the voice above and beyond his own logic, an evil torment in the night willing him to do its bidding. Having made it through these many weeks and also completing his missions made him question whether or not the whispers were a better guide than his own judgment. Ethan leaned in toward the mirror and the reflection engaged identically. Nearly eye-to-eye with his alter ego, Ethan spoke truth to power.

"I'll see you tomorrow." No truer words ever spoken, off to bed he went.

XXVIII.
ARTISTIC LICENSE

The date was Thursday, 8 November 1888. Only one day before Ethan's return through the Flicker doorway, only one victim remaining, he woke early, just before nine in the morning, with his singular mission in mind. It seemed like years since he had been in the 21st Century. He still had the presence of mind to realize that the things *Time* had forced him to do during his visit here had warped and twisted his thought process about the world, both worlds. Professor Ethan LaPierre would not return through the portal the same man he was before he made the leap of faith into the past. After everything he had done and all he'd experienced while there in 1888 Whitechapel, he'd not just profoundly changed, he had become an entirely different man. It would require every last ounce of energy to suppress the newfound rage and silence his addiction to it. He laid very still, lost in the ether, lost in time itself.

Ethan knew he would have to conceal his amorous inclination toward his young Maggie, should he see her again. As a strong motivation during his undertakings in the 19th Century, she was now and forever a part of it but would remain unaware of the roll she'd played in his mind's eye during this mindless abandon of reason over these past months. He would play these events like a poker hand, close to the vest. He'd bluff his way through the debriefing, knowing all too well that the truth would hurt many, mostly him. Ethan knew he could not risk the possibility that they would not understand that he did what he had to do. With that thought he rolled out of bed. It was time.

His final day began by laying out three complete ensembles of clothing on the bed: what he would wear for the day's preparations, what he would wear that night for his interlude with Mary Kelly and finally, what he'd be dressed in for his return home. Once outfitted in his local attire, Ethan's first order of business was to go to the bank on Whitechapel Road and withdraw his remaining funds. He'd planned to seek out the manager to offer a bribe of sorts. By means of a "charitable donation" made in cash (one at the man's discretion to distribute), Ethan wanted all record of his account discarded. It needed to disappear with him. His best guess? The money would disappear, going directly into the banker's pockets. It was not uncommon in the 19th Century (nor even the 21st for that matter) to buy someone's loyalty and his expectation of the manager did not go unrealized. He was in and out of that bank in no time with what money he needed in hand, all the remaining funds gone but not forgotten by a banker perfectly willing to keep his mouth shut for a price.

Returning to his room, occasionally peeking down the stairs, Ethan waited until everyone in the lodging house had stopped by the kitchen for lunch before moving on. After the traffic died down he went there to set up a large pot to boil and sterilize all of his surgical instruments, with the exception of the eight-inch blade. His plans for the day were underway. Once they were thoroughly cleansed, any contaminants removed, he dried them as well, neatly placing them into the duplicate medical bag he'd purchased for his trip back into the future. He had to be methodically prepared for any contingency, ready in advance to make the leap. Knowing he'd have ample time mattered not as Ethan was obsessed with the details of his mission. The Flicker doorway would still be wide open for the full twenty-four hours of November ninth, to allow enough time for him to return at his leisure without feeling rushed. Acting in haste due to a smaller window of opportunity, too brief of an access period could cause critical mistakes to be made. Ethan had considerable time to think everything through, including what he would do once he returned to the future.

By the completion of his outdoor errands, he'd already begun to feel the bitter cold setting into his bones as the sun began setting. The rain had moved in, dowsing him enough to require a change of attire earlier than expected. Redressing into his "work" clothes for the final encounter of his stay, he stared into the mirror, thinking *"This is who Mary Kelly will meet in a matter of hours...when she meets her fate."* Cold and calculating, he snickered at the image then moved away from the looking glass. He'd seen enough. As each task was completed, his pocket watch continually kept pace to tick-tock away the minutes, the excruciating hours of anticipation. As he waited an anxiety revisited him, once again building to a crescendo, a fever pitch. Undefined and uncontrollable, the same feeling that consumed his consciousness the previous night returned with a vengeance. It didn't fall neatly into a category or a subset of emotions but was instead, an integral part of the equation. Not fear, not dread, more like butterflies fluttering about in the pit of his stomach, much like the feeling one has before embarking on a first date with a new partner. Thinking about it, Ethan decided it was all part of the play, that sensation one gets while waiting in the wings, waiting for his cue to step onstage, as if for the first time, but it was not stage fright. No. He knew his lines, his part in the play. Every cue, every mark, each and every move he would make, all committed to memory. Ethan even knew when and where to exit the scene of the crime and yet, still, there it was again, taking up residence in his gut, lodged in his throat.

Packed and ready to go, on his mark, Ethan still had nearly six hours before his stage cue. He used the time wisely to finish writing a pack of lies in his fake journal. Having been not in the least hard-pressed to find the identical diary with the leather binding, same type of bond paper within, he found it readily available on the open market. Documenting the encounters with these five women in an entirely different way, Ethan scribed eight entries dating back to his initial arrival up to and including tonight's "Scope" mission. He was meticulous, planning to name one of over thirty suspects in his report to appease The Consortium brass. Countless embellishments, bells and whistles, occupied his mind to pass the time while recording the *fictional* version of history. As he wrote, he found it harder than he thought to simply make up this story as he went along. In fact, he found the fiction rather boring, not nearly as fascinating as his true account of events. Generalizing these encounters, he wrote descriptively about having to stay hidden in the shadows without intervening while each woman was brutally murdered by this 19th Century killer. He filled in the gaps with his experiences of the smells of the city, the taste of the food, especially those bangers and mash he'd grown so fond of, sharing the raw experiences of being back in history. He wrote eloquently about how much time he spent secluded in his room, never exploring the streets and people of the time, never interacting with the police and certainly not having any personal interactions with any of the locals in any way, especially any of the victims. He created the perfect portrayal of the perfect Scope. Anything and everything The Consortium wanted and needed to know, the epitome of a Flicker Project done right. Lies, all lies. Yet it was not quite perfection, not yet. There was still one more mission. One more woman. One more victim. Ethan had killed her a hundred times in his mind. Detached from reality, he was ready to go.

There was no protocol, no training; no standard procedures for what Ethan had to improvise almost from the moment he stepped through the Flicker. All he had at the beginning were his wits and his knowledge but somewhere along the way he was introduced to a friend, an ally, a partner in crime. *Time* approached him in the manner befitting a newly discovered relative, a brother in arms constantly watching his back, front and sides for whatever was coming his way. Oh sure, like any brother of lesser age, Ethan was teased and tormented by *Time* but it was done out of love, to make him more of a man, to make him stronger, building his character.

It was nearing one in the morning on this rainy November 9, 1888. Finality and beginning merged. Ethan was unshaven, dressed up in his second to last physician's suit he had bought in London back in September. Over it he wore the long coat with trimmed astrakhan collar and sleeves, in his hands a pair of leather gloves. Standing beneath an overhang as the rain began to subside, knowing his encounter with Mary Kelly would begin on this corner of Thrawl and Commercial, though guised in the doctor's apparel, Ethan would not be carrying his medical bag for this meeting. He had only brought the blade of familiarity and assistance to him which was concealed in a roll of clean rags from a supply stored in his room, all of it then wrapped up in plain brown paper and twine which Ethan was holding under his left arm as a parcel. He had put on the red felt hat and pulled it nearly over his eyes. Here on Commercial Street on an early Friday morning there was more exposure than any of the locations where he had to meet with his victim. Traffic was considerable and he did not need to draw attention from anybody other than the players from history, one being Mr. George Hutchinson. The sole witness of his interaction with Mary Kelly, he was a local worker, hard up and hoping to receive pity from her, asking to give him "one" on credit. She, needing money herself, passed up his penniless offer for a far more lucrative one, both profitable and logical, a prime night engagement.

It was two in the morning when Ethan spotted Mary walking in his direction on Commercial Street. Lifting his head to reveal his face from beneath the brim of his hat, hoping she would remember their brief encounter the evening before, as Mary approached him she did, indeed, recognize the man who had helped her up from an embarrassing spill in the mud outside the candle shop. She stopped to talk with him, beaming with both gratitude and, considering his apparel, the hope of a potential customer.

"Sir?" She opened their discussion with a nod.

"I thought last night you took the term *dirty work* a bit too literally. Are you all right, lass?" He asked as he put his hand on her shoulder. They both laughed.

"All right." Mary responded, lowering her head, still slightly humiliated.

Her thick, Irish brogue accent was the only discerning difference between her and Abigail, the other clone who was evidently cut from the same cloth. Her smile, her laugh, even the way she looked up at him with her big innocent eyes, she was astonishingly similar to the other girls. She leaned in towards his ear, rising to her toes to get closer as if to share a secret, whispering her message.

"I was beginning to wonder if you had a voice, as you didn't speak a word last night. That was a shock to me, a man left speechless!"

"You'll be alright for what I have told you." Ethan joked as he kept his hand on her right shoulder.

They began walking together down Commercial Street toward Dorset. Ethan was well aware that Hutchinson would follow them all the way to Millers Court, as he testified to the local authorities. He would first eavesdrop then later report parts of the conversation he overheard between them. Ethan had the dialogue memorized. He knew he would have to pause, speaking with her at the entrance to Millers Court for about three minutes according to "the script". Ethan needed to justify the parcel beneath his arm, the one concealing the long blade that had a destiny with its victim. Improvising the tale of a shy artist who wanted to sketch her lovely female form in the medium he carried in a wrapped package, he offered her a generous payment to do so. That the discourse was awkward, the whole rendezvous making him visibly uncomfortable added to the allure for the young woman.

"All right, my dear. Come along. You will be comfortable." It was all the man, Hutchinson, could hear Mary say from their conversation.

Ethan put his arm around her then began to enter Millers Court. Mary turned to kiss his cheek. As she did so, she noticed a few drops of the earlier rain still clinging to his face. Reaching into her bag to retrieve a clean handkerchief to wipe him off, she realized it was missing.

"Oh! I seem to have lost my handkerchief."

Ethan reacted immediately to her remark, pulling out his own red handkerchief then presenting it to her, the perfect gentleman. Under watchful eyes of the witness, the two of them headed down the narrow passage toward Mary's room. Once again, the advantage went to Ethan knowing the play, lines memorized, all the players and points where the characters would make their exit. Historically, George Hutchinson would never pass by Mary's room or dare to look inside. Instead, he would wait at the alcove in hope that Ethan was a quick customer and he would still have a chance to talk her into a complimentary carnal encounter. He would stay there waiting until three in the morning, leaving as a regional clock chimed in the distance. Ethan knew he'd be alone with Mary. He knew he'd be alone with her all night. He never broke continuity with cause, no matter how mad he'd become, a man on a mission.

"It's nothing fancy, mind you." She unlocked and opened her door.

Mary's room had all the creature comforts of a prison cell. Police photographs of her death and the room she'd expired in were burned into Ethan's brain from the hours of studying every detail, yet they served no justice to actually standing in this tiny domain. There was a twin-sized bed and bedside table to the right as he entered the room, a table flat against the opposite wall underneath two small windows, one of which was broken and covered over with rags and a man's coat to keep the cold air outside from seeping in. A small fireplace hosting a tea kettle filled the opposite wall of the room from the entranceway. It was drab and dark, nothing cozy about it but to Mary, it was home. She leaned over to light her new half penny candle.

"Will you need more light to paint my portrait?"

"This will do for now." Ethan said politely, uttering the prophetic words.

"You may take your coat off, if you'd like." Mary began removing layers of her own clothing, comfortable in her own place, be it ever so humble. She was likewise comfy with him, the artist, excited about having her image rendered on canvas.

The fact that more than a month had passed since the "Double Event" occurred, doing business on the streets of Whitechapel had resumed to a certain extent. People began to let their guard down as things slowly but surely got back to normal. Mary's lack of an inquiry pertaining to Ethan's identity was proof enough. Evidently, he'd gained her trust in front of the candle shop. She never even asked his name, let alone that of an alter-ego, nor did he offer it. Mary's guest was welcome in her home, not a hint she might suspect him of being Jack the Ripper. No. Not him.

"I'd rather keep it on for the time being if you don't mind." Ethan fumbled with the package beneath his arm as well as his words.

"If it's to your liking, sir. Might you want me to build a fire to warm you?"

"No, thank you." Placing the package down Ethan turned toward her. "Actually, on second thought, why don't you go ahead, prepare one but don't light it, not yet."

Mary shrugged her shoulders and did as she was asked. With the chore finished a few minutes later, she walked over to Ethan. Looking up at him with her flirtatious smile, she spun around once in place like a schoolgirl showing off.

"No one ever asked to paint me before!"

Ethan refocused his attention on the package, unraveling the twine.

"Is there really paper and pastel in your parcel there that you'll use to draw me, sir?" There was respect, reverence in her voice. After all, he was a professional, his manner of dress and his speech reassuring her of it. There was something different, something special about this man. He was not the usual local street vermin she had grown accustomed to and acquainted with over time.

"Yes, direct from France where I studied under the great artist, Ethan LaPierre."

He dared the cosmos, risked using his own name as a blatant, arrogant challenge to the Universe. Ethan smiled knowingly. Deity. Untouchable. The director and the star of the play. His artistry would soon be displayed on the skin canvas of a young Irish lass. His artist's brush would be in the form of a blade, as sharp as his memory.

"Afraid I don't know much about art or France or anything else, for that matter."

Mary joked lightheartedly at her own expense, a self-deprecating humor Ethan found charming as he smiled her way again. Continuing to disrobe while he looked on in silence, Mary took her time. She made an effort on Ethan's behalf, seductively loosening up the strings of her blouse, dropping her skirt to the floor. Folding layers of clothing over a chair, her boots got propped by the fireplace. Once it was ignited, they'd be nice and warm for the morning. Mary would never see the glorious light of day again. When she'd reached the thinnest undergarment, he stopped her before completely undressing, leaving her in only a slightly tattered white cotton chemise.

"No, please. Leave this on. It will add a bit of mystery for the viewer."

"Do you mean your painting, my likeness might become famous?"

"I assure you, it will." He coyly replied.

Her implicit trust in him bore no relevance to Ethan. He was center stage, a role to play in history. Their scene was set and tonight, he'd be the "artist-in-residence". This was to be Ethan's final encounter, his masterpiece. Destiny placed him on that stage and handed him the perfect script. Directing himself to get on with it, the actor had a job to do. There he stood in that enclosed room with hour upon hour in which to do his detailed work. He asked Mary to position herself on the bed, lying on her back. She followed instructions well.

The night table next to the bed was elevated above the mattress, obscuring her vision of what was in the package Ethan was unwrapping on the top of it, prompting Mary's curiosity. Trying to prop up on her elbows to see his instruments of artistry, Ethan put his hands on her shoulders and made the physical suggestion that she stay prone on the bed.

"Just wanted to see all the pretty colors."

"Oh, don't worry, you will, but only if you're a good model and lie still for me."

Ethan fiddled with the paper and loose rags hiding the knife to make it seem he was compiling his parchments in preparation for a rendering then he leaned toward her. "You do have a beautiful neckline. Would you mind turning your head to the right, facing the wall? I'd truly like to capture your profile."

Flattered by the compliment, Mary acquiesced to his better judgment, an artistic flair for the dramatic, turning her head to face the opposite wall from the side of the bed where Ethan stood. Nothing but the portrait on her mind, it had been thirty-nine days since the Ripper last struck. For too many, making money was a much greater concern than a murderer in their midst, especially one who seemed to have vanished into thin air, until now. There was nothing else on her mind but fame and fortune.

Even though the broken window had been insulated in a makeshift manner, the cold night air still seeped into the room, causing a drop in temperature, enough that when Ethan dug the knife into the left side of Mary's neck, steam pushed out from a deep wound, the heat of her blood escaping like a puff of smoke. Before she could utter a sound he covered her mouth with his hand then began rapidly sawing away at the flesh just below her jaw line and across her throat, creating the appearance of a crimson necklace. Blood sprayed out like a geyser, redirected by its impact with the sleeve of his coat, deflecting backward to the wall Mary's bed was fixed against. After the initial spurts, pulsing up and out of her throat, it oozed instead, forming a pond. Her only attempt at thwarting the attack came instantly, bringing up her right hand as a reflex. Trying to scream, trying to free her mouth from Ethan's palm, her hand met the blade, cutting the back of it wide open, slicing her thumb to the bone. Pulling it away in an instinctive reaction to the pain, Ethan went in for the kill. The blade's persistent jagged motion gaining momentum, he leaned in harder, launching all of his weight behind the knife. Pressing on Mary's face, desperately seeking the sound and physical sensation of the serrated blade meeting the bones of her vertebra to indicate his success, once detected, he drove it home with purpose, dragging the full length of the steel across her larynx, clear through to the left side of her throat. Ethan's entire focus was on the immediate and lethal near-severing of her head. His visual focus, however, remained fixated on peering with pleasure into the windows of her soul. The expression in those eyes stabbed him right back, penetrating Ethan as deeply as the knife he'd plunged into her neck, maybe deeper, perhaps to his soul if one still existed at the core of a monster.

"Yes. Yes. Yes." Ethan repeated the words with a whisper, as if lost in the throes of a passionate liaison, at the height of orgasm; an acknowledgement that what she was doing to him, for him, was a pleasure beyond all measure. As the blood escaped her body, what had been stolen from him the night of the double murders had been retrieved. It became an almost unbearable anticipation. Still holding his hand tightly over her mouth, the last moments of the life she cherished unfolding under Ethan's knife were expressed by the intoxicating anguish in her eyes, that helpless gaze she shared with him as she stared from the left corners of their sockets. Mary could not scream. Any air remaining in her collapsing lungs seeped through that bloody gash, bubbling to the surface of a gaping wound in her neck before it could ever make it to her shredded vocal chords. Her eyes were doing the screaming. He could hear it, music to his eyes. A symphony orchestra, visual stimulation, a visceral composition rivaling the works of Mozart or Beethoven, its emotional complexities were astounding, a private concert of pain for an audience of one. Then Mary's eyes went dead. This concert was over but he still had an encore performance of his own yet to come. He was satisfied with what he'd rendered thus far, enjoying his work.

Over the course of events, experiences he'd had while visiting the 19th Century, of all his interactions, the one constant conductor of the symphony, director of the stage and confidant of a killer was *Time*. Yes. Certainly there were moments when his accomplice was a benefit to Ethan but, as of late, he was growing weary of the tiresome constraints put upon him. This was the moment when Ethan would liberate himself, no longer a slave to the mere seconds and minutes *Time* allowed, no longer subject to its whims and flights of fancy. He'd been entrusted to sanctify the annals of history. This time he had power over *Time*. He would finally take what belonged to him during the expansive window of opportunity he had in which to do his work, to create his final masterpiece. He would have the hours, the privacy, the blade and the body of this young woman. Mary. She was his canvas, his model and his muse on which Ethan would paint the broad strokes and fine lines of history, writing her place in history in blood. It was 2:30 in the morning.

Unlacing her chemise undergarment in an erotic manner, it was no longer white, saturated with her blood. All the while, Ethan continued staring into her dead eyes. He fantasized about a scenario not unlike this between himself and young Maggie, but there would be no need to cut her throat. There would be no struggle, no disguise necessary. Ethan wouldn't need to masquerade as an artist or anyone else. He could be himself and she would succumb, surrendering her will, her body and her life. He would make the role he'd play, his own. In time, he would have her all to himself, claiming her soul. He'd have to wait for Maggie Daley but would first exercise his patience on the form of the woman who now laid dead on the bed beside him as he sat on the edge, studying his blank canvas. Pulling away the chemise to expose her entire naked body, the darkness of the room obscured his view which would not do. He'd dealt with that when he had to perform his work on Catherine Eddowes in the shadows of a London street, relying strictly upon *Time* to guide his hand exactly in accordance with what history had recorded. No. Ethan would not allow his invisible ally to dictate the conditions of the final, most detailed work he'd been tasked with, so he stood from the bed, retrieving the half penny candle she had bought previously when she'd done her muddy-Maggie impression outside the candle shop. Carefully moving it across from the table to the bedside, requiring more than ambient "mood" lighting, he sought out another candle. Finding one half-burned but still very useful, he lit it as well then placed it on the bedside table, illuminating the nude, motionless body of Mary Kelly. Adequate for his purposes, Ethan stood above her, assessing, planning the work, a role he'd have to perform, taking his time, for quite some time. He drew from memory, every written report and photographic detail of the death of the woman in front of him, charged with duplicating or rather, repeating the episode to precise specifications. Postmortem descriptions chronicled by Dr. Thomas Bond and Dr. George Bagster Phillips allowed him to burn into memory every disfiguring cut that had been made, that he'd have to do. Ethan's arrogance reemerged with his determination for absolute accuracy.

Enlisting the long coat as a buffer between the blood and the clothing he had on underneath it, Ethan pulled Mary's body closer to the edge of the bed nearest him then turned her face to the left. In his mind, even in death, she could still watch his mastery as long as her eyes were open. Picking the knife back up from the table, he then positioned his left knee between the now open and separated legs of his victim. Reaching up with his right hand, he grabbed her right breast and pulled it up from her body, providing a defining line to use as a guide then began slicing it from her ribs, quite like old western tales of Native American's scalping their mortal enemies. Cutting in a circular pattern around, under the breast tissue, all the while pulling the nipple and surrounding skin straight up and back towards Mary's face, he cut until he completely severed the breast, leaving in place only the exposed ribs and thorax. Almost fully off balance, Ethan caught himself in a tumble with his right arm, breast in hand, just above Mary's left shoulder, her dead eyes staring at her own body part. He quickly repositioned himself, repeating the act in the removal of her left breast. He held the second one in his hand, seemingly weighing it in as a "pound of flesh", amazed by both the texture and heaviness of it.

"Well, I wouldn't want to carry these around all day." He said in jest.

Ethan turned and placed the second breast down near her right foot then jabbed the tip of the blade into her calf about five inches above the ankle and just pulled in through the skin and tissue up to her knee. He then turned his focus to fileting away the surface on down to the bone from her right knee along the inner thigh up to and partially including her right buttocks. Standing next to the bed, he then performed the same cut on her opposite inner thigh. Laying the knife beside her for a moment, he turned to the bedside table, gathering the rolled out brown paper and rags he had used to conceal the knife, moving the package over to the table by the window. He returned to the bed, lifting each fileted portion of her inner thighs, laying them flat, neatly on the mostly vacant bedside table, careful not to disturb the burning candles. Once a man on a mission, now a monster in a methodical mode, engrossed with the procedure, there wasn't a single shred of human decency in the horrible acts he was performing, no hint of remorse. Even psychopaths would deem him a psychopath.

Stepping over to the rags, Ethan grabbed one to wipe the blood from his hands, as it was making it slippery to hold her skin and the knife handle. Meticulous in his madness, he repeatedly wrapped the rag around each finger, to clean every crevice, any place in which it had already begun to coagulate. While doing so, he peered out the small windowpanes overlooking Millers Court, thinking about how beautiful it was at that time of the morning, how lovely the wet cobblestone appeared, a street illuminated by gaslight streetlamps. Across the courtyard were two adorable kittens rummaging through a few discarded wooden restaurant crates. It made Ethan smile. He watched them playfully scurry around for several minutes before backing away, viewing his own distorted reflection in the rippled glass. Staring into his own eyes, into the mind of a madman, he walked over to the fireplace then set the rag atop the tinder Mary prepared for him in advance, planning to warm and comfort her artist.

Before continuing his required chores, Ethan hovered over her disfigured form, focusing his eyes on the area where both elongated cuts along her inner thighs met. Unaware of his facial expression while he stared at the woman's vagina, it disturbed him to imagine how many men had penetrated this twenty-five year old. Imagining all sorts paying for the pleasure of what was, at least at one time, a sanctified orifice intended for the union of two people in love. Was it fifty? Was it a hundred men or more who had stuck her with an unclean erection along their return from a night of drinking or a stinky, sweaty work shift? Who would want her? He was doing Mary a favor and perhaps dissuading other women who were considering this line of work by discouraging them from walking the streets, instilling the fear they would be the next to be butchered. Perhaps his work in this Dark Age had even affected the future decisions of young Maggie, history influencing her personal story as cosmic ripples resonating in the 21st Century. The vast majority of men who worked with her down in The Valley at the Flicker trials, including Colin, wanted her and would fuck her if she let them for a price. She could retire, not wanting to continue her education. In the depths of his warped, twisted mind, he fathomed himself her Savior, perhaps performing a public service for all womankind, it had been a true labor of his love for the opposite sex.

Ethan picked the knife back up from the edge of the bed and went back to work with even more focused, resolute determination. Using his right hand, he felt around her torso, finding the costal arch between the ribs where he would continue cutting. He first cut into her abdomen just below the sternum, making the incision just wide enough for Ethan to stick the four fingers of his right hand down into it, right up to the knuckles, giving enough of a hold of the skin and tissue to pull up at it and away from the body. The temperature in the room was biting cold. Resting his hand inside of her for a few moments to warm his fingers, he then lifted the gap and continued in a sawing motion along the line below the ribcage on each side. Before the section became too long and hard to hold onto, he carved a large section off by slicing across her stomach, freeing the section of flesh, allowing him to place it neatly on the table atop the two filets of thigh already there. The surface of the small table became his personal butcher block as he cut away the rest of the exterior of her midsection then down to the pubic area, carving the large piece in two, again for easier handling. In time, he'd place those pieces on the table, as well. The dual action of slicing, pulling away the flesh reminded Ethan of a tough fatty steak he once had at a pub in Bristol, no doubt attributed to Mary's younger, tighter form as opposed to the others he had ravaged, all of whom were almost double her age. It could also be that by now, with time to spare, applying more painstaking scrutiny to his work, he was more attentive to every detail permeating all of his senses in the confines of this private little room. A visible steam lifted from the viscera into the chilled air. The smell of bowels and blood filled Ethan's nostrils, as it had with his previous victims. The odors of death had become a familiar, almost intoxicating aroma to him, the scent of a woman.

Placing the knife between Mary's legs, with all her internal organs exposed, he needed to recreate the photograph he had memorized from the police and historical files. Using both hands, Ethan lifted her intestines out of her body cavity, placing them on the right side of her torso next to her hip, only grabbing the knife to sever the connective tissue, completely removing them from her abdomen. He'd take his time removing her uterus and kidneys, positioning them along with her right breast beneath her head like a fleshy pillow. He cut out her liver, laying it at her feet then removed her spleen and placed it to her left side on the bed. Once again, he put the knife down to gather up a few rags to wipe off his hands and the handle of the knife. Like an artist in his studio he took a few steps back from the body, his body of work in progress to inspect it, making certain of the precise positioning of the organs and segments of flesh he had removed to identically duplicate the historical photographs of the crime scene.

Suddenly Ethan felt a little hungry, having worked up quite an appetite. Taking a break, he was able to find some leftover fish and potato Mary had from her earlier meal near the fireplace. He took a pause from the work and stood, pensively peering once more out the window. The kittens were gone. He picked at a small package of food as if he were relaxing at some park on a sunny day without a care in the world. There was no pressure from *Time* in this place. No interruptions or constraints. He could quietly work, savoring every bite as well as every nuance of the event, a final required effort in commitment to the instilled Scope directive to maintain historical integrity, creating a scene in its original conditions before exiting the stage. Taking one last bite, wiping his hands on his overcoat, Ethan turned back toward the lifeless corpse lying on the bed. He wasn't done with her, not yet. Poised on the edge of the bed, careful not to sit on the spleen at her hip, he leaned in close to her face to speak with a ghastly figure, a mangled ghost.

"Thanks for the meal." He said softly before leaning in, kissing her on the lips.

Abruptly pulling away, in spite of the fact that she wasn't protesting his intimate advance, he paused to reflect on her eyes. Realizing for the first time that Mary did *not* have green eyes like his Maggie, he'd found himself shocked by the revelation. Instead, her eyes were pure blue, as deep as the sea; liquid crystalline blue eyes. He leaned back in and kissed her once more, running his tongue across her motionless lips. He tried. He really tried to make it work between them, but she was no Maggie. She was too easy. She was a whore.

The word "rage" is usually reserved for the irrational actions of the sane. What was building inside Ethan went far beyond this description, well beyond reason. He began shaking violently from the anger he felt, the kind of anger only betrayal could manifest. Grabbing the blade once more, Ethan leaned back in towards Mary's face, but not for another kiss. Mumbling under his breath, he brought the knife up to her eyes as if to show her the object of his vengeance.

"You bloody bitch!" Gritting his teeth, the words spewed as pure venom. "Fake, fucking slut. You are *not* my Maggie. You will never be her. I see your façade. You will not fool me again. You will not look like her, not anymore." He then proceeded with her defacement, vile and vulgar in his intent.

He dug the knife deeply into her lips in vertical cuts, puncturing, shredding and spreading apart the tissue, running down to her chin with cavernous cuts due to the blade length and its force. He then shoved the blade through her upper lip, piercing her nose cartilage. An overwhelming rage, the raw emotion of it caused him to cry. Mary was a bitch, a common slut. They were all disgusting bloody whores and they deserved what they got from him. They deserved more but as *Time* had cheated him with the others, this one would have to suffer the justified indignities for all the rest of them. He continued, slicing off her nose, serrating the skin atop her cheekbones. Her eyebrows were carved away as he kept cutting, slashing across her face until nothing was left of her identity but a mixture of twisted flesh and tissue and muscle. As his tears flowed like blood, Ethan stood from the bed, slashing along both of her arms, lashing out in animated ways, the inner pain of these women toying with his mind and his heart. *His* heart! Ethan stuck his right hand back through the incision, past Mary's sternum, grasped her aorta, pulling down as he applied the knife to its connective tissue, freeing her heart from its valves. Since she fucked with his heart he would tear hers out of her inert body. He stood up, backing away from the gutted shell of a carcass, placing the heart and the knife on top of the rags and brown paper set open on the table near the window.

"Oh! Murder!" Hearing the cry from outside, Ethan peeked through the window expecting to spy a witness gawking inside at the gruesome scene. Nothing. Perhaps it did sound too far away for someone to have been peering in. He began to wonder if, in his rage, the outcry was again in his head, like the cries of "murderer" he heard in his room on Bakers Row. Still keeping vigilant watch at the window, Ethan took the lower part of his coat, lifting it up to his face to wipe away his obstructing tears with the fabric lining. Dropping it down again, the wool brushed against the chain of his watch, reminding him to check the time. 4:04 a.m.

What little light emitted from the candles on the table or the streetlamps outside, Ethan noticed the expected bloodstains on the fabric of his coat. He took one more rag from the parchment paper and washed his hands clean as best he could with the water from the kettle in the fireplace then dried them with the rag before throwing it into the tinder along with the blood-drenched coat, extra papers, rags and finally, Mary Kelly's heart. By striking a match from the matchbox nearby, he ignited all the items in the fireplace. As the fire began building higher, Ethan could better see his artwork in the room as he began to carefully and perfectly position the body in the manner it would be discovered later that morning. Turning her head to the right side, her left arm across her gaping stomach, her legs spread and the right knee bent, applying the images of history burnt into his psyche, to set the scene "as is", there to be revealed to the horrified witnesses and authorities due to arrive in several hours, this final *fait accompli* for the world to accept. Yet, he was likewise burning new memories as he paused for a time, staring at what was once a woman, gazing at his work, his dirty but necessary job well done. It was his masterpiece of origination and replication in its truest and highest form of flattery to the original artwork which, as it turned out, was an original creation of his own, after all. Admiring the view, it was almost beautiful as an act of perfect evil. Light cast by a now raging fire revealed something he missed in the darkness, bloodstains still remaining on his hands.

Daring the risks of overstaying his welcome and tainting his gilded association with *Time*, he stayed lost in the moment, reflecting on the fact that "it" was all done! For more than two months he had survived an existence in the past. It was a journey begun with the most invisible of intentions, planned to perfection. It simply wasn't the plan of history to give this traveler such a pass. The frightening fee was his soul and mind to fulfill the predestined, ordained ordeal of ritualistically and gruesomely murdering these five women. Ethan stood silently still in the tiny room with his last victim when internally the sudden shock wave of implication and condemnation hit him like a meteor from the sky and brought him to his knees.

There was, for an instant, a glimpse of his former "self", before his hands were forced into this heinous role and subsequent perversions of character and morality. It manifested itself in a momentary panic attack as he struggled for oxygen. Ethan's chest tightening, his vision constricting into a tunnel form, he closed his eyes and recalled his training in self-discipline with the military brigade officers of the FTC. The training he had received was meant for a much more benign scenario but it was nonetheless adaptable to any case, including gathering himself in the aftermath of his actions, realizations and forthcoming role he would have to play upon his return home. Amidst the insanity and loss of identity over these many weeks, Ethan could still muster enough of a scientific mindset to understand one thing. He had to return through the Flicker. He never existed in this time in history. He was never here. He was only a stain like the stains on his hands and immortal soul. He was only a visitor in time and it was time for him to go home.

Opening his eyes, he had effectively regained control of his breathing and focus on what still needed to be done. His confidence restored to its distorted proportions, he rose to his feet to take one more look around the room to make sure it was truly picture perfect for the local authorities to find. The fireplace was fully ablaze with the burning evidence. It was the proper time to say goodbye to Mary Jane Kelly, to the room, to this world and to this century.

XXIX.
GONE BUT NOT FORGOTTEN

In the early morning hours, the cold, damp elements bit his cheeks and nipped at his heels as Ethan took the path back to his lodging. Deprived of the long coat he burned to ashes, the blade in his pocket, he tucked his hands under each armpit and kept his head down, marching along at a brisk pace; a processional of one. The term "short-timers disease" applied as the countdown to his departure from this era had begun, his return to a 21st Century world was no longer measured in months, weeks, or days, but instead, in hours. One, two, three, four, five, six. A militant cadence he established was a much needed distraction, a disciplined approach to this journey, dragging him along, back from the lunatic fringe his mind had reached the edge of during the final murder.

"Control it. Easy lad." He tutored himself through an anxiety check. It was not just a twisting of his psyche. He was plagued by the nagging paranoia of detection, being so close to completion of this mission. Thus far, it had gone without incident, no glitches in the system yet an irrational fear of becoming somehow compromised in the final hours took hold in his mind. To be thwarted by some shortsighted action on his part so close to completion or to carelessly falter after more than two months of determined, diligent and cunning movements would be an unbearable failure. He knew more than ever before, this was the time to be most cautious, avoid tempting fate, to be prudent in every step he took. His final destination, Flicker.

One, two, three, four, five, six, seven, eight, nine, ten, eleven, twelve…

From time to time, Ethan would look up from the corner of his eyes as the clock continued to race, gauging his surroundings, catching a glimpse of an early morning traveler, someone off to somewhere, just like him. Many erroneous statements were made after the slaying of Mary Jane Kelly, a few reports of her being seen by others, citizens along the streets witnessing her alive for hours after her death. His thoughts traipsing in and out of madness with each step, Ethan wondered if he'd gone crazy, *imagining* the event rather than committing the slaughter of a woman. Were these eyewitness accounts accurate? No. Although obscured, Ethan could still detect dry bloodstains on his fingertips and the edges of his sleeves. He could feel the weight of the blade handle as he reached into his pocket to stroke the murder weapon. This had surely happened.

Then who did these people see? Perhaps it was like the old turn-of-the-century photographs of ghosts. So, what if it was the spirit of Mary Kelly walking the streets later that morning as she had done so many times before her death? There was still another possibility. What if it was mistaken identity? Many prostitutes of that time wore the same kind of attire, layer upon layers of skirts, boots and bonnets. Couldn't it be people spotted a woman who merely resembled her? Or, maybe it was Abigail. Except for the difference in the shapeliness of the two women the resemblance was remarkable, easily mistaken for one another, especially on a crowded street.

And what of Abigail? Would Ethan happen upon this mortal worshipper again, once more before departing? Could she have been watching, following, maybe even stalking him since their last encounter? Was she standing just outside the little room where he sliced his last victim apart? Was she the one who had cried out in the dark of night? "Oh! Murder!" If so, to maintain his anonymity, he would have to silence Abby before leaving, having no choice but to kill her.

"No worries." He thought it through. *"She would consider it an honor and feel privileged to have me cut her into scraps for the homeless hounds on these streets."*

Then like the flip of a coin, the arrogant, erudite and entirely self-possessed side of Ethan's insanity took charge.

"Stop it! She wasn't there. No one was there." Applying his logic to perfection, everything he did was perfection and nothing would or could be altered. Dr. Arthur Bridgeman would remain a fictitious, unrecorded and unimportant name in history. The entire event was perfect. He was perfect.

There were really no vestiges left of the man who stepped through Flicker back at the end of August. Certainly there was the memory of who he'd been at one time. Memories of family, friends, his love of teaching. He knew he was Ethan LaPierre in name only. Once an innocent boy, later a man of morality and humility, he could not afford to be *that* Ethan to do what he had to do here in this century. He couldn't afford to return to being that man once he stepped back through the vortex. He did not want to, anyway. That sheep of a man who let years pass him by as opportunities in life, for love, were laid at his feet and yet he sidestepped them to avoid any pain. In retrospect, he'd lived a half-life. Now, Ethan was empowered with the necessary tools, all the proper skills to navigate his surroundings, whatever the time period or place happened to be. He was now the master of his domain and his dominion was the bloody fucking Universe, according to him, and he would know because he was a god. It all made perfect sense. The soldier returning home, not with mental trauma but prowess to command everyone and everything in his realm. His comrade, *Time* would accompany him through the Flicker back to the LHC, with him for eternity. Standing shoulder-to-shoulder, they would defeat any adversary.

Though his thoughts were all over the place, Ethan had the presence of mind to pick up a discarded tarp from the pile of trash just across the street from his lodging, from the same heap that sheltered Abigail from sight as he had watched from above. It seemed so long ago to him now, more like a dream. Making it back to his flat just past 4:30 a.m., without incident, as expected, Ethan became delightfully intoxicated with the aroma of fresh-brewed coffee as he walked in the door. Either it belonged to the night manager or just one of the early workers who'd already left for the day. Ethan helped himself, pouring a cup without asking, as the kitchen, for the moment, was empty of occupants. While enjoying the coffee he set the kettle of water to boil, preparing to later sterilize the surgeon's blade one last time before reacquainting it with other instruments resting on the desk in his room. They would travel together, inside the duplicate medical bag Ethan had purchased for the occasion of his return. Bringing the mug upstairs along with the canvas tarp he had claimed with reason, Ethan began the process of preparing for his journey home.

Home. It would have a different feeling now. That apartment he knew and grew to love, on the outskirts of the Oxford campus, could feel uncomfortably foreign to him. Ethan feared he would forever feel like a caged animal when enclosed in those four walls. He had lived more of a life during the time he'd spent in the room where he now stood than he ever did during all those years he'd wasted away in his luxury, tech-savvy flat.

Collecting himself first, Ethan then proceeded with his final travel preparations by gathering up every item of clothing he had purchased here, as well as the initial physician's attire he had worn entering this era. Stuffing whatever would fit inside the original medical bag, after all the time he devoted to its cleansing, he could still see the bloodstained lining as he opened it to receive other incriminating evidence. A pitcher of fresh water at the ready for his disposal. Ethan had filled it in advance, now patiently waiting for the sun to arrive on this new and last day in Whitechapel. Biding his time until the sun would penetrate his room through the window, once it made its grand entrance, Ethan began collecting all the remaining clothing, shoes and accessories he could not stuff into the medical bag and, along with what he was wearing, tossed all of it onto the discarded tarp. He bathed his body, all the while staring at himself in the mirror, deep in thought. Ethan knew he was gazing at the visage of a god. After shaving clean the beard and his moustache, he ran his hands along his face, slowly transforming his exterior into a previous persona. Now it was time to dress the part of Dr. Arthur Bridgeman again. The elegant attire he'd bought in London, fit for a fine physician, was enlisted to assist him in completing the look. Virtually identical to the suit he'd arrived in, none the worse for wear, it hadn't had any wear until now, having been saved for this momentous occasion.

Dressing the part one last time, once he had tied the replicate dress shoes, Ethan stood to admire his appearance in the mirror. "Voilà! Dr. Bridgeman has returned!" Once again, staring down his reflection in the looking glass, he then realized that clothes do not make the man. This time he'd have to wonder if the demon staring back would, like *Time*, follow him into the future. The man's disturbed mind being duly occupied, he retrieved the blade, pre-wrapped inside of several rags. Ethan headed downstairs, finding the public kitchen vacant and his pot of water ready for boiling. He hovered above it as the steam began to rise, escaping the water, sweeping across his newly exposed skin, the sensation a welcome one. Watching as the blade boiled, keeping an eye on his timepiece as well as his surroundings,

Ethan remained ever mindful of the mission, prepared to intercede should anyone come sniffing around, perhaps a fellow tenant who might become curious about what he was cooking. Of course, no one intruded on his task.

Nearing 7:30 a.m., the knife sterilized, Ethan returned to his room. Standing in the middle of the rug, there he remained just looking around. All of his items packed and ready to go, he paused to reflect upon the past months spent in these quarters, taking a few mental snapshots as mementos. Time spent with Polly and Abigail but mostly his time alone there would haunt him the most. The ghosts, the nightmares, the dreams, the fever and the food. He'd lived a lifetime and *Time* had changed his life. His departure surely bittersweet, if his leap had been designated a one-way trip through the Flicker, Ethan was certain he would not only have survived during these times, he would have thrived. But it was not a one-way trip. He was expected home. The foreseeable future upon his return, Ethan was expected to report on the journey. He was expected to tell them a story and they expected a true one.

Gathering the last of his personal belongings, it included something that did not belong to him. Retrieving his borrowed copy of "Robinson Crusoe" from the desk, he would return it to its rightful home in a cubbyhole in the hallway, placing it back on the shelf from which it came on his way out the door. That tiny little library had, at times, been his saving grace. Over time, he had read every book in the collection. Meager as it was, they were firsthand classics of his time, as well as their own, and it was a privilege to have access to them, revisiting old friends when he was deeply, desperately lonely, longing for some company. In fact, Ethan was quite sure all the literature had literally saved him from the depths of insanity. Of that, he could not have been more mistaken. Nothing could save him from himself.

Ethan put on his coat, picked up the tarp and medical bag then tucked the book under his arm. Turning to face back into the room from the hallway, from the same spot where Polly and Abigail once stood, from the same doorway which glowed as a pair of *angels* made their entrance, he quietly closed the door on his 19th Century world. Walking downstairs, he replaced the book in the alcove then in rather bland, unceremonious style, stepped over the threshold and out the front door, exiting the lodging house without speaking to anyone. There'd be no point now trying to cover his tracks; nothing more could potentially taint his anonymous, clandestine mission. He turned right on Bakers Row then left on Hanbury Street, eventually reaching the corner where Hanbury, Commercial and Lamb Street met, just on the northern edge of Spitalfields Market. It was 8:12 a.m. and the Flicker door was just a few minutes' walk to the north but Ethan had one more stop to make. One more mission.

Whether it was his quick pace, brisk morning air flooding his lungs or this sense of accomplishment going to his head, he was practically floating along the surface of the streets beneath his feet. Ethan was euphoric, delighted with his performance and the outcome of this project. Knowing precisely where he was going, in moving forward, his mind was free to wander back in memory. Stepping lightly, something whimsical about his cadence, sentiment was building and brewing, biding its time. Observing the people in passing from beneath the brim of his hat, he considered the implications, cast into an irreversible role, one he'd be forced to play for the rest of his life. What did the future hold? He could see he'd be forced to stay in character as the persona of Professor Ethan LaPierre, the man they knew in 2020 expected to emerge on the other side of the doorway, bringing with him an amazing story. With that notion, Ethan drew in a deep breath and smiled.

Of the many thousands of faceless, nameless women who worked the streets of Whitechapel during this era, the five women who'd met their fate beneath the blade of a man from the future would be properly acknowledged for the roles they played in history. He'd see to it. In fact, he demanded it of himself, considering what he'd already done. Jack the Ripper's victims would no longer languish in obscurity, all but lost in the annals of time, overshadowed by his damned pseudonym. Now they, too, would live on in infamy by the same hand they'd died by. He would reanimate their souls. He silently vowed to do his part on their behalf, intending to write about them in the future. They'd no longer be listed merely as "victims" of a serial killer. Instead, these five women were deserving of the world's respect.

Mary Ann "Polly" Nichols
Annie Chapman
Elizabeth Stride
Catherine Eddowes
Mary Jane Kelly

He would honor them in ways they had never been before. Their horror stories would be told in greatest detail, shared with all to read. He would write about them! He would lecture on all of them to his university students. Yes! He would declare himself their advocate, their only existing voice. Ethan was left speechless by his own thoughts and aspirations. Stopping dead in his tracks in the middle of the street, tears began to swell up in his eyes. Out it came, this bursting of the dam within his emotional walls. He began sobbing irrepressibly as the thought of devoting himself "in memoriam" touched him deep in his soul, finding the last nuances of his former self. He doubled over as if all the weight of guilt and responsibility pulled his head forward, overcome with feelings he could not control. After a few moments, Ethan began to slowly catch his breath, finally able to stand upright, only to find himself in tears of diabolical laughter.

"Oh my God! That's bloody hilarious!" Ethan exhaled the words, still trying to catch his breath.

A slow, sly, callous grin crept onto his lips. Oh, of course, it made perfect sense.

He stood at the main entrance to Spitalfields Marketplace as customers stepped all around him. He coldly calculated the depths of human depravity to which he was willing to sink, considering the endless possibilities of using their names to his own advantage. *"I am fucking brilliant!"* Anyone witnessing it would think the man was sobbing. Rather, Ethan was laughing hysterically, maniacally at his own cleverness. Paying "homage" to them in this way would appear entirely altruistic. He would be admired for doing so. His smart move would actually be a slight of hand committed with words. He would make a career of them! Ethan's insidious grin widened into a broad smile.

He was a god capable of exploiting them, once again, his grand and graceful power of resurrection and everlasting life. Illuminating the "victims" would allow their killer to lurk in their shadow, effectively redirecting a white hot spotlight from the predator onto his prey. There would be no harm done. They were already ghosts so they would not care as long as he made them as famous as himself. By protecting him, they would not have died in vain. Elated, Ethan realized he would escape any scrutiny. No searchlights casting suspicion upon him, he'd refocus his attention on them, in honor of their sacrifice made, paying the ultimate price for fame. *"Perhaps it was a bit cynical but such is the way of the world, be that world old or new."* He thought silently. Pulling it together, he moved on into the marketplace, navigating his way through the light crowd. Thinking about the future as much as he'd dwelled in the past, Ethan would find his way to merge the two worlds and it would be his saving grace. There was method to his absolute madness. Not only was he a master at stealing lives, he was also fast graduating to stealing all hope, a killer of dreams.

Ethan reasoned that the victims, these five women, in fact honored him or the persona he assumed during his travels in this time and place. Especially Mary Kelly, bestowing her blessing on him in more ways than one to be sure, but one way more specific than the rest. In his feverish delirium, when faced with both his angels and demons, Mary sat atop his body. With her rage and retribution, she'd plunged the knife into him over and over. During his maddening nightmare, she spoke. No. She decreed and condemned him to live, to survive. Ethan felt her hatred at the time it was happening, processing the hallucinations as a curse bestowed, yet, now it was clear. Her words were prophetic to a fault. What she truly sealed was the fate of his identity. He would live on forever in the annals of history, not as Dr. Ethan LaPierre but as the infamous, notorious serial killer "Jack the Ripper". The dark, clairvoyant prediction of eternal terror, he was the terror that was about to leap more than one hundred and thirty years into the future.

Many of the market vendors would get a late start of it on Friday, as opposed to Saturday's merchants. Most were beginning to set up wares to be purchased. During this morning ritual, several metal drums were ignited with waste materials from the nearby trash heaps, keeping them warm, a type of recycling for their own purposes. This was to be Ethan's last stop on his path to the portal. Stepping between two of the wooden produce stands over to a burning barrel strategically placed for both the vendors to share, he laid the replacement medical bag in his right hand down on the ground beside him. Ethan lifted the original medical bag that contained some of his old clothing and his previous journal inside and held it in front of him for a moment before tossing it into a fiery grave. What remained wrapped up in the tarp followed it into the barrel. He could have simply grabbed the new bag, turned and continued on to his final destination. Instead, he spent his last few minutes in the 19th Century facing the flames of his existence, watching yellow smoke billowing from the metal can, following the embers with his eyes, rising up to meet an overcast morning sky. Ethan wondered which ashes were from the blood of his victims being released into the air. Which telling streak of smoke came from Abby, blowing him a bloody kiss? Were they parts of his words, confessional pages of the journal he could never bring back? Looking down into the bowels of the blackened pit to see the incineration of the leather bag and its contents, garments in the tarp, they were burnt offerings to other gods in tribute, hoping for returned blessings from his peers. The true tale of his journey was going up in smoke and flames along with any fragments of the man Ethan once was before stepping through the flame-like doorway some months ago. Will o' the wisps, they were, whispering his deepest, darkest secrets as they went, telling tales of woe to a marketplace full of people but no one was listening to them.

Ethan could not help but smile as the smoke wafted up in his face, stinging his eyes as he gazed into the open pyre. He could feel the ghosts of his victims hovering around him. He saw them in the smoke, each smiling down upon him in tribute to his cleverness, uncanny abilities to navigate a series of complex tasks over so many weeks involving an extensive cast of characters without being detected. *"Bravo!"* His satisfied smile was in homage to his friend and ally *Time* who, although toying with him a few times, never betrayed a confidant nor his confidentiality. *Time* had helped him make it through this mission. The "job". Ethan's grin grew as an inferno engulfed any and all evidence remaining in that barrel. Oh, he wasn't going to move until the last of it disintegrated, disappearing into the ether, not because he was still paranoid about being discovered but because it was a ritual necessary for him to let go, to say his goodbyes to the women and the world he *changed* forever in history. He too was forever changed. As the last bit of the bag burned out of existence Ethan picked up the other one at his feet and walked away unnoticed. It was 8:47 a.m.

Approaching the entrance to the small alley where the Flicker door awaited him, Ethan surveyed the area and even passed by it, covertly glancing down the corridor to the brick wall several times, making certain that no one was watching him from the street or a window above. Due diligence was tantamount, he was nothing if not thorough. The last thing he needed was to return to the year 2020 and read about a historical claim from some homeless vagrant seeing a man in fancy clothing passing through a brick wall in Whitechapel during the time and crimes of Jack the Ripper. Dreading a return to an alternate reality, he made sure he couldn't be tracked to the future. Dissecting every detail of this mission from the start, here he stood at the finish line. Confident his entrance into the alley wasn't witnessed he quickly slipped in and down the narrow, twenty foot long passage. Reaching the end of an alleyway he placed the bag down long enough to remove the pile of crates he placed in front of the wall where the Flicker should be, clearing his path. He snagged the bag then stood facing the invisible doorway, taking into his lungs a deep breath of this place and time. Holding it inside the same set of lungs that once rejected it as poison, the act was oddly comforting to him now. How many times he thought of this moment throughout his stay, knowing the hazmat team awaited his arrival, one of several in shifts, prepared for him, aware the time could and would vary but would be on this date. If he did not jump through as scheduled, missing the window of his expected arrival, it would be protocol to reset the Flicker, sending someone back to an earlier point during his mission to assess the reason for his absence. To his knowledge, no one had come to call because he was still right on schedule, the stickler for details. Ethan took one more look over his shoulder at the empty alley then raised his free hand, reaching out, through the wall, confirming the presence of the invisible door. To both his relief and fear, his hand passed directly through the solid brick structure. With one more deep breath he stepped through Flicker, a flash of pure, white light.

XXX.
THE FORESEEABLE FUTURE

Ethan's eyes were instantly forced to make a necessary adjustment, much like strolling into a dark cave after being out in the brighter desert sunlight. The corridor was shadowed. He saw beyond the glass encasing of the decontamination chamber, what looked like several hazmat crew members dressed in yellow from head to toe. As Ethan let out his breath and began to speak he drew in his first breath of air from the 21st Century in over two months, inhaling clean oxygen in the containment unit. The sterility and purity of the environment sent Ethan's head spinning, causing him to immediately become dizzy and disoriented, collapsing to his knees then quickly losing consciousness, blacking out. Gone.

The sounds of voices surrounding him, medical team members hovering above him, all the beeping and buzzing from monitors near his head, Ethan began to regain consciousness, greeted with what could be best defined as a pressure migraine. He didn't know how long he'd been out but he was now flat on his back being wheeled along on a gurney, wearing an oxygen mask which obstructed his view, worsening the pressure in his head. His vision was grainy, at best, but Ethan could faintly see the familiar LHC fluorescent lights passing overhead while ushered along, flanked by medical staff on either side of the stretcher.

"P? Can you hear me? You're alright mate. Just breathe."

Ethan tried to refocus. The voice was familiar. It was most likely Colin Bishop who was holding Ethan's hand inside his oversized glove. Straining to see through the glass mask covering the face on the suit leaning over him, obscuring the visage behind it, he could finally see that it was, indeed, his best friend Col.

"Hang in there, mate. You passed out. They are taking you to the med lab now, to check you out." The raw emotion of worry was detected in Colin's words.

All Ethan could do to respond was give him a big thumbs up with his free hand, but it was only free momentarily before a second glove grasped that one, as well.

"Look who's here to welcome you home!" Colin blurted out excitedly.

Turning his head to the other side of the gurney, Ethan followed the hand which had just grabbed his own, scanning upward, tracking the yellow arm of the hazmat suit to the mask covering the face of Maggie Daley. The intern smiled down at him with a few visible tears streaking her cheeks. They had both been waiting for him.

"Hello, professor!" Maggie stated gleefully. "It is wonderful to have you back!" In spite of her voice being muffled by the mask, the sincerity in her quivering words was unmistakable. There she was – his muse, his inspiration, his Maggie.

Ethan returned his gaze to the ceiling lights passing above him. The oxygen rich headache was depleting him of energy, focus and ultimately, consciousness. Before fainting again he smiled, saying something barely audible from beneath his mask. Those around him could only make out one word of it before Ethan passed out cold. He said the word "God".

Given the weekend to rest undisturbed before The Consortium would begin the debriefing, a barrage of tests conducted on the returning time traveler, Ethan knew it was only a matter of time before he'd have to address the details of the jump. The dizziness and headaches subsided by the end of the first day in this heavily-guarded infirmary room at the LHC. He had become so accustomed to the deplorable smells of Whitechapel that when he passed through Flicker into the untainted air in the lab he was overcome by the drastic change in atmospheric conditions. It required some hours for his brain and lungs to get reacquainted with purer air. Regaining his senses by midday Friday, Ethan knew if anyone from the staff or a list of approved visitors came into the room and saw his eyes open, all the questioning would come too fast and too soon. Thankfully, the areas surrounding his room were quiet enough to hear a pin drop so, if he heard any footsteps approaching, he could feign being sound asleep. Most of the traffic would come from medical staff charged with monitoring his meds and vital signs. He had EKG sensors and some kind of intravenous fluids connected to him which several nurses came in to check on frequently. While his eyes were closed he'd recognized the voices of Anson and Colin hovering over him on a few occasions, telling anecdotal stories about Ethan like he had died. He was bursting at the seams to tell them how right they were. The man they'd once known was indeed dead, killed a mere three days into his jump by two murderers: one he would never meet, the other he would meet literally face-to-face in the mirror or in passing a pane of glass, as his own reflection. Killed by the events he was forced to simultaneously perform and watch. Killed by Jack. Killed by *Time*.

By Saturday Ethan could no longer pretend to be sleeping it off. An examination would result in an instant diagnosis, discerning that he "should be" alert, completely recovered. Too much make-believe and this playacting would raise suspicions. As an educated man of substantial intellect and training, including the medical research he did for his jump, Ethan knew, at least for a little while longer, he could falsify a status of being in a weakened condition and only have visitors for small periods of time but once the nurses then doctors passed word that he was awake, the jockeying for position would begin, his peers lining up for a chance to speak with him. Ethan played it for as long as he could, for all it was worth, taking his time to think as the patience of others wore thin. Detecting some shuffling beyond the door, it became somewhat loud, disturbing his peace of mind. The doctors, holding true to their oath of serving their patient, ordered most to leave, stating too much excitement was not in Ethan's best interest. The star-struck audience, those awaiting with bated breath, diminished rapidly, forced to shelve their curiosity until Monday along with the rest of the debriefing council.

The first familiar face to visit him was no surprise at all. As the director of the program, Anson carried the most clout. His project clearance gave him the priority position, first contact, even above Colin Bishop. Ethan peeked through the slits of his eyelids, observing Anson enter like a cartoon character, maneuvering his hefty frame as quietly as possible through the room on his tippy toes, gritting his teeth in an effort to be silent. Ethan could not hide his delight in the image, chuckling aloud as he opened his eyes to receive his first guest. Arriving bedside, his voice drowned out anything electronic making noise in the room. Nothing soft spoken about him, its resonance, that deep baritone, caused Ethan's sternum to vibrate.

"I figured you were tiring of all the pretty nurses tending to your needs. Thought it might do you good to see my face." Anson laid his hand on Ethan's shoulder.

Ethan began to mutter a counter to his wit before Anson stopped him.

"Quiet now lad, you need to rest your voice. There'll be plenty of time for you to talk once your debriefing begins come Monday." Glancing around the room, he felt compelled to comment further. "You and I may both need to 'check in' here for a vacation after all of it is said and done."

Both men grinned at each other before Anson turned to leave. Stopping near the door, he returned to Ethan's bedside, leaning toward him with a serious expression.

"I flipped through your journal, lad. I know you identified the Ripper in there." After a dramatic pause, he continued. "I'd just like to hear it from your own lips."

There was a silence in the room which probably seemed like minutes to Anson but was only a few seconds as Ethan stared back at him blankly then the corners of his mouth turned ever so slightly into a smirk before he spoke one word.

"Kosminski."

Anson smiled then turned again to leave. Ethan watched him going. The instant before disappearing through the ward doorway he saw Anson make a clenched fist and elbow jab, gesturing as if he'd just thrown a strike in a bowling tournament or won a big bet. Ethan gave him precisely what he wanted and would give the rest of The Consortium exactly what they wanted, too: a perfect Flicker project. Ethan had completed enough questionnaires, surveys and Valley trial paperwork as well as all his Scope research to predict how the next week would follow. Now a god, he could readily manipulate the process and convince them of his cover story, meticulously catalogued in his journal, information Ethan would soon begin to impart flawlessly. In numerous interviews at various departments, verbal as well as written testimony, he would elucidate every angle of the leap until every participant in the process was satisfied. An exhaustive effort in terms of time invested, Ethan made it look easy.

No Scope had ever been tasked to make a jump then bring back hard evidence. Bringing any modern recording devices, be it audio or video, would and could not be permitted to pass back in time. Should anything be lost or stolen, the technology could lead to quantum time shifts due to reverse engineering. No, the reasoning for the intense ethics scrutiny was because every Scope had to be trusted enough before being sent back to be taken at their word of what they witnessed when they returned. There would be no true scrutiny of Ethan's jump. Any remaining doubt would have been removed well before his journey into the past. He knew they'd take his word as gospel. "Gospel". An appropriate term when hearing a god speak. Ethan did not fancy himself "Thee God", more a philosophical deity who understood telling the truth to mere mortals would only harm their fragile psyches. He needed to provide them the security blanket they required to reassure them all was right in their little world view. Only he knew the *truth* and would take it with him to the grave.

"Fucking Scopes, always on their bloody backs. You training to be a hooker?"

Ethan immediately recognized the voice and began to smile before opening his eyes. Colin was propped in the doorway to his room.

"Hooker?" Ethan said, raising his head. "My good man, at my rates, I'd prefer you use the term *Lady of the Evening*."

Colin approached, his arm extended in advance. The friends shook hands, Colin keeping the greeting playful, just under the length of discomfort. Ethan knew he'd been missed these many weeks and knew Colin would want to spend as much time as possible with him during the debriefing. Yet, Ethan purposefully insisted that his longtime friend not be allowed to partake in any of the meetings, nothing that didn't directly involve Colin's part in the project, citing the stringent rules of impartiality, his excuse for any perceived slight. Colin was the best friend of the *Ethan* who had jumped into the past but he posed a threat to the *Ethan* who returned. He also posed a threat to Ethan's **new** best friend, *Time*. The two men only spoke for a few minutes and only superficially, discussing nothing of substance. Colin knew the protocol. If he were to ask anything about the mission, he knew

Ethan could not and would not respond, the line in the sands of time clearly drawn by The Consortium.

The debriefing process was as unoriginal and predictable to the deity known as Ethan as he'd expected. What was scheduled as five full days of anticipated intense recall and documentation took just over three. Ethan asked Anson for the paper trail part of the process; no actual paperwork, but rather, transcripts on tablet to forward with more efficiency. He completed every question asked of him in nine hours flat. The interviews and examinations, of course, came up clean and absolutely concise. The play's the thing and Ethan was playing all of them for fools, replaying the entire experience like a concert violinist in the orchestra pit, knowing the tune all too well. Mostly he wanted to speed up the process, to get the hell out of there and back to England, as there was still a small paranoid voice nagging at him with the thought: the longer he stayed, the greater the chance he would be discovered. Finally, after all the tests and interrogatories, he was allowed to return off-site to his humble but comfy staff quarters, to a cold, gray room on a cold, gray Thursday morning. Ethan unlocked then opened the door to living space that now felt foreign and unfamiliar. Somewhat disoriented by a change in venue, he missed the brightness of the LHC infirmary but here, at least, he had some privacy. Here, he would spend the last few hours resting then packing his belongings before heading back over to the complex for the final project review, a formal meeting with the Debriefing Council before catching his flight back to England later on that afternoon. After a long, hot shower he dressed for the far cooler temperatures, common in early November. Finding his dapper suit hanging in the closet where he'd left it, Ethan reached inside the pocket of his trousers. His fingers found it, his precious antique timepiece embossed with the three-legged horse… his only friend. If he had anticipated it might be missing, it wasn't the case.

Ethan opened it up. It hadn't been wound for over two months, the time stopped at 3:26. Had it stopped around the same time he was beginning to carve up his first victim, Mary Ann Nichols? Regardless of the timing, a more puzzling and troubling consideration entered Ethan's thoughts. Having first purchased the timepiece while doing one of his run-throughs in 21st Century Whitechapel, what were the odds he'd find *his* original watch, then purchase it again in the 19th Century? He was certain Abigail had lifted it from his room as her token, a keepsake of her love for a god. It seemed unlikely she would pawn it or sell it, no matter how desperate she got. Perhaps she'd kept it until her death and descendants sold it instead, unaware of its sentimental value, finding its destiny in an antique shop, back in Ethan's hands once again, one hundred and thirty years later. When he returned to England he would have to do some deeper research on this timepiece. Right now, he had to get to that final meeting on time, his final role play. Packing up what little he'd brought with him to Switzerland, the time had come to return to the LHC complex where all the department heads would report their findings compiled from all their examinations of Ethan to the Flicker Director, Dr. Anson Van Ruden.

Ethan's transportation van arrived right on schedule, the drive back to the LHC taking longer in daytime traffic than it had in the wee hours of the morning when he made the jump months ago. Pensively staring out the window, taking in all the splendid scenery, his view of the Swiss countryside was breathtaking as a series of snapshots taken in memory of his trip. Saying nothing to his driver for the duration of their journey, it never occurred to him to engage the man. Ethan was saving all his energy for the onslaught he would undoubtedly deal with upon his arrival. Sure enough, when the van pulled into one of the many access points at the LHC, one of The Consortium valets escorted him in to their large meeting room. Most of the key players were already present, mulling around with their cup of coffee or tea in hand. Ethan was approached with offers of congratulatory handshakes from all he passed as he made his way to the one seat positioned on the opposite side of the table, place holders bearing the names of the principle participants, wireless microphones at the ready. There were several photographers / videographers granted exclusive access to the proceedings, permitted by The Consortium to record this historic event, just as every part of the project, before and after, was documented for posterity.

As Ethan made his way over to the seat reserved for him he heard that familiar, bellowing laughter. Anson Van Ruden was making his presence known, arriving in his usual larger-than-life style. Loud and boisterous to the point one could not help but notice and pay attention, a large assortment of manila folders tucked underneath his left arm, he began greeting everyone with handshakes and high-fives all around. It was as festive an atmosphere as one might expect, as there was much to celebrate given the successful outcome of the project. Anson was jubilant about it, launching his words into the stratosphere, causing an eruption of applause.

"There he is…Ethan LaPierre, time traveler extraordinaire!" Anson exclaimed. Holding his arms outstretched, he maneuvered around the table to Ethan, embracing him with his Swedish one-armed bear hug, literally lifting him off the floor to the amusement of the onlookers. Anson was a ham, eager to meet with the press corps present at these times.

"Let's get this silliness done with so you can finally go home, lad. Yes?"

Ethan could only smile and nod in approval as Anson was crushing his lungs, leaving him unable to speak. Anson released his hold on Ethan then put the burley arm free of folders around the Scope's shoulders for publicity shots. As the cameras flashed (telephone cameras were strictly prohibited) all the professionals inundated Ethan, blinding him for a few moments. In that surreal circumstance he was drawn back in mind to the same effect he'd experienced when jumping through the Flicker so many weeks before, flash after flash, visualizing the faces he encountered during his excursion. Polly, Annie, Mary Kelly, the faceless reflections of Elizabeth Stride and Catherine Eddowes, even Abigail. Eternal worshippers of an immortal god.

As the camera flashes diminished, it was as if time was both playing tricks with him and slowing down the speed of the event to make it even more torturous. There, standing in the room was Maggie. He thought he'd only imagined her when he was being wheeled away from Flicker to the infirmary upon his arrival. Colin escorted her into the meeting. After Ethan's weekend of recovery, he'd requested not to have any visitors during his down time between the debriefings, mostly to avoid any idle conversation with Colin, though he certainly would have enjoyed a little down time with Maggie. As he stared at her she gave him a smile and nod as if to say she was happy and proud of him. Of course she was! She worshipped him, as did the others. Over the next several hours Ethan sat quite still listening to review board summaries of the debriefings, already knowing their conclusions.

"The project Scope performed his mission with the utmost ethical and objective perspective the department could have designed, executed with integrity. The result provided clarity and closure, resolving the more than century long mystery without any foreseeable alterations to the current timeline." Project hearings closed.

The finale of the meeting ended with dozens more publicity shots, opportunities to hobnob and handshake with his worshippers. All the while Ethan's intermingling kept him preoccupied, his eyes kept searching the room for Miss Maggie, craving a glimpse of her. Almost fixated on the object of his affection, she was a vision, her purity and youth enticing beyond measure to the man who longed to be alone with her instead. As more and more committee members filtered out of the room, Ethan could see more of her. Dressed in a formfitting emerald green blazer and skirt, that color made her eyes leap across the room. She must have known she was a knockout when she looked in the mirror and Ethan was certain she chose it for him. Maggie appeared so much more mature than he remembered. She had grown into a beautiful woman in only a few short months. Still shaking hands, accepting congratulations, he'd be momentarily distracted, engaged in the pleasantries of this event but would repeatedly return his focus to her the first chance he got. Had Maggie noticed him noticing her? At one point she crossed the room. Ethan followed her with his intense gaze, watching with rapacious eyes as she floated through the crowd. Suddenly, an encounter of another kind occurred as she was passing Colin who didn't look at her but was instead, staring directly at Ethan. For the first time during the meeting, their eyes locked, something Ethan had actively avoided. The expression in them did not speak of admiration or abiding friendship but of bewilderment. Colin held his stare for the moment then broke it, turning to deliberately glance at Maggie then back to Ethan. There was no mistaking an accusation. Ethan looked away, revealing far too much of his new persona through his obvious hunger, his salacious lust for Maggie, something Colin had never seen in his eyes before.

Although his fiduciary relationship with Anson still seemed intact, Ethan knew the bond with Colin could not continue. They had been far too close before his jump and he'd spot the smallest of character changes which could hinder Ethan's plan to rule the future as a deity. Ethan turned his attention to collecting his documents and personal items showing only the top of his head to the room. Once he finally looked up again he noticed Maggie had departed the meeting. Colin was with Anson at the entranceway, apparently in a deep discussion, both speaking softly, uncharacteristic of Dr. Van Ruden. Colin appeared agitated via his gestures. Anson kept shaking his head in response to Dr. Bishop's diatribe. Ethan could feel the tension building and knew precisely what was being discussed. . .him. Lowering his head again, feeling scrutinized in the extreme, when Ethan looked up to meet Colin's stare, his "friend" abruptly exited the room. Anson turned toward Ethan, giving his protégé a satisfied smile and a big thumbs up before following Colin out the door and out of sight.

Ethan knew Colin was going to be a problem and possibly a bigger one when they returned to England. Once they were back at Oxford he'd have to distance himself, separating from those on campus who had known him most intimately well, those who would see how he had changed. He had no choice but to abandon a friendship. Ethan had made certain he would return on a different flight than Colin and Maggie. The months he'd spent in that small room in 19th Century Whitechapel had not only altered him, it had transformed him into this isolationist, something more than the sum of a man. Ethan was a monster, a madman, a god. He would return to teaching and to his home on campus but he'd keep to himself, disassociating with those he'd once held close. The insatiable hunger to witness abject fear in the eyes of a woman under his control was there, the addiction to their surrender to his blade, his power. It was his deep desire to observe what could pass for either fear or love. Passionate, unconditional, undeniable, uncontrollable fear or love. Ethan's life would no longer be that of a sheepish tutor redundantly sequestering himself in books, there to keep company with the women of history. Rather, he would be a wolf in sheep's clothing, forever to remain on the prowl. He was certain of it. He was Jack the Ripper.

***

"This grieved me heartily; and now I saw, though too late,
the folly of beginning a work before we count the cost,
and before we judge rightly of our own strength to go through with it."
Daniel Defoe "Robinson Crusoe"

Epilogue
FALLING INTO PLACE

The month of April in the year 2021 was the heaviest logistical schedule at The Valley Flicker trial site because the days were getting longer and the weather was optimum to accommodate the increased backlog of project reenactments. The crisp morning air was refreshing, the sheen of dew still glistening atop the blades of grass as sunlight beamed through droplets, casting diamond lights along the valley floor. The temperature at this time of the day was still on the cool side and wouldn't warm much before noon, much to the delight of the LHC trial site crews, all of whom had smiles on their faces this time of year, the elements too pleasant to complain about. It was when they most enjoyed their work.

At the moment there were five Flicker trials underway. One trial was concealed beneath a giant-sized black tent, closely akin to an old circus big top. That particular trial was one unique night time historic event of record. Being shrouded in darkness allowed the participants to do run-throughs, day or night. On the outer boundary of The Valley, standing on top of the hill adjacent to the observation tower, the solitary woman surveyed the landscape. From her vantage point overlooking the expansive facility, grounds buzzing with activity, she could see vehicles of various sizes and models moving along the roads. She wasn't paying much attention to what normally inspired her, preoccupied by what she'd read in the morning edition of "The Sun", the horrible headline stating:

"Copycat Killer Continues In Whitechapel"

"To the frustration of local authorities and Scotland Yard no leads have surfaced regarding the death of another woman in the Whitechapel district of London. Found last weekend, the corpse remains unidentified, the body brutally mutilated in what appears to be an homage to the infamous 'Jack the Ripper' who terrorized the same region during what became known as 'The Autumn of Terror' in 1888. Forensic specialists have been called to the case. Police now believe this to be the third such type of ritualistic copycat killings since early January of this year, coinciding with a release of the publication of the successful, yet closely guarded 'Flicker Project' in which a Dr. Ethan LaPierre identified, or, in project linguistics, 'spy-glassed' an original suspect in the case, Aaron Kosminski, as the notorious 'Jack the Ripper'. The spokesman from Scotland Yard stated the investigation was ongoing, focusing on the possibility that the new published report triggered someone seeking the same level of notoriety. The first two murder victims being women in their early twenties, currently unidentified...."

"Excuse me! Ms. Daley! Ms. Daley!" The rather overzealous, if vigilant young intern they'd all nicknamed "Mercury" (as he was always running messages in and out of The Valley to various recipients at light speed) fast approaching, waving her down, he had attracted the attention of the project professional he was seeking out. Stumbling through swampy muck, the soft, soggy, springtime sod was clutching at his feet. Maggie smiled, fascinated by the way history tends to repeat itself.

"Mind yourself, mate!" Maggie responded, erring on the side of caution.

The student apprentice was holding a black notebook with one word embossed on the cover: "Classified." Racing to reach her with it in his outstretched hand, the wiry lad was gleaming as he handed it over to her.

"Congratulations, mum!" He was struggling to catch his breath.

Maggie stared at the intern, confused for a moment before it finally hit her.

"You mean?" She paused.

"Approved! Practically this instant! Dr. Van Ruden just called the office and he said to get the initial Scope paperwork over to you, post haste!"

The young man took a deep breath to slow down and think. He looked up to the sky over his thick plastic glasses.

"He also told me to tell you, beggin' your pardon, mum, but he said this, too: 'Tell Margaret to get her ass ready. We'll be drinking at Oxford next Monday.' Ms. Daley, allow me to be the first to say 'Congratulations!' on your Flicker approval and your title as Scope in the project. Fuck yeah! Sorry mum...my language."

"No, no. You're right!" Maggie remarked. "Fuck yeah! Thank you!"

The student ran off toward the tower, almost losing his footing, nearly taking a spill down a long, steep hill into The Valley below as Maggie watched Mercury fly. Finding him endearing, suddenly a pensive, contemplative expression furrowed her brow as her thoughts turned to a more innocent time, a more innocent girl right here in the same predicament some months ago. Thinking back further, to her childhood, she could not recall a time when she didn't know about Jack the Ripper. He was an integral element of English folklore, a part of the vernacular, the subject that would never go away, more famous than infamous. She could not believe some lunatic took inspiration from the press release of a successful jump as an opportunity to kill innocent women and grab headlines. Innocence lost. She unfolded the newspaper again, laying it on top of the folder. Maggie stared at the article in abject terror, in utter disbelief.

In the beginning of the Valley trials for "20/20 Hindsight", well before she was selected as an intern, Maggie became engrossed with the program since she was the project Scope's assistant at Oxford. She did her own research. As she did, Maggie learned all of the gruesome details of the case. She felt so badly about the way these women lost their lives but more so, how their identities were trumped by a fictitious name. It truly terrified her to think there was someone out there duplicating these horrible murders. It was then the thought occurred to her that *she* could fall victim. Not merely her mortality but her identity. Not that she was a princess or anyone of importance to anyone else but herself. The cold chill of fear passed through her, undoubtedly the same exact fear women shared in 1888. The possibility existed that everything she was as a person, as a woman could be buried with her, just as history did with the victims of Jack the Ripper. In her research she discovered the sickening course of society, the depressing truth that every serial killer stole more than lives. The perpetrators stole headlines. These women had *real* names. They had lives and loves, pains and pleasures that everyone has, if they fortunately lived long enough. To be robbed of a full life is truly unfair. To be robbed of its remembrance is simply inhuman. Maggie trembled at the thought. There was never any redemption for the women of this story. It was never told, never even written about by the Scope who'd gone back to witness these atrocities. Jack the Ripper, a faceless manifestation, still ruled history, still popular, more fascinating than ever. With one deep sigh, tucking the newspaper with its horrible headline underneath her arm, she abandoned it in lieu of the great story about to unfold in the binder she received.

"More bloody paperwork." She began to glance over page after page of "legal" and "ethics" forms to fill out, already drowning in a sea of black and white.

Maggie Daley had become part of the privileged tribe, not in the sense of being inducted into the exclusive club of Scope candidates, an honor in its own right, but having been blissfully influenced by Anson Van Ruden while she was at the LHC, introducing her into a realm of rock music from the 60's and 70's. Flipping through her delivered documents, Maggie donned the earphones connected to a smartphone. Listening to her favorite classic rock station, effectively chasing images of carnage from her mind, she replaced them with one of her beloved songs from the legendary rock group "The Guess Who". Maggie cranked it up, singing along from the hilltop.

"These eyes cry every night for you, these arms long to hold you again.
The hurtin's on me, yeah but I will never be free, no, my baby, no, no
You gave a promise to me, yeah and you broke it, you broke it..."

In a trance, Maggie must have momentarily gotten lost in the music because she never sensed the approach of somebody from behind, most likely originating from The Valley car park just beyond the hilltop. Reacting out of reflex, startled, she felt the unexpected contact of a hand upon her shoulder. Maggie spun around, expelling a soft shriek of surprise. Stepping back from who touched her, almost falling down the steep hill, she regained her balance over the terrain just in time. Removing her earphones, Maggie's expression was one of joy and elation, recognizing a familiar face, one absent far too long.

"Well, hello there stranger."

Fini

ACKNOWLEDGEMENTS

First and foremost, we must thank our parents for their endless, bountiful love and support, their encouragement and heartfelt belief in our mutual ability to bring this story to fruition. Over the course of time required to breathe life into a concept, they remained a constant source of inspiration and reassurance, listening, offering guidance and advice and especially perspective regarding this unique collaboration of heart and mind. A desire to see us succeed akin to our own, this project became a reality because of their confidence in both of us to make it happen in spite of every obstacle along the path of a remarkable journey. Reminding us that perseverance is the key which opens virtually every door in literally every aspect of life, including this labor of love, we honor and cherish them above all else.

There are those who epitomize the word "friendship", those who comprehend the true meaning of the word and likewise understand "love" as a verb. Nikki Salach and Sue Darnell are two such individuals, giving generously of their time and talent to enhance this offering to the world. These two women were always there for us, at a moment's notice to contribute to the cause. In the midst of their busy lives they took the time, made the time to help make magic happen, sharing our commitment. We remain eternally grateful, humbled by their service to the greater good.

Our appreciation is extended to Mike Covell and Len Miller, gentlemen aware of the intricacies of this tale and our compelling desire to tell it. Aficionados both, the subject matter is near and dear to them. Literal experts providing an insightful, thought-provoking approach has been an invaluable resource to us while enduring the dark side of a story which ultimately sheds new light in the world.

With our grateful hearts, thanks are extended to Alison Pierce Cotton for always making us look better than we do in real life. She is a true artist behind the lens.

ABOUT THE AUTHOR

George R. Lopez is a military veteran, serving as an intelligence officer in the U.S. Air Force during the Cold War. Living in Europe for three years of his tour of duty, he fell in love with its history. After being honorably discharged he has since made his home in Florida. Eventually much of his training led him into the field of the paranormal where he excelled, fast becoming an accomplished, well-respected member of the community. Creator and host of his own network, as a radio broadcaster, a prolific lecturer and spokesman for positive ideals regarding investigation of the supernatural realm, George brings a much needed pragmatic perspective to this endeavor, in avid pursuit of the truth. From veteran to researcher, now author, this story blends his natural artistry with an insatiable curiosity, brewing in his analytical mind for a quarter of a century before finding its way into the world in print.

Andrea P. Perron is the author of the supernatural trilogy "House of Darkness House of Light", the true story behind the major motion picture "The Conjuring". As a 1980 graduate of Chatham College in Pittsburgh, Pennsylvania with a B.A. in English and philosophy, she went on to become first an entrepreneur then later a counselor by day, meanwhile spending decades in the theatre as an actor and singer by night. Now, as a lecturer and apprentice paranormal investigator, she travels extensively, speaking on various subjects in the field from spirituality to extraterrestrial activity. "In A Flicker" is her first collaboration on a project, what she describes as a true labor of love, bringing to light an otherwise dark story with a profound message for humanity.

inaflickernovel.com
George R. Lopez@officialinafli2

Printed in the United States
By Bookmasters